RANDOM MELODY

DETECTIVE ROBERT WINTER

SERIES

William Michaels

Varzara
House

Varzara House
Orlean, VA

Published by Varzara House

Library of Congress Control Number: 2019902327

ISBN: 978-0-9998161-1-0

10 9 8 7 6 5 4 3 2

v8g

ACKNOWLEDGEMENTS

Special thanks to the state, county, and federal law enforcement officers and members of the military who have graciously provided their insights and expertise, especially Captain Luke Durden of the Fairfax County (VA) Police Department, Sergeant Brian Dunford of the Boston Police Department, Deputy Sheriff Alex Armstrong of the Fauquier County (VA) Sheriff's Office, and Robert Dunford, Superintendent (ret.), Boston Police Department. Also many thanks to Guy Williamson, Kim Pursche, and Deborah Atella.

Police procedures and policies differ across jurisdictions, and any errors and omissions are the sole responsibility of the author.

RANDOM MELODY

CHAPTER 1

Rick Singleton lowered the master volume slider on the mixing board until the sound in the studio was barely audible. The raucous cacophony, sounding more like a car crusher at a junkyard than music, curdled his eardrums.

On the other side of the glass, the bass player, who called himself Oz the Magnificent, raised his pierced eyebrows at Rick. Rick gave him a big smile and an enthusiastic thumbs up as he simultaneously dropped Oz's playback volume to zero. The guy not only couldn't hold a bass line, but rarely managed to hit a single note in the key the song was in. Which was pretty difficult, if you thought about it.

Rick slipped on a pair of headphones, not even plugged into the board, so he wouldn't have to listen as Oz lit into a long series of painful runs.

Rick wondered for the hundredth time how this band—the Crash Heaves—had managed to get a recording deal. Rick's own music was so much better than theirs—if for no other reason it had a *melody*—and yet after toiling away for years he couldn't get an A&R guy from a big label to listen to his stuff even if he paid for it. Not that he hadn't tried. He'd offered money, off-the-books recording time, anything he could think of, to no avail.

Oz finished his riff with a flourish, swinging his Fender bass into a microphone stand, which dropped onto the drum set. Oz twisted around like a puppet drawn to the cascading equipment, ripping out his guitar chord. Rick should have signaled Oz for another take, but figured the painful screech of an amplifier short would barely be noticed on a Crash

Heaves release, it might even improve it. He gave Oz another big thumbs up and faded the track.

A wild-eyed face appeared in the window at the back entrance to the studio. The band's lead singer, Lasher, waiting his turn in the green room. Lasher was stoned, as he had been since the band had arrived at the studio, and that was four days ago. Rick had yet to see him eat a single calorie, unless you counted the tea bag Lasher had swallowed thinking it was a melt in the mouth package of coke.

Rick did a little blow now and then, but not while working, and certainly not while recording, he was a *professional*. Those Seventies bands had managed to play stoned out of their minds, but while Rick felt he could write, he was a realist; he was no top level player. That's why he'd teamed up with Gerry back in high school, the guy already a musical prodigy. Unfortunately, Gerry was long gone.

Oz had fallen back onto a duct taped Naugahyde sofa, a throwback to the days when Larry, the owner of the studio, recorded bands laying down multiple tracks simultaneously. Rick had heard too many tales from Larry of the heady days of rock and roll, wild sex in the studio, and wouldn't go near the sofa himself for fear of what diseases it harbored. As for Larry, he wouldn't know how to even turn on a digital board, so other than putting in an appearance to glad hand the new bands, he was hardly around.

Rick shut off the recording light. Lasher didn't move, so Rick banged on the window to get his attention, pointing to the studio and mouthing *You're up.*

Rick swiveled in his chair at a knock on the mixing booth door, trying to cover his look of dismay with some semblance of a smile at who peered through the glass. "Hey, Rudy, Oz just finished up."

Rudy, the assistant manager of the Crash Heaves, dressed like he had just stepped out of a casting call for a late career Elvis movie: white flowery shirt, white pants, white shoes, even a white belt. Except where Elvis had a little pouch in that outfit, Rudy swam in his clothes. "How did it sound?"

Rick didn't think Rudy's job had anything to do with the band's music, but Larry had said Rudy would be paying the bill, which was already considerable.

Rick gave Rudy the same exuberant thumbs up. "Vintage Oz, Rudy, vintage Oz. Want to hear it?"

"Nah, as long as it had energy. Did it have energy?"

"Enough to power the board," said Rick. "That guy can really light it up."

Rudy flashed a set of blinding teeth that matched his outfit. "Good, good. Who's next?"

"Lasher is going to lay down the first layer of vocals." Rick gestured to the studio, where Lasher had his head pressed against the glass like a little kid puckering up to goldfish in a bowl.

"Great, Lasher. Man's got a set of tubes. Listen, do you know how much longer we're going to be here? In the studio, I mean?"

Rick bit off his first answer, which was that they could leave anytime, it wasn't like the second or third or even tenth takes had improved on the original cuts. "We have all the tracks for five, this is number six."

"Whatever. So that sounds like a few more days?"

"At least," said Rick.

"Okay. Listen, the band is running a little low on, you know, fuel."

Rick's first thought was that Rudy meant energy, or food, but Rudy's furtive eyes hinted at a more illicit sustenance. "What do they need?" Rick asked carefully.

"You know, something to keep the creative spark going. We had hauled a pretty good stash from Houston, but . . ." Rudy put his hands out in a *what are you going to do* gesture.

Shit, the guy was asking Rick to score some blow. First he had to suffer through the Crash Heaves's music, and now Rudy was asking him to keep them high. Rudy looked surprisingly sober, which could only mean he had given the last of his own stash to the band. Cautiously Rick said, "How much are you talking about?"

Rudy's lips moved with no sound, a human drug calculator. "I dunno exactly . . . fifty eight balls, maybe? And a half pound of weed. Oh, and Lasher has all these problems with his back, he's running out of oxy, a hundred of those would be good."

Rick blinked, maybe the Crash Heaves's music had scrambled his brain. Rudy was asking for enough drugs to satisfy a small arena. He did his own calculations in his head. Thousands of dollars. Not to mention the cost of the lawyer if he got caught; no way he could argue that much was for personal use. "You sure?" he asked. "For the band?"

"Oz wants to throw a party, and the guys have hooked up with a few locals, plus what they need, hey, it all adds up. And if Lasher doesn't stay juiced, we'll never get the recording finished, and we have the Boston gig in just two weeks."

The Boston gig. Another achievement the Crash Heaves didn't deserve, the kickoff to a twelve city tour. Rick could barely get himself booked at Marburg's coffee shops while the Crash Heaves would be kicking it at the TD Garden. Life was unfair, but this was ridiculous. What the hell did these guys have that he didn't?

Other than a local source for coke, that is. Rudy was out of his element up north. "I might know a guy," said Rick. The problem was that Rick's normal—and rather infrequent—buy was an eight ball and a few dime bags.

"Great," said Rudy. "Bring him by with the stuff."

Like that was going to happen. Rick picturing it, asking Doc Miles to come in person to sell to a stranger, loaded with enough illicit weight to put them all in federal prison. Rick was struggling for a way to not sound unhelpful, while at the same time getting Rudy to forget his offer to help, when the studio phone lit up.

Rick snatched at it. "Studio."

"It's Larry. How are those Crash Heavies doing?"

"The Crash *Heaves* are doing just fine," said Rick. "I'm actually talking to Rudy right now."

"Okay, I get it, you can't talk. Make him feel special, you know what I mean? Those guys don't know shit about the price of anything, I'm charging them fifty percent over the going rate. I can't believe the label is letting them get away with this."

Rick mentally corrected Larry: *Letting you get away with it, you mean.* "Maybe the paperwork isn't complete?" Rick was trying to talk in code in front of Rudy. What he meant was, *Maybe they don't have a contract?* Which would reassert some sense of fairness into the musical world, although Larry would be out a bundle.

"Nah, they're good. When do you think they'll wrap?"

"Could be a while yet." Rudy appeared absorbed in Larry's Grammy on the wall, so Rick whispered, "No hurry, right?" Confirming Larry's desire to keep the clock running.

"We've got that chick Candy coming in again on Tuesday. She pays *twice* the going rate. In the meantime, do whatever it takes to keep on the schedule."

Rick didn't know what was worse for his ego, a band that could barely play but had a contract, or a rich bitch who wanted to buy her way into stardom. Candy was hot, though, she had that going for her. And truth be told her voice was okay, no worse than a dozen other pop divas on the charts.

Not that Candy had given Rick the time of day, though her personal assistant Miranda had given him a few looks.

In a single inspirational heartbeat Rick put together a breathtaking plan: impress Miranda with some smooth talk and a good time, then get to Candy through her. Candy's money would probably land her airtime, and if Rick could get her to sing one of his songs . . .

Rick didn't have enough cash for fast food, but Rudy had just given him the keys to Fort Knox. "Sure, Larry, I'll manage it."

"You better, kid."

Rick hung up, Larry's meaning clear. Rick had to solve the Crash Heaves's problem or else he wouldn't be around long enough to even see Candy on Tuesday. Rick desperately needed this job, he was barely making ends meet with all the medical bills for his mom.

Rick did another set of calculations. If Rudy and his buddies were so oblivious to recording session rates, maybe they'd be as equally out to lunch on local street prices. "Rudy, about your stuff. This isn't exactly a big city like Houston. Everything costs a little more, you get me?"

Rudy shrugged. "Whatever. We may not have brought enough product, but we certainly have enough cash. The band got a big advance."

That clinched it for Rick. He'd have to take the risk.

If Rick played his cards right he'd keep a little of Rudy's money for his trouble and use it to charm Miranda. Miranda would get him close enough to Candy to make his pitch, and he'd be on to songwriting heaven. He'd finally have enough money to take care of his mom and get back to making music instead of recording other bands.

A crazy set of ideas, but music careers had been launched on far less.

Rick stood up. "So Rudy, when can you get your hands on this cash you've been hauling around?"

CHAPTER 2

Rudolph "Doc" Miles eased himself gingerly into his hot tub. Still September, and it was already frigging cold, he couldn't imagine what the winter would be like.

God he missed Miami . . .

He'd had a good run there. He'd concocted the Medicare scam early on in his career, memorizing the best mix of diagnostic codes to load every conceivable charge on the government, whose auditors didn't know the difference between a tendon and a tenderloin. The only downside was that Medicare meant *old* patients, and they talked and talked and talked, taking Doc's noncommittal grunts as interest in their life stories.

He'd switched from seeing three patients a day with fifty billable diagnoses to fifty patients a day with three scripts each, mostly for oxycodone. His new patients were acutely aware they were in his office to get a piece of paper and not give Doc any more details beyond being in pain from some imagined injury. Doc, in fact, had done more talking himself, helpfully suggesting it was probably their back or neck that hurt the most. Backs and necks offered a trove of non overlapping diagnosis, lumbar pain, spinal stenosis, spondylolisthesis, fibromyalgia, and that was before even getting started on the cervical and thoracic vertebrae. He could write twenty patients up for back pain without having to dip into the vague soft tissue injury diagnosis that set off red lights in insurance company reviews.

Unfortunately, other doctors hadn't been as circumspect, and soon there were more task forces tracking oxy than there were doctors in Florida. Doc experienced a sudden urge to go skiing far to the north, which had brought him, via Canada, to the Boston area. Since no one ever moved *to* New England from Florida, Doc figured it would be unlikely any authorities would look for him here, especially since he was not really practicing, although he had rented an office for appearances. A sign on his door said *No insurance plans accepted*, which kept things nice and quiet.

Doc reconnected with the snow bunnies who wintered in Florida and eased back into the business, going light on oxy and instead satisfying the needs of the rich, mostly fentenyl and adderal. His willingness to quietly help with their addictions had brought him their thanks not only with overpriced office visits, but presents of all kinds: watches, a Jaguar, and literally kilos of coke. At first he just used the coke as a sort of friendly calling card to potential new clients, but later had carefully sold a little here and there. When that gig became as lucrative as the prescriptions he tapped into his old Miami network for supply.

The strains of Bach Harpsichord Concerto Number One melded with the bubbling spa water. Doc leaned back and picked up one of the six phones—all throwaways, virtually untraceable—behind the tub. Each of his current special customers had a dedicated ring tone. Doc had a penchant for the classics, and chose ring tones to remind him of who was connected to each phone. In this case, a guy nicknamed Harpy. Harpy, harpsichord. Kooky, but it worked for Doc.

"Hey, Harpy."

"Doc. How's it hanging?"

Doc automatically looked down between his legs. "Fine, what can I do you for?"

"My friend, he wants to have a party. I was hoping you'd help with the decorations."

Burner phones or not, Doc and his customers were smart enough to speak in an innocuous code. Harpy wasn't looking for drugs this time, instead, he wanted bling. Fake bling, to be exact. Doc had stumbled on this side line by accident when a rapper with a back problem had come into his clinic wearing enough gold to start his own QVC line of jewelry. It had taken Doc almost half an hour to realize the rapper wasn't there for an imagined illness, he really *was* in pain. Doc told the rapper his problem was the twenty pounds of jewelry on his neck, a surefire way to strain the cervical vertebrae.

The rapper explained it was image, man, he needed an edge to make it. Doc was surprised the rapper hadn't made it, how else could he afford all that bling? After Doc had given him a morphine patch, the rapper had let loose about all the gold being fake and that good fakes weren't cheap. In exchange for a free sampler of pain medications, Doc got the name of the rapper's bling supplier. One thing led to another, and Doc, always looking for a legitimate enterprise to explain how he could afford his house and cars, was in the fake bling business.

Doc asked Harpy, "Are you looking for streamers or disco balls or hanging party lights?" Streamers were thick gold chains, disco balls were diamond necklaces, and hanging party lights were large earrings, usually rubies.

"We're good on streamers," said Harpy. "But my friend wants to show his new acquaintance how he treats his special friends."

Doc got the message. Harpy's boss, a dull, short balding accountant who made a ton of money helping launder money, was trying to impress some hottie, and he wanted to invite her to a party where some hired hookers would wear the fake bling and all coo about the accountant's generosity. "No problem," said Doc. "You have a budget in mind?"

"My friend said ten is fine, he'll go twenty if you find something breathtaking but not gaudy."

Twenty grand. If she was worth flashing twenty K in fakes Doc wanted to meet the accountant's hottie himself. Doc said, "Got it."

"You need anything up front?"

"I know you are good for it at delivery." Doc rarely extended credit, but he made exceptions now and then for the customers who had the dedicated phones. None of his drug customers were big users themselves, mostly aides and assistants to the rich folk, the power people. These helpers weren't glorified gofers, they were paid well and made shit happen, the go-betweens to the underground economy, to the drugs. It wasn't like a pop star or a senator was going to buy his own coke. Best of all, they were a tight knit group of professionals. No one blabbed, because if they did, they'd never work again.

Doc hung up, feeling pretty good. He had a ton of bling around and might have what Harpy needed in stock. It was a perfect side line; he could actually keep it in the house, he had bona fide receipts. Fake jewelry wasn't illegal. Not declaring the income from renting it was, but as far as Doc knew there were no fake jewelry task forces.

He cranked up the spa jets, trying out all the buttons. The top of the line, music equipped spa had cost over ten grand, the house addition to hold it another eighty, all worth every penny. His back still hurt from his own—unfortunately not feigned—lower back problems. An oxy would be nice right now, but Doc made it a practice never to be a seller and a customer.

A titter of laughter from the adjoining bedroom. Probably Tricia, the younger one. The first night Doc had met her she claimed to be eighteen. Doc wasn't so sure, so he had dangled a pretty blue vial of fun under her nose until she coughed up her license. The other one, Gina, looked older and acted it, stoic about the tit for tat due Doc for providing pharmaceutical grade powder. Once she was high she loosened up well enough.

Tricia giggled and skipped out into the addition, stark naked. "You didn't wait for us!" she pouted.

"I didn't want to disturb your show." Doc suspected Tricia had been watching cartoons.

Tricia dipped her hand in the water. "It's so hot!"

"That's why they call it a hot tub."

"You're so funny, Doc." Tricia eased dramatically into the spa, playfully flicking water at Doc, who believed she actually thought he *was* funny, less an indication of his ego than her simple mindset. It was fine with him. She was enthusiastic with a killer body, and he was a fifty year old soon to be tub of lard with once strong arms starting to sag. If he didn't have candy he'd never get laid unless he paid for it with cash. "Where's Gina?"

"I think she's waxing for you."

Waxing maybe, but most likely for a boyfriend, not Doc. Gina's male friend was a never mentioned reality between her and Doc. Normally he'd not stand for that, and twenty years ago he would have found the guy and taken care of the situation, but Doc had other uses for Gina, and the arrangement kept her focused. "And how about you?"

Tricia played her part, cuddling up under Doc's arm. "I know what you like, Doctor Doc."

Doc laid his head on the padded backrest and wondered how long he could stay in the hot tub before shriveling up into an oversized prune.

Gina padded out from the bedroom, even more naked than Tricia on all the parts that counted. Her one surrender to modesty was a thin sliver of platinum chain around her neck, a glistening emerald, matching her piercing green eyes, artfully dangling in her cleavage. Nothing fake about it, a gift from Doc.

Gina's gesture cinched it for him. He decided he'd stay in the hot tub until spring.

CHAPTER 3

RICK HADN'T BEEN to his mother's house in a week. Each day made it harder to go. The screen door banged against the siding, reminding Rick he needed to fix the closer.

The now familiar smell greeted him as he stepped inside, childhood memories mixed with impending sadness and finality. The small ranch had always seemed confining to Rick, and even with just his mother living there, now felt smaller. He wove his way through the living room, especially tight with the hospital bed.

Rick bent to give his mother a kiss on the forehead. "You look good today." She actually looked the same, which wasn't good at all, bluish, wrapped up in thick flannel pajamas, even though the room was hot as a greenhouse. Her hair, once densely black, was so thin the bedside lamp reflected off her scalp.

"I'd be better if you came by more often."

"I'm sorry. It's been crazy busy at the studio." Rick rolled the tray table of half eaten blended pablum away. He could no longer identify the food. "You aren't hungry?"

His mother's eyes flicked away. "I ate something."

Rick hated this part, trying to convince both of them that food would change her prognosis. "Maybe I can bring home one of those chickens from the market, you always liked those."

Her eyes, protruding over her shrinking skin, softened. "I think I'd eat more if you sat with me at night. I hate eating alone."

"Doesn't Sherry sit with you?" Sherry was the private day nurse.

"For breakfast."

"And lunch too, right?"

Again her eyes flicked away. "She's not always here for lunch. She had to take on another job."

"Jeez, Ma, when did this happen?"

"After your check bounced."

"I fixed that. I did, really." Rick had, but it had taken a week. His mother's social security was barely enough to pay for the utilities and insurance and food, let alone cover a private nurse. Rick was trying to make up the difference. Last month the property tax bill had forced Rick to empty his checking account. "I can't believe Sherry went and got another job."

"Don't blame her. She needs to pay bills too. She's a good woman and shows up every morning."

"I've got something going to make extra money. Once that happens I can get a nurse for the evenings too." Now it was Rick's turn to look away. "I'm trying, Ma, I really am."

"I know, Rickie. I don't want your money. I'm worried about you not having enough. Don't you think it's time to get a real job?"

They'd had this conversation so many times it was like a dance, each sentence choreographed. To his mother, and his long deceased father, music would never be a real job. "I have the studio work."

His mother jumped to another longstanding topic. "And before I leave this world, I want to see you settled down. Someone who'll take care of you when you get old and sick. You don't think of that now, but when the time comes . . ."

"Don't talk that way, Ma."

"And I mean a good woman. You're too easy going, too gullible."

Rick had once made the mistake of helping a girlfriend make a few car payments. In his mother's defense, she'd been right about that girl-friend.

"And no one in the music business. Those girls are trouble. Who knows what kind of men they've been with. And all the drugs."

"Speaking of drugs, Ma, are you taking all your pills?"

"Don't change the subject. Why don't you call Rebecca's daughter, Mary? She's such a sweet girl."

"You need anything, Ma? Some help getting up?" She was too proud to tell him she needed help going to the bathroom; Rick had learned this from Sherry. Nothing in his life had prepared Rick for the embarrass-ment of having to help his mother clean herself in the toilet. Not only for him, but for her; this debilitation more visible than the cancer itself.

"I'm fine."

"No really, Ma, it's okay. Let's go."

She didn't protest as Rick pulled back the blanket, lifted her legs over the side of the bed, and eased her down the narrow hall, the walls closing in on them both with every step.

THE WORST PART ABOUT Doc's relocation north—besides the shitty weather—was rebuilding a network of trusted worker bees. He wasn't looking for partners, or confidantes, just a few reliable helpers who could keep their mouths shut. Doc didn't trust anyone but himself with the big picture or the extent of his operations. The fewer involved, the less chance for leaks.

It was harder than it sounded, given the nature of his business. Most of his primary contacts for bling, blow, and muscle required tapping into someone else's network. It also meant that every so often he'd have to return the favor.

Which was why he was right now sitting at a picnic table under a viewing area pavilion out by the small regional airport. Cold and gray, the middle of the workday afternoon, the place was virtually deserted. Doc would have far preferred to be inside a warm and cozy restaurant, but you never knew where there would be cameras.

Doc didn't know the guy he was going to be meeting with, which meant he wanted to keep any possible eyes to a minimum. A sign proclaimed the parking lot was under video surveillance, so Doc had left his car a few blocks away and walked.

He was wearing a newly purchased leather jacket. The stiff material accentuated his portly frame, but the jacket did wonders against the never ending cold wind. In the off chance anyone wondered why he was sitting there, he held a lit cigar, a nice Montecristo.

Jose, one of Doc's contacts in Miami, had asked Doc to screen a Boston guy named Frank who had been recommended as a reliable delivery driver. If Frank worked out, Jose promised Doc he could borrow the driver when he wasn't busy. On the call Doc and Jose had commiserated on the difficulty of getting good help.

Doc's Cuban smoke was down by half, the guy was late. Not a good sign for a delivery man. Doc would wait until the cigar was almost done, then he'd pack it in. Sitting in the cold was enough of a favor for Jose, they'd be even.

Two men, looking far more comfortable than Doc in their leather and in the cold, walked in from the parking lot. One was gesturing, animated, long stringy hair past his collar, the other mostly quiet.

The quiet one, shortish dark hair, trim beard, hands at his sides said, "You Doc?"

Doc focused on the other guy, especially his hands, deep in his jacket pocket. "Who are you?"

The dark haired guy answered. "I'm Frank. Mutual friend said I'd find you here."

"Who are you?" Doc repeated to the other guy.

"Paulie. Friend of Frank's."

Doc took a hit from his Montecristo, got a nice glow going. "Take your hands out of your pockets."

"What?"

"Do as the man says," said Frank.

"Fucking cold," said Paulie, but he pulled out his hands.

Doc let out the smoke in Paulie's general direction. Jose didn't say anything about *two* guys. Surprises were rarely good. "You must have me mistaken for someone else."

Paulie scoffed. Frank said, "Maybe. My friend says you know a guy named Jose."

"Jose is a really common name." That was all Doc was willing to give up. No way he would let a stranger know he was connected down south.

"What's with the song and dance, old man?" said Paulie. "We're looking to do business."

Doc took another long hit on the Cuban. "Come to think of it, I had a gardener named Jose. You two gardeners? Looking to pull weeds, rake leaves?"

"Fuck you talking about," said Paulie. "We move shit."

"Shut up, Paulie," said Frank. To Doc he said, "Don't mind him. He's learning the ropes for when I need shotgun on a longer ride."

Doc stood up. As far as he was concerned, the interview was over. "Find yourself better friends," he said, and walked away.

*   *   *

DOC WASN'T SURPRISED to hear the hasty footsteps behind him. He was on a narrow pathway which ran through a line of evergreens, heading more or less toward his car.

Doc turned, Paulie bearing down on him. Predictable.

"Nobody disses me like that," grunted Paulie.

Already Paulie's hands were coming up, no weapon, Paulie maybe figuring Doc to be an easy beat down. Doc took one last hard draw on his Montecristo and waited, unperturbed. When Paulie was two steps away Doc quickly moved to the side. Big as he was, Doc was still agile. Doc pushed at Paulie's shoulder, spinning him half around, and smashed the glowing tip of the Cuban into Paulie's eye.

The reaction wasn't immediate, yet the agonizing scream made up for the delay. Both of Paulie's hands came up to his face. Doc tripped him, Paulie falling with no hands to break the fall. Doc kicked him hard in the kidney. "That's for making me waste the rest of my smoke."

Doc strolled out past the evergreens, examining the remnants of his cigar. Jose now owed *him*, and Doc might consider a box of Cubans as repayment.

Jose was right, good help was hard to find.

RICK WAITED UNTIL the studio was empty, which didn't take long. The Crash Heaves were taking a toll on the entire staff. On days like this, Rick often had second thoughts about whether working in the music industry was a good idea. He wanted to *be* an artist, not just work with them. He was as good as half the bands who had come through Larry's studio, and most of those bands were in the big time, not wannabees off the street. Every so-so song was another reminder of why Rick should be on the other side of the window, in the studio, not working the board.

Music had been part of his life since he was five years old, banging away at his mom's piano, doing air guitar imitations of Slash and Steve Vai. He could sing Beatles' songs before he could read, play scales before he could do arithmetic. His father had owned a bar, his mother helping out as a waitress, and Rick would sit on a stool after school as they got ready to open, an old jukebox blaring classics. A teenage babysitter would whisk him away before the bar opened, but he must have absorbed the music, because even at her house he'd be pattering away at sofa pillows arranged on the floor like a drum set.

As he often did when alone in the studio, Rick stuck a thumbdrive in the board, running his own creations through the monitors. Larry could be a jerk, but he had great equipment. Twenty years ago, in recording studios all over the country, the amateurs had paid the rent, long lines of dreamers putting their ideas onto media. Bad as some of their music was, they were efficient in the studio, the clock ticking, pay per hour. With the advent of digital music bands could do demos at home, not even needing the proverbial garage. Even big names recorded tracks in personal studios, assembled for ten percent of what a full pro studio cost. The old studios were closing down, especially the indies. A few still hung on, like Larry, due to his contacts, his good equipment—a lot of it bought from bankrupt competitors—and oddly, his out of the city location, some bands preferring to get away from the rush, just like an author would hide out in a cabin to write a book.

Rick listened critically to his own music, fighting the urge to be a perfectionist, but knowing he'd never be satisfied. The trick was to decide what really needed to be changed versus what only he would notice. The song playing now, a brisk major chord upbeat track, was meant to be the first song on an album, the enticer. It had the appropriate tempo and energy, but it wasn't quite right. Rick hit a few switches, redirecting the output from a straight play to the mixer, adjusting the sliding pots. The levels were too uniform across the play, the song needed more dynamics.

He fiddled for a while. It helped him relax, putting him back in the mood of a musician. He hadn't laid down a vocal track; he was an okay singer, but this song needed a range he didn't have. In his head he sung along with the voice he wanted. Bryan, a guy who had sung lead for his and Gerry's best band, would have killed these vocals.

The band that had *almost* been signed. Rick glanced involuntarily at the wall where Larry's Grammy hung. Larry had worked at The Magic Shop as an engineer, a legendary studio for decades, and had done fine work, using equipment that would now seem woefully difficult to work with. Though a lot of that took place before Rick was born, Rick and Gerry had a link to that Grammy. Through a friend of a friend of a friend, which was how musical dreams often took wing, they'd managed to get one of their songs in front of an A&R guy at the very label which had released Larry's Grammy hit.

The memory still haunted Rick. Just out of high school, he and Gerry were in New York, sitting in a conference room of a major record company, listening to *their own* music through the monitors, as the A&R guy, whose name was Steve Loci, tapped his fingers on the table, nodding. Rick almost peed his pants when Steve called in one of his buddies and played it again.

The rest of the conversation was as clear in Rick's mind as was the music now pulsing from the control room monitors.

"Sounds good," Loci had said. "Nice hook. But I gotta know, is this all hours in the studio and overdubs, or can you do some semblance of it live? No one makes it these days without a tour."

Rick jumped in before Gerry could go into too much detail. "Sure, Steve, sure. That little spot after the chorus is a doubling, but we could run that through the board in real time."

"That's okay, everyone does a little mix of live and prerecorded," said Steve. "I mean, how about the rest of the band?"

Rick glanced at Gerry, hoping he wouldn't let slip that their keyboard player had just moved to the west coast for college.

"We're all good," said Rick. "When do you want to give us a listen?" He'd prayed it wasn't the next day.

"I have two weeks on the road, I'm actually going to be in Boston after that." Loci pulled out his card, sliding it across to Rick. "Call this number to set it up."

All the way back to Massachusetts Gerry had worried about the keyboard player, but even Gerry's pragmatism couldn't bring Rick down. *They were on their way.* Years of practice and songwriting and fighting with his parents over his future would finally be replaced with a career in music, he and Gerry were going to get their songs in front of the world . . .

They scrambled to find a keyboard player, harder than they had thought. They finally found a guy who agreed to do the play through, and Rick had put in the call to the label.

Only to find out that Steve Loci was not there. Not just not in the office, but gone from the label. Rick, on the phone, couldn't think straight, the secretary's clipped words a dagger in his lifeblood.

He'd hung up in a daze, and it took a week of calls to find out where Steve had gone. They left a dozen messages at Steve's new label, only to finally reach a harried assistant who told them the label was looking in a different direction. Translation: sorry, you are shit out of luck.

Now, almost ten years later, Rick was no closer to success than he had been then. For his music, that is. Unfortunately, he was physically closer to musicians and songwriters who had made it, rubbing shoulders with them every day, which only made it that much more depressing.

He cranked up the volume, slipping away into the magic of a good song, a reminder of how far he had come, and how much farther he still had to go.

CHAPTER 4

Rɪᴄᴋ sᴀᴛ ᴀᴛ ᴀ table in Marburg Park, downing his second overpriced Monster from the concession stand. He'd been in the studio until five in the morning with the Crash Heaves because the lead singer kept messing up the lyrics. Rick really wanted to just go home and sleep all day, but he had the twenty thousand of the band's money, and didn't even trust himself with all that cash.

A zippered portfolio holding the cash sat on the table. Rick knew enough to treat it—or pretend to treat it—casually, like it was merely his reading material. An unadorned blue book bag lay against his feet.

It was warm for September, the tables dotted with internet surfers, readers, coffee drinkers. Mostly older people, a scattering of moms with younger kids.

A perfect place for a drug deal, according to Doc.

Rick had bought drugs from Doc before, although never this quantity. That Doc sold to him at all was an oddity only due to Rick once before being in a similar situation as a go-between. Rick's boss Larry had eyes for a Latina who'd shown up at one of his parties. When she told Larry she needed something picked up, Larry order Rick to run the errand. Rick was at the party as hired help, so he didn't care if he was being sent to pick up feminine products.

The woman had given Rick the keys to her Corvette. The address turned out to be a doctor's office, Rick wondering what kind of doctor kept evening hours? Rick never made it to the office; a pasty skinned, fat guy with thinning hair and almost invisible eyebrows carrying a portfolio case met him in the parking lot even before Rick got out of the car. The guy gave Rick a once over, glanced at his phone, told Rick to pop the trunk, walked around back, closed the trunk, and said to Rick, "I put a case in the trunk. Bring it to her. Don't make any stops, don't open the case. Got it?"

Rick nodded woodenly, realizing he was making his first drug haul. A few blocks away he stopped the car, thinking it through. There were drugs in the music business, sure, and while Rick's life wasn't exactly on a yellow brick road, this wasn't a detour he ever wanted to take. But it was a little late to pull out now. What was he going to do, drive to the cops, say, hey, I might have some dope in this expensive car I'm driving, which also doesn't belong to me?

Back at the party, Rick handed the portfolio to the Latina. She thanked Rick with a big hug, like he had just saved her life. She reached into her tiny purse and handed him two hundred dollar bills and disappeared into the bathroom.

A month later Larry had a thing going with her, and Rick ran a few more similar errands. The third time, he spoke to the fat guy for the first time, asking if it would be okay if he could also buy a little of whatever was in the portfolio now and then, Rick having figured out from the dust on the drama queen's nostrils it was coke, and likely a far higher quality than Rick ever got.

The fat guy—who Rick now knew as Doc—had said, "I don't know you, and I don't do nickel and dime." Doc's way of saying Rick didn't look like he had the money to make it worth his while.

Rick wasn't upset, the guy was just being careful. "How about I just do an add on with the next pickup?"

The doctor said, "That's between you and her."

It had been fine with the Latina, and even after she and Larry had moved past each other, Rick had done small piggybacks onto her buys a few times, even doing the pickups for her.

This was going to be Rick's first buy on his own, which the Latina had graciously set up in exchange for Rick getting her the private phone number of the lead singer of a hot band that had recorded at the studio.

So here he sat, with the book bag and the portfolio, nervous but knowing the drill. If Doc used other delivery men Rick had never met them, it had always been the fat man himself.

Who plopped down in the small metal chair as Rick was looking the other way. Doc was wearing a dark blue fleece sweater and wool pants, way too many clothes for the weather.

"Thanks for doing this," said Rick.

"We haven't done anything yet," said Doc. The doctor—Rick still wasn't sure if he was a real one—placed a matching zippered portfolio on the table, indicating he was at least open to the deal. Rick fought the urge to look under the table for a book bag. Rick nodded toward his own portfolio. "She said twenty would make it worthwhile for you."

"I still don't know you."

"I'm just a guy, I admit," said Rick. "You know what I do, who I come in contact with. They're in, they're out. No names. Shit, I bet some of them don't even remember *my* name."

"Need to keep it that way. That is, if we do anything."

Rick said, "If I was going to be a problem, I would have been a problem already. And believe me, the band I'm helping out, this is definitely for their own use." What Rick was trying to communicate was that the Crash Heaves would be the last group the cops would use to set up a sting. The doc still seemed to be undecided, so Rick, bordering on desperation, added, "The studio gets its share of people who might be more your kind of—client. I can make the introductions."

The fat man tapped the portfolio with a pudgy finger. "Your piece?"

Rick knew music, not about dealing. "Whatever you think is fair."

The doctor leaned forward, peering into Rick's face. "When was the last time you used?"

Rick wondered if there was any way to tell, maybe the guy *was* a doctor. Or a psychic. Again Rick went with the truth. "Three weeks maybe? I've been in the studio day and night with the band this stuff is for. I don't use much at all, and I never use when I'm working."

The doctor leaned back. Rick never knew whether it was what he said or whether Doc read an EKG of drug history in his eyes, but the fat man pulled a cheap phone from his pocket and slid it under the portfolio. "Use this if you have something for me. The number is stored. No details on the phone, just ask for an appointment."

Rick realized he had crossed some kind of threshold, and considered taking the opportunity to ask for a little extra product. He never got the chance.

Doc said, "Remember, I'm a doctor, not a bank. No credit." He eased himself out of the tiny chair, picked up Rick's portfolio and empty book bag, and waddled off.

Maybe Doc was a psychic after all.

*   *   *

THE DRUGS SPURRED the Crash Heaves into productivity, but everything bogged down on what was scheduled to be their last day, the band pointing fingers at Lasher for being off key, at Oz for being off the beat.

Corey, the producer, tossed his coffee cup in the trash and said, "Shit, here we go again."

"They've done this before?" asked Rick.

"Whenever they're not high. All their latent real musical skills pop back out." Corey got up, stretched. "I'm out of here."

Rick glanced at the clock. He was supposed to get things wrapped by the end of the day and they still had overdubs to do. "What time are you coming back?"

"I'll check in every few hours. Or call me if they get motivated, you know what I mean?"

"Larry usually keeps a bottle of tequila in his office," offered Rick.

"Don't even think about it," said Corey as he walked out. "Booze puts them to sleep."

Rick turned off the sound from the studio, he had to think. If the band didn't get out on time their problem was going to be Rick's problem, seeing that the rich, double-fee-paying Candy was scheduled for tomorrow. Just as important, the pre-production meeting with Miranda was set for this afternoon. Rick was trying to figure out how to move things along when Larry came into the control room.

"What the hell is going on? I just saw Corey walking out."

Rick gestured toward the studio. "A little creative disagreement."

"Damn metalheads. You need to get them out of here. I don't need them wrecking the place before Candy comes in."

Rick actually thought most metal bands were easier to deal with than the pop divas, but he didn't want to get in an argument with Larry. "I'll take care of it."

"You'd better."

Rick filled in the blanks. With all the studios closing down, engineers were easy to get. Rick couldn't afford to lose his job. "I'll take care of it," he repeated.

Larry stormed out, muttering about metalheads and the old days. Rick watched the band argue through the glass, an old fashioned silent movie. He didn't think reminding them about the deadline, or even offering up a few musical ideas of his own, was going to help, so he just called Rudy.

"Hey Rudy, it's Rick. Listen, the band is getting a little off track. Corey thinks maybe, you know, a little pick me up might be in order to get them focused?"

"I'm sure he's right. But we're all out."

"Out?" Rick had delivered all the drugs Rudy had asked for.

"We had a little party last night which turned into a big party. The stuff went pretty fast."

"So there's nothing you can do?" asked Rick.

"Actually, I was just about to call you."

Rick's phone buzzed with a text. Larry: *I don't hear any music!*

Soundproofed as the studio was, Larry's office was close enough to pick up the vibrations.

"Shit," said Rick.

"What?" asked Rudy.

"Nothing." Rick grabbed at his hair, why couldn't anything be easy? "I'll take care of it for you," he said to Rudy. Which was all Rick seemed to be doing, taking care of other people's problems instead of his own.

RICK SCURRIED AROUND the studio, jamming the detritus of the recording session into an industrial trash bag: plastic water bottles, high dosage caffeine drinks, crumpled tissue paper. He'd long ago learned to wear latex gloves for this part of the job.

He had managed to get the Crash Heaves out on schedule, but it had cost him dearly. He had made a frantic call to the guy who had been Rick's coke source before Doc. Hearing Rick's desperation, the guy charged Rick extra, forcing Rick to use up the cash he had made on the Crash Heaves transaction, leaving him nothing for his plan for Miranda, who was going to show up any minute.

The band had soaked up the blow like a sponge, greasing them for the rest of the session, although Oz had managed to break a microphone stand in his exuberance. It wasn't especially expensive but even Larry would notice a dangling boom, so after dumping the trash Rick dragged it down to the basement storeroom.

The basement was a tribute to the studio's history, stacks of old tube amplifiers, guitar pedals, even reel to reel tape machines. Larry hadn't been down here in years and no doubt had lost track of what had been stashed away.

Rick had barely made it back upstairs and cleaned up when Miranda arrived. Rick's best smile wasn't faked; after being holed up with the band for over a week, she was a sight for sore eyes. Not to mention the potential she represented.

"Good to see you, Miranda."

"Rick." She held out her hand, all business like, carrying a chic brief-case. She was wearing a fringed jacket over a white tee shirt with tight black pants. Her brown eyes were a little small and close together, but she did a good job with makeup, giving her lashes a little curl.

Rick normally did meetings in the control room when he wanted to impress someone, but figured Miranda was immune to that, so he ushered her into the utilitarian conference room. He got her a bottle of water from the fridge without asking, making sure to give her a glass.

"Things good?" he asked, sitting across from her.

"Good enough. Candy keeps me busy." Miranda looked around the empty room. "We expecting anyone?"

"Just me. I can get Larry if you want, but between the two of us, he's just going to turn around and repeat everything you say to me. It'll be faster this way, less chance for miscommunication."

"Okay. But we need to tell him Candy is running at least a day or two late. She's stuck on the last couple of songs."

"What do you mean, stuck?"

"She's got writer's block. She's out at the house."

The *house* was the Carter family estate, a ten thousand square foot mansion that frequently graced the pages of architectural magazines. "That's okay," said Rick, not believing his luck. *Candy needed material.* All he needed to do now was get his songs in front of her . . .

"Once she arrives," said Miranda, "Candy must have two bottles of Pellegrino with fresh lemon always available. The temperature of the studio should always be at exactly seventy one degrees. I will bring her special tea."

"We have a hot water kettle."

"We'll bring our own." Miranda frowned. "Aren't you going to write this down?"

"I know you are very good at what you do," said Rick. Trying not to sound boastful, he added, "So am I."

Miranda gave him a look. "Okay. No smoking in the studio or any room where Candy will be." Miranda opened her satchel. "A catered lunch at one, every day. Here's the menu. If you can't get good goat cheese around here I'll have it driven in from Boston. And this separate menu, for when her new producer is here."

"Who is?"

Miranda paused. "You're going to find out anyway. DeVaughn."

"Kendall DeVaughn? Holy shit, how did she manage to get him?"

"It's no secret Candy's first albums didn't do much. She refused to use any of her daddy's money on them, because he hates the idea of her being in music. But since she is, he's not going to let a Carter fail. He brought in DeVaughn."

Rick recognized the possibilities. "DeVaughn can make Candy a star."

"Which is why we need to treat him right. He still wants to hear the final demos, and Candy doesn't think she has enough material. Which is why she's still writing."

"I'll personally make sure everything is perfect," said Rick. If he could convince Candy to use even *one* of his songs on a DeVaughn produced album . . . "For the food, we'll use Cuisino—same one as in the city. You know it?"

Miranda gave Rick her first real smile. "You do know what you're doing, don't you?"

"We aim to please," said Rick. "And we'd do that even if Candy wasn't working with Kendal DeVaughn."

Miranda made a little shake of her hand, indicating the room. "What are you doing here?"

Rick understood her question. If you know what you are doing, why are you working out in the middle of nowhere? Larry's studio was well respected, but this wasn't exactly Los Angeles or Nashville. Rick was about to launch into his history, his songwriting, his dreams of making it big. He'd been on the receiving end of those stories, they always sounded like the excuses of losers. Instead he said, "I'd rather hear *your* story, but at someplace nicer than here."

Miranda tidied up her papers, noncommittal. "Anything you get around here besides coffee and goat cheese?"

Though Miranda was far more discreet than Rudy, Rick immediately deciphered her code. She wanted to see if he could score some drugs, either for her or Candy. Or both.

Rick said, "Look, I know what you do, you make things happen. So do I. The engineering is just part of my job. We get together, I'll bring more than just my history."

Miranda looked him over, Rick's heart pounding, trying to hold it together on the outside. He was glad he'd worn a nice shirt and a great pair of shoes, women like Miranda noticed shoes.

Diffidently, she said, "I might have some time tomorrow night."

Rick gave himself a mental high five. Step one, complete.

RICK AWOKE to complete silence, the mixing board lights coming into focus like a B-movie producer's idea of a psychedelic trip. The hall lights were out, turned off by timers. It was almost ten p.m.

He'd been dreaming not of fame and fortune, but of a conversation with Candy. Not in a conference room, but Rick yelling to get noticed through a huge PA system, like those old stacks in the basement. But even though he had the gain maxed out, Candy wasn't listening.

Rick had no doubt Miranda was expecting him to provide some party drugs. She looked all business, but he picked up a definite vibe that carrying a fancy portfolio case hid her wild side, not smothered it.

His immediate problem was that he had nothing for Miranda. He'd used everything he had to save the producer's schedule and Larry's profits and maybe his own job, but Miranda wasn't going to be able to put that on a tray and snort it up her nose. Rick needed some cash, and fast.

Cash. Larry had all that unused equipment gathering dust . . .

More than dust, Rick found out when he made his way back to the basement and started pulling the piles apart. A vintage Vox AC-100 amp, the same amp the Beatles had used in their 1964 U.S. tour, was buried behind a piece of crap Peavy cabinet. Unfortunately the Vox was also buried under a layer of mold, which Rick didn't have the time to clean off. Too bad, the amp was probably worth a bundle.

Rick had never stolen anything in his life, unless you counted the supposedly valuable Canadian pennies he'd snatched from one of his not so good friends in the fourth grade. The kid had a jar full, so Rick had figured he'd never miss any. Rick learned a few valuable lessons that day, one being that a lot of what people said was bullshit, and the other being that if you were going to steal something, better to take what wouldn't be missed.

Rick's plan was to hock some equipment and buy it back when he finally got a few songs sold. But as he uncovered hidden gems of gear he became more pissed off at Larry. All this classic gear didn't deserve to be sitting in a damp basement. His old partner Gerry would be able to make that Vox sing.

Rick slumped on the edge of a busted Marshall stack. Thinking about Gerry always made Rick a little maudlin. He and Gerry were going to be the next Lennon and McCartney, or at least the next Steely Dan or Dave Matthews and Tim Reynolds. Rick's uncle, a small town lawyer, had even prepared a real, legal contract between them, agreeing on a fifty-fifty royalty split for all their songs. The piece of paper wasn't really needed, but it made Rick feel like a professional at seventeen.

Gerry could craft a hook out of theory, and though he could outplay Rick in his sleep, Rick knew how to give the songs punch. They'd been the perfect complement since high school, Gerry years ahead of his age in his skills and musical chops, Rick writing lyrics, putting together a band, getting them gigs. He saw nothing but runway to a successful takeoff and a career in music.

When graduation rolled around Rick hadn't even thought about college, it would just get in the way of music, and why lay out money for a future payoff when they were already making more than any of their friends? Far from rich, sure, but enough to give music a full time go of it. Gerry, though, had as much skill in math as he did with music. The day Gerry told Rick about his acceptance to MIT was the saddest day of Rick's life, even worse than the loss of the record deal.

Rick toyed listlessly with the fabric on the edge of the Marshall cabinet. He'd managed to convince Gerry to defer his admission; after all, Rick was good at convincing people. But after the recording contract hadn't materialized they were back on the same treadmill, playing local clubs. Good bands were a dime a dozen, and making it big would mean a move to the West Coast or Nashville. Rick would have left in a heartbeat, but Gerry was more interested in equations than music notation, and after two years he started college. He gigged with Rick and the latest iteration of the band for a few months, but then dropped out, leaving Rick with notebooks full of songs but no partner.

Rick kicked over the lightweight Peavey cabinet. Dreaming about a future that would have come about from a lost past wasn't going to do him any good now. Time to make a new future. Rick grabbed a Marshall head that looked halfway decent and hauled it up the stairs.

CHAPTER 5

B Y ELEVEN THE NEXT MORNING, Rick had almost a grand of cash in his pocket. He'd driven to Boston early and had unloaded the equipment at two different pawn shops. Most of the stuff was pretty old and no one asked for purchase receipts.

Rick didn't think a grand was enough to interest Doc, so he went back to his usual recreational use source. Rick bought what he thought he'd need for Miranda, leaving himself a few hundred.

It was a good thing he did. When he'd called Miranda to set up a time she said she was in Boston and wanted to eat at a new Chinese restaurant there. Rick had just driven back from Boston, but he figured he'd recover the gas money from what he'd save taking her for cheap eats.

Miranda was already at the restaurant when Rick arrived, a post modern glass and red chrome noisy joint with uncomfortable looking chairs. Tonight Miranda was wearing a woman's business suit, the whole nine yards, jacket, matching skirt, heels. He almost didn't recognize her.

"Sorry I'm late," Rick said, although he was right on time. Miranda leaned forward like she expected a kiss on the cheek, so he gave her one.

"I finished up early. I don't have my car. You'll have to drive me home."

That sounded good to Rick, the night getting off on the right foot. A momentary bump jostled his mental ride when he checked out the prices on the menu, how could Chinese be this expensive?

Rick did some calculations in his head, hoping Miranda wasn't a wine aficionado. Fortunately she ordered a Paloma, another good sign; a little tequila might soften her up for his pitch.

She drank half the glass in one swoop. "Shit, what a day."

"Trouble?"

"Candy asked me to sit in on the lawyer meetings for the preparation of her royalty contracts for videos and overseas play. I don't understand half the words they use. They could be dragging out the meetings just to run up their fees."

"What does Candy say?"

"She never goes, she's still writing. She'll see the final contract, but her lawyer—actually, her father's lawyer—will have the last word."

"So why does she want you there?"

Miranda finished off her drink. "She trusts me more than she trusts her father's lawyers." She looked around hopefully for the waiter. "I'm famished."

Over the meal they made small talk until Miranda finally came up for air. "I better stop," she said, eying a platter of duck. "I'll burst."

"With the menu you showed me for the catering, I had you pegged for a vegan."

"That's Candy. I have to eat all that crap when I'm with her, it makes me crave meat."

"How'd you two get together?" asked Rick.

Melanie crunched on a fried noodle. "We were both waitresses at the same restaurant."

"Candy? A waitress?"

"Yeah, right? Candy kept hearing about the downtrodden ninety nine percent during her freshman year at Wellesley and decided to learn about the masses for herself. So she took a summer job at a tourist spot on Cape Cod. Got her hands dirty."

"And?"

"Other than having to serve hamburgers—she was already vegan— she actually seemed to like it. You've met her, haven't you?"

"Just briefly. I was helping out on the board when she did her demos."

"She's got two totally different sides. One part of her is the typical rich kid, knows what she wants and just gets it. But she has this down to earth side too. No one at the restaurant had any idea she was rich. I never even associated her name with the family." Miranda was working on her third drink, she'd switched to margaritas. "I'm not telling you anything people don't already know."

She said it in a way that made Rick think she was talking out of school, so he changed the subject. "What about you? How'd you get from the waitress gig to working for Candy?"

"My mom was a personal assistant for a senator. She taught me a lot about the job. It didn't hurt that Candy's father knew the senator, too. Connections." Miranda picked the slice of lime off her glass and sucked on it suggestively. "Plus, you know, I'm not as good looking as she is, so when we are together everyone will be looking at her and not me."

"You're plenty good looking."

"Don't humor me. I got nothing on Candy. But I'm more fun."

Rick gave her a little eyebrow wiggle. "I bet."

"What's your story?"

Rick sensed she wasn't really interested, so he gave her the short version. "I'm a songwriter and musician, pop rock mostly. Doing the engineering work to pay the bills in between gigs."

"What do you play?"

"I'm okay on guitar, bass, drums, even keyboards, but not amazing at anything."

Miranda puckered her mouth around the lime wedge. "Wow, an honest musician."

"I *am* good at songwriting, especially lyrics." Rick waited a beat to see if Miranda took the bait; he didn't want to sound like he was selling, not even after her three drinks.

"I have to hit the ladies'," she said.

Rick waved for the check. Thank god he had the blow.

THEY'D BEEN IN THE CAR less than five minutes when Miranda shuffled in the seat and did some gymnastic move under her skirt. "I hate fucking pantyhose," she said, kicking off her shoes and wadding up her nylons. She rolled down the window and tossed them outside.

Rick figured that was as good of a segue as he was going to get, so he reached into the armrest and pulled out a CD case. "You might like this better."

Miranda squinted at the title. "Jeff Beck? Really?"

Rick glanced over as she pried open the case. The inner tray had been hollowed out into smaller sections, each filled with coke, along with a small glass straw. "It's his best album. Blow By Blow."

Miranda laughed and pulled out the straw. "I knew I'd like you."

RICK'S HEAD WAS STILL FOGGED the next morning at the studio, so it took him a while to register the implications of the fact that Candy Carter herself had arrived with the band. He'd partied late with Miranda. Or more accurately, Miranda had partied all the way home from the restaurant, in the parking lot of her apartment, and, once inside, had gone through most of his coke as fast as she had the Chinese food.

Rick had done a few lines himself, and they'd traded tequila shots. He had worked the conversation around to his music, promising Miranda he could fix Candy's songwriter block in one shot. He played Miranda a few songs off his phone and transferred the files to hers. The audio sucked, but it was the best he could do. Miranda told him it was a great idea, then promptly fell asleep, the tequila beating the blow in a photo finish.

Candy being in the studio hopefully meant she was going to use Rick's material. He didn't have a chance to ask Miranda; she barely gave him a second glance, shadowing Candy around as the band got ready. She'd got more sleep than Rick and looked better than he felt.

Candy's musicians were pros, finishing more tracks in the first two hours than the Crash Heaves had in two days. Candy sat in the studio, bobbing away to the beat, looking hot, sunshine natural blond hair, her big blue eyes bright, dressed in distressed jeans and a loose tee shirt that said, "Eat less chikin." Larry's nephew Gus, the senior engineer, ran the board. Even though Rick was second fiddle in the control room without much to do he didn't have a minute to talk to Candy about his songs. Miranda had vanished soon after the session had started, only reappearing just before lunch with two shopping bags. In between songs she pulled out a bottle of kombucha and waved it through the window to Candy.

"Take five, everyone," said Candy.

Rick followed Candy out into the hallway, hoping to corner her, but bumped into Larry popping out of his office. Miranda was on her phone, setting up a publicity shoot.

Or trying to. Candy wagged a juice drink bottle in Miranda's face. "It's got malitol! How many times do I need to tell you, only natural sweeteners!" Candy tossed the unopened bottle in the trash. Larry soothingly hustled her into his office.

Stymied, Rick hovered around the hallway. Candy's bass player caught his eye.

"Need something?" asked Rick.

In a raspy half whisper, the bass player said, "Any place I can sneak out for a smoke?"

"Sure," said Rick. "Come on." He led the bass player out the back entrance. When Rick walked back down the hall Miranda was still on the phone, and Candy was just coming out of Larry's office.

Rick caught her before she reached the studio. "Hey Candy, I'm Rick."

She gave him a perfunctory smile, no hint of recognition to either his face or his name. "Hi."

"Uh, just wondering what you thought of the songs."

Even less recognition now. "Excuse me?"

Rick tried again. "Miranda said you needed a few more tracks for the album—"

"I'll have them done in a few days. We'll keep the schedule, don't worry. I just told Larry." She pushed past Rick into the studio.

Rick felt like an idiot, Candy obviously had no idea who he was. Miranda got off the phone and followed Candy, but Rick took her arm and half dragged her into the conference room.

"Hey," she said, pulling away.

"Hey yourself. You said you'd give my music to Candy."

Miranda looked genuinely confused. "Did I?"

Rick *was* certain about playing his music for her, but not much else about the night before. "Yes you did."

"I don't remember."

"I put the songs on your phone. Candy just told me she's still short a few tracks. You'd be helping her out. And me."

"Remind me again why I'd do that for you?"

Rick bit off a mean retort. "How about we party again?"

Miranda shrugged. "I get invited to a *lot* of parties. You're not the only one wanting Candy to listen to some music."

That was possibly true, although Candy, even with her record deal, was no Adele, and right now Rick couldn't trust his bullshit meter, he wanted this so badly. "What would be a fun party for you?"

"Like last time, but maybe you could stay a little longer." She narrowed her eyes to slits, no doubt her idea of sultry. "And bring more entertainment."

Rick forced a smile. "Tomorrow night okay?"

CHAPTER 6

RICK LAY AMIDST the crumbled sheets, Miranda's heavily sprayed hair itching his stomach. She was babbling, some story about a trip to Paris she'd taken with Candy. Rick almost regretted not having brought a bottle of tequila to go along with the blow. It might have slowed her down, but he wanted her to be lucid so this time she'd remember her promise to get Candy to listen to his music.

As it was Miranda had done a half dozen lines already. Earlier, when Rick hadn't bit at her sultry eye come-on she'd practically mauled him, ripping at his clothes. The sex had been overly loud, Miranda moaning like a porn star. The combination of Miranda not really being his type and the need to focus on his plan kept Rick a little removed from the action.

He was about to launch into his spiel just as Miranda said, "You're cute. I like dark eyes and curly hair."

Rick was about to say something nice in return but Miranda wasn't the listening type. She went on, "And you're a pretty nice guy."

Rick's antenna tensed, that was usually the intro to either a *we're just friends* blow off or a *let's be a couple* speech. "Thanks," he said carefully. "You're pretty nice yourself."

"I mean, I barely know you, but I feel I can talk to you. I can't relate to all the people in Candy's world, you know what I mean?"

That seemed harmless enough, so Rick said, "I hear you."

"They have so much money. I'm the only one around her who isn't rich."

"Must be tough," said Rick.

Miranda rolled her finger around his shoulder. "Candy treats me okay, most of the time, but the rest of them look at me like I'm not there. You should see the parties. Caviar, champagne fountains. Guests show up in limousines, the women with more diamonds than Tiffany's. I get a clothing allowance from Candy, but I always feel like I'm dressed in rags. For Candy's sixteenth birthday they had Kylie Roman as the dj. I heard he cost fifty grand."

Rick was thinking about the money he'd seen thrown around by other successful musicians at the studio. "With that much money, you have to spend it somewhere."

"You got that right. The Carter family has ten cars. Who needs ten cars?"

Rick thought having a few nice cars wouldn't be so bad, especially since all he owned was a no frills Kia.

"I mean, it's so unfair," Miranda went on. She leaned over Rick for the tray on the nightstand and did another line of blow.

Unfair was having to sleep with a personal assistant to get good music listened to by an unproven artist, thought Rick, but he kept his mouth shut. He took the tray from Miranda, did a little bump. Not too much—it was all he had left—just to keep him focused on the task at hand.

Miranda plopped back on Rick's chest. "I mean, I have dreams too. I don't want to be a personal assistant all my life."

The conversation threatened to drift into downer territory, so Rick said, "The parties must be fun, though?"

"Kind of stuffy. I could throw a mean party, but they'd never let me." Miranda brightened. "*There's* an idea. I want to have a really big, *fun* party, invite people I've met through Candy. Impress them, just like Candy's family does."

Rick made a noncommittal *hmm* sound.

Miranda was warming to her own inspiration. "Lots of coke all over the place, like I was rich. The best booze, great music."

"That's a nice dream," said Rick. Parties were to the music world what golf courses were to business—it was where deals got done.

He was trying to figure out how to get the conversation back around to his music when Miranda threw a heavy leg over his and straddled him. "You want me to get your music to Candy? It's going to take more than a roll in the sack. Get me enough coke to throw a party for my friends, and I promise you Candy will listen to your songs. And I'm not talking my BFF's, I mean a *real* party. A big party. With enough left over to share with a special friend."

"A boyfriend?"

"For a friend it would be good for you to impress, you know what I mean?"

Rick figured she meant someone up the food chain in the Candy entourage, or maybe even Candy herself. Just because Candy was a vegan didn't mean she didn't put pure stuff up her nose. "Sure, Miranda, no problem."

Rick made Miranda do all the work the next go around, his mind preoccupied with how to get that much blow.

IT WAS A GOOD THING Rick wasn't on the board the next day. Between Miranda's physical needs, the coke, and worrying about his own problems, he hadn't slept. Miranda, in between sweat soaked tussles, wound her party story so tight it was now a gala.

Though he'd given up trying to dissuade her, Rick hadn't fully committed to a deal. What Miranda was asking for was many thousands of dollars he didn't have. And she certainly could be playing him for a sucker. For all he knew she did this all the time, sucking desperate songwriters for all they were worth with empty promises of floating their creations in front of Candy and her money.

Kendall DeVaughn entered the studio regally, even though he was dressed in a body hugging silk tee shirt and distressed jeans. Rick was impressed by DeVaughn's work; he'd given the Midas touch to a few songwriters. Rick knew better than to hit DeVaughn up with his own music; not only would Larry hit the roof but DeVaughn would see Rick as nothing more than an amateur.

At lunch, though, Rick slipped a thumbdrive of his music into the board and piped it into the studio, a little background groove. Good dynamics, which he felt was missing from the tracks he'd heard so far from Candy.

Before the track reached the chorus the studio was empty, everyone hitting the conference room where the food was laid out. Rick kept the music playing, then drifted over that way himself, hoping Miranda would invite him in.

All he got from her was a look that made it clear all he had done for her last night wasn't carrying over to today. She wasn't looking too hot herself, but Candy didn't seem to notice, giving Miranda a long list of to-dos.

After the conference room cleared out Rick forced down some left-overs and hurried back to the control room. Gus was at the board, and Rick's music had been turned off.

Time to come up with a Plan B.

DOC MILES HAD JUST BEEN on the receiving end of a great backrub from Tricia when the strains of Schoenberg's String Quartet Number 2 wafted across the room. Doc still wasn't sure how he felt about atonal music, which was why he had chosen it as the ring tone of the burner phone for the new kid, Rick. Doc hadn't decided about Rick either.

Tricia brought him the phone. "Yeah?"

"I have an investment opportunity you might be interested in."

"I only invest in sure things."

"Well, then maybe not. I don't want to waste you time. But it's a small investment with a potentially large payout. I can't guarantee it's a sure thing."

Doc was passably impressed by Rick's response, although he sensed where the conversation was going. "How short are you?"

"I need five."

"What's this big opportunity?"

"A way into a client who would be worth way more to you than I ever will be."

"I have a lot of clients. Give me some reference."

"The woman I drove for in the past? Way more than her."

If Rick could link Doc to a customer who would be interested in that level of weight, it would be worthwhile for him. "I don't need publicity."

"None for you, and this potential client has a lot of reasons to be very discreet. Family reasons."

Which meant she was monied. Doc was warming to the kid, he knew how to communicate. Partially because of that, and partially because he was feeling loose from Tricia's backrub, he decided to let it play. "Better not come empty handed. I might consider an investment, but you have to have some skin in the game. I told you, I'm not a bank."

Doc was feeling good, not generous.

*   *   *

RICK DIDN'T TRY to read too much into the fact he was meeting Doc in his office for the first time. The office was warm, yet Doc was over-clad as he had been every time Rick had seen him, a heavy sweater vest, a wool sport coat. Today he wore a tie, like he was a real doctor. Rick still didn't know, even though the sign out front had said "Rudolf Miles, MD." The office was as stuffed as Doc, heavy books on built-in shelves, monstrous expensive looking mahogany furniture, leather lined boxes, a lingering scent of a fine cigar.

"Thanks for seeing me on such short notice," said Rick. Actually it had been a whole day, but he needed the time to borrow a few more pieces of equipment from Larry's basement. Still short, on his way back from the pawn shops Rick stopped off to see a musician who had eyed Rick's vintage Roland Overdrive Space Echo and custom pedal set at a gig. Rick hated to give them up. They had a lot of memories attached; he'd used them in his first band with Gerry. But if he was forced to sell his gear he wanted it to go to a musician who would appreciate and take care of the equipment.

"I've got clients coming in," said Doc. "Make it quick."

Rick had plenty of practice making pitches, he'd been doing it since he was sixteen trying to get gigs. "I've got an in with a personal assistant to Candy Carter." Rick thought that would have been a good enough hook, but Doc looked blank. "As in the Carter family."

"That means what, exactly?"

"Old Boston money. Not flashy, but the family goes way back, movers and shakers behind the politicians. Lots of charity work."

"I'm not from around here. Is this old money as in they *were* rich and only have the name left?"

"No, it's old money in that they can't spend what they earn on it fast enough. The daughter—Candy—wants to be a pop star. She's got a good enough voice, and the looks. That puts her in a very special club. A club with money. Rich people who party."

"And with all this money she needs you?"

"I'm not going to bullshit you, she might not. But her family doesn't step foot on the other side of the tracks. The closest they come to normal people is the hired help. If the family wants anything you don't buy in a Balducci's, *someone* has to get it for them. Especially if they don't want people to see them getting it."

Doc lowered himself into his thick leather chair, but didn't offer a seat to Rick. "And you know the personal assistant?"

"Intimately and getting closer. She's the conduit for whatever Candy needs." Rick hesitated, letting it sink in. "These people want the best of everything. And they are willing to pay for it."

"And this investment idea of yours?"

Rick tried not to talk fast, this was the dicey part. "I prove to the personal assistant that I'm reliable and can get her boss good quality product, as needed, and in quantity. Big party quantity, if need be. For that I need more than a few eight balls. And,"—here Rick was totally honest—"they all have to think of me as more than a runner. Otherwise I'll get cut out." He held Doc's eye. Rick wasn't trying to pretend he was Doc's equal in the power game, just that he was more useful than a simple delivery boy. "If I get invited to the parties, I'll have more opportunities to meet the right people, which means *you'll* have more opportunities."

Rick had slid over the part about the first party being for Miranda and her friends. If all went well, he'd get his music in front of Candy, sell Miranda's friends some first class blow at a nice markup, and have enough to pay back Doc. Going down a path he dreaded, but he'd make sure it was a very short detour. A year ago Rick wouldn't have even imagined taking this risk, a month ago he would have talked himself out of it. Yet being so close to his big break made him willing to take the chance. How many Candy's would he meet in his life?

"What are you proposing?" asked Doc.

"Three ounces, at an appropriate discount. I pay a quarter up front. Whatever you think is a fair arrangement on anything that comes through later." Rick wanted to be a musician, not a drug dealer. After he got his songs in front of Candy Doc could do his own deliveries.

"Once it gets rolling, I could cut you out," said Doc, no emotion at all in his voice.

Rick spread his hands. "I know. That's why I'm laying it all out for you. Show you I'm telling it like it is."

Doc tapped his fingers on his spotless leather blotter, the room quiet enough for Rick to hear the fat man's deep breathing. "How much do you know about the white powder?"

Rick shrugged. "I'm just recreational. I can tell good from bad."

"What did you think of my product? The piggyback?"

Rick wondered if this was a test. "Cut once, maybe?"

"Give the man a prize. The woman you were picking up for, she's not so discerning. I have even better offerings. Still cut, but purity is overrated, sometimes deathly so."

"Candy is very discerning and particular in everything she puts in her body."

The fat man gave Rick a hard stare, Rick trying not to sweat, the hot room not helping. Doc said, "I don't deal with addicts, you get me? You'll have to do something for me before I decide if I'm going ahead."

"Sure, you name it," said Rick, unable to hide his nervousness.

Doc smile was humorless. "You know that Marriott in Waltham?"

"I can find it."

"Room 1209. Be there in an hour. Bring your investment capital."

The doc stood up, indicating the meeting was over. "I kind of like you kid, but don't fuck with me."

Rick nodded and slipped out, sweating, and not just from the warm room.

DOC MILES SLOWLY ROTATED his big desk chair so he could reach the controls for the stereo. He punched up Offenbach, just the right mix of contemplation and hidden promise. Who knew what this Candy what's-her-name might amount to, but she was certainly the type of customer he liked. He'd heard about old Boston money, and had no real path into those people. This might be it.

On the other hand, it might be a waste of a few grand. Not a big loss, in the great scheme of things. He'd laid out way more than that in free blow for the right potential client. But he wasn't going to be hustled. Getting taken for a few grand was just as bad as getting taken for ten times that amount, at least as far as reputation was concerned. If word got around he could be scammed, he'd have to move back to Florida.

Which wouldn't be so bad, if it weren't for the DEA. Maybe Arizona. Did rich retirees snort coke and rent fake diamonds?

Doc listened to the rest of the Offenbach, then called Gina.

*   *   *

RICK PAUSED OUTSIDE the door of room 1209. Would Doc send him all the way out here to get rolled for a measly fifteen hundred bucks? Doc would have to pay for the room . . .

Or maybe not. Some goon could be coming along any second to stick Rick up as he waited like an idiot in front of an empty room.

The carpeted hallway of the hotel was quiet and deserted. Fingering the cash in his pocket, Rick knocked, suffering through a few long seconds of shaky anxiety before the door opened. It was no goon.

A really, *really*, hot chick with incredible green eyes wearing a white bathrobe beckoned him in, her bored look doing nothing to detract from her allure. If this was a stickup, Rick might just volunteer. He followed her inside, and only when the door clicked shut did Rick force his eyes off her rear. A simple hotel room, king size bed, small writing table, one lounge chair, a lamp. The bathroom door was closed.

"You can look around if you want," she said.

Rick wondered if this was part of Doc's test. "No, I'm okay." He wasn't really, since dangling a half naked sexpot in his face would be a great way to rip him off. He shoved his hand in his pocket to be sure he hadn't already been robbed of the cash while he'd been distracted.

"I'm Rick," he said.

"Duh, you think I'd let you in if you weren't?"

Rick didn't mind the snide, he deserved it. "What's your name?"

"Does it matter?"

Rick shrugged. "Your rules."

"No, Doc's rules." She moved to the work table, pulling a tray and a small box out of the top drawer. "Remember that. *Always* Doc's rules."

The woman was just Rick's type, offhand sexy cool, looking good and fully aware of it, almost no makeup, auburn hair to her shoulders. Above average height, toned thighs poking out of the bottom of the short robe, a tattoo on her ankle. Confident, not at all worried about being in a hotel room alone with a guy. She was to Miranda what a movie star was to the second runner up at a county fair beauty pageant. A *small* county fair.

"I hear you do a little blow," she said, not looking up.

"A little," Rick agreed.

"A little for one is a lot for another, that's the million dollar question, isn't it? Or in your case, the five thousand dollar plus question."

The woman opened the box, revealing a very large quantity of white powder. On the tray was a thick envelope, a spoon, two straws, and a flat plate.

She turned to Rick. "In the envelope is what you came for. Doc's standard high quality product. This," she indicated the open box, "is a more than generous sample. Doc doesn't mind working with recreational uses, but he hates addicts. He's willing to let you use as much of this sample as you want, right here and now. Without even digging into what you came to pick up. Only you have to make a decision first."

Rick's eyes flicked back and forth from the coke to the chick. He was too distracted to figure out what she was getting at.

The auburn beauty lazily undid the belt of the robe, pulled it open, and let it slide to the floor. She was completely naked underneath, and hard as it was for Rick to believe, her body was even better than he had imagined, and he had been aiming high.

She nodded toward the tray. "You can have that, or me. And before you ask, both is not an option."

Rick hadn't even considered both. No one could be *that* lucky.

CHAPTER 7

RICK SUNK INTO the deep cushions of the white Lawson sofa, trying not to spill his scotch. He didn't remember the sofa from the last time he had been at Miranda's. He didn't remember her having scotch either. Miranda doing her best to impress the guests.

The guests and the loud hip hop music were overflowing into the hallway, the women far better looking than some random invite list. It was an indication of either Miranda's lack of concern for being upstaged—which Rick doubted—or her desire to invite the most connected beautiful people she knew, even if the women were more attractive than she was.

He tapped his hand against the breast pocket of his jacket, making sure the coke was still there. He still couldn't quite believe he had managed to score that much high quality blow. Who would have guessed that passing Doc's creative drug test was better than a perfect FICA score? In the hotel room, he'd barely taken a look at the free sample, far more interested in the woman. Would an addict have really turned her down?

She'd laid a line of blow down the middle of her chest, arching her back to offer it up. Rick chose the chest, not the powder. And because he had, here he was, five grand of coke in his jacket pocket. And a special gift, an exotic deep blue vial which she said was Doc's best stuff, meant for his top customers. Rick got the message: the vial wasn't for him, it was for Candy. He'd brought it tonight, on the chance that Candy would be here.

Miranda, wearing a red designer dress and flashy heels, crossed the room on the arms of two hulking guys who looked like they had stepped right out of a men's health magazine. She looked better than Rick had ever seen her, yet after Doc's test woman even the made-up Miranda paled in comparison.

Miranda must not have spotted him, otherwise Rick was sure she'd be all over him for the party favors. She lasered in on the oldest woman in the place, fortyish, platinum hair, chic dress, funky sandals. Miranda took the woman's arm and steered her away from her drooling audience. The two guys stood a respective distance apart, a cross between bodyguards and servants.

A white coated Chippendale's honorary member stood numbly behind the small bar. Rick eyed the Highland Park single malt, three hundred bucks beyond Rick's price point. Rick assumed Miranda had another guy on the hook for bringing the scotch. Hopefully Miranda hadn't also promised the booze supplier she'd get his music in front of Candy, that would suck big time.

A petite brunette, a purple streaked lock bisecting her forehead, tottered over on too high heels. Rick gestured for her to order first.

She gave Rick a real smile. "Thanks." She fanned her face with her hand, her dark pink nail polish waving like a flag. "Hot in here. I'm Lavender," she said. "You a friend of Miranda's?"

That was a good question. Rick wasn't sure how to describe a relationship that was somewhere between a one night stand and a dope supplier. He countered with, "I'm the engineer where Candy records."

"Really? How exciting is that?"

"It has its moments," said Rick. "How do you know Miranda?"

"I work for Aaron Fisher."

Fisher was the head of Morgan Publishing, a big music publisher. "Quite a list of artists you got there. How exciting is *that*?"

"It has its moments," she said, laughing as she took a big sip of her daiquiri.

"You know these people?" asked Rick. "Who's the blonde with Miranda?"

"That's Suzanne Michin. As in Bitchin Michin. She invests money for the Carter family."

"That's some nickname."

"Don't cross her. She'll cut off your balls if you do. See those two guys with Miranda? She brings them everywhere, even to parties. Word is they are part of Candy's bodyguard staff, but one of them does the friends with benefits thing with Miranda. They're tough, but I'd rather have them after my throat than Suzanne."

"Miranda seems to be okay with her."

"If Candy's father tells her to, she'd cut off Miranda's balls, no matter how much Candy likes Miranda."

Rick didn't think it his place to inform Lavender about his first-hand knowledge of Miranda's anatomy. For all he knew, Lavender would dime him out, and he'd be finding out up close and personal whether Miranda's bodyguard slash boy toy was as tough as he looked. "Quite the impressive crowd," he said.

Lavender shrugged. "Not bad, for around here. I go to these parties in New York you wouldn't *believe*. But Miranda does good suck up, plus no one wants to take a chance she'd whisper the wrong words in Candy's ear, and it might get to her daddy." Lavender leaned over to Rick, adding in a conspiratorial whisper, "Actually, I hear Candy is still trying to go her own way from daddy, and might not tell him shit."

"That's why everyone showed up?" asked Rick.

Lavender gave him a big wink. "That, and Miranda promised us all amazing blow. I hope it shows up soon, I'm getting bored. No offense."

Rick polished off his aged scotch. "None taken. I'm getting a little bored myself." He looked around the room; no one seemed to be listening, not even the Chippendale carved torso. "I happen to know where that blow is. You want a sample before the balloons fall?"

Rick's phone buzzed just as things started to get interesting with Lavender in the apartment stairwell.

Miranda. "Where are you?"

"Just stepped out for some fresh air."

"I hope you brought what I asked for."

"I do what I say I'm going to," said Rick, hoping Miranda took the hint; this was a two-way street. "I'll be right there."

"Her Highness calling?" asked Lavender.

Rick held up the coke. "I did promise."

Lavender finished her snort. "This is great stuff. I hope you are getting something good in return."

"That makes two of us," said Rick.

He left her in the stairway and wove his way back through the packed hallway into Miranda's apartment. He found her bookended between her football player friends, who gave him a Secret Service stare.

"Relax," said Miranda. She let Rick give her a kiss on the cheek. "You can start passing out the party favors."

Rick had a sudden image of Miranda's two bodyguards announcing they were narcs and cuffing him. He looked from one to the other, trying to figure out which one was more likely to be boffing Miranda, would a narc do that? It was hard to tell them apart, they might have been twins, Tweedles Dee and Dum.

Rick shoved the envelope in Tweedledum's hand. "Probably more impressive to your guests if it comes from you," said Rick.

Miranda brightened as the exchange was made. She leaned up to give Tweedledum a kiss on the cheek. "Be a dear and spread the cheer."

Tweedledum moved off and Miranda said, "I hope you have a special stash for my special friend."

Rick was about to pull out the blue vial when he noticed how close Tweedledee had shifted toward Miranda, going from bodyguard to body friendly. Rick edged away from Miranda's personal space, picking up a definite vibe between them. Damn. Miranda had been bullshitting him about giving some product to Candy. If he had a few more scotches under his belt he might have called her on it, but didn't want to get her pissed and not hold up her end of the deal.

Rick left the vial in his pocket and instead pulled out a small bag of coke which he'd split off from the main stash. He was saving it to sell, but it was the best he could do. "Extra high quality," he said, hoping Miranda wouldn't notice the difference.

Tweedledee pulled the bag out of Rick's hand, put his arm around Miranda, and said, "Come on, baby, let's get us a little privacy."

TWO HOURS LATER the party was peaking, guests still arriving. Rick figured the coke would run out soon, and he wanted to be gone well before then. He kept trying to corner Miranda, but her special friend was like a toll booth, and now his look-alike was back.

Rick waited until Miranda tottered off toward the bathroom, followed her down the hall, and pushed in behind her.

"Hey," she said, her eyes glazed.

"Just want to chat," said Rick, locking the door behind him.

"You're jealous, aren't you?" she said, giving him a leer.

"That's it, exactly," said Rick. "But I should have expected there would be guys all over you."

"Damn right."

"I did my part. Now it's your turn."

Miranda preened in the mirror. "Shit, my eyes are red."

"Miranda—."

"Yeah, yeah, I hear you. I'll talk to Candy about your music."

Rick wasn't going to trust Doc's five thousand dollar investment—more, depending on what was in that blue vial—to Miranda's whims. "How about sending her a text right now? Get it out of the way."

Miranda fumbled through a drawer for more makeup. "Soon as I get back to where my phone is."

Rick whipped his phone out like a six shooter. "Here, use mine."

"Are you serious?"

"Come on. You got to admit, I brought the best."

Miranda finished with her makeup, Rick sweating. Tweedledee wouldn't be too happy if he caught them in the bathroom, and Rick's gut told him that Miranda would go back to the well for more coke before paying off. He held the phone in her face.

Miranda threw her mascara back in the drawer. She looked worse, going from slightly over made up to a Goth caricature. "You have to do one more thing for me," she said, taking the phone but making no move to dial.

Oh shit, thought Rick. *Here it comes . . .* "What's that?"

"Have a big smile on your face when you follow me out of the bathroom," she said, brightening. "You're not the only one I like being jealous."

THE BURNER PHONE let fly the strains of *Windy* just as Doc was about to lower himself into the spa for his nightly warm up. It had been a long day, a series of minor but compounding annoyances, and the spa and a scotch would be medicinal.

Windy, though, was the ringtone of one of his very best customers, a stormy eyed newspaper reporter named Jennifer. Jennifer's success at getting scoops was a function of both her brains and her ability to work for days with almost no sleep, courtesy of Doc's blow. Not only discreet, she was married to a part time instructor at a law school, who supplied intrepid attorneys in training with the wherewithal to make the grade.

Doc took one last look at the spa and answered the phone. "Don't tell me, there's a shortage of arepas in Miami," he said by way of answer.

"There's a shortage all right, but it's not arepas."

Doc knew Jennifer wasn't due for a shipment. "The usual?"

"And then some. I got a promotion. Getting transferred to the London desk."

"That's good," said Doc, yet not feeling it. Moving a little coke via car or even common carrier was one thing in the states, a totally different animal overseas. "Your husband okay with this?" Meaning: *will he still be buying my product?*

"He's coming with me."

Doc didn't let his disappointment show through. "Don't over pack, they are really clamping down on luggage." Knowing Jennifer would get the message: don't get caught hauling drugs through customs.

"I hear you," said Jennifer. "I was wondering, do you have any friends in the U.K.?"

Another source, she meant. "Sorry," said Doc.

"Too bad. Good friends are so hard to replace."

Which was why Jennifer had continued to buy from Doc even when he moved north. She could easily source in Miami, but her position required discretion, and she'd come to trust Doc's carefulness.

"What's your timetable?" asked Doc.

"Very soon." Jennifer's voice softened. "I'll miss you, Doc."

Which answered the other part of Doc's timetable query. Jennifer's nostrils, and all those of her husband's students, were out of his life.

"Me too," he said, and hung up before he got depressed.

DOC FORCED HIMSELF to think of the spa as an indulgent reward he could only earn if he found a way to replace the lost income from Jennifer's move. He picked up another burner from the row, the name *Lloyd* penciled on a piece of masking tape across the phone. Lloyd was his second biggest customer by volume, but up and down in frequency, depending on the timing of the parties he supplied.

Doc rarely reached out to his customers, the idea reeked too much of selling insurance. When Lloyd answered he seemed as surprised to hear from Doc as Doc was at himself for making the call. "Yeah?"

"Just me," reassured Doc. "I'm doing a little long range planning due to a recent spike in demand, just wondering how your schedule is looking." Lloyd didn't respond, so Doc answered the likely question. "Not a matter of price, just logistics."

"The calendar is light," said Lloyd. "Nothing for the foreseeable future."

"Let me know if there's a change," said Doc, and clicked off.

A bad feeling gnawed at him. Doc picked up another phone, this one marked *Eva*. A successful actress who loved to party and share the wealth, Eva had been with Doc since her regular doctor had refused to renew her pain medication after a twisted ankle.

It was decidedly not Eva who answered the phone. "Yes?"

"I must have the wrong number," said Doc.

"Miss Eva is no here," said the woman.

Doc was working through the list of possibilities of why this woman would be answering a burner phone. "I'll call back," said Doc.

"Miss Eva will not be able to talk for a while," said the woman. "She has gone to—"

There was a mix of urgent Spanish in the background. Doc didn't need to be fluent to pick up the words, "Gulf Shores Recovery."

Eva, it appeared, was in rehab.

"Goodbye," said Doc, more to the money than the woman.

Doc no longer felt like he deserved either the spa or the scotch. He slipped into his Turkish bathrobe as he plodded to his home office. An old fashioned index card box sat in full view on the desk. Doc had long ago learned that whatever you locked up would appear valuable to a thief; leave it out in the open and no one would give it a second glance.

He dropped into the chair, the leather sticky on his arms. Each card held a name, the first names accurate, the last made up. Innocuous information accompanied the names: *met at Joe's party, buys commercial buildings, collects old lamps*. Each was a code for a customer, with lots of fake cards mixed in. Doc didn't trust this information to a computer. Even Gina didn't know the code.

Doc did a mental calculation as he worked through the names. The number of defunct customers was more obvious when viewed all at once. Not only the drug buyers, but the bling renters. Doc had a few other deals going, fake medicinal cannabis cards, real jewelry delivery of indeterminate origin mixed in with his fake bling, even a string of auto quick lubes. The cannabis card business dropped every time a state lowered the penalty for possession, the jewelry caravan dried up when the Stilwell brothers got sent up, and the lube business was flat with all the new cars needing fewer oil changes.

Shit, he'd gotten lazy. With the move and the house renovation, he hadn't been reseeding the pot. He wasn't broke, not by a long shot, but would be at his current cash burn rate.

He leaned back in the chair, the spa all but forgotten. Had to get more irons in the fire and fast.

CHAPTER 8

Rick overslept, the result of way too much single malt at Miranda's party. If he ever made it big, he vowed to have a scotch bar in his house, and another in his limo.

A limo would have been good this morning, because limos came with drivers. Rick eased his Kia slowly across town to the studio, not sure if he'd pass a breathalyzer test six hours after his last drink.

The party had still been in full swing when he had left, sucking up Rick's—actually, Doc's—blow like human vacuums. Rick had made his escape the minute Miranda sent the text to Candy about his music.

Rick was supposed to open the studio, not that anyone would be there at nine in the morning. So he was surprised to see a Range Rover parked in front. Even more eye opening was Candy Carter leaning against the hood, her long legs poking out from a pair of Daisy Dukes, doing more to wake Rick up than a pot of coffee.

Rick, wishing even more than ever he had that limo, parked the Kia a respectful distance away and jumped out. "Hey Candy. Sorry, we weren't expecting you until later."

"That's still the plan. I got this text, I didn't recognize the number, but since not many people have my private phone, I checked it anyway. From Miranda?" Candy said it like she still wasn't sure.

"That's my number," said Rick. "Miranda didn't have her phone on her." He worried how Candy would take that, so he added, "I ran into her at a party."

"The text said you've got some songs?"

"I do."

"Who else have you written for?"

Just the fact that Candy was here hinted at not only writer's block, but desperation. "I had this band. Well, me and this other guy were the nucleus. We actually were about to get signed, I mean really, we were at the Arista office . . ." Rick doubted Candy cared about the details. "I'm not going to lay a sob story on you. The deal fell through. But I can write. Let's go inside, you can decide for yourself."

Candy's hesitation was the longest ten seconds of Rick's life. Rick was about to pull out his phone and play a track right there, crappy audio and all, but Candy said, "Okay, might as well. I'm here."

Rick fumbled the keys in the lock and ushered her inside. He snapped on the lights and led her to the control room. Normally he'd offer her a drink, but he didn't want to give her time to change her mind or get turned off by their unbranded tea.

He slipped his thumbdrive into the board as soon as Candy sat down. "This first song is called *When Worlds Collide*. It's about—well, you'll see. It would add a little edge, you know?" Rick realized he was babbling. He hit the play button and held his breath.

The track kicked in, naked through the JBL studio monitors. It was an old song, written and originally recorded with Gerry, who sang lead, Rick harmonizing. Rick had updated the drum and bass track, giving the song more punch.

Candy listened attentively, Rick trying not to stare at her for any hint of a reaction. Partway through she started tapping her foot, Rick almost jumping out of his chair. By the end she was nodding.

"Nice dynamics." she said. "You do the vocals?"

"Just harmonizing. You could change the key and be all over it."

"Yeah, up an octave after the turnaround. That would make it more intense at the end. Play the chorus again, will you?"

Rick was happy to oblige. He fought the urge to highlight how the song would be a great lead in to Candy's album. After the chorus played he turned down the sound, the song becoming a movie soundtrack in the background. "Again?"

"No, I got it. It's okay. Not really much of a hook, but it has—tension. I need some tension. But—it builds, but doesn't resolve, you know what I mean? I'd want to get some release in there."

"Huh." Rick's estimation of Candy's musical abilities went up about five notches. Normally he wasn't keen on taking advice about his music, unless it was from someone very good, like Gerry. He reran it from the bridge. "Maybe if we go to the tonic . . ." he pointed in the air at the right place, "here?"

"That might work," said Candy. "Yeah, I think so." She stared at the ceiling, humming, Rick hearing her transform his creation. His and Gerry's creation, actually. A veritable thrill shivered him, he was *working*. Creating. On the verge . . .

"I do have my own edgy song I was working on," said Candy. "I could go with what I have. With DeVaughn's help and his name I know I'll get airplay and it will be a successful release."

Rick crashed, struggling to hide his disappointment. Oddly, her tone didn't match the certainty of her words. "Why don't you sound overjoyed at that?"

Candy's eyes flared. "I want my music to succeed because it is *great*, not just because of DeVaughn and money. I want people to say *of course* DeVaughn produced her, because her songwriting is incredible, he's just the icing to take it to another level."

"I get it, I do. Let me play you another one." Rick had originally planned on playing his most recent work next, figuring it would best tie in to what was on the charts. But Candy was all about hooks, maybe too pop for her own good. He needed something that sounded current but had a tinge of pop to appeal to Candy's style. Catchy angst.

He spun through the song list, again going back to an older cut, one where Rick sang lead. "I wrote this a long time ago with another guy. It's called *Never Believe*. It would be right in your vocal sweet spot."

The song wasn't a toe tapper, so Rick focused on Candy's eyes. At the chorus her entire face changed.

After the last chord had drifted away, Candy said, "Play it again."

Rick's fingers shook as he punched up the replay. After the song ended the silence in the room almost sucked Rick off his chair. Fearing he had lost her, he sputtered, "You could change it up."

Candy looked like she was going to cry. "No. It's—*perfect*."

Rick turned away, fighting back his own tears. It was one thing to believe in your creation, it was another to get such an emotional reaction from someone who obviously knew about music. Candy could have told him she loved him and wanted to have his children and it wouldn't have affected him as much as her response to his song.

Not even ten in the morning, giddy thoughts pinged uncontrolled in Rick's head. Above all, the need to commemorate this moment. Which made him think of the special coke for Candy. He pulled the little blue vial out of his pocket. "Want to celebrate?"

"What?" she asked.

Rick put his finger to the side of his nose and sniffed. Candy's blank stare said it all. Her eyes flicked to the vial with no hint of comprehension.

Rick's was comprehending for the both of them. Candy either had no interest in a little nose candy, or had no clue what he was talking about. He scratched an imaginary itch on his nose, but Candy had obviously caught on.

"I'm really careful about what I put in my body," she said, not sounding angry, but in a tone that was setting the record straight. "I don't care about what people do on their own, but not on my dime."

Rick choked back his distress. What was he thinking? The woman brought her own tea bags, she was a vegan. Of course she wouldn't be into drugs.

Which wouldn't be good news for Doc. Rick would have to figure out how to deal with that. But right now . . . "Sure, I get it." He closed his fist around the vial, praying she hadn't written him off with his stupidity.

Candy pointed to the thumbdrive. "So those are all yours?"

The two songs he had played for Candy had been mostly written with Gerry, although Rick was still the co-creator and owned half the rights. So said their written agreement. Rick answered very carefully. "I didn't do all the singing and play every instrument, but it's all my work." That sounded too legalistic, so he added, "Just like your stuff, you use other musicians."

That must have done the trick, because Candy said, "Can you make a copy for me?"

RICK SAT IN his car in the studio lot, staring at the vial of coke as the last rays of the sun shifted the glass from a bright cerulean to an ominous midnight blue. It had been a long day, Rick carried along by the excitement of his possible arrangement with Candy. She hadn't treated him any differently during the recording session—in fact, she hadn't said a word to him—reminding Rick of the tenuousness of his position. Candy could find a new song any day, could use only her own material, shit, she could forget all about Rick and he'd be back where he started.

Which wasn't a very good place. Except for the blue vial, he had nothing for Doc. No new A-list customer, and no cash for the coke that had greased Miranda's party. What he had carved out to sell on the side had gone up Miranda's and her boy toy's nostrils.

Miranda. She certainly liked the blow. If he could get her to buy the vial . . . He'd have to give her a discount, especially if she knew that Candy had liked his music.

He could get more for it on the street, but it would have to be cut, and he didn't know shit about selling drugs. With his luck the first deal he set up would be with a narc.

He was a songwriter, about to make it big, not a drug dealer.

Miranda's it was.

THE MUSIC BLARING on the other side of Miranda's door suggested the party was still going on. No wonder Miranda hadn't been at the recording session that day. Rick banged again on the door, gave up, and called Miranda's phone.

Amazingly, she picked up. "Calling to thank me, right?"

So she knew. "In person," said Rick. "I'm in the hallway."

The door opened. Miranda's made up eyes were extra smudged, her lipstick coating a sloshing wine glass like a kid's finger painting. She grabbed Rick by the collar. "Hey Keith, look who's here!"

Keith, it turned out, was Tweedledee, even more imposing in sweatpants and shirtless. He looked very much at home, especially when he put his arm around Miranda's waist.

Rick didn't want to give Keith any idea he was there for personal reasons. He pulled out the vial. "Got some of that top line stuff here. In fact, maybe higher than top line, if you can believe it. Not cut at all." Rick wasn't sure of that, but it had to be purer than what Doc had already supplied, or why else the magic vial? "To thank you for your help with Candy, I can give you a great discount. Two grand."

Miranda giggled. "Wow! That's a lot of money." She put her arm around Keith. "That's a lot of money, isn't it, baby?"

"I could get much more than that on the street," said Rick. "And I already helped you out by supplying your party. This is just a little extra appreciation."

"It's not appreciation if you are charging for it," said Keith.

Rick should have called first, this wasn't going well. "How about half for nine hundred? I bet there are two ounces in here."

"Let's see," said Keith, grabbing the vial out of Rick's hand.

"Hey . . ."

"That still doesn't sound right," Miranda said. "Especially if you don't even know how much you got. Does that sound right to you, Keith?"

"Nah, I don't like the sound of it."

Rick's eyes were glued to the vial. "I'm sorry, I can't do any better."

"Really," Miranda said. "You could've never gotten Candy to listen to your songs without me. If she decides to use them you'll make plenty of money."

"Look," Rick said, his voice unsteady. "You can't just take this stuff. It's really not mine. I owe money on this." He reached for the coke.

"Not our problem," said Tweedledee. The vial disappeared in his huge fist. "You can go now."

The big man was faster than Rick expected, because he hadn't even seen Tweedledee's other hand come up. With an offhand gesture Rick was propelled back into the hall.

"No, really, you don't understand," said Rick. "I can't just—"

The door slammed in Rick's face, and the only result of his pounding was the music getting louder.

CHAPTER 9

Rick whacked his hand against the door. "Miranda!"

No answer, though the music took on a new sound, urgent. It took a second for Rick to realize it was his own phone ringing. He snatched at it. "Miranda, I need that stuff back, really, you have no idea how screwed I'm going to be—"

"Rickie?"

Rick's brain wasn't working right, in fact, nothing was working right, he could barely stand. He didn't even think to look at the caller ID. "Who is this?"

"Rickie, I fell down."

"Ma?"

"You don't recognize your own mother?"

"Are you all right?"

"I can't get back up. I didn't want to bother you, I called Sherry, but she didn't answer."

Rick pictured his mother on the floor, crawling to the phone. "You're okay, though right? You made it up?"

"Not yet, I'm trying."

"I'll be right there. Just wait for me, you hear!" Rick was already running for his car, trying not to sound as panicked as he felt. "Don't move!"

Candy watched DeVaughn's face as the last strains of *Never Believe* whispered through the room, courtesy of the amazing Apogee speakers and the best lossless digital player money could buy.

"Where did you find this?" asked DeVaughn.

"The house engineer at Larry's wrote it. His name is Rick."

"It's good. We can make it a hit. Just needs better vocals."

"I know. But even as it is—it's like . . ."

"Like he wants something really bad," said DeVaughn. "It comes through the lyrics too."

"You think?"

"Sure." DeVaughn fiddled with his phone. "Does he have anything else?"

Candy wasn't fooled by DeVaughn's sideways question. What he was suggesting was that Rick's song was better than her material. "Tell me the truth."

DeVaughn raised an eyebrow. "How honest do you want me to be?"

"Brutally."

"You'd be surprised how many artists tell me that and then throw a fit."

Candy looked him right in the eye. "I look like the throw a fit type?"

DeVaughn put down his phone. "Okay. Your music is good. You'll get airplay, get noticed as up and coming. Set you up for the next album."

He was sugar coating for sure. Candy prodded: "But?"

"A *lot* of artists get noticed as up and coming. Too many. You'll have a leg up because, frankly, they won't have as much money behind you, and they won't have my name. It's just a fact of life in the music business."

"I'm sensing there is more."

"Remember I told you that even with the best production, good material, and a lot of marketing muscle, it's still fifty-fifty at best having a hit?"

"Yes."

"This song," said DeVaughn, waving at the speakers, "done right, changes those odds. Not one hundred percent, nothing is. But we'd have to screw it up for it not to chart. If you can sing it with that *feeling* flowing out, wanting it. Not only will it be a hit, you'll go from being one to watch to *the* one to watch."

"It's that good, isn't it?" Normally that would have pissed Candy off, she was proud of her work. Except DeVaughn was right. This song *was* better than anything else she had planned for the album. Which also meant it was better than anything she had ever created.

Not an earth shattering realization—there were thousands of great songs out there. Candy just never thought one would pop up out of the blue from a no name engineer.

DeVaughn said, "Not quite yet. But in my hands, it will be."

"I want to be known as a songwriter. How will it look if I didn't write my first big hit?"

"That's your ego talking. It won't be the end of the world, you won't be the first artist to start that way. But it might not come to that. This Rick guy. Will he agree to list you as co-writer?"

Candy thought about Rick's not so hidden excitement when he'd played his songs for her. "He's pretty desperate. He wants it bad. I think it's what you hear in his voice on this song. I think he'll do whatever it takes to make it. Anything."

"So what did you tell him?"

"I didn't make any promises."

"Good. He'll agree once he sees how big we'll make it."

"There is one thing. I'm not sure what to make of this guy Rick. He's kind of . . . strange."

"A strange guy, in the music industry? Are you kidding?"

Candy smiled. "You know what I mean."

"How is he strange?"

"I don't know. I mean he seems like a nice guy. A little intense. He might have a coke problem."

"What makes you say that?"

"He pulled a vial out like it was standard equipment."

"You want to be in music, you have to deal with it. Just because you're clean doesn't mean everyone else is going to be."

"I know, believe me, I know."

"You think he's a serial killer or something?"

Candy laughed. "I can't really put my finger on it. I have a hard time trusting people who do a lot of drugs." Candy winced, not exactly sure where DeVaughn stood on the whole drug experience.

"What do you need to trust?" DeVaughn said. "If we use his song he'll sign a contract. After that, you'll never have to talk to him again."

RICK RAN UP the walk at his mother's house, pulling out the key. He didn't need it, the door was open, bright light beyond. He had a crushing thought the house had been broken into.

"Ma!"

It wasn't his mother he found in the kitchen, but Sherry, the nurse. "Look who's here," she said.

"Where's my mother?"

"She's in bed. Keep your voice down, I'm hoping she fell asleep."

"Is she okay?" Rick was heading down the hall.

"Leave her be."

"I'm just going to check." The door to the bedroom was ajar. A thin line in the bed was the only hint of his mother. It took forever for Rick to be convinced that the tiny movement in the blanket was real, proof of her breathing. He gently eased the door shut.

Back in the kitchen, Sherry was drying her hands on a dishtowel. A heavily set woman of indeterminate age, her hair was pulled back in a tight bun. A large birthmark on her neck looked like an old tattoo, blending in with her dark brown skin.

"What happened?" Rick asked.

"She fell."

"Christ." Rick pushed at the air with his hands. "She couldn't get up?"

Sherry folded the dishtowel. "She's getting weaker. That's why I don't let her sleep in the hospital bed in the living room. Walking her back and forth will help keep her muscles going."

"I got here as fast as I could."

"It's going to happen again. I can't always be here."

"What's this about you taking another job? You didn't warn me."

Sherry pointed at him. "I did *so* warn you. After your check bounced. I love your mother, but I've got responsibilities of my own. My youngest is out of work again."

"We can't just leave her alone."

"No, *you* just can't leave her alone."

"Sherry, if I'm not working, I can't pay you."

"You working twenty four hours? You can at least sleep here."

Rick's apartment was no Taj Mahal, but it was almost as big as this entire house. As worried as he was about his mother, he'd go crazy here. "I'm working on getting more money. You can be here all day, and I'll get a night nurse."

"Or you could start thinking about a nursing home."

Rick shook his head. "She won't. Not yet. And—once my dad went into one, he went downhill fast. I'm not sure I can deal with it."

"It's not about you."

Rick collapsed against the counter. "I know that. I just need a little time."

"Whatever you are cooking up, you better make it fast. I can't always be available to come running at all hours."

Rick's pocket buzzed. Doc's burner phone. Shit, just what he needed.

He held up his finger to Sherry, pulling out the phone as he went into his old room, now stuffed with the accoutrements of his mother's illness, walkers, canes, toilet risers. He sat in the foldable wheelchair, staring at the phone.

He was already depressed, might as well get it over with. "Yeah."

"I expected to hear from you by now," Doc said.

"Sorry, Doc. I've just been crazy busy."

"What's going on with my new client, the singer?"

"I haven't been able to talk to her alone. But tomorrow, for sure."

"I'm not getting a good feeling about this."

"Really? Why? There's no problem."

Rick translated Doc's silence as *That's bullshit.* "Honest, Doc. Everything is cool. This woman always has an entourage. It's not the kind of thing you want me bringing up in front of a bunch of people, right? I need to catch her in private."

"You need to pay up on the other merchandise I floated you."

"Yeah, I'll be by on—," Rick did some fast thinking, trying to figure how much time he could ask for—"in a few days."

"No, junior, I'll send somebody to pick it up."

The line went dead. Rick rocked the wheel chair back and forth, neither the motion nor the familiarity of his old room making him feel the least bit better.

TRICIA TORE OPEN the UPS box like it was a Christmas present. She was naked, as she almost always was at Doc's house. Doc liked watching her, she had an exuberance that made him feel young. Even knowing the box wasn't for her, Tricia was still having a good time.

Gina was lying on the other end of the sofa from Doc, a notebook balanced on her flat stomach. No youthful exuberance from her. Not for boxes, anyway. Doc knew from experience that she could turn on the excitement at the right time. She was likely faking it, which didn't bother Doc all that much, as long as she didn't overdo it.

Tricia used a long delicate nail to peel away the last of the packing tape. Tissue paper flew like a windswept cloud. Tricia held up a gold chain as thick as her dainty wrist. "Is this real?"

"If that were real, dear, I don't think it would come in a UPS box," said Doc.

Tricia ducked into the chain, the links falling to her waist. "It *feels* real," she said. "It's so heavy!"

"And ugly," said Gina.

"That ugly pays the bills," said Doc.

"*I* like it," said Tricia, skipping into the hall. "I want to see what it looks like on me."

Doc tapped Gina on the foot. "Catalog it," said Doc. "And all the rest."

Gina was already writing on the pad. "I always do."

As Gina unwound herself from the sofa, a squeal of delight split the house. Tricia had no doubt reached a mirror.

"Let Tricia unpack the rest," said Doc. "It's more fun to watch."

Gina shrugged. "You know what you're doing, Doc. But I wouldn't trust her if that bling was real."

Doc didn't need to raise his voice. "I don't trust anyone that much. Even you, Gina."

Gina, to her credit, didn't look away. "I'm not stupid, Doc."

"Which is why you're doing the inventory instead of Tricia."

"I know where I sit."

Doc detected just a hint of irritation in her voice. Gina didn't like to be doubted, even less of being second to Tricia. A younger Doc would have slapped her for that. He could play all the favorites he wanted. But the combination of her and Tricia was a good thing, and who needed two cats fighting?

Instead Doc said, "Why don't you come sit over here?"

CHAPTER 10

"THE KICK LEVEL is clipping the channel," said Gus. "Christ, Rick, get your head out of your ass."

Rick's fingers were on the mixing board, which swam in his vision, a confusing mix of options. He pulled his hands away like the board was on fire. "What?"

"The kick, damn it. What are you, deaf?"

Rick's mind was on everything but recording. His mother. Doc. Not even the sight of Candy in the recording booth was enough to get him focused. "Sorry, Gus. Got a lot going on."

"The only thing going on is getting this mix right for Candy."

That woke Rick up a little. The last thing he needed added to his shitstorm of troubles was getting Candy pissed. He lowered the slider on the kick drum.

He was just getting back into it when the door opened and Liz stuck her head in. "Rick, there's someone out here to see you. Says it's really important."

Shit. Doc looking for his money. Rick doubted it was Doc out there, he must have sent the green eyed woman from the hotel. He looked up at Gus.

Gus was already taking over the board. "Go. You're pretty useless anyway today. But make it fast."

Rick was hoping to see the woman again, but not for this reason. Maybe he could sweet talk her, get a few more days. Escaping the control room for a few minutes would also give him a chance to get Miranda alone and beg for his money.

It wasn't the hot auburn haired woman in the waiting area, but a very tough looking dude who made Miranda's friend Keith look like a parody of a movie bad guy. Keith was big, but this guy was mean. He had a buzz cut with a pockmarked face, wearing a leather jacket over a tight camo stretched shirt, black pants, and boots. He jerked his head toward the door.

Rick got as close to the guy as he dared. "I haven't got it," he whispered.

The guy's features never wavered, he just jerked his head again.

Rick eyed the back exit. Even if he managed to get away, he'd have to come back to the studio eventually.

Rick opened the door and was shoved outside. He stumbled, the bright light a laser into his head. The guy in the leather jacket propelled Rick around to the side of the building and pushed him up against the cinder block wall.

"Doc wants his money."

"I don't have it. Not yet."

"Doc wants his money now."

The guy's cologne was as mean as he was, an ominous assault on Rick's nostrils. Rick fumbled for his wallet, pulled out all the bills and held them up. "It's all I've got on me."

"That's like sixty bucks. You expect me go to back to Doc with sixty bucks? You won't be the only one who'll get his ass kicked."

"I'm waiting to get paid for the stuff. As soon as I do, I'll get it to you, I swear."

"You sold it?"

"I had to spread some around, to get good with Candy's assistant, like I told Doc. I sold the rest, I'm just working on collections." Rick tried a joke. "Just like you are."

"I don't work on collections, I *make* them." The guy grabbed Rick by the shoulder and slammed him back against the wall, Rick's head bouncing off like a basketball, the pain excruciating.

"Come on, man . . . I can't give you what I don't have!"

"Consider this an incentive," said the goon, banging Rick against the wall again.

"I get the point! Bashing my head in isn't going to get you any money!" Rick felt the back of his head for blood.

"It's not my money, it's *Doc's* money."

"I need to talk to Doc, I can explain everything!"

The goon pushed Rick to the front of the studio. Rick hadn't noticed earlier, but there was a black Mercedes SUV parked in the lot.

"Doc's here?"

"He wants to talk to you too."

"So you banged me around even though Doc wanted to talk to me?"

"Needed to get you focused. So you wouldn't lie to Doc."

Rick, ready to lie through his teeth to Doc, now frantically reassessed his plan as he was propelled to the Mercedes.

The back window rolled down without a sound. Doc was sitting in the back seat, not looking very pleased. The goon still had his hand tightly wrapped around Rick's arm.

Rick tried to shift the conversation away from the money. "Hey, Doc! Listen, about Candy. She's in there, I should be able to get her alone today."

Doc didn't even glance at the studio. "We'll get to that. Right now, I want my money for the rest of it."

Shit. "Sure, Doc, sure. I just need a few days."

Doc drummed his fingers on the window sill. "Give me back the blue vial. I'll give you a day to cover the rest. Now that Kevin has communicated the priorities."

"I—I don't have it."

"Kev will drive you to pick it up." Doc flicked a tiny piece of lint off his thick sweater. "If there's any problem, he'll take you for a longer ride. You get my point?"

"No, that's not it. I don't have the vial."

Doc's eyes narrowed. "I thought you said you hadn't connected with this Candy chick?"

"I haven't. I gave it to Miranda. Candy's assistant. Candy trusts her with everything."

"She in there now?"

Rick didn't see how he could lie about that. "Yeah, but the studio's not very private."

"Bring her out. We can talk here."

"Candy might not let Miranda leave just because I ask."

Doc shrugged. "No problem. Kev, *you* go get this Miranda."

Kev let go of Rick and headed toward the door.

Desperate, Rick said, "The Candy thing isn't going to work, but I got a better deal for you!"

Kevin was at the door. If he got in the studio everything would go sideways real fast, Rick's job would be history, no money at all for Doc or his Mom, no music deal with Candy. "Doc, please, you gotta listen!"

Doc said, "Kev."

Kevin froze like he'd been zapped, Rick almost falling down with relief. "Doc, I'm sorry, I blew it. At least with Candy. She's not into the white powder, but I'm sure her big money friends are. I know Miranda is. Now that I've worked my way into their circle it will only be a matter of time before I find another Candy."

"Shit, junior, anybody can maybe make a connection *someday*. You know how many guys try that same sales pitch on me? If this Miranda is a good conduit, what do I need you for?" Doc looked past Rick. "Kev, go get her."

"Wait, wait! I have something *big* going down, it's worth more than everything you gave me. Way more!"

Doc held up a finger. Rick, too scared to see if that was for Kevin to stop, pushed on. "I've got a songwriting thing in the works with Candy. She's going to put my music on her new album. She's got tons of money invested, a big producer, she's going to sell millions. I'll pay you double what I owe you!" Rick was babbling, still listening for the sound of the studio door behind him. "Triple!"

Doc dropped his finger. Behind Rick, the door banged as hard as his head had hit the wall. Rick, frantic now: "Listen, Doc, did you know that six dudes split two million on one song they wrote for Bruno Mars? And one guy got half a mil from a song that never even got on the radio but was used in a potato chip commercial? There's a lot of money in music."

"Who the fuck is Bruno Mars?"

Rick stumbled, who hadn't heard of Bruno Mars? "He's a singer. Writes most of his own stuff, but uses other material too. That's what I'm doing for Candy, writing some of her songs."

"And this makes you rich how?"

"The songwriter gets a cut every time the song is sold. And even when it is just played. Automatically." Rick waved toward the front seat of the SUV. "You turn on the radio right now, a song is on, whoever sings that song gets money, the songwriter gets money." Rick didn't think now was the time to go into the details of how little the songwriters got for airplay.

Doc drummed his fingers again. "How do you know this Candy will have a hit?"

"Half—shit, ninety percent—of music success is who you know, the connections, how much marketing muscle is behind it. You think the stuff you hear on the radio is just the best singers? Candy's got the basics, and the looks, but what will get her into the game is *money*. She's going to buy her way to the table. She's got a big name producer, Kendall DeVaughn, who wouldn't waste his time on artists who don't have a chance."

"So that's what you're offering me? Some piece of your split, *if* this Candy makes a record, *if* she gets a song on the air, *if* she gets a hit? I can't spend ifs."

Doc had it about right, but Rick needed him to buy in. It wasn't hard to put the belief in his own voice, it was his dream too. "I won't lie to you, it's not a sure thing. But Candy has a *lot* vested in this, her money, her name, her family reputation. There's no way she's going to walk away until she makes it *big*."

The studio door banged again, Miranda's voice cutting into Rick pleading his case. "What's this all about?" she whined.

Rick made one last play. "Doc, this is a lot better than moving coke. Totally legal. What difference does it make if you get Candy's money from her nose or from her music? It's all money."

Rick felt Miranda at his side, and the looming presence and cologne of Kevin. He kept his eyes on Doc, trying to convey sincerity, belief, promise.

Doc turned to Miranda. "Is Candy going to be as big as Bruno Mars?"

CHAPTER 11

D OC STARED out his office window at the sparkling layer of morning frost. Frost. In fucking October. He had to find a way to get back to a warmer climate, and soon.

In the meantime, he had to keep the cash flowing. Not being in Miami definitely hurt his business. Even the bling rental business had taken a hit. There just weren't as many rappers in the Boston area as there were in Miami.

Doc turned from the depressing outdoor scene and speed dialed Dwayne. Dwayne was a rapper, a bona fide customer of Doc's legitimate, tax filing, tax paying costume jewelry rental business. That Doc's customers paid in cash or in cocaine for most of their rentals wasn't any business of the IRS.

"We got a new shipment," said Doc. "Nice heavy chains, just the way you like them."

"Sounds good, man. Not so thick they don't look real, though."

"Just right." Doc understood Dwayne's concern. No one would believe a one inch thick chain was real gold unless it was worn by a really big name. "Sixteen millimeters."

"Better not be that herringbone."

Doc spun his chair back to look outside. The frost was still there, which meant he needed to be patient with Dwayne. If he pissed off one of his best customers he'd never escape this cold. "Cuban link. Like the one's I've been getting you."

"Same deal?"

"Yeah. I'll get you photos if you want."

"Nah, just yanking your chain. Get it? What's your girl think of it?"

Dwayne was aware Doc always had women around. "She loves it. I had to pry it off her."

"She's got good taste, even though she's with you. Just send it down."

"On the way." This was normally the extent of the conversation with Dwayne. "Got a question for you," said Doc.

Dwayne's voice grew cautious. "About bling?"

"No, about music. I've got this kid who owes me a fair amount of coin, but he doesn't have cash."

"You in a new line of business, Doc? Becoming a banker, maybe?"

For all his bullshit, Dwayne wasn't as stupid as he often sounded behind his mostly made up persona. He was asking Doc if he'd become a loan shark.

"It's a one time thing. The kid's in the music business. He tells me he's about to score some money from a song he wrote. It's gonna be on some chick's album that's supposed to sell a million fucking records and then he'll have enough to pay me back. Wondering if I should let him ride a bit, see how it plays out. Or go another route." The other route would be to have Rick's head banged against the wall again. Much harder.

"Long shot," said Dwayne. "Chick's name on a big label would be a better bet."

"I don't know about the label." Doc listened to music, he didn't know shit about how it got made. "Her name is Candy something."

"The only Candy I know is a stripper."

"The kid says her daddy's got some money." Doc downplayed it, none of Dwayne's business.

"That helps. Music is like politics, man, money buys access, promotion. What else she got? She a dime?"

Doc could never keep up with the slang. He took a guess based on what he'd be asking. "I haven't seen her in the flesh. I found a few photos on line, but you know how that goes."

"She got a producer?"

"Kendall something."

"Kendall DeVaughn? He's the real thing. Bet he's got at least two walls in his house full of gold records."

"The kid says he's going to make money from the song."

"Is she buying the song outright or giving him royalties?"

Doc hadn't even asked Rick that question. "Don't know yet."

"If he's smart, he'll go for royalties. I wrote a song that ended up on Sleazy-A's last album and my cash register rings every time an album sells or if the song gets played somewhere. Made me fifty K. So far. Money keeps rolling in, like clockwork. Got me an accountant just to deal with it."

"Shit." Doc was impressed. He couldn't believe there was so much money in rap. "You had a special deal?" What he was asking was, did this Sleazy-A owe Dwayne the same way Rick owed Doc? Maybe Dwayne was getting all Sleazy's share.

"Nah, usual five percent."

"A lot of songs make it that big?"

"Not many. I've got raps better than what I gave Sleazy. It's a game, fitting the right song with the right artist. We've got a different vibe, this cut worked better for him."

"But it's possible?"

"The best thing your boy has going for him is that your piece of Candy got her a big league producer. DeVaughn wouldn't be doing it if he thought she was crap, no matter how much they offered him. If her daddy's footing the bill for the promotion, and DeVaughn's putting his name on it, shit, she's ninety percent there."

The sun finally came out, reflecting off the icy dew, blinding rays shooting into Doc's office. He put his hand on the warm glass. This might work out after all. "How long does it take for the songwriter to get the money?"

"Won't happen overnight, but once it starts, it just keeps raining. You gotta make sure you have a lock on the royalties. If your boy sells his material outright, that's all he gets."

Doc grimaced, thinking of the pressure he'd already put on Rick. Nothing wrong with pressure, unless it made Rick do something dumb, like try to get the money he needed to pay Doc back by selling his song rights to Candy. "How much would a song get sold for?"

"Depends on who's selling. If he doesn't have a track record, could be just a few thousand bucks. Maybe even less."

For all Doc knew, Rick might settle for a few thousand bucks. He'd need to get to Rick fast.

Dwayne was on the exact same wavelength. "Think your boy will play ball?"

"He will after I have a talk with him."

"Make sure you get a lawyer who knows about music deals."

"Lawyer?"

"Shit, man, this is a business. Get it in writing."

Doc thanked Dwayne and hung up. His first thought was that he owed Dwayne one, maybe slip in a few freebie chains.

On second thought, if Dwayne was making beaucoup dollars from songwriting, he could afford what Doc was charging him and more. Next shipment, the rental price would be a bit higher. Good fakes weren't cheap.

Doc pushed a button on his desk, opening the drapes all the way, letting in the welcome sun and warmth. Did another speed dial.

"Sterling. Need you."

"I'm due in court in fifteen. Phone okay?"

Tyler Sterling, Doc's lawyer, understood the sensitivities of phone calls. Sterling didn't ask questions he didn't want answers to.

"This will be quick. I got a guy who is going to cut me in on royalties for a song he wrote. Any way to make sure that happens?" *Legally*, was the unspoken word.

"He can't write you a check?"

"He hasn't earned them yet. It's for a song that isn't even out."

"Hmm. You'll need paper."

Sterling sounded like Dwayne, everyone a fucking lawyer now. Doc hated paper. Paper meant a trail. "I was hoping to avoid that."

"You could trust the guy to just pay you when he gets his cut."

"That's one option," said Doc. "I was thinking of something more automatic, like the money just shows up in my account."

"Then you definitely need paper."

"Shit." Doc fiddled with the remote for the drapes. "What's the downside?"

"Is the guy legit?"

Doc wasn't sure how to answer that. How legit was a kid who was willing to move coke for him? But Rick didn't have a record, Doc had checked that a long time ago. "He's good."

"Then it shouldn't be an issue. There won't be anything more than a contract saying he's entitling you to whatever per cent. We run it through an LLC, your name doesn't even appear on it. Simple. I can get it all for you, it's boilerplate."

One thing Doc appreciated about Sterling was that he didn't pretend all legal work was reinventing the damn wheel. He charged top dollar, but that was more for discretion. "What do you need?"

"Text me the guy's name. I'll leave blanks for you to work out. You can fill in the percentages yourself, just make sure he initials anything handwritten."

Another thing Doc appreciated, Sterling understanding that there might be a little coercion involved with this particular deal. "Thanks."

"Don't thank me yet. Your song makes it big, you'll have plenty of taxes to pay."

That, thought Doc, wouldn't be all bad. A few more taxes would nicely cover up the big house he planned on building somewhere far away and warm.

CHAPTER 12

RICK PULLED INTO the studio lot just as it started to rain, forty minutes late. Liz, the receptionist, was sitting in her car, giving him the evil eye.

Rick unlocked the door and she dashed in, bitching. "Now my hair's all wet. Where the hell were you? If you got here on time . . ."

"Yeah, yeah, good morning to you, too," said Rick. As he flicked the lights on a black Mercedes SUV pulled into the lot. "Shit."

Rick wasn't awake enough to spar with Doc, he'd been up half the night taking care of his mother. He had done his best, but she needed a night nurse. Without sleep he wouldn't be in any shape to make enough money for a nurse or to pay Doc back. Something had to give, likely him.

Liz yelled at him as he walked out. Rick tuned her out, she was the least of his problems now.

He stood by the back of the Mercedes, the rain slapping at his cheeks, not able to see though the tint. But it wasn't the rear door window rolling down, it was the driver's. Kevin jerked his head. "Get in."

Rick's mouth must have been open, because the harsh taste of liquid acid was on his tongue. His lips fluttered, a fish begging for water. This was the ride Doc had threatened him with. "I need some more time," he sputtered, sounding like the rain.

The rear window slid down a few inches. "Get in the fucking car."

Doc's window rolled back up, but Kevin's did not. Rick reached out for the door handle.

"Not the back, you idiot," said Kevin. "Up front, where I can see you."

Beat my head against the windshield, you mean, thought Rick, but he stiffly walked around the car. He could only pray that nosy Liz was watching and would remember the car, in case Rick didn't come back.

Rick turned in the seat to face Doc, his body tense, expecting a blow from Kevin at any minute.

Doc was wearing his usual heavy sweater. "About time you showed up," said Doc.

"I had some personal business to attend to."

"Getting me my money?"

"I swear, I'm working on it. But my mom is sick, I'm trying to take care of her."

"We all have our crosses to bear. Right now, you are mine. You think a guy like me needs a cross?"

"No, Doc, really. I don't want to be a problem. If this thing with Candy comes through—"

"If?"

"When, when. Candy told me that DeVaughn went for my song. She's going to use it, definite." Rick tried to keep the pleading out of his voice.

"That's good to hear. You getting royalties, right?"

"We haven't talked specifics." A royalty would be good, but with Doc hounding him Rick would have taken cash. "I bet I'll be able to get everything I owe you in one shot." Rick winced, that didn't sound good enough. "More than enough. Pay you extra for the trouble."

"I don't want you to sell the song."

"What?"

"That's right. Get a royalty cut."

"But—Doc, you know that's less of a sure thing."

"I thought you said this chick is good? And with backing?"

"She is, but—royalties could take a while to come in. Candy's a perfectionist, shit, it could take her months to release."

Doc shrugged, or at least that's what Rick thought he was doing, his head moving up and down like a fishing float over his sweater. "What, you think I need this money to pay my electric bill?"

"No, not that, I just—." Rick glanced over at Kevin, who wore his usual hard stare. "I thought you were in a hurry."

"You let me worry about the timing," said Doc. "But just to make sure we're all singing the same song, so to speak, we're going to formalize our little deal."

Rick couldn't imagine anything more formalized than sitting within striking distance of Kevin. "Whatever you say."

"Always, kid, don't forget that. Kev, give it to him."

Rick's shrunk against the door, his arm coming up defensively as Kevin moved. Instead of a blow, Kevin dropped a stack of papers in his lap.

Doc said, "That's a contract. Between you and one of my companies. It gives me the right to half your royalties. Sign it."

The document must have been radioactive, because Rick couldn't bring himself to touch it. "Half the royalties?"

"You negotiating?"

"No, no." Rick gingerly picked up the document, trying to focus. His mind was racing ahead. Half the royalties could be a lot of money, but it could also get Doc off his back for good. "So if I sign this, I don't have to pay you what I owe you?"

"As long as the royalties are at least five times what you owe me."

"What if they're not?"

"Let's just say the next time Kevin shows up and tells you to get in the car, I won't be in the back seat."

Rick got the message, his eyes jumping to the words. It looked straightforward enough. There was nothing he could see about the minimum payment, but of course Doc wouldn't put down on paper that he was going to break Rick's knees if he didn't get paid.

Rick didn't want to miss anything in the contract, not that he had a choice. If only it wasn't so hot in the damn car.

"Come on kid, I ain't got all day."

"Sure, Doc, just want to make sure . . ."

"Give him the fucking pen, Kevin."

Kevin shoved a pen in Rick's hand, a nice Cross. Maybe another joke from Doc, the only cross he bore was a gold pen. Rick was near the end of the last page, a paragraph entitled Representations. *The signee represents that he is the sole owner of the intellectual property . . .*

"Doc, uh, one little problem."

"You miss the part I said about negotiation?"

"It's not the terms. It's this sole owner thing. I wrote these songs with another guy. That means I'm not the sole owner. Candy knows, and she's going to expect the royalties will be split."

Doc didn't raise his voice, but his displeasure was obvious in the way he leaned forward. "I thought you said the song was yours?"

"It is. I mean, I wrote it with a friend, back in high school, for god's sake. I changed it, and Candy will change it again. I don't know the law, but he is probably due half."

"You should have told me this."

"I wasn't trying to hide it. I figured I'd get money from Candy, pay you off, give him his share if anything was left. He'd be happy since he wasn't expecting anything."

"Or not mention it to him?"

Rick would definitely have given Gerry his share, but this wasn't the time to convince Doc he was a good guy. "I didn't think it mattered."

"Well, it does now. Who is this other guy?"

"Do we need to get him involved?"

"He's already involved, he just doesn't know it yet. Get him on board."

"Doc, I haven't talked to him in forever."

"This will be a good time for a reunion. If you don't convince him, I'm sure Kevin can."

Rick wouldn't wish Kevin on anyone, especially Gerry, who wasn't exactly the rough and tumble type. "I'll get with him as soon as I can," said Rick. What the hell was he going to tell Gerry?

"Give me back that contract," said Doc.

Doc made notations on one of the pages. "I just changed the percentage you are giving me from fifty percent to seventy five percent. I'd make it a hundred, but I want to make sure you stay motivated. Initial the changes I made, and sign it. Now."

Rick did as he was told, his fingers shaking so badly he didn't recognize his own signature. At this point, he would have given up all the money just to be free of Doc. Rick's name would still be on the music, which was what counted.

"What's your friend's name?" asked Kevin.

Rick looked to Doc for help, but Doc just held out his hand for the contract. Rick surrendered. "Gerry. Gerry Hennig."

"And where can I find Gerry Hennig, should the need arise?"

Rick frantically thought of how he could save Gerry a trip from Kevin. Even if he lied his ass off, Doc would find him sooner or later, it wasn't like Gerry was in hiding. "He's getting a PhD at MIT. That's in Cambridge."

"I know where it is, shithead," said Kevin.

"Hey, Kev, that's no way to speak to the kid. We're partners now, after all." Doc tucked the papers in his portfolio. "And partner, don't forget to give Kevin the pen back."

CHAPTER 13

Doc LAY HIS HEAD back against the seat. "Why can't anything be simple?"

"Something I can do?" asked Kevin.

"Just drive. I need to think."

The Mercedes pulled out of the lot, smooth even over the potholes. Doc didn't care where they went, the car was warm and cozy, and Kevin knew to keep his mouth shut when Doc needed quiet time.

He should probably just let the whole song thing go. Chalk it up to a bad deal. Point Kevin at Rick, be done with it. Collect what he could, it wasn't exactly a ton of money.

Not to mention the paper trail.

The Mercedes stopped at a light, the wipers flipping side to side, huddled pedestrians snapping in and out of focus. A woman with a bright pink ski jacket crossed in front of the car, holding an umbrella, her steps bouncy, maybe listening to ear buds.

Doc hated ear buds as much as he hated the cold. Ear buds ruined even the best music. Three other pedestrians crossed, all bopping along, wires running into their coats like plugged in zombies.

"What kind of music you listen to, Kevin?" he asked absently.

"Mostly rock, a little hip hop."

"You got a stereo?"

"A what?"

"You know, speakers, an amp, a CD player."

"I use my phone."

Shit, thought Doc, another one. Although he hadn't hired Kevin for his musical appreciation, it was still depressing.

"How much you spend on your collection?"

"I don't keep track. I guess I buy a couple dozen songs a month, they're only about a buck each."

Didn't sound like much to Doc. "You know any musicians? People who make a living at it?"

"One of my cousins plays a fiddle in an Irish dance group."

"Hard way to make a living."

"He bought his Da a boat and paid off their mortgage, so I guess he's doing okay."

Doc found that hard to believe. Who the hell listened to Irish dance music? "Your cousin, he have a side job, like you?" Meaning, does he do anything illegal?

"Just the music," said Kevin. "Big money in music he says, if you hit it right."

They had reached another light, more plugged in zombies controlled by their mp3 players appearing out of the mist. Doc grunted. Maybe there *was* good coin to be made with this music shit.

Doc rang up Tyler Sterling. "Might have a problem with that paper you sent over. I got the kid to sign on, but it turns out he had a writing partner. Can you fix that?"

"Same way. Get the other party to give over his piece to your partner, or directly to you."

"A share of a share?"

"Or an outright buy. Even more straightforward. He sells all his rights for a flat fee. Simple."

Doc liked simple. "I'll send you the guy's name. Pay him a visit, have the paperwork with you, make an offer."

"How much?"

"Size him up." Doc remembered what Dwayne had said, about the value of music written by an unknown. "Use your judgment up to a couple of grand. If it gets beyond that, I'll send someone else."

Doc hung up. Sterling could be persuasive, but only in a lawyerly way. If Sterling couldn't get Gerry fucking Hennig to get on board, there was always Kevin.

RICK DID A crash and burn in the studio bathroom, his rush of adrenaline depleted after his escape from Doc's hot car and Kevin's hard fists.

He splashed cold water on his face and stumbled out into the studio corridor just as Candy and her entourage were arriving.

"Hey," she said.

It was the warmest syllable she'd ever uttered to him. Rick perked up, her smile a faster jolt than Doc's best blow. "Hi. I'll get the rest of the lights on."

Candy was wearing a white tee shirt with *Candy* written in retro script, superimposed over an updated yet forties style image of herself, long legs thrown over a piano.

Candy caught him staring. "Like it?"

"Nice," said Rick. His next line would normally be, "And the shirt isn't bad either," in a Groucho Marx impression, but he bit it off just in time.

"It's the mockup for the album cover. I'll get you one, if you want."

"Wow, thanks."

Candy squeezed the wetness out of her hair. "We're having party at my house the week after next, build an early buzz for the album. Publicists, people from New York. You're invited."

Miranda, who'd come in behind Candy, mouthed at Rick, "You owe me."

Rick stood there for a second, feeling like an idiot, but too thrilled to move. He'd deal with Miranda later. He had Doc off his back and Candy giving him a smile. Things were turning around. So what if he had to fork over royalties to Doc? He could live with this. "Wouldn't miss it for the world."

"Good. Let's get going, we've got a lot of tracks to lay down."

Candy brushed by, giving Rick's arm a squeeze. It wasn't romantic, just friendly, he knew that, but he felt like one of the team already, the inner circle. Not a technician, here today and forgotten tomorrow, but an artist. *A songwriter.*

Rick watched Candy walk down the hall toward the recording room, riding so high on the turn of events he didn't want to miss this opportunity. "Candy?"

She turned, her hair still messed up from the rain, looking like the proverbial girl next door, approachable. That cinched it for Rick. "This isn't really important," he began, trying to downplay it, "but at some point, can we discuss the, uh, arrangement for my song?"

Candy squinted. "The music or the rights?"

"Well, I'd be interested in helping on the music, but only if you want, after all, it's your album, and you got DeVaughn." Rick laughed nervously. "But you know, it's my baby."

"I'll always listen," said Candy. "I can't promise anything."

"Of course. About the other thing . . ."

Candy gave him a look that deflated Rick like a gunshot into a hot air balloon. He'd blown it. Fuck, he should have waited . . . "I mean, I just wanted to say, whatever works for you. Standard royalties, if that's okay."

"You don't want anything up front?"

"No, I'm in this for the long haul. I won't feel right making a dime unless you are killing it."

Candy turned on her thousand watt smile. "Right answer. I'll have one of my father's lawyers draw up the papers."

She disappeared into the studio, Rick almost peeing his pants with relief, but she immediately reappeared. "Wait, didn't you mention a co-writer? Is he going to be a problem?"

Rick was already shaking his head. "Not at all. He's out of music. Besides, his share would come out of my cut anyway. Anything I get him will be like a Christmas present."

"Get it on paper," she said.

RICK HAD NEVER had so many emotional jerks in one day. One minute he was depressed over his mother's situation, then scared to death of Doc, seeing a way out, achieving his lifelong dream of being a songwriter, having a hot chick invite him to a party, and now this. Rick thought Gerry would go along, but he had to be sure.

In writing sure.

He ran into the control room, firing up the board, then rushed back out into the hall, turning down the thermostat to Candy's desired temperature. The heat reminded him of Doc, everyone making Rick do paperwork.

Gus was talking to Candy and the band. Rick slipped into Larry's office and dialed Gerry, who he hadn't spoken to in over a year. Come on, come on, pick up . . .

"Gerry! It's Rick, how's it going?"

"Rick? It's fine, you okay?"

"Yeah, yeah, all good. Real good, as a matter of fact." Rick knew he should do more chitchat, warm up, but this was his old friend. "Listen, I don't want to keep you, but I need to talk to you about something important."

"I'm just heading out. I have a class to teach."

"Is there some time we can get together? I'll come to Boston."

"Sure. Next month, maybe? Around Thanksgiving? It slows down."

"No, no, it's kind of a time critical thing. How about tomorrow?"

Gerry laughed. "Rick, I have my orals next week. I don't have time to eat."

The door popped open, Liz. "They want you."

Rick held up a finger. "Gerry, I got to go. Here's the thing. I might have a deal for one of our old songs, I need to talk to you about it."

"Good for you. Do what you need to do."

"But our deal, remember? The partnership?"

"Rick, I got to go too. I'm sure it can wait a few weeks."

"I need something on paper. Listen, I can get us some money, it's not like you're going to get rich teaching math or whatever you're going to do, are you?"

"Sounds good, Rick, whatever you say. After orals. Gotta go."

"Gerry! There's a party coming up, music people I want to meet. I can get you in, we can get it done then."

"You know I hate parties."

Rick didn't want to play this card, but he was desperate. "Come on, Gerry. You left me kind of high and dry, remember? This could be my one shot." Rick didn't have to fake pleading. "Please."

There was a long silence, Rick crunching up the papers on Larry's desk in his fist. "Come on, Gerry. Cut me a break here."

"When is it?" The sorrowful tone in Gerry's voice knifed into Rick like Candy's frown, Gerry making it clear he was disappointed in Rick playing the guilt card.

"Week after next, I'm not sure of the exact date, I'll let you know. After your tests, though."

Another long silence, Rick feeling terrible, already thinking of ways to apologize, to make it up to Gerry.

"Okay, Rick, I'll try to make it."

Rick hung up, not feeling as good as he should have.

CHAPTER 14

Detective Robert Winter squinted at the looping script spray painted on the plate glass windows of TheraRex, a company he'd never heard of in a new industrial park on the east side of Marburg. Normally he couldn't read graffiti worth a shit. This particular addendum to the otherwise unadorned glass, however, didn't take any special skills to decipher.

"Somebody doesn't like these guys," said Winter. "*People die from TheraRex greed.* Ouch."

Daniels, the uniformed cop standing next to him, said, "It *is* a pharmaceutical company."

"Still," said Winter. He didn't recall reading anything about a patient dying from drugs made by a Marburg based pharma company. "So exactly why am I here?"

"Thought you'd be interested," said Daniels. "There was another spray paint job across town about three weeks ago. Different company, different message." Daniels pulled out a small notebook. "Stop sourcing from overseas sweatshops."

"Another pharma company?"

"Nope. Westside Tool. They make industrial machinery."

"Huh. Some kind of political protest?" mused Winter.

"You're the detective. I'm just pounding the pavement. But I wouldn't have called you if it was just two acts of vandalism. Westside Tool got *another* spray job last week. Same kind of message. 'This company supports child labor.' This time it was on a wall *inside* the building."

"Someone broke in to spray paint a wall?"

"From what we can tell, no one broke in at all. No sign of forced entry. Workers showed up in the morning, it was just there. Visible from the street though."

"Pissed off employee?"

"We thought so too. Captain Logan put Hendricks on it. He checked the employees, no recent firings, no one with a record."

Hendricks wasn't a detective, but was next in line, one of the more senior uniforms. "Hendricks on the way?"

"He's got that training thing in Boston this week. We've taken photographs, done a perimeter search, but I thought you might want to see this for yourself."

Winter didn't think it was much, but he did get a rush from finding connections between crimes. "I'll take a look. Send Cindy the photos of both scenes. There's a guy I know in Boston who works the gangs, he might recognize the style." Cindy was the department criminologist. She was also much better than Winter at computers and anything electronic, but so was just about everyone else in the department.

"Doesn't look like gang tag to me," said Daniels.

"Me neither," said Winter, and went inside.

THE GUY STANDING next to the reception desk was late thirties, thin, with light brown hair and a perfect three day beard, who didn't look anything like a pharmaceutical executive. A ruddy skinned man in a set of overalls stood in the corner next to a bucket, with a ladder balanced against his leg. A receptionist, a petite twenty something redhead with a pixie haircut, sat behind a curved wooden counter, pretending not to listen.

"Mr. Schmidt?" asked Winter. "I'm Robert Winter. Any idea who did this?"

"Not a clue. Although pharma companies are on everyone's shit list. Except of course the people who work here and whose lives get saved by drugs."

"Your drugs?"

"Maybe someday. We do early stage research. We don't even have any drugs out."

Winter gestured toward the paint. "Then why this?"

"It doesn't make any sense. Whoever did this doesn't know squat about how the pharmaceutical industry works."

"Neither do I," said Winter.

"Do you go spray painting diatribes on pharma company walls?"

"You've got a point there." A stream of employees entered the lobby from the office. Mostly young, dressed casually like Schmidt, chinos, polo shirts, even some jeans. For once Winter didn't look out of place in his cargo tactical pants. No one gave him a second look.

"Not very corporate," commented Winter.

"I don't care what people wear, as long as they get their work done. Might as well be comfortable."

"I need you to talk to my captain," said Winter. "That's what I keep telling him." He watched through the window as the maintenance man swiped a rag across the glass, smearing a line of paint into a blob. "When was this done?"

"Overnight. We're not sure what time. The security camera doesn't pick up that part of the window."

"Any problems lately? Fire anyone?"

"No and no."

"You don't have a security guard?"

"You sound like Sven Miller. He's on our board, keeps telling us to get more security. But his brother runs Baron Protection, so he probably mentions that to everyone he meets."

Winter knew Baron Protection. Winter wasn't a devious person by nature, but had learned to think like a crook when he needed to. "You think he could have had this done? Drum up business for his brother?"

"Not likely," said Schmidt. "We have conflict of interest rules. If we did hire outside security, it couldn't go to his brother's company. It would have to go to one of their competitors."

BACK OUTSIDE, Winter watched the attempt to clean off the glass. The man was struggling to get at the spots where the spray had dripped into the edge seams.

Winter pulled out his multitool, swung out the knife, and scraped along the bottom of the sill. "Might need to use a razor blade on this," he said.

"I think so too," said the man. "I figured Mr. Schmidt would be happier if I got the words blocked out first, even if it leaves a mess."

"Good idea," said Winter. He scraped along the bottom of the glass for a while, just trying to be helpful. Winter wondered how the vandals wielding the spray cans would feel about someone splashing paint on their stuff, no matter how creative the drawings. Maybe that would be a good punishment, spray their wheels or their expensive sneakers. The thought made him happy enough to clean off the entire bottom sill.

WINTER TOOK a slow stroll around the building to get a feel for the place, trying to imagine how the vandal had approached. Around back, four squat air conditioner compressors sat in a fenced off service area lane.

Winter was about to continue on when a quick furtive movement in the alley caught his eye, his hand going to his gun. The wind blew through the gap, swirling papers and leaves, carrying to Winter the unmistakable sound of distress.

Except it wasn't human. Winter relaxed, listened again to make sure, and became certain when a furry head poked out, followed by a plaintiff wail. A cat, which appeared to be stuck.

"Hey, buddy," said Winter. "You okay?"

The cat looked at him and cried. Winter didn't know much about cats. It was pretty obvious, though, that this one needed some help.

"Hang on, I'll get someone with the key." Winter didn't know why he was talking to the cat, but something in his voice must have triggered an interspecies understanding, because before he took two steps the cat let out a sound that reminded Winter of when he had stood helplessly by while his wife had gone into labor. He couldn't bear that then, and couldn't now, but this time he could do something, so he stuck his foot on the chain holding the padlock and hoisted himself onto the fence and over.

The cat mewed as he approached, giving him a pitiful look. Somehow the animal had managed to get stuck in a narrow slot between the compressors. The cat was breathing rapidly, it's mouth open, which didn't look good. Winter tried pulling at the sheet metal frame next to the cat, it barely budged. He slipped out his handkerchief, which he carried all the time but used for everything else other than blowing his nose, wrapped it around his hand, sat on the ground, braced his foot against the compressor, and grasped the sharp edge of the metal near the cat. The metal bent easier than Winter expected, cut into his hand,

and he fell on his back, banging his head. The cat leapt out and onto Winter's chest.

Winter wiped the blood with the handkerchief and was trying to figure out how to get back out with the cat when it ran between his legs and under a narrow opening beneath the fence.

"You can get through there but couldn't get by that compressor?" said Winter.

He climbed back over the fence, expecting the cat to run off, but it just sat there looking at him. A thin blue collar with a bell suggested it belonged to someone. "Go on home, you."

Winter checked the collar, no tag. The cat looked clean and well nourished and not only didn't mind Winter's touch, but rubbed up against his leg.

Winter picked the cat up, carried it around to the parking area, got in his car, and drove around the block. The cat, content, curled up in his lap like this happened every day.

NO ONE ANSWERED at the first house, but at the second Winter got lucky. "That's Maureen's cat, next door."

Maureen was a plump middle aged woman. "Oh my god, Jasper!" She banged her way out, Jasper giving her a contented yawn. Until the woman noticed the blood and screeched.

"It's not his, it's mine," said Winter.

"Are you okay?"

"Just scraped myself. Your cat managed to get stuck in a compressor behind your house."

"That's my Jasper. Always trying to find a place to hide. That's why I put the bell on him."

"You might want to put your name on a tag, too," suggested Winter gruffly. He was more pissed at the woman than the cat.

"I keep meaning to do that. Did he jump out at you when you found him? It's a game he plays."

Winter shook his head and walked back down the steps, his fingers starting to throb.

"Thank you!" yelled the woman.

Winter raised a bloody hand and waved without looking back.

CHAPTER 15

T YLER STERLING TURNED his BMW M6 onto Memorial Drive in Cambridge, easing up to a building sporting typical old school college architecture, large windows, Ionic columns, *Aristotle* carved out in the frieze.

He found a rare parking space—Memorial Drive being one of the last streets that didn't have meters or require a resident permit—across from the building. He took the time to fix his impeccable tie in the visor mirror. Sterling always looked his best. Once you started taking things for granted, once you got sloppy, you made mistakes, you missed opportunities. Sterling hated missing opportunities. Opportunities meant money.

Normally he would have handed off this particular visit to one of the gofer law firms he used for minor cases. That is, if the client had been anyone but Doc. With Doc, nothing was minor.

He'd met Doc in Miami, where Sterling spent part of every winter. Sterling had been at one of those slightly gaudier than chic, slightly more free spirited than elegant parties that was so Miami. A mini universe of opportunities for Sterling, potential clients galore. The music had a heavy Latino emphasis, as did the crowd, those not olive skinned by birth so evenly tanned they might have been.

All except one man, an older, incongruously pale, going on overweight guy, as far from the beautiful people look imaginable, cocooned in a thick—although Sterling had to admit, nicely cut—cashmere suit jacket that was too warm by half.

Out of place as the big man seemed, he was shown an uncommon deference, his champagne refilled before he lifted his finger, powerful men Sterling recognized stopping for a word, listening attentively. This treatment immediately put the man on Sterling's radar as someone to get closer to, or fear.

Perhaps both.

Sterling had been right on both counts. After a year of not quite so chance encounters, Sterling had been introduced to Doc. At the time they met, Sterling didn't quite know what Doc did for a living. Basic research ruled out politics, real estate, and the other relatively legal activities that brought power and prestige. Doc did have an office but didn't practice in the big money area of plastic surgery.

It had to be drugs.

Sterling had been careful with his clients. It was one thing to represent a big construction conglomerate that bent the rules on getting city contracts, it was another to be mentioned in the same newspaper story with a drug kingpin. Yet Doc appeared to be different. Sterling had a sixth sense for those who were as discreet as he was.

He'd been right about the opportunity. His new BMW was the latest gift to himself from the work he'd done for Doc. Doc had sought Sterling out after a surprise move north, proving again that no matter how big a fish you were in your own pond, once you jumped to another body of water, you sought out the familiar. Sterling had made himself indispensable to Doc since then.

Sterling pulled the photo of Gerry Hennig out of his portfolio. Both the photo and Gerry had been easy enough to find, courtesy of an MIT website page which listed not only the faculty but all the grad students. Sterling had also found Gerry's home address, working back from his listed cell phone.

The directory said Gerry had an office in Building 2. Inside, footsteps echoed in a large foyer. An impossibly young looking student with her head in a book sat at a small reception table, her dirty blond, straight as straw hair completely covering her face.

Sterling ignored her and took the stairs to three. Gerry's office door was open. Gerry was sitting in a swoop chair that had been in vogue when Sterling had been an undergrad, staring at an old style blackboard covered in symbols. Gerry would have won a masquerade party award for the stereotypical geek, uncombed medium brown hair, skin even paler than the norm for cloudy Boston, square metal framed glasses, a plaid shirt. Sterling doubted he was much over a hundred and twenty pounds.

"Gerry Hennig?"

Gerry held up a finger, his eyes glued to the blackboard. Shook his head, turned to Sterling. "I'm Gerry."

"I'm Tyler Sterling, I'm an attorney. Mind if I come in?"

"I'm just on the way out. What do you want?"

"This won't take long," said Sterling, sizing up Gerry, making minor adjustments to his approach. "I can see that you are busy. Getting a math PhD, at MIT no less, is quite an accomplishment."

"How do you know so much about me?"

"A mutual friend of my client told him. Rick Singleton."

"Rick told you to come see me?"

Sterling sidestepped. "I understand you and Rick wrote songs together years ago. I also understand you are no longer in the music business. I have an opportunity for you to help yourself out."

"Help me out how?"

Sterling gestured vaguely at the office, the blackboard. "All of this is expensive. I'm sure you could use a little extra cash."

"Once I get my PhD I'm going to be able to get a good job."

"Yes, yes, of course," said Sterling. "But you're not quite there yet, are you?"

"What's this got to do with Rick and the music?"

"My client might want to use a song you wrote with Rick. The song will go through some changes, but my client, who is a very careful man, doesn't want to have any complications, so he's willing to buy your share of the song rights upfront. For cash."

"Is this the song Rick called me about yesterday?"

"I assume it is. I have the details here," said Sterling, tapping his portfolio.

"Who is your client?"

"Does it matter, really? They're offering you a thousand dollars for something that's been sitting on a shelf for years. It's just collecting dust, right?"

"A thousand dollars?"

"That's right. Think about that math." Sterling keyed in on Gerry's reaction. The offer hadn't seemed to impress him. Maybe another tack would work. "If you don't mind me asking, Mr. Hennig, why did you choose math?"

Gerry's head bounced like a bobblehead. "That's what got me

interested in music, it's like math. Did you know that you can actually build mathematical models of recurring themes in hit songs?"

Sterling didn't know and didn't care, but he said, "That's interesting. So the music was just a sideline? It's actually the math that drives you?"

"Yes, it's the numbers. They can be as beautiful as a melody."

"Then your old songs can't really have that much interest for you. It's not like you are going to go back into the music field, are you?"

"No, never."

"So what's the harm in selling some old song rights?"

Gerry got up, slipping his phone into his jeans, floating on his skinny waist. "Probably nothing. But I'm not going to do anything until I talk to Rick."

Sterling tried another ploy. "You and Rick are good friends?"

"We were. Still are, I guess, we just headed in different directions. I love math, Rick loves music."

"You'd be helping Rick if you sell your song," said Sterling. "You get your math, Rick gets his music."

"I'll talk to him about it. I'm going to see him at a party."

"There's some urgency to this due to a production schedule."

"I said I'm not doing anything until I talk to Rick."

Here Sterling would usually up the offer as an inducement, but he sensed it wasn't about the money with Gerry, at least not the kind of money that Doc had preapproved. Sure, ten grand might do it, but ten grand would make Gerry suspicious. Ten grand would make *anyone* suspicious.

"Maybe you could discuss it with Rick before then," suggested Sterling.

Gerry was at the doorway. "I have to go. I've already spent too much time talking to you. Sorry, but I've got orals coming up. I have to focus on that."

Sterling moved aside, this deal wasn't going to get done today. He'd need something to appease Doc. "The party you mentioned, where is it? I could be there with the paperwork, we could handle all the business in two minutes. A gift toward your PhD."

"You'd have to ask Rick," said Gerry. "I'm getting in through him. It wouldn't be right for me to invite you."

Sterling smiled. "I know a lot of people, maybe I could get my own invitation."

Gerry looked Sterling up and down as if noticing him for the first time. "If you can, I'll see you there. I really got to run."

Gerry reached past Sterling, locked the office door, and sprinted for the stairs.

IN THE FOYER, the young blond woman was twisting her hair into a curl as she talked to Gerry. Gerry fidgeted nervously from foot to foot, Sterling recognizing the unmistakable signs of a introverted guy getting a little female attention.

The girl smiled a not especially attractive smile, but it was enough to wiggle Gerry into a near jitter. When Gerry finally managed to pull himself away the unheard communication spoke volumes to Sterling.

He waited until Gerry left before approaching the young woman. That Sterling hadn't been able to get a deal done with Gerry wasn't unexpected, that was the nature of deals. What was a problem was what Sterling was going to tell Doc. Maybe he could salvage this day after all.

"That's one smart man," said Sterling.

The blonde didn't even ask who Sterling was. "He certainly is."

"You seem to know Gerry pretty well."

The blonde blushed. "Okay, I guess."

"Maybe I'll see you at the party."

"You're going to the party at the Carter's estate?"

Just to be sure he'd heard the right name, Sterling said, "Gerry's in a nice club."

"I had no idea. The Carter family, can you believe it? I hope he invites me."

Sterling hid his smile, and, feeling a little better about his day, didn't burst her bubble.

CHAPTER 16

DOC LAY FACEDOWN ON the extra wide massage table in his solarium. The room was dry and very hot, a cross between a perfect martini and an enticing woman.

"You're very tight, Doc," said Tricia, her long delicate fingers probing at his shoulder blades.

Tricia made up for her lack of skill in shiatsu with not only enthusiasm but a willingness to also be naked while performing her ministrations, even though Doc knew he probably looked like a beached whale.

Tricia shifted her hips on Doc's ample butt to get better leverage. He didn't have to turn over to know that her tongue was peeking out of her dainty lip in deep concentration. "That's good, right there," he said, not sure himself whether he was talking about where she was sitting or where she was rubbing.

"You should let me do this every day. You're too busy."

Dumb as she was, the woman always said the right thing. "If I'm not working, who's going to pay for all your clothes?"

Tricia giggled. "Who needs clothes?"

"You say that now. Next time we're out, you going to go naked?"

"Sounds like fun. If you want me to, that is."

Doc was considering the possibilities when the adagio from the Cello Concerto in C Minor drifted over the room.

"Should I get that for you, Doc?"

"Yeah." That would be Tyler Sterling. The concerto had been long attributed to JC Bach, but had actually been written by another composer, Henri Casadesus. Just like Sterling, a face behind a face, a mask. "Tell me good news," Doc grunted into the phone.

"You pay me to tell you how it is, not just good news."

"I pay you for results. It sounds like you didn't get any." The tightness in Doc's shoulders, which Tricia had partially rubbed away, was back. He shrugged Tricia off, ignoring her yelp.

"I couldn't get him on board. He said he wouldn't sign anything without talking to Rick first."

Doc already didn't like Gerry Hennig. Too stupid to see what was good for him. "Maybe you didn't push him hard enough."

"What did you expect me to do? Break his arm?"

"You're supposed to make it so I don't have to push that button. I got another guy for that kind of work. In case someone needs incentive." Doc let the threat hang in the air.

"I can't advise you on that. I *can* tell you about how to get another crack at him, and maybe parlay it into a bigger opportunity."

"I'm listening."

"Hennig said he's going to see your kid Rick at a party. We can get to them there, do all the paperwork in one shot."

"Or I can drag Rick's ass to Hennig, accomplish the same thing."

"That would get you the songs, but you'd miss the parlay. This party they are going to, it's at James Carter's house."

"Who the fuck is James Carter?"

"Boston money."

Doc sat up on the massage table too quickly, his head swimming. Tricia hustled over with a towel, patting like a hummingbird at his forehead. Doc brushed her off. "Must be the father of the chick who is going to use the songs. Rick mentioned he had some money."

"Big time money."

"Sure, sure." Doc had lived in Miami, he'd seen plenty of big time money. "So?"

Sterling's voice, patient. "Doc, I got money. You got money. This is a different world altogether. This guy could buy and sell the Kennedys. James Carter won't accept anyone with his family name looking like a failure. He's going to make *sure* his daughter is successful, even if he has to buy every radio station in the country and make them play her music 24/7. That kind of big time money."

Doc said, "Not sure how that helps me. Old time money might not be interested in my line of business."

"You might be surprised. And even if not the Carters personally, there's all the people surrounding them, layers upon layers of money. Carter has his hands into everything. His wife has a fashion business with her own line of clothing. Not to mention who else might be at that party now that the daughter is into music."

Doc understood where Sterling was heading. The fashion business was almost as doped up as the music business. "Opportunities," said Doc.

"Exactly," agreed Sterling. "It wouldn't hurt to expand your local social circle more. This is a group even I'd have a hard time getting you into."

"I'm not a party crasher. I want the wheels greased first."

"Sure. Although if the party is being thrown by the daughter it might turn out to be one of those events where people just show up. But I'd advise you to take the long view. Get in good with the daughter through the songs. At the right time, let her know that you hold the rights."

Doc said, "I hear you." It made sense. Get into Candy's inner circle, use them to get to the movers, shakers—and users—around the family. Could be a gravy train.

"There is one problem," said Sterling.

"I was just starting to feel better, and now there's a problem."

"This guy Hennig could mess things up. If he doesn't get on board, and someone later claims Candy stole the music, or Hennig sues, it's going to get messy. Old man Carter will pound Hennig into submission, run over him like a speed bump, but they might still drop the song. And you don't want that publicity. Your deal with Rick would be made public. Even with the LLC, even with a dozen LLC's, the word would get out you're behind it."

Sterling didn't have to spell it out. Doc was doing pretty good lying low from the feds, this would put him in the papers. Worse, the word might get out exactly how Doc got into the deal in the first place.

"Draw up more paperwork," said Doc. "Spell out how Rick gives me half his rights to any *future* songs. All of them."

"Might be a hard signature to get."

"You let me worry about that," said Doc, and hung up.

DOC DANGLED his legs over the massage table, kicking back and forth, weighing the possibilities. Candy's family could leapfrog Doc into a wealth of clients, the type of relationships it had taken him years to develop in Miami. There he had met customers through his medical office; it was a very small step from prescribing Oxy and fentenyl to bored rich housewives to supplying them with coke. He didn't have that channel open to him here. Even if the Carter family wasn't the ticket, surely it would open up a lot of doors. Maybe Massachusetts wouldn't be so bad after all.

He hated the idea of more legal agreements, that dreaded paper trail, but Sterling's idea was a good one. In the meantime, he'd deal with this Hennig problem. Kevin used a different kind of persuasion than Sterling and would talk sense into Hennig.

But too many people knew that Kevin worked for Doc. Doc was already one step too close to Rick, it would be a mistake to have a direct connection to Gerry Hennig in case this got ugly. Rich people were great clients, but it was senseless to make them enemies. Doc was looking for opportunities, not battles.

Doc was still working it out when Tricia, who he'd forgotten all about, tentatively asked, "Would you like a drink, Doc? Maybe a little music?"

Music. Just like that, Doc had his answer.

CHAPTER 17

W INTER FINISHED his notes from the day, picked up his coffee, felt how cold the mug was, and set it back down. Cindy, the criminologist who sat at the front of the detective squad room, wheeled her chair back toward him. Her hair was blond today, which might or might not have been her real color, her locks an ever changing rainbow. For all Winter knew, she was a natural blond who gave herself a blond hair job.

"Your friend from Boston got back to us on that graffiti at TheraRex," she said. "He said it doesn't look like any gang tag. Unless—and these are his words—Marburg has a gang of nerds."

"Was that his entire contribution?"

"He did mention something about if you needed some practice doing real detective work, like with actual criminals, rough guys, you could go to Boston, he'd show you the ropes."

Winter held up his bandaged hand. "We got rough right here in Marburg."

Cindy peered through her bangs. "You want me to let him know you got scratched by a cat?"

"It wasn't the cat. I was bending a half inch thick steel panel with my bare hands."

"Okay, superman," said Cindy. "I'll keep your secret."

Winter hadn't been expecting much from Boston, but ruling out a gang tag at least took one possibility off the table. Hiring a gang to do the work also seemed farfetched.

He picked up the file on the graffiti vandalism. The other detective, Hendricks, had reinterviewed the owner of the tool company, looking for a connection between the two businesses.

Hendricks couldn't find one. No shared employees, either past or current. No shared suppliers, customers, or owners.

The notes indicated that the tool company had a security guard on the premises. The guard came on shift at five p.m. when the receptionist left, and stayed until one. Anyone entering after five would be checked by the guard. Before going off duty he did his rounds and locked the place up.

The vandals had managed to spray inside the building during the night, since the wall they painted was right behind where the guard would have been sitting. Yet no one had checked in after regular closing hours.

Winter leaned back in his chair, staring at the ceiling. It was his preferred method of looking for connections, using the white—or in the case of the station, dingy off white—surface as a blank canvas, where he could create a possible set of linkages between crimes.

On the far left of the ceiling, just next to the florescent light that used to buzz so loud Winter had removed the bulb, Winter drew an imaginary box around Westside Tool. Two black dots indicated where the spray paint had been left, one on the outer wall, one inside.

On the other end of the ceiling, another box, this one for TheraRex. One thick dot there, indicating the paint on the window.

Now he'd try to put lines between the boxes. If he could find a connection—if there even *was* a connection—it might help him figure out the who and why of the crime.

Winter scratched at the bandage on his hand. It didn't hurt, just itched like hell. Damned cat, spending his day hiding, instead of clawing furniture or whatever the hell cats were supposed to do.

CHAPTER 18

MALCOLM WASHINGTON, known to everyone on the street as Third Eye, shuffled along the tree lined strip between Memorial Drive and the river, his eyes jerking in every direction. He'd been around, not only Boston, but other cities, Providence, New Haven, even New York. Yet he'd never felt so jumpy as he did right here in Cambridge.

The Rids he'd done earlier weren't helping like they should. Usually Malcolm could ride a nice high all day from the Ritalin, giving him a confidence that exuded so far out of his body people on the street bounced away from him like he was a super magnet. Today, almost nothing.

He lost track of where he was, the buildings all the same. Turned around, bumping into two joggers. "Watch the fuck where you're going," he spit out.

The joggers, white dudes in sweats, earphone deaf, didn't even turn around. Malcolm couldn't believe it. If this was his neighborhood, knives would be out by now.

He fingered the blade in his jacket pocket. Be ready next time.

Got his bearings, back the other way, leaning against a tree across the street from the building with the big windows. Stupid, all that glass, someone could come up and shoot you right through the window.

There was no place to hang, it wasn't like a corner where he'd look at home just standing there. Everyone was moving, jogging, riding bikes, walking. No one just chilling. No one watching the world, looking for action. Just movement.

Worse, no place to hide, do a quick pipe. He had a little ice with him, even a little hit would get him back on track. But all those windows.

Doing a pipe on his corner wouldn't even get a cop to stop. Over here, who knew. It wasn't like anyone else on the street was even smoking a joint.

He was waiting for the dude Gerry that Dwayne had told him to put a scare in. He'd got to Gerry the day before, recognizing him from the photo Dwayne texted. But he only managed to corner Gerry for a few seconds, the dude with two other guys, coming out of his apartment building. Malcolm figured they'd split when he crowded Gerry against the wall, but they just stood there, too stupid to know what was good for them. Lots of eyes, lots of cell phones.

Malcolm's own phone blared, the ringtone one of Dwayne's raps. Malcolm didn't have much to tell him. He let it ring while he pulled a ball point pen from his jeans. The ink had been replaced with crushed ice, and Malcolm did a deep snort.

He answered the call. "Yo."

"You find him?"

"Yeah." Malcolm was half focused on Dwayne, half focused on waiting for the speed to hit.

"Yeah?"

"Couldn't put the big fear in him, too many eyes and ears."

"He say anything?"

"Started babbling about why's everybody bothering him, some dude named Rick, a lawyer, weird shit, didn't make sense."

"Get him to make sense."

"Working on it." Dwayne was blocking Malcolm's high. He cradled the phone and did another hit from the pen.

"You snorting, Third Eye?"

"Fuck no." Then, "Just a little pick me up." Malcolm turned around to see two frumpy bitches whispering to each other, pointing at him. "What you looking at, ho? Never seen a brother?" The two women didn't move. Malcolm started at them, which loosened them up quick, running.

"Fuck you at?" asked Dwayne.

"Cambridge. Guy goes to school here."

"Maybe get him where he lives."

Malcolm sometimes thought Dwayne had been off the streets too long, all the music making him forget how the real world worked. Dwayne was a long way from their days together in Providence. "Tried that. Hard to get him alone there, I think he got roommates. Seen the lights on after he gone."

"You been on him all the time?"

"Shit, you know how few brothers are around here? I'm sticking out like—." Malcolm couldn't think of a good example.

"My limo in a snow pile?"

Dwayne usually gave Malcolm a laugh, but he wasn't in the mood, maybe the ice hitting, wanting to argue. "Don't be throwing that up at me, you and your limo."

"Chill, Third Eye, chill. Don't mean nothing by it. You know you can come down here anytime, I'll get you your own car if you want."

"Don't want no car." Malcolm hadn't driven a car since he was fourteen.

"This is important to me."

"Yeah, yeah. I got other shit to do too." If he was going to be hanging around, he'd rather do it on his own block.

"You don't need to be debating the guy. Just tell him to do what the lawyer wants."

"Still got to get him alone," insisted Malcolm.

"Then get him alone."

Malcolm rubbed his head, didn't he already have this conversation? His hand was jerking, the ice finally kicking in. "All he does is go from his apartment to this big ass building near the river. Practically sleeps here."

"Get him on the way, then."

Three more joggers in tight spandex bounced by. Malcolm wasn't doing nothing but talking on the phone but they automatically veered away as they approached, one of the dudes actually moving the woman to the middle, her protective hero.

Pissed Malcolm off, like it wasn't his street too. Pointed his finger at them like a gun, gave them a smile as he mimicked three shots. The hero tripped, probably having a heart attack, Malcolm laughing. Almost as good as the ice.

"Third Eye, you there?"

"Yeah, I'm here." The three joggers anxiously peered over their shoulders as their jog turned into a sprint. "Hey Dwayne, you want me to just pop the guy?" Malcolm had been practicing with a newly acquired Ruger 9 which he got in trade for two piece of shit Ravens.

"Shit, no." A pause. "Could you do that?"

Malcolm looked over at all the windows. "Easy."

DWAYNE COLEMAN, aka Outta Here, sprawled out on a lounge chair by the pool at the Delano hotel. He wasn't here for the rays, his skin so dark the sun didn't stand a chance. He wasn't here for the crowds, either; the Delano was tiny, he'd go to the Fontainebleau for that.

But the Delano still got traffic, on every tourist list of places to see in South Beach. Dwayne liked the way he stood out at the pool, not only was he one of the few black men, but his ebony skin against the white covered furniture made him a veritable tuxedo.

He wore long black pants but was shirtless, his skin broken only by three thick gold chains—one actually real—and a half dozen tats. One of his women, Sassy, a full figured in all the right places smooth skinned black woman who had a great ass, was sitting on his right, reading a copy of *Essence*. At her feet, another magazine, casually opened to an article about Dwayne.

On Dwayne's other side sat Polo, his legs spread wide on the lounge like he was riding a horse. Polo's real name was Jamal, but he'd once been caught wearing a polo shirt on the street and after realizing he couldn't shake the nickname, absorbed it and now wore nothing but polos, no matter what the weather.

Behind Dwayne's dark sunglasses he was checking out the women, but unlike most men with a woman by his side, when he saw one he liked he didn't hide his interest, but took off his glasses and looked right at her. The first time he did that Sassy gave him some lip, and he told her to shut her mouth. The second time she just gave him a look, and Dwayne slapped it off her face so hard the bruise lasted days. Since then she hadn't seemed to notice who Dwayne stared at.

"Twenty minutes," said Polo.

Dwayne gauged the crowd. "Fifteen."

"By name?"

"Okay, twenty." They were betting on how long it would take for Dwayne to be recognized. Twenty minutes was about average for the middle of the week. "And we don't need that magazine," he said to Sassy.

Sassy flicked the page closed with a bronze nail polished foot.

Dwayne knew why she had the magazine out, hoping Dwayne would be recognized fast by a woman walking by, it put him in a good mood. When he was in a good mood he tended to be extra generous with the blow.

Two young white girls, maybe high school age, had their heads together across the pool, pointing at him. Both snapped pictures with their phones but didn't make a move to come over.

"Shit, three minutes," said Polo. "A new record."

"Jail bait don't count," said Dwayne. "Got to be a real woman."

"Never asked, how about men, they count?"

"Only brothers."

"Lots of white people listen to hip hop."

Dwayne, not taking off his glasses for the jailbait, looked over at Polo. "Exactly how many white friends you got?"

Polo, staring at the two girls, said, "Depends on what you mean by friends. Might be two more right there."

"Keep it in your pants, Polo. We're building a brand, not looking for that kind of publicity." Polo's comment did make Dwayne think about Doc, the whitest dude he had ever seen. "Phone," he said to Sassy.

Sassy reached into her oversized bag and pulled out a burner for him. Doc's name was listed in the contacts as *Albino*.

"Been working on your problem," said Dwayne, without preamble.

"And?"

"Hard to set a meeting with that guy."

"My lawyer got to him in a few hours."

"We ain't planning on having the same kind of discussion your lawyer probably had," said Dwayne. "Need to get him alone so he can focus on the message."

"I hear you," said Doc. "But the clock is ticking."

"What you need this guy for, anyway? Signing away his life insurance?"

"Just a business deal."

Dwayne figured that was bullshit, you didn't twist a guy's arm for a legit business deal. Although the Gerry guy was at MIT. "He a mad scientist with a new invention?" he probed.

"He's just an impediment," said Doc.

Doc sounded even cagier than usual to Dwayne. Whatever Doc was after, it had to be valuable, otherwise why go to all this trouble to get some nerd to sign paperwork? "My boy did start a little conversation. Your future business partner gave him some lip, said we should be talking to Rick. Want my man pointed at Rick instead?"

"You just need to worry about the one guy."

Doc, probably on a burner too, but still dodging the question, making Dwayne even more intrigued. "Want us to up the pressure? Make your problem go away permanently?"

A pause, Dwayne not sure if Doc was worried about what to say or considering the idea. Dwayne had never killed anyone, not yet, although Polo had cut a few, and Malcolm was itching to do more than that. Malcolm had done the fake drive-by that had launched Dwayne's career. Ever since that day, Malcolm had been looking for a reason to take the *fake* out of the drive-by, maybe even walk up to some dude and pop him in the face for no reason.

"No, this needs to be legal," said Doc.

Dwayne laughed, he couldn't help himself. Doc, legal. "You don't want this to look bad, you better find us a different venue."

"Only place I know he's going to be is at a big party."

"What kind of party?"

"That music I talked to you about. Rich chick using the music is going to be throwing a bash."

"DeVaughn going to be there?"

A pause. Dwayne sensed the hesitation, Doc deciding what to tell him. Doc must think him stupid if he thought Dwayne couldn't figure it out.

"Why?" asked Doc.

"If DeVaughn is going to be there, I can get my man in, no problem. My producer and DeVaughn did two albums together."

"I think this place will be more for the lawyer approach, not yours," said Doc.

Dwayne bristled, Doc telling him it was no place for lowlifes. He let it go, no need to piss Doc off now, Dwayne wanted to see what was going down. But he'd remember. "Send him too, if you want. But it won't hurt to have some extra incentive."

"I'll let you know. In the meantime, keep on the guy."

Dwayne hung up, thinking. If Doc wanted legal, what was he doing leaning on this nerd Gerry? Doc must have plenty of muscle he could use, what did he need Dwayne for?

It had to be something big. Dwayne knew Doc was loaded, so it had to be *really* big. Certainly worth more than what Doc was paying him for leaning on the nerd. That other guy Rick had to be in the mix too. Dwayne was going to figure out Doc's angle and see how he could get a piece.

Dwayne was so intrigued by the possibilities he totally missed the chic tall brunette until she was standing over him. A little old for his tastes, thirty, thirty five, her age compensated by high cheekbones, a flawless complexion, two carat diamond studs, a ring bigger than Dwayne's thumb.

She gave Dwayne a million dollar smile. "Love your music," she said. "Nice to see you, *out here*." Just a slight emphasis on the *out her*e, a play on his name. She knew.

Dwayne tossed his sunglasses onto Sassy's lounge chair, holding his other hand out to Polo for a slap.

"Thirteen minutes," said Polo. "Nice."

Doc HUNG UP with Dwayne, uneasy. Not exactly sure why, but sensing he'd let out a little too much information.

He dialed Kevin. "Where are you?"

"Followed the kid from the studio. Sitting outside a house he went into. Mailbox says *Singleton* on it. Wait, there's this woman coming out. She's wearing one of those nurse's uniforms."

"The kid said his mother was sick. Must be her house."

"What do you want me to do?"

"Make sure the kid sees you. Keep up the pressure."

"Want me to go in? Pay a visit to the mother?"

"Not yet." But it wasn't a bad idea, thought Doc. Not at all.

CHAPTER 19

WINTER SAT in complete darkness. He did this often at home, falling asleep in his chair while staring at the ceiling doing one of his connect the dots crime connections, only to wake up in the dark. Right now though, he wasn't at home, he was in the basement of TheraRex, sitting on an old leather banker's chair that he had to admit was pretty comfortable.

He was here, oddly, because of the cat. The woman who owned the cat said it hid all the time and jumped out on people. After he'd discovered the linkage between TheraRex and Westside Tool, he'd worked through the possibilities of why the vandalism had been committed and how.

Winter had a pretty good feeling about knowing the former, the why. Tonight he was pinning down the how.

The vandals hadn't got what they wanted from the tool company after the first paint job, so they'd hit it again, the second time inside. If Winter's idea of their motive was right, they'd have to hit TheraRex again as well, to ramp up the pressure.

There had been twelve days between the first and second acts of vandalism at the tool company. Today was thirteenth days after the spray painting at TheraRex.

It was Winter's third day in the basement.

He was here because there was no place else to hide in the building without risk of discovery. He knew because he'd checked.

The stairway to the basement was just past the entrance to the offices, not three steps in from the lobby. If the receptionist was in on it, the basement was a perfect place to hide, a jumble of desks, broken chairs, and portable shelving. And behind the storage shelves, the larger leather chair in which Winter now sat, invisible to a casual basement visitor.

Winter knew the place by heart, having walked it until he could run the imperceptible gap from where he sat to the entrance door in pitch darkness. The CEO Schmidt knew he was here, as did his ex-partner Brooker, who Winter had noodled over the problem with.

Captain Logan knew too, but had told Winter he wasn't paying for overtime. Unless, of course, Winter caught someone.

Winter figured the vandal wouldn't take the chance of entering early in the day. Even with a good hiding place, why risk it? Better to get buzzed in by the receptionist late in the afternoon, hide until after dark, then do the deed.

The first day, Winter had waited until past six, but no one had come down to the basement. Winter figured it was about four now. He didn't bother looking at his watch; he'd learned long ago that checking the time made stakeouts drag. It would either happen or it wouldn't. He'd brought water, a few energy bars, and a piss bottle, not wanting to chance going back upstairs to use the bathroom in case the vandal was on the stairway.

Of course, his vigil could all be a waste of time. But during the few hours each day he'd spent alone, Winter managed to work out only two other possibilities for the how and why of these crimes—other than sheer randomness. And while he firmly accepted the reality of randomness, he'd also learned that seemingly unconnected crimes often had a tiny thread that tied them together. Like two coils of rope, connected by a single gossamer string of fiber.

Winter had just taken a sip of water when a single click broke the silence. He froze. A circuit breaker? Another click. It could be the door, but the overhead light did not come on. Yet Winter had become so attuned to the room he sensed a difference, a change in the atmosphere.

A barely audible scrape, a subtle change in the air. The basement door was being opened.

Winter still held the bottle of water in his hand, not wanting to move a muscle. He relaxed his shoulders, knowing that straining to hear a sound only made it harder to place.

Without warning the overhead light snapped on. A man had taken a single step into the basement, the door still held open with one hand. He looked to be in his thirties, lithe, dark haired, wearing a midnight blue shirt and dark pants. He could have been an employee, perhaps entering the basement for the first time, just confused.

Winter waited.

The man looked carefully around the room. When his eyes swept Winter's hiding place Winter willed himself not to move his head or even shift his eyes.

The man eased the door shut. He took out a flashlight, shining it around the room, even though the overhead light was still on.

Definitely not an employee.

The circuit box hummed, the man redirecting the beam, but from what Winter could tell, didn't panic. So he was not only the guy Winter was waiting for, but he was trained as well. Possibly ex-military.

The man's head cocked, and he turned, bringing the flashlight around, making another slow sweep as he crossed the room.

His body shifted, tensing, and fluidly leapt over a desk, bolting for the door. Winter was already moving, pushing through the path he had prepared, blowing through a tall stack of empty storage bins.

Winter yelled, "Stop, police!" but the man ignored him without even turning, yanking the door open and rushing out.

Winter caught up just as the door closed, grabbing at a trailing arm. Winter wrapped his fingers around the guy's bare wrist while simultaneously ramming his shoulder into the door, catching the intruder's exposed lower arm in the gap. The man swore but didn't scream. Winter dug his fingers into skin, opened the door a few inches, and slammed it again on the guy's arm.

Winter twisted the trapped arm. "Hold still," he ordered.

But the door came flying out at him, and even braced against it Winter was pushed back, the guy was strong. Winter struggled to hold on as the man slowly yanked his arm out of Winter's grip.

"Asshole," gritted Winter, realizing he was losing. He didn't risk pulling open the door in case the man had a weapon. For a long few seconds there was a stalemate, and then the intruder's other hand slinked its way through the gap, a can of spray paint pointed at Winter's face. Winter ducked just as the spray let go, the sickly smell overpowering.

Winter, pissed, kicked the door as hard as he could, let go the pinned wrist, and grabbed at the can, twisting it back around as he yanked the door open and jammed his hand around the fingers holding the can.

A full jet of bright red paint hit the wall like an arterial blood spray. Winter got a good dose on the guy's head and face before the intruder managed to break free, Winter's hands now covered in slick paint. Winter ran up the stairs after him, emptying the last of the can on the guy's back.

Winter slipped on the stairs, and by the time he got up the door to the main floor slammed, the guy making for the lobby. Winter pulled out his phone, hit speed dial. "He's coming out. You won't miss him."

"Got it," muttered Brooker, who sounded wide awake and ready to go for a guy with angina who had been sitting in his car out front for a few hours. Brooker, technically on medical leave, was bored and had jumped at the chance to help Winter, even if it meant holding down the front door.

Winter looked down at his pants, splattered with red paint. One of his newer pairs, he'd already relegated the *last* pair for painting.

"Asshole," he said again, to no one in particular.

CHAPTER 20

DOC'S BREATH left a ring of condensation on the French doors. Long past sunset, he could barely see past his back patio, yet it somehow even *looked* cold.

The side door opened two rooms away, yet fingers of frigid air raised the hairs on his neck. Gina, out for a pizza run. How that girl could eat so much cheese and stay skinny was beyond him.

Doc didn't allow delivery people at the house. Years ago, back when he was a poor medical resident, he'd had to share an apartment. Having two roommates was worse than the back to back shifts at the hospital. The loss of privacy, the mess, the smells, every minute reduced to the lowest common denominator of his roommates.

He'd supplemented his meager income by pocketing a few pills from patients too far along to need them. One night his industrious roommate was making up nickel bags of weed; his own side income. Doc was always careful about not having any drugs out when visitors came, but he figured his roommate was okay. It was a mistake Doc never made again.

Doc's roommate wasn't so cautious, and the pizza delivery guy was in the apartment before Doc could throw a magazine over his multicolored pile of pills. A week later, the apartment was robbed, nothing missing except the drugs.

Doc suspected the pizza guy, an acne scarred string bean who bopped waiting to get paid for the pizza, a walking advertisement for uppers. Two days later Doc ordered a pizza from a public phone outside the pizzeria—back when there were public phones, with their wonderful anonymity—and followed the delivery guy. After getting no answer at the empty looking house address Doc had provided, the guy drove to a corner and did a window drug transaction. After the car drove off, Doc asked the customer where he could score some pills. The buyer, wired, hadn't even questioned Doc, flashing a ziplock bag of pills, which Doc instantly recognized as from his stash.

Doc called the pizza parlor, complained about not getting his pizza, and this time was waiting on the front step when the delivery guy showed up. The window rolled down, and Doc twisted the string bean's head back while at the same time grabbing his shoulder and pulling. It was amazing what a medical school knowledge of anatomy could do. The guy couldn't see Doc's face, but his agonizing wail was pretty clear.

Doc leaned into the car. "Where's the fucking drugs?"

The guy held out for about five seconds, until Doc drove a forearm into his throat. A feeble hand pointed down. Doc reached under the seat and pulled out a baggie of mixed pills, much depleted. Disgusted, Doc yanked the string bean's shoulder, Doc's medical brain wondering if he could break the guy's neck right there. He never found out, because a gaggle of rowdy students turned the corner.

That was the first time Doc had been robbed. The second time, Doc actually found out he *could* break a man's neck with his bare hands. It was harder than he thought. After that, he decided not to use his hands whenever he had to kill someone unless he had no choice. There were other tools and other people for dirty work.

A phone rang, one of the burners. Doc raised the thermostat before answering.

"Hey, Doc, what's shakin'?"

Dwayne.

"You got good news, right?"

"First hand. I ever tell you I'm a firm believer that if you want something done right you gotta do it yourself? I decided to take matters into my own hands. Got myself invited to your boy's snazzy party."

Doc didn't think he was hearing right. "What?"

"I got friends in all the right places. Called my producer. He told me all I had to do was get my ass to Mass, show up at the door and be ready to hit the floor."

"You did *what?*"

"Catch up, Doc. You wanted a little pressure on the Gerry kid, I'm going to make it happen. Me and my man Malcolm."

Doc was quickly cataloging how many people knew of his connection to Dwayne. More than one, which was already too many. "Let your guy handle it, Dwayne. Go find yourself another party."

"Too late, man, I'm already here. Place is hoppin'."

Doc leaned his head against the wall. "This is supposed to be low profile."

"Why is that, Doc? This is just a little business deal, right?"

Doc didn't like the undercurrent of curiosity in Dwayne's voice. "Don't fuck this up. Just do what I asked, put a little pressure on Gerry, get him primed for my lawyer."

"Sure, sure. A little pressure. I'll keep you out of this, Doc, don't worry. Who knows, maybe Gerry gets a little beat down, people see me, put two and two together, and my stock on the street goes up a leap. Kill two birds with one stone. Get me a million more song plays."

Doc couldn't believe Dwayne could be such an idiot. "You're crazy."

Dwayne's voice turned cold. "Watch who you calling crazy, old man. I see things nice and clear, get me?"

Sweat dripped down Doc's arms. His eyes focused on the thermostat. Seventy eight. Not high enough to bring on a sweat. "Don't fuck this up," he repeated.

"Hey man, gotta run, I see DeVaughn."

The line went dead. Dwayne could blow Doc's carefully crafted plan wide open. He'd made a mistake bringing in Dwayne to deal with Gerry too soon after asking the rapper questions about song royalties. Egomaniac as he was, Dwayne wasn't stupid.

Dwayne would get to Gerry, who Sterling had talked to about the royalties. Dwayne would put two and two together easily enough, giving him a big hammer to hold over Doc's head, not to mention what Dwayne already knew about Doc's drug business. Even if Dwayne didn't do shit tonight, Doc might have to rough up Gerry to sign the papers. If any piece of it went sideways, Dwayne could blackmail Doc for more than just a piece of the music. Doc could picture the headline: *Songwriter coerced to give up rights to hit song to a drug dealer.*

Had to stop Dwayne.

CHAPTER 21

RICK WAS BLOWN AWAY by the Carter's estate even before he made it into the house. A massive wrought iron gate supported by stone pillars reeked of power and big bucks. A guard house made the entrance look like an embassy. Rick's Kia was in line between limos, a sickly dab of mayonnaise between two T-bone steaks.

The limo was waved through. Rick rolled forward, giving his name, expecting the third degree, but the guard flipped through his clipboard, nodded, and pointed Rick up the drive, his eyes already on the limo behind Rick.

The drive wove its way past a long line of mature floodlit trees. After a bend the house practically jumped out of the dark, bright as a night game at Fenway, limos unloading in a circular drive. A young kid with a flashlight pointed Rick to a road which led around the side of the house, where a sea of cars were parked in a grassy field.

Rick texted Gerry as he walked toward the house. *I'm at the party, where are you?*

Two couples in front of him, dressed in cocktail outfits, the woman stepping precariously in the grass on stiletto heels. Rick, in a jacket, now worried he should have worn a tie. He'd expected music people, which normally meant tee shirts.

Not even in the house yet and he'd already fucked up.

No answer to his text, maybe Gerry couldn't hear his phone over the pulsating music.

One of the men up ahead was pointing off toward the house. "There's two pools, one on each side. Fresh water and salt water. Heated, of course."

"Of course," a woman said, laughing.

"Place is frigging huge. You could get lost looking for the bathroom if there weren't twenty of them."

"You sure we can get in? It's not like we got our own invite."

"You're with me," said the first man. "Party like this, everyone brings friends. Don't sweat it."

Rick followed the couples through the maze of an impeccable English garden. A portico large enough for an orchestra, guarded by three story columns, led into the house. The couples turned that way, joining a flock at the stairs, reminding Rick of the entrance to the big church his mother took him to as a kid. These guests would be kneeling at the feet of the Carter's money.

Rick felt out of place, this wasn't his crowd. He instinctively turned the other way, knowing Gerry would as well. If Gerry had even bothered coming.

A wide stone walkway led around the side of the house. Rick followed the tangy air, emerging through a boxwood hedge, the Olympic sized saltwater pool before him.

On the patio, he'd only taken a few steps when a white coated waiter appeared with a tray of champagne. Rick grabbed one and slipped into the house through the open patio doors.

Twenty minutes and two champagnes later, he'd covered only half of the main floor, weaving his way through the crowd. Gerry should be easy to spot, he'd be standing off alone, or looking for Rick. All Rick saw were couples and groups.

Where the hell was Gerry?

DOC FUMBLED with the two phones. From his own phone he texted Kevin, asking exactly where he was. On the burner, Doc punched in Dwayne's number for the third time, Doc didn't even trust burners to hold a call list.

No answer, again, Dwayne ignoring him. Doc had sent Kevin to Boston to do a big ecstasy pickup, of all nights. Doc was half hoping Kevin had broke down and was close enough to get over to the Carter's estate to deal with Dwayne, even if it meant losing out on the ecstasy.

Kevin texted back he was already in the city. No help there. Doc would have to deal with Dwayne himself.

On the way out he grabbed his black silk suit jacket. It was a *party* he was going to, after all. The jacket held his usual collection of party favors, Xanax, Klonopin, fentanyl, a collection of opioids, colorful vials of powder, all discreetly tucked away in custom tailored pockets. Doc knew the jacket so well he could find what he wanted without looking.

Halfway out the door his brain focus kicked in. He detoured to the hidden safe behind the garage circuit panel where he kept his supplies. The box was separated into colored bins, organized by purity level. Doc lingered over the cut but still high quality product. That might not do it. In the white bin, enough pure blow to buy a house. He slid pouches in his coat; if he couldn't convince Dwayne to back off, he could buy him off.

In the Mercedes he hit the button to reset the seat position. Not only did he have to get his hands dirty dealing with Dwayne, he had to drive as well. He fucking hated driving.

DWAYNE JERKED his head at Malcolm. "Stay close, but not too close, you get me?" Dwayne didn't have a posse, and Malcolm wasn't massive enough to be a bodyguard, but one look at Malcolm's wild eyes was deterrent enough.

Dwayne nodded at a few people he recognized, not too friendly, giving off the vibe he was as important as anyone else here. Looking good, silk shirt, tight black pants, five hundred dollar green Adidas Pharrell's on his feet. Three gold chains, two real, the other one of Doc's good fakes, trippin' on it, Doc's bling on his neck as he screwed Doc over.

The chick Miranda giving him the house tour wasn't his type, too short, only her ass giving her a pass. The night was young, he would do better. In the meantime, she knew her way around, claimed she was Candy's assistant.

"You live in Boston?" asked Miranda.

"Got a few cribs. Stay in New York when I'm recording."

"I didn't see you on the guest list." Dwayne gave her a look, she didn't cringe, moving her stock up a notch. "Not that it matters," she said. "I only know because I drew it up."

"I was telling my pro I was heading to New York and he says, 'Dwayne, you gotta hit this Candy girl's party.' I figured I could take a little detour, stop by, say hi to some of the boys." Dwayne tossed Miranda a little thrill. "The ladies, too."

Miranda's tongue did a slow roll over her upper lip. "Of course."

"You doing the guest list and all, you must know Rick?"

Miranda teased, "I know lots of Ricks."

Dwayne didn't know Rick's last name. Dwayne took a stab. "Works with DeVaughn."

"Rick Singleton. Sure, I know that Rick." Letting it hang.

Anyplace else Dwayne would have slapped her, and not on the ass. Jerking him around. Ballsy, though, he gave her that. Be good to tame her down later. Right now: "Yeah, that's the dude. Someone suggested I connect, we might be able to do some business."

Miranda's frown suggested doubt, but she said, "I saw him around. There he is, over there."

Dwayne followed her eyes to a white guy near the patio sliders, alone, checking his phone. Nudged Malcolm, who nodded.

Miranda said, "Rick's working with Candy. He's an assistant engineer."

"Right," said Dwayne. Still couldn't pin it down. Doc wanted a thumb on Gerry, who knew Rick. Rick just a fucking engineer. What could Gerry and Rick have that Doc would want?

Miranda moved in closer. "You're not going to dump me for Rick, are you?"

Which was Dwayne's exact thought. Before he could blow her off, Miranda said, "Oh shit, there's Candy. She needs me." Miranda gave him the sultry eyes. "There's a very private cabana out by the pool. I'll be there in a bit if you want to get a better handle on this." She turned her ass into his body. "Don't tell me I didn't catch you checking it out."

Dwayne gave her a noncommittal flick of his wrist. Maybe he'd do her, maybe not. She might be useful if Doc's deal was connected to the money behind the party. Something big was going down. Dwayne wanted a piece, if for no other reason to get a thumb on Doc's neck. The bling was good, but Dwayne knew Doc had been screwing him on the price.

Find out what Doc was up to, get some cred by having Malcolm do a beat down on Gerry, hook up with a chick. A three-fer.

An inked white dude with a big camera was snapping photos of Sickboy, a rapper Dwayne recognized, talking to some suit. Sickboy respected Dwayne, tweeting about Dwayne's last release. The photographer had to be from a music mag.

"Third Eye, go find the Gerry guy," said Dwayne.

"Bring him here?"

"Too many eyes. Just hole him up. Make sure he gets the message, you hear?"

Malcolm's eyes lit up. "How loud?"

"Enough so anyone who sees him knows he got a visit."

"Yo." Malcolm bopped off through the crowd.

Dwayne made his way over to Sickboy and the suit. Sickboy was preening for the camera, doing a Mos Def wave like he didn't want his picture taken, sucking it up. Dwayne let him have his space, no need to step on it. The suit was smiling, comfortable, he must be in the business.

Sickboy spotted Dwayne, pointed, an invitation. "Filling my earbuds with your rap all day," said Dwayne, which was bullshit, but Sickboy wouldn't know that.

"Man knows his music," said Sickboy.

The suit said, "You wrote *Stealin It* for Zoom Zoom, right?"

Dwayne didn't mind hearing that. "So did." Even better, the camera dude had turned his way, already snapping. Dwayne let him get a few with Sickboy and the suit, and then, much more important, angled his shoulders so he'd have the crowd at his back.

Dwayne spotted another photographer who shot for BOYZ, a fine hip hop blog that had given his music good words. "Be movin'," he said, doing a bump with Sickboy.

A waitress in a stiff white coat cut him off. "Can I offer you something, sir?" Very blond, very blue eyed. A little old for Dwayne, but still tight.

"Your tray's empty," said Dwayne.

The waitress didn't blink. "What is it you are looking for?"

"More a who than a what," said Dwayne.

"I could help with that," said the woman. After a beat she added, "Later."

Dwayne was liking this party. "I got business now. But a drink would be good. Not some of that bubbly, put some Hennessy in my hand. You do that?"

"There's XO at the bar, but I know where I can get you some Collector's Blend."

"That's good, that's good." The high end spirit would be smooth, but right now he didn't want to wait. "Be moving around," he said.

"I'll find you."

Dwayne let the black photographer see him. The photographer started snapping away, knowing the game. Three chicks gathered around, tight dresses, flashing bling, stiletto heels. Perfect. One of them recognized Dwayne, asking him to sign his name just above her left breast, cameras firing away.

His audience grew, the now inked hottie doing the introductions like they were lovers from way back. Dwayne let her talk, she was doing good.

The photographer gave him a nod, he'd got what he needed. If his blog ran the photos, and Malcolm did his job, Dwayne would pass the word that some skinny white dude had crossed him in a business deal, and Dwayne had made him pay. The street would put two and two together, Dwayne having the balls to do a beat down at a fancy party.

Malcolm would do the actual deed, but no one would remember Malcolm.

"There's Candy," said one of the bitch posse.

A mighty fine chick was making her way over, nodding and helloing just about everyone she passed. Young, twenties, nice body, leather leggings, a denim top, low boots. Confident, not only owning the place but looking it. Dwayne's audience parted like the Red Sea.

Candy said, "I like your kicks."

Dwayne lifted up one of his size twelves. "I'd trade you, but you'd swim."

Candy laughed. "Look better on you than me even if they were the right size. I got some Yeezy's though."

"Yeezy's are good," agreed Dwayne.

"I'm Candy," she said.

"He's Outta Here," piped up one of the bitches. "Dwayne."

Dwayne liked that Candy didn't ask why he was there, liked her even better when she said, "I listen to *Flight Beats* when I'm chilling."

Dwayne had done that one with Ultra Z. Not his favorite, but he didn't give a shit, because the photographers had taken a renewed interest now that Candy was on the scene.

Dwayne was trying to figure out how to pump Candy for dope on the Rick guy, she might even know the score about Doc. Had to be tied to her, or at least her money.

Too late. Candy said, "See you around," moving off. A few of

Dwayne's newly acquired posse followed along in her wake.

The blond waitress materialized at Dwayne's side. "Your drink, sir."

Dwayne barely glanced at her, draining it. Not the way to appreciate good cognac, but he had to move. He dropped the empty on her tray and headed for Rick.

RICK COULDN'T keep up with the arrivals. He no sooner had covered the room when the teeming mass rolled over, new faces everywhere. He hung by the door, knowing that if Gerry showed—if he hadn't already seen the overwhelming crowd and skipped—he'd do the same.

Still no response to his texts. Rick wondered if Gerry didn't want to break it to Rick he hadn't come.

A black guy wearing ten pounds of gold chain headed his way. Rick, thinking he might be security, said, "Candy invited me."

"So I heard. You're working with her and the man DeVaughn. We got a mutual friend."

Rick didn't recognize the guy. "Who?"

"Doc."

Not the connection Rick wanted to hear. "Doc?" he said, noncommittal.

"Just talked to him. When I told him I was going to be here, he said, 'You should find my man Rick.'"

"Yeah?"

"Doc thought you might need a little help getting Gerry to sign."

Rick didn't like the sound of that. First Kevin hanging outside his mother's house, and now this. Doc turning up the heat, as if Rick needed reminding of the hole he was in. He'd barely slept the night before, scared shitless. "I haven't found Gerry."

"My man Malcolm is rounding him up right now."

"That's not a good idea. Gerry should hear the deal from me." Rick was looking over the guy's shoulder, trying to spot Gerry. "What's your name?"

"My mark is Outta Here, but you can call me Dwayne."

That sounded vaguely familiar to Rick. "You're in the music business."

Dwayne flashed a smile. "That's why Doc thought I could help. I hope you got a good piece of the deal."

"The usual. I mean, I haven't really finalized it with Candy, but I assume that's what it will be."

Dwayne's eyes narrowed. "Right, Candy. Just talked to her. Big money behind this one. And DeVaughn too. Should be a sure thing."

"Let's hope," agreed Rick.

"I shouldn't be telling you this," Dwayne lowered his voice. "But I'd hate to see you get screwed, you hear me? You got to watch out for Doc, he's a friend and all, but it's all about him."

"I know what I'm doing," said Rick.

"Just sayin'. Let's go see your friend Gerry, make sure we're all rapping from the same sheet music."

Rick was getting mixed vibes from Dwayne. Doc obviously had clued Dwayne in and pointed him at Rick, yet Dwayne was warning him off. "I better talk to Gerry alone first."

"Sure. Take you to him."

Rick was ushered out the patio door, Dwayne's grip a vise. "Where we going?"

"You don't want your business heard by all those ears, do you? I know a private place."

Dwayne half forced Rick down the patio steps, along the pool, and toward a dimly lit cabana next to a sizable pool house. "There's no one here," said Rick.

"They'll be along. In the meantime, let's celebrate your deal." Dwayne twisted one of the links on his chain and out popped a metal canister. "My custom snuff bullet." He offered it to Rick. "It's from Doc."

Rick wasn't too keen on getting high right now. "Don't want to tamp your stash."

Dwayne twisted another link and snorted from the bullet. "Got plenty."

Maybe a little pick me up wouldn't be so bad, get him focused. Rick did a hit.

"Doc's a tough negotiator, but he provides first class shit," said Dwayne.

"No argument from me," said Rick.

"Listen, maybe I could offer you a better deal than Doc."

"Not sure I got any options," said Rick, although any deal would be better than what Doc had him cornered with.

"Always options."

Rick didn't hide his confusion. "I thought you were a friend of Doc's."

"Customer. We do some business now and then. Doc will understand, it's only business. If I make you an offer, he can always counter."

Rick didn't see Doc as the counter-offer type. Not to mention what he owed Doc already. "No disrespect, but I'm kind of locked in."

Dwayne did another hit, waved his hand at the grounds. "You grow up in a house like this?"

"Shit no."

"Me neither. These people—and people like Doc too—you think they know how people like me and you grew up? How we live? Sure, I'm making it good now, but it ain't been easy. I bet the same for you. You think they give a shit about us?"

Rick took another snort. "Candy's been good to me."

"She's slumming."

"There'll be a contract."

Dwayne looked up, his eyes very focused. "Surprised Doc wants it that way."

"He insisted."

Dwayne looked back toward the house. "You got your piece in writing yet?"

Dwayne seemed to know most of what was going on, which meant he was close to Doc, so Rick admitted, "With Doc. Not with Candy."

"Candy in on this?"

"Well, yeah, the songs—"

Dwayne's phone rang, a tune Rick vaguely recognized. Finally placing Dwayne, it was his music.

Dwayne listened to the call, then said, "You did good, Third Eye, have that talk with him." Clicked off, did a huge hit, laughing. Said to Rick, "I see the picture. Shit, got to hand it to old Doc. Man always has a plan."

Rick, feeling the buzz, said, "I better go find Gerry."

"Told you, my man will bring him here."

"Why do you want some Gerry when you can have me?"

Rick jumped at the voice which came from the darkness beyond the cabana. Miranda.

"Baby girl, we doing a little business here," said Dwayne.

Miranda looked back and forth between Dwayne and Rick. "I'm good at business." She gestured toward the snuff bullet in Dwayne's hand. "Got a taste for me?"

"What you got to bring to the meeting?" asked Dwayne.

Rick tried to warn her off with his eyes, the last thing he needed was Miranda involved. She didn't even look at him, all her attention on Dwayne and the blow. "I work for Candy, remember? If this has anything remotely to do with her, I can help."

Dwayne said, "Maybe you can, maybe you can at that." He gave Miranda the bullet and they alternated hits.

The pool house is unlocked," said Miranda. "Nice and private." She wiggled her butt at Dwayne.

Dwayne laughed. "You got moves, I'll give you that. You got something to do needing private?"

Miranda took another huge hit, her eyes already as glassy as Dwayne's. "Don't you?"

"Depends."

Miranda dropped to her knees in front of Dwayne. "Have it your way."

Rick had no interest in being a one man audience. He backed off, using Dwayne's moans as cover to hide his footsteps as he rapidly slipped back toward the house.

DOC HAD NO PROBLEM finding the Carter estate—so large it was visible in his map street view—nor in getting onto the property, the security guard taking one look at his Mercedes and waving him in, Doc not needing a story. A kid had even offered to valet the car, which Doc had declined. The fewer people who remembered him, the better.

On the porch a huddle of men were drinking brandy, the distinctive scent of Cohibas filling the air. Sterling was right, this was big money, he had to get into this circle. First, though, he had to deal with Dwayne.

He'd barely made it to the front steps when a familiar figure squirreled out of the house, intently making her way through the garden. Miranda, Candy's assistant. Doc had grilled her on Candy at the studio. She'd certainly know what was going on, so he followed her.

He peered through the arched pathway opening between the English garden and the pool. Thick clematis vines hid him from view while still allowing him to clearly see the trio of Dwayne, Rick, and Miranda by the cabana.

She'd spooked Rick, popping out of the shadows, Rick jumping. Maybe Rick hadn't been expecting her, interrupting him and Dwayne. No doubt Dwayne was pumping the kid for information on Doc's deal.

Had to get to Dwayne, but not with witnesses. No figuring what Dwayne might blurt out. Miranda could be a real problem too, her being close to Candy.

For now, just wait.

Dwayne twisted one of his gold chains, Miranda's hand out. Doc bet Dwayne was wearing the chain Doc had sold him with the hollowed out links. Miranda and Dwayne did a few hits, then Miranda was on her knees, Rick backing off.

Rick spirited along the far side of the pool toward the house. A laugh snapped Doc's eyes back to the cabana, Miranda dragging Dwayne into the pool house.

Shit.

Rick was lost in the crowd on the back patio. Doc weighed the options. Be seen with Rick at the party, or be seen by Miranda?

He could always get to Rick. Better to stay on Dwayne.

Two women picked their way down the patio steps, champagne glasses in hand, ritzy dresses, bling flashing. They turned into another path to the garden, Doc hearing them behind him, nervous laughter, then the unmistakable nasal intake of a snort. A dealer's dream. The connections he could make tonight if he wasn't having to deal with fucking Dwayne.

More reason to shut Dwayne up. The last thing Doc needed was the Carter's well of opportunity spoiled by Dwayne's big mouth.

The pool house door opened, Miranda stumbling out, her hair a mess, working her heels on as she made her way back toward the party.

The man himself appeared in the doorway, buckling his belt and calling out, "You'll be reading about me!"

Doc was already moving. Dwayne, mouthing a indecipherable rap, was groping at his chain, Doc on him before Dwayne even zipped up.

Dwayne's eyes were in and out of focus, flying high. "Doc! We got business to talk, yes we do."

"Where's Gerry?"

"Don't worry, I got my man Malcolm softening him up."

Doc pushed Dwayne back into the pool house out of sight. Dwayne half stumbled, spinning around.

"No way to treat your partner," said Dwayne.

"We aren't partners."

Dwayne's eyes swam into focus. "Better watch your attitude, old man, or I'll cut you out totally."

Doc sized up Dwayne, the younger man taller, more muscular, but he was stoned. Doc had a hundred pounds on him and bet he had more beat downs under his belt than big talking Dwayne. "What the hell are you doing here, making all this noise?"

"Told you. Gonna get a little press, street cred, no grandstanding required. A little number on the Gerry kid, word gets around, you hearing me?"

"You don't know what's going on, you're going to fuck it up."

"You think I'm stupid? You're running a deal with the kid. I may not have all the details, but it's all about the rich bitch Candy and her music. Big money, or else you wouldn't care. You don't know shit about the music business. You're going to cut me in." Dwayne fingered his chain, coming up empty. "Hey, you carrying? Let's celebrate our partnership."

Doc's first instinct was to wrap the chain around Dwayne's neck. He checked himself, first instincts often had bad consequences. Softening his tone, he said, "Always willing to talk." He pulled out one of the bags of uncut coke, drifting it under Dwayne's eyes.

"Good, talk, now we're talking," said Dwayne, holding out his empty link for a refill, immediately taking a hit.

Doc would have warned any other customer to go easy, this was the pure stuff. As far as Dwayne was concerned, his heart could explode for all Doc cared.

Which planted the seed of an idea in his head . . .

"So you talked to Rick?" asked Doc.

"Yeah, yeah, I got the drift, you two got a hook into the Candy shop bank, through the music." Dwayne's eyes glittered. "Am I right or what?"

"Something like that," said Doc, watching Dwayne's pupils dilating in and out faster than the beat of the music from the house.

"The paperwork part kinda threw me. Didn't sound like you, leaving a trail. That's why you need Gerry, right? He's got his fingers in the pie, you got to cut them fingers off."

Doc waved his hand. "Gerry's just icing, but he knows enough to ruin it—for *all* of us. That's why you have to call off your man. Get Gerry out here, we can all talk it over."

Doc must not have sounded convincing enough, or the coke was sharpening Dwayne's bullshit meter, because Dwayne said, "We don't need to talk, no, no. Whatever you got going on paper, I want a piece. A big piece. If you can put your name on paper, you can put mine on too."

"It's not like that."

Dwayne muscled up to Doc. "Then fucking make it like that!"

Doc didn't budge. If Dwayne thought being in his face was going to scare him, Dwayne really didn't know shit. "I got this under control. Let's not screw up a good thing."

Dwayne poked Doc hard in the chest. "*Your* good thing. I want *my* good thing. You've been fucking me over for years on the bling, you don't think I know that?"

"You're free to take your business elsewhere."

"You know what? I don't think we need to be partners, I don't see what you bring to the party. I can get bling and blow anywhere, I probably got better connections in Miami than you do, you fat coward, hiding up here."

Dwayne was pushing the wrong button. "Don't go there, Dwayne."

"I'll go wherever I want. I'll waltz into that big fucking house right now and tell little Miss Candy all about you. She know how you make your living? Does her daddy? Bet he'd be happy to hear his little lily is mixed up with a drug dealer."

It wasn't the accusation of Doc being a coward, it wasn't even Dwayne calling him fat. The first was a bully's misconception, the second was fact. What *did* push Doc down a new path was Dwayne bringing the entire music deal tumbling down, and at the same time poisoning Doc's chances of wheedling into the Carter's fortune.

No fucking way he was going to let a gangbanger turned rapper screw up his plan, maybe screw up his life.

Time to get on top of this, right now.

As Dwayne shakily tapped out the last of the coke from his link, Doc turned away, feigning surrender. Slipping his hand into one of his special pockets, he fingered a fentanyl, expertly flicking open the capsule with one hand.

Doc had the bag of coke in his other pocket. He reached in, spilled most of it out into the pocket, and let the near empty bag slip to the ground. Dwayne tracked it like a bird dog. Dwayne stooped to pick it up, bracing himself on one knee to refill his chain.

Doc switched the open fentanyl capsule to the pocket with the loose coke, mixing the concoction with his fingers, a poor man's speedball. Dwayne was still fumbling with the chain.

"Here," said Doc. He held out a handful of the mixed powder. "Maybe you're right. I can use help figuring out the music business. Here's a peace offering."

Dwayne's needs overwhelmed his suspicions, not even questioning the loose powder. He tipped Doc's hand into the empty link, spilling four figures worth of coke.

"Now let's work this out," said Doc, waiting for Dwayne to do another hit.

Dwayne did. "About time you saw the light." He wavered, his neck looping like an asp, a full minute passing before he unsteadily rose to his feet. "Need some air, man."

Dwayne pitched through the door, blinking in the relatively brighter light. Muscles twitched in his neck and face like he was standing on a live wire.

A high pitched scream from the direction of the house split the air. The music abruptly squawked out. Three fast heartbeats of utter silence, then more screams, building to a cacophony that made the now silenced raucous music sound smooth in comparison.

Guests spilled out of the house, fireflies of cell phone flashes firing, a mass confusion so powerful Doc could feel it press against him all the way down by the pool. Then, so loud as if it had been run through the speakers, a woman yelled, "Oh my God! Call an ambulance!"

Screaming again, so distracting that Doc missed exactly when Dwayne had started laughing. Only when Dwayne broke into a garbled rap and grabbed at him did Doc turn away from the house.

Dwayne's eyes were wild with delight. "Got him good, got him good. My man, Third Eye, he got him good."

"What are you ranting about?" demanded Doc, although he had a bad feeling.

"I told my boy Third Eye, show him the light, you feel me, Doc?"

Another plaintive wail from the house. "He's dead!"

Dwayne laughed so hard he had to clutch at his chest. "Third Eye was looking to make his bones. I bet he got his wish, hey, hey."

"Gerry? He killed Gerry?"

"What's it sound like to you?"

"Shit, you crazy gangbanger pretender idiot, you know what you just cost me?"

"Not more than I just bought, I'm gonna be famous, you know how many pictures got taken of me? Street will put two and two and it comes up Outta Here, all me, no pretender gangbanger, I put a man down right in front of all these people. Everybody be talking about me tonight. This here is *real*, man."

Doc had heard more than enough. Gerry dead by Dwayne's man, a connection a moron could trace right back to Doc if Dwayne kept blabbing. Doc hated connections even more than he hated a paper trail.

His fingers clenched around his remaining fentanyl, crushing the capsules to pulp. He grabbed Dwayne's chain, yanking it against his throat as he shoved his knee into Dwayne's back. Dwayne did what Doc expected him to do, because it's what they all did. Dwayne grabbed at the chain around his neck, his mouth opening like a funnel.

Into which Doc slammed his palm, full of the fentanyl, crushed capsules and all. Dwayne gagged, Doc pulling the chain hard. When he let go, Dwayne gasped for air through his mouth, swallowing the pills. Doc making sure, clasping his hand over Dwayne's mouth.

Dwayne jerked like a shotgunned dummy, Doc yanking the chain, using it to drag Dwayne toward the pool, spurred on by the shouts from the house. No doubt dead Gerry was drawing everyone's attention.

Doc held his fingers to Dwayne's neck, his old medical skills once again useful. Dwayne's pulse was in overdrive, the carotid artery bleating like a cow. All that fentanyl on top of the coke and Dwayne could be gone in seconds.

Doc wasn't one to take chances. He kept his pudgy, but no less utilitarian, hand over Dwayne's mouth and nose. Only when he heard a siren in the distance did he push Dwayne into the pool.

Sometimes first instincts were right after all.

CHAPTER 22

MARTIN RYDER STOOD a few feet from the gruesome body, close enough so no one would think he didn't have the stomach to deal with it—not like the rook who had thrown up—but far enough away so there would be no chance of getting blood on his new shoes, a pair of Bruno Magli's that had set him back half a week's pay. He had bought them for this very opportunity, a visit to the home of the upper crust. He hadn't been expecting it would be for a dead body, but he took what he could get.

"You saying no one knows the victim?" asked Ryder.

The uniformed cop by his side, a tall bony guy whose name Ryder had already forgot, said, "Not that we've found, but Burkett is asking around." The cop hesitated. "A lot of guests. Maybe Mason could go help."

"What, and puke on more people?" Ryder knew the rookie was in earshot. Serve him right, teach him a lesson.

"I could go," said the tall cop. "People might start leaving."

"Uh, Detective?" said Mason. "A lot of people already left. They were driving out when I got here."

"And you didn't stop them?" Ryder couldn't believe the incompetence. No wonder the Marburg force had brought him in, the place really needed new blood. He jerked his head at the rookie. "Go block the drive. Think you can handle that?"

"Yes, sir."

Ryder flicked his finger at the body. "Let's see if he has ID." The EMTs had long since finished up.

The dead guy, who looked to be in his late twenties, although it was hard to tell with his head all bashed in, was lying mostly on his stomach, his legs twisted together, as if he'd tripped. If he had, it was pretty clear that his injuries didn't come from a fall. He'd been beaten, and badly. Cut too.

He was wearing tan khakis, a blue stiffly pressed button down shirt, and inexpertly polished scuffed loafers. He didn't fit the image of a fancy party guest, and Ryder wondered if he was a crasher.

The uniform fished in the khakis and gingerly removed a thin wallet. "Rear left pocket," he said.

According to the Mass driver's license, the dead guy was Gerry Hennig, aged twenty-six, with an address in Boston. The wallet contained credit cards but no cash.

"What have we got?"

Ryder jumped at the voice, he hadn't heard anyone walk up. Fucking Winter, sneaking up on him.

Ryder handed Winter the license. As usual, Winter looked more like a guy you'd see on a shipping dock than a detective, military style cargo pants, a denim shirt—decidedly unpressed—black sneakers. And a fucking hoodie.

"Cambridge. Maybe a student," said Winter. "A little out of place."

Which was exactly what Ryder had been thinking, but he wasn't going to admit it to Winter. "Don't jump to conclusions. For all you know, it's his house."

"No," said Winter, absently. "House belongs to James Carter. He only has one child, a daughter named Candy."

Of course Winter would know. Winter knew everything about Marburg. Unlike Ryder, Winter had grown up here, and would probably never leave. "Still could be related," said Ryder.

"Maybe." Winter bent over the body, seemingly unperturbed by the blood and gore. "EMTs move him?"

"No."

"Huh." Winter stood up, looked down the long hallway. "Maybe he was running. Anyone check to see where this blood came from?"

"Third door on the right," said the tall cop. "Lots of blood there."

"You didn't mess up the scene, I hope," said Ryder.

"I was careful. Just cleared the room."

From the stairway rose an angry male voice, "You can't just keep us here!"

"This is a crime scene," muttered Ryder. "No one gets to leave until we say so."

Another voice from downstairs. "Just be patient, please. If you all help us out we can get you on your way faster."

"Logan's here," said Winter. "He'll take care of it."

Which was precisely what Ryder was afraid of. Captain Logan, another of the old guard. Probably friends with the owner of the house, more than likely willing to let possible witnesses leave. Not because he was shady, just sloppy.

The uniform's radio squawked. "Are you with the detectives?"

"Right here."

"Tell them there are guests leaving."

"Didn't Mason block the gate?"

"I don't know, I'm out back. There's another exit, some kind of service road by the garages."

"Shit," said Ryder. "What a clusterfuck."

Another uniformed cop came down the hall, carefully avoiding the bloodstained rug runner. "It's worse," he said. "There's a dead guy in the pool."

CHAPTER 23

ROBERT WINTER half listened to Captain Logan dole out the detective and officer assignments. Right now he was more interested in the party guests and staff—the ones who hadn't already bolted.

The guests stood in small groups, an eclectic group, a little on the younger side but a handful of middle aged and older, white, black, a few Latino. Well dressed, what Winter's daughter might call chic. She'd look right at home here. The staff, in white tuxedo jackets, huddled in the corner.

Winter recognized a few guests, a Marburg ex-councilman, an exec at a bank where Winter had helped figure out an embezzlement. Winter hadn't been in this house before, but he knew of it well enough, the family one of the richest in the state, old money from Colonial times. As a kid Winter had snuck on the property with his friends to play capture the flag, the estates along this road owning acres of wooded land.

Logan was assigning duties. "Ryder, you and Crosse are on Hennig. Owens, you and . . . ," Logan looked around, spotted Winter in the back of the group. Winter gave him a curt shake of his head. Logan, getting the message, said, ". . . O'Dowd are on the deceased in the pool. We got a name on him yet?"

"EMTs didn't find ID. Might be on the bottom of the pool," said one of the officers.

"Get some big lights out here," said Logan. "Try to get a photo that isn't frightening and show it around. Same for the man upstairs."

Winter tuned out again. The detectives and cops knew all this, Logan just had to get the ball rolling. After everyone had split off, Winter said to Logan, "Brooker would be helpful."

"He hasn't been cleared for duty," said Logan. "Can't have a guy with a heart problem running around."

"They probably got an elevator here, we'll keep him off the stairs."

"No," said Logan.

"He might know the family," argued Winter. "In case we get stonewalled."

"You expecting stonewalling? Something you want to tell me?"

"No. Never heard a whiff of this family doing anything wrong. But you know, big money, lots of lawyers."

"Can't risk it," said Logan. "Sorry."

Logan sounded like he meant it, so Winter let it go. "Don't assign me with anyone."

"You shook me off on Owens, you got a problem with him?"

"No, we're good. We did the stolen credit card thing a few months ago, remember? It's just—if you hook me up permanent, Brooker will think he's finished."

Logan, not unkindly, said, "You need to prepare yourself for that."

Winter had been trying, he really had. "Not for me, for him. He's going nuts sitting at home. Just keep me solo a little longer."

"Okay, for now. The move is away from permanent teams anyway, you know that. Be good for you to work with Owens again. Crosse, all of them. Even Ryder. Especially Ryder."

Winter knew what Logan left unsaid. Ryder, and the other new, younger detectives the Marburg force had been pressured to take in, were there to change the culture away from the old timers like Winter and Brooker. And even Logan. "Maybe you could work with him," suggested Winter.

"Nice try," said Logan. "In the meantime, I'll keep you on utility SWAT. You can co-ordinate between the two cases, find the connection. You're good at that."

"If they are connected," said Winter.

"Two men show up dead at the same party, at the same time? What do you think?"

Winter was good at finding connections between seemingly unrelated crimes, but he'd learned the hard way that *finding* connections wasn't the same as *looking* for them.

"Interviews are going to take all night," said Winter. "Brooker's probably awake."

"Nice try," repeated Logan.

WINTER WANTED to see the other body before helping out with the interviews. On the way to the patio the ex-councilman caught up with him.

"How long is this going to take?" he asked Winter.

"We'll have to get a statement from everyone."

"I didn't see anything. I was right in this room, nothing happened here. I just heard some screaming. That's my statement."

"Works for me, but it might not for Captain Logan. You should talk to him." Winter didn't blame the guy. It was late, he had been sleeping himself when the call came in, all hands on deck for this one. Marburg, a city of a quarter of a million people, got its share of deaths, but rarely two at once, and never two in the home of a rich family. "Sorry."

"Logan is here?"

"He just went up the stairs. You can't go up there, but he should be down soon."

Winter left through the patio doors. Cold outside, a breeze blowing into his face, he was glad he wore a hoodie. He wasn't into the latest technology except when it came to clothing, he would have killed for windproof tops when he had been in the service. Stuff the military didn't have then he could get at any sporting goods store now.

Jimmy O'Dowd, one of the detectives Logan had assigned to the pool death, was cornered between three middle aged women, all dressed in sequined gowns, bitching and moaning about not being able to leave. O'Dowd's eyes pleaded for help from Winter, who shrugged. O'Dowd turned to the side and gave Winter the finger out of view of the women.

At the pool one of the officers was setting up high intensity lights. Two EMTs were standing by a gurney. Andie, the crime scene tech, was taking photos. David Owens, a tall black guy with big shoulders and no hips, had tucked his tie in his shirt so it wouldn't get in the way. He was bending over a body at the edge of the pool.

"First uniform on the scene pulled him out of the water," said Owens. "He was already dead." Owens wasn't smoking but it always sounded like he'd just swallowed a diesel exhaust lungful of fumes.

Winter had seen a few pool deaths. Most involved booze or drugs.

"Get a chance to look around yet?"

"Just got here. Feel free."

"I'll wait for the lights," said Winter. "Don't want to step on any-thing."

The dead man was black, Rasta braids, dressed in dark clothes except for a pair of bright green sneakers. Twenties, maybe. Three long gold chains hung loosely around his neck.

"I doubt he was in the water very long," said Owens. "Somebody would have seen him."

"Pretty dark down this end." Winter made a note to himself to ask guests if the party had extended to the pool. "M.E. will be out, maybe she can give us a quick take."

"No, she won't. She's at some convention in California. There's an assistant, but I doubt he's going to stick his neck out with a guess until the autopsy."

Winter squatted near the body. Unlike the other dead man inside, there were no indications of trauma.

"Could have fallen in," said Owens. "Got a little drunk, whatever."

"Have an accident at the same time a guy is getting beat to death in the house?"

"You're the connections expert. You tell me. Maybe he killed the guy inside, couldn't live with it, came out and drowned himself. Tidy."

Nothing about this scene looked tidy to Winter. He stepped back as Andie snapped a photo of the dead man's face.

"Can you get a copy of that to my phone so I can try to get an ID from the guests?" asked Owens.

"Sure," said Andie. "But only on your department phone."

"I hate that one," said Owens, but he pulled it out.

Andie did the transfer, then said to Winter, "How about you?"

"Can't," said Winter. "Don't have a department phone."

"He doesn't even have a smart phone," said Owens.

"You're kidding."

"No, really." Winter stood up. "But I'll help with the interviews anyway. I'll ask around for a guest list."

"Working on that," said Ryder, who had just walked up with O'Dowd.

"Already solved the one inside?" said Owens.

"Funny," said Ryder. He held up his phone. "Send me this one's photo too. Let's make sure we ask everyone about both of the deceased."

Owens rolled his eyes at Winter. O'Dowd, his voice flat, said, "That's a great idea, Detective. Maybe we should get names and addresses of the guests as well?"

"You guys are a riot," said Ryder. He stooped over the body. "Anyone check his pockets?"

"Nothing," said Owens. "Hey, those are nice shoes you're wearing."

"I guess," said Ryder, sounding pleased. "Expensive enough."

Owens said, "Too bad, then."

"What? Why?"

"You're standing in a puddle of salt water. You'll never get the stains out of that soft leather."

Ryder jerked back, flicking water off his shoes. Winter fought to keep from laughing. O'Dowd didn't bother trying. Ryder, muttering, headed back toward the house.

"That was mean," said Winter, his laugh escaping.

"Guy's an asshole," said Owens.

"He has his moments," agreed Winter.

"When he's an asshole?"

"When he's not," said O'Dowd.

Winter waited for Ryder to clear the area, then, in what he thought was a pretty good Ryder imitation, said, "You two, make sure you ask everyone about both of the deceased."

"Fuck you," said O'Dowd.

Winter, feigning offence, said, "For reminding you of what to do?"

"No, for leaving me with those three women. I thought they were going to tear me to shreds. Another five minutes and we'd have had another body."

RYDER SLIPPED INTO a bathroom, balancing his foot on the sink so he could see the damage to his shoes. They didn't look bad, a few little rings, probably would come right off. Owens must have been jerking him around, knowing Ryder was into clothes. He hated all that sick cop humor.

He ran the water, stuck his finger in the flow, dabbing at the water spots. Pulled out his monogrammed handkerchief, cringing at the waste, it would be ruined. Spotted a guest towel, which certainly cost more than his handkerchief, but on the other hand, it had probably been handled by a hundred guests, full of germs anyway. He used it to dry his shoes as well as he could, washed his hands carefully, found a clean towel to dry off with, checked his hair in the mirror, and tightened his tie.

Back in the main room, Judy Crosse waved her cell phone at him. She was wearing the female detective equivalent of a suit, dark gray pants, boxy black jacket, a white blouse. Ryder thought she might not be half bad looking if she lost a few pounds, wore some makeup, and grew her hair out of the butch cut.

"Guards gave me a guest list," said Crosse, her Boston accent obvious to Ryder even in six words. "Just texted it to you and everyone else."

"Let's line them up, get statements," said Ryder.

Crosse nodded toward a bald guy on the other side of the room. "Captain wants us to start with him."

"Witness?" asked Ryder.

"Ex-councilman. Friend of the Captain."

Ryder's first thought was to make the bald guy wait until the end. No special privileges. On second thought, helping out a politician might not be bad for his own career. "Okay, I'll take him."

"Let's work our way around the room, meet in the middle. Captain already made an announcement about taking statements."

"Be more helpful if he did a few interviews," said Ryder, as he headed off.

WINTER WAS TRYING to figure out how he could ask the guests about the dead men if he didn't have a photograph. The department secretary had given him a tablet which he'd half leaned how to use, but he hadn't thought to bring it. One of these days he'd have to get a modern cell phone, instead of the push button one he carried and mostly kept turned off.

Inside the house, the guests were restless. While it was unlikely any one of them had committed the Hennig murder—there was just too much blood to not have splattered on the killer—they all still had to be interviewed.

A mini ruckus broke out in the corner, where Ryder was wrestling a photographer for his camera. Winter headed over.

"Give me that," Ryder demanded.

The photographer deftly held his camera out of reach over his head as he pulled out a laminated card. "I'm with a bona fide press organization," he said. "You can't have my camera."

"What's the problem here?" asked Winter.

"This guy is taking photos," said Ryder.

"Half the room is probably taking photos," said Winter. To the photographer, "Who are you with?"

"BOYZ. Hip hop glossy and blog."

"Never heard of it," said Ryder.

The photographer said, "Never heard of you either. Don't mean you ain't real."

Ryder muscled up. "Watch it."

"I got this," said Winter.

"What, you know hip hop too?" said Ryder, but he moved off.

"Thanks, man," said the photographer.

"Don't thank me yet. He had a point. You might have a photo that could help us out. You been talking shots all night?"

"Since the arrivals. Candy's assistant Miranda brought me in."

Winter must have looked blank, because the photographer said, "It's a publicity party for Candy's album."

"Hip hop?" asked Winter. He didn't know shit about current music.

"Nah. Pop stuff. But it's all connected behind the scenes. The producers, the distributors. I'm here more for the other guests who are here, you get me? Everyone scratching each other's back. A little publicity for the rap and hip hop artists here, and they return the favor, invite the rock and pop people to their bashes."

"If you say so," said Winter, not quite getting it. "Your photos could help."

"Not looking to get anyone in trouble. Ruin my reputation."

"Might help you a lot if you had the killer's picture in that little box," suggested Winter.

The photographer said, "You get a subpoena to cover my ass?"

"Sure, if it comes to that. In the meantime, can you just show me a little of what you have? I won't take your equipment."

"I can live with that." The photographer turned the camera toward

Winter, flicked a thumbwheel, and started working though the images.

Typical party shots, mostly small groups in conversation, drinks in hand. Winter said, "Stop."

The frame showed three men, two black and one white. One of the black men had braids and three long gold chains.

"You know that man?" asked Winter.

"Sure. That's Outta Here. Good music."

"Outta Here?"

"His music name. His real name is Dwayne Coleman. He just goes by Outta Here, or sometimes Outta Here Dwayne. I got some better shots."

"Who's Dwayne talking to?"

"The black dude is Sickboy, I don't know his real name, I should, he's had his share of hits. No idea who the white guy is."

Winter looked around the room. He didn't spot either of the two. "Seen them around?"

"Not since the cops showed up. But, you know, lots of people split."

"Tell me about it," said Winter.

RYDER, STILL PISSED from the run in with Winter, tried to keep his voice calm as he talked to the politician. The bald guy didn't know anything about the deceased men. He was there only because his law firm handled some of the Carter family businesses. Ryder did learn that the party was for the daughter, Candy.

The bald guy pointed Candy out. She was standing in a group of six, obviously the center of attention, perhaps as much for her looks as for her money. Ryder detoured from his planned starting point and headed her way.

Ryder gave Candy Carter a well deserved twice over as he crossed the room. She was dressed in denim, leather, and boots, not Ryder's favorite look, but she pulled it off. He buttoned his suit jacket as he approached, hoping she wouldn't notice his water stained shoes.

Candy was talking to a crew cut guy wearing a loose suit; Ryder's first impression was ex-military. The discussion appeared to be all one sided, the guy taking it like a soldier.

"Ms. Carter," Ryder said. "I'm Detective Martin Ryder. I'd like to talk with you."

Ryder flinched as Candy redirected her intensity toward him. "Did you find out who did this?"

"Not yet. We could use your help." Ryder switched to the man. "And you are?"

"Darrell Light. I was on security at the front gate tonight."

"Are you carrying a weapon?"

"I am. I already declared it and showed my carry license to one of your officers."

Ryder jerked his head. "Wait over there. I'll talk to you after."

Light moved off and Ryder turned his attention back to Candy, whose eyes were unfocused, looking far less in control up close. "He work for you long?"

"He works for my father, not me. Part time. We don't have full time security, just for the event." Candy pulled at her hair. "What a disaster."

Ryder figured she meant the crime, not her hair. Or maybe not. "We're you expecting trouble?"

"No, of course not. We just wanted someone down at the gate. We have other staff, but they were all busy with the party, otherwise they would have done it."

"What can you tell me about the men who died tonight?"

"One of them was Outta Here Dwayne?"

Ryder assumed she was talking about the dead guy at the pool. "We're working on positive identification." He showed Candy the photo.

"That's him." Candy's lip quivered. "I can't believe this happened here."

"How about the other man? Gerry Hennig."

Candy gave a slow head shake. "The name doesn't ring a bell. Do you have a photo?"

Ryder poised his hand over his phone. "It's pretty gruesome."

Her eyes narrowed. "I'm not a child."

"Okay." Ryder showed her the photo, watching her reaction carefully. Her face whitened, which appeared to be more shock than recognition.

"Jesus," she said.

"Sorry." Ryder turned his phone away. "Anything you can tell me?"

Candy hugged her arms, pulling her jacket tighter. "I don't recognize him, although in that condition I'm not sure I would have."

"If you didn't know him, how did he get invited?"

"Probably a guest of a guest."

Ryder flicked through the guest list. Sure enough, there was Hennig's name, he should have looked already. "I don't see anyone named Dwayne. What is his last name?"

"Cole, Coleman, something like that. He just goes by Outta Here. Hip hop singer. You can google it."

Ryder waved his arm around the room. "Fancy party like this, you don't keep track of the guests?"

"Excuse me? This is *my* fault? I didn't realize there was a law you have to track your guests at a private party."

Ryder put his hands up in mock surrender. "I didn't mean it that way. We're just trying to piece it all together."

"We've never had a problem at a party," said Candy. "My father is going to hit the roof."

"Is your father here?"

"He's in Europe on business. My mother is at the winter house in Palm Beach. This isn't exactly their type of event."

"Why is that?"

"Most of the guests are in the music industry. A few are friends of the family who come sniffing around looking to make connections. There were a lot of people here I didn't know, it's no big deal." Candy looked up toward the balcony. "My father is going to be *royally* pissed."

Ryder figured that was the least of her problems. "Who did the invitations?"

"Miranda, mostly. She's my personal assistant."

Ryder couldn't quite imagine why a twenty-something would need a personal assistant, but on the other hand he wasn't entirely sure how people this rich lived. Already he'd been wrong about assuming that the guest list would be strictly monitored. He still wasn't sure he believed it hadn't been; Candy might be hiding something.

"I'll want to talk to Miranda. What's her last name?"

"Dell. She's over there, long brown hair, wearing the black dress with the spaghetti straps. Talking to that tall guy—I don't recognize him."

"He's with us," said Ryder, painful as it was to admit it. Winter. "So your family used security. How about cameras?"

"We have a few, but none inside the house. My parents are very private people, they don't like the idea of being recorded. One of my father's friends had his camera feed hacked, pictures all over the internet. There's a camera on the front gate, one on the back entrance, a few more—Polly can tell you."

"Polly?"

"Polly Cooke. She runs the house. She's—." Candy looked around. "I don't see her, or most of the staff, for that matter."

Ryder jotted down the name in his notebook. "I'll find her. How well did you know Dwayne?"

"I met him tonight for the first time. I mean, I know his music."

"Did he seem okay when you talked to him?"

"I guess. We barely spoke. Just to meet, say hello."

"You weren't surprised to see him here?"

"I told you, I didn't know everyone. Guests bring guests, I'm sure you've been to enough parties."

Not like this one, thought Ryder. "So you don't know how he ended up here?"

"Miranda might have invited him, or more likely Kendall did. My producer, Kendall DeVaughn. He knows everyone in the industry."

"You doing hip hop music?"

Candy appeared relieved not to be talking about the dead men. "No. The publicity crosses over more than you think, ever since all the duet collaborations became popular few years ago. You know, a pop artist doing a song with a rapper, hip hop inspired rock, stuff like that."

"Where were you when you first learned there was a problem?"

"I'd just gone to the bathroom. I heard a scream, more than one, I came running out, someone said a man was hurt upstairs. I started to go up, one of the guests—Jacque LaChance—he stopped me. He said a man had been beaten up."

"This Mr. LaChance, he was coming down the stairs?"

"He was on the stairs. I'm not sure if he was heading up or down."

"Then what happened?"

"I told him to call an ambulance, he said one was on the way. I would have gone up but Jacque was pretty adamant." Candy pointed to Ryder's cell phone. "Now I understand why. I came back down and tried to calm everyone down. Speaking of which, my guests want to go home. How long are you going to keep them?"

"I'm afraid it's going to be a while," said Ryder. "We need to talk to everyone." And not give them a chance to get home and change out of clothes that might be blood spattered. Unless, of course, Hennig's killer was long gone, which was more than likely. "Can you point out Mr. LaChance?"

"I don't see him."

Ryder said, "Excuse me." He texted Crosse, told her to ask around about LaChance.

"If you are done with me I'm going to go find Polly, get coffee out here."

"Okay." Ryder recognized the signs; Candy was busying herself to take her mind off of the deaths. He pulled out his card. "If you remember anything at all about these two men, please call me." He fingered the card. "One last thing. We're not sure how Dwayne died—he was in the pool. He might have just fallen in. Did he look—under the influence to you?"

"He seemed pretty coherent."

"Is this the kind of party where—you know, people are imbibing? Besides the alcohol?"

"Not in front of me they wouldn't. They know how I feel about drugs."

"But you said you didn't know a lot of the guests."

"I can assure you, no one got any drugs from me or my staff. I don't drink either, but I know it's the way of the world, so we serve it. And it's legal. No drugs."

Ryder pushed. "Still, one of the guests could have been outside, getting high?"

"Anything's possible."

Which, Ryder thought, was unfortunately true.

CHAPTER 24

Before Winter had exchanged ten words with Miranda Dell he had come to the conclusion that she was a sad person. It wasn't because of the drink she gulped—always turning away from the room as she did so—or her semi disheveled hair.

Just *sad*, underneath the overly enunciated slow speach, the little black dress, the opulent surroundings.

Winter still needed to be sure she wasn't reacting personally to either death. "I understand you were in charge of the invitations?"

"Pretty much. I have a list of publicity people and media. Candy added a few names, so did her producer, Kendall."

"I didn't see anyone from the local paper."

Dell laughed, a dismissive cackle. "The locals aren't exactly our target market."

"How many were invited?"

"About a hundred."

Winter did a quick count in his head of just the people he'd seen on the way in and by the pool. "Huh. There's that many people here now, and I heard a lot of guests left."

"Kendall might have invited a bunch without telling me, wouldn't be the first time he's kept me out of the loop." Dell's eyes darted away. "It's an incestuous business. People just show up." She slurred over the word *incestuous*.

Not for the first time, Winter was glad he didn't have a ton of money or have to live around people who did. "That happen a lot? Party crashers?"

"I've been to parties I was invited to, and lots more I wasn't. It's not like people stroll in off the street. There was a list. But if you were with a guest they'd let you in." Dell sucked away at her ice cubes. "The more the merrier."

"What can you tell me about the man who died upstairs? Gerry Hennig."

"I don't know him, but the name rings a bell, did you check the list?" She pulled out her cell phone, scrolling through. "Here he is, he was a guest of a guest." She held the phone up for Winter to see. "Rick Singleton."

Dell was surprisingly unperturbed. Winter wasn't sure if she hid it well or had prior experiences with crime filled parties. "Is he here?"

"He was, I haven't seen him for a while."

"You know him?"

"He works at the studio where Candy is recording."

Winter couldn't tell if Dell had a habit of not answering questions directly, or if she was drunk or high. "Excuse me," he said. He motioned over one of the uniforms. "Are all the guests in this room?"

"Mostly. Detective Crosse is doing her interviews in the next room. The staff is in the kitchen with Officer Carter."

"Anyone out on the grounds looking for other possible witnesses?"

"Captain Logan is organizing that."

"Ask him to spread the word to look for a Rick Singleton. I want to talk to him right away."

Winter turned his attention back to Miranda Dell just in time to catch a fleeting sharpening of her interest. In Rick Singleton maybe? "This Rick a friend of yours?"

"I didn't invite him. Candy did."

Dell had flirted around the answer once again. Winter would come at her again after he talked to Singleton. "And you didn't know Gerry Hennig at all?"

"You got a picture?"

"No. We'll show you one later." When you are more sober, thought Winter. "He was beaten up. That sound like something one of your guests would do?" They would be checking the entire list for prior arrests for assaults, but it didn't hurt to ask.

"I can't imagine who. Candy, she's pretty straight."

Winter shifted his body as Dell picked up a new drink. In response, she turned even more to the side as she sipped. Winter glanced behind him, saw Ryder talking to a blond woman. Winter guessed that's who Dell was hiding her drinking from. "You work for Candy for a long time?"

"Few years."

"You got to meet a lot of her friends? The people here?"

"These aren't exactly friends. More like who she needs to make the big time."

"You don't approve?"

"It's the music business. Got to know the right people to make it."

"Tell me about Mr. Coleman."

Dell appeared confused. "Who?"

"Dwayne Coleman. I'm told he goes by the name Outta Here. A rapper."

"Oh. I like his music. He does hip hop, it's more than just rap."

Winter wasn't sure what that meant. "He was here alone tonight?"

"He had people around him at the party, he might have come with them."

She'd hesitated a bit too long for that reply to satisfy Winter. Maybe she wasn't as drunk as she let on. "Anyone in particular?"

"I saw him talking to one of the photographers. Some women too. You know, guests. I don't keep track of who talks to who." Dell added, "Why are you asking about him?"

"He was also found dead tonight."

"Dead? Where? *Here?*"

"In the pool."

"Are you sure? I mean, are you sure it was him?"

"Black man, braids, twenties, had these green sneakers."

"I can't believe it." Dell's eyes darted around the room, as if looking for an escape. "Shit," she muttered.

"I assume you know him personally? I'm sorry for your loss."

"No, nothing like that, I just met him tonight."

"You seem pretty upset."

"This is going to be bad for Candy. Two people ending up dead at her party? Her family hates publicity, they aren't even happy she's doing music." Dell took another drink, this time not turning to hide. "How did he die? Did he get beat up too?"

The question was a natural one, yet Winter noticed it had been delivered in feigned indifference.

"No." Winter let it hang, watching Dell's eyes. She looked like she was going to press it, reconsidered, thinking way too much. She raised her glass to her lips, not appearing to notice it was empty. "What did you talk about with him?"

"Nothing really. I told him about the house."

"He knew a lot of people here?"

"I told you, it's incestuous. A lot of music around, but it's a small world at the top."

"Did Dwayne know Rick Singleton?"

"Rick's not in that world. Not yet, anyway. He's grabbing at Candy's coattails."

Dell hadn't answered his question. Winter shifted. "Was Mr. Coleman on the guest list?"

"No. He'd be someone who Kendall might have invited. You should ask him. He's over there by the stairs, leather jacket, skinny tie."

Winter was trying to figure out another way to get past her possible evasions and pin her down when Ryder walked up. "Ms. Dell? I'm told you made the guest list. Is the one the guards have up to date?"

"Yes, but we were just talking about how a lot of people here are not on the list." Dell frowned at her empty glass. "Are you done with me? I need another drink."

Before Ryder could ask a question, Winter said, "Sure, but don't leave yet, okay?"

After she walked away, Ryder said, "I need to talk to her."

"You should. Maybe you'll have better luck than I did." Winter brought Ryder up to speed. "She's not all there. She's either got this weird obtuse way of talking, or she's hiding something. I think it would be better if we find this Singleton guy first, get his story, see if it matches up. Give us another angle on her."

"We should be doing all these interviews at the station."

Winter looked out over the crowd. "We couldn't *fit* all these people at the station."

RICK WAS HIDING in a closet bigger than his bedroom when a man down the hall yelled, "Police! We need everyone downstairs." Rick heard the bedroom door open, the call repeated, but no one came to the closet, and the voice drifted off down the hall.

Rick collapsed back into a pile of storage tubs, too numb to cry. Gerry. Although Rick hadn't seen Gerry in forever, they'd been as close as brothers once. Now he was dead. If he hadn't invited Gerry . . .

Rick had been roaming through the house looking for Gerry. Three white jacketed waiters rushed past him down a back stairway and out a door, Rick's Spanish just good enough to pick up the words *dead guy*. Rick, maybe too high for his own good, had walked up the stairs. On the other end of the hall, two men, one in a suit, the other a hoodie, were standing over a prone body, cops nearby. Rick heard the name *Gerry Hennig*, his body reacting faster than his brain, backpedaling. Voices below in the kitchen area spooked him from going back down. He went up, along a long hall, slipping into the first room.

He lost track of time, more muffled voices, separate sets of running footsteps along the hall. The bedroom door opened, Rick trying to figure out how he could explain why he was hiding in a closet. Female voices, loudly whispering, sharing an exciting secret. "I got his picture! Here's one with me in it. I'm going to post it."

Disbelieving laughter. "No, you can't!"

"Why not?" A giggle, then, "Can you believe it? Look, I'm with a dead guy."

That was enough to light Rick up, it was his friend they were talking about. He pushed to his feet.

"We should have got his autograph. *Outta Here Dwayne*. This is going to make him more famous than Tupak."

"Who?"

"Grow up. *California Love? Dear Mama?* Sometimes I don't know about you Cecily."

Rick half listened to them half argue, sinking back to the floor. What was going on here? Gerry, Dwayne, both dead?

He was screwed. It wasn't going to be hard for the cops to figure out he'd been talking to Dwayne, and even easier to find out he'd invited Gerry. He'd look suspicious for sure. Maybe they'd even try to pin it on him. He hadn't done a thing, but Candy would drop him like battery acid.

Maybe he *was* to blame. Gerry was dead because Rick had invited him. But who would hurt Gerry? Hardly anyone even knew he'd be here.

Shit. *Doc*. Doc had talked to Dwayne about Gerry, about getting him to sign the papers. What had Dwayne said? Something about his friend finding Gerry at the party? Rick's head was buzzing, he couldn't think straight, he hadn't done much blow but it must have been really pure, his heart still pounding.

His pulse beat so hard it filled his ears, so loud he didn't even hear the closet door open.

THE YOUNG WHITE guy being pulled along by the uniform looked nervous as hell to Winter, wide eyed and jumpy. The officer said, "Found him in a closet."

"We'll take it from here," said Ryder. "You're Rick Singleton? I'm Detective Ryder, this is Detective Winter."

"Maybe we should take this elsewhere," said Winter, jerking his head toward the guests.

They walked through an archway to an adjoining room, smelling of food that had been sitting too long.

"I understand you invited Gerry Hennig," said Ryder.

Singleton nodded too many times, his fingers flicking restlessly, his eyes dilated. Winter recognized the symptoms. Singleton was high, but without the blunting effect of alcohol he'd seen on Miranda Dell.

"It's true then? Gerry's dead?" Singleton's voice held a hint of hope.

"I'm afraid so," said Winter.

"Shit," said Singleton. "Can I sit down?"

Ryder looked like he preferred to pin Singleton to the wall, but Winter said, "Sure." Singleton awkwardly perched on a stool against a wet bar.

Singleton asked, "How did it happen?"

"It looked like he was in a fight," said Ryder. "When did you last see him at the party?"

"I didn't. I didn't see him at all."

"You invited him, didn't you?" pressed Ryder.

"I did. But we didn't come together. I was supposed to meet him here, I couldn't find him. I wasn't even sure he showed up." Singleton's hopped up eyes clashed with his gloomy demeanor. "He didn't even answer my texts."

Ryder didn't look convinced, but Winter sensed true sorrow from Singleton. Still, he wouldn't be the first murderer who'd had second thoughts. "Can you show me your hands, please?" asked Winter.

Singleton didn't hesitate, holding up his hands. Winter couldn't see a drop of blood. Singleton could have washed up, but from what he'd seen of the way Hennig had been beaten and cut, Singleton would likely have splatter if he'd been the attacker. Singleton hadn't even asked why Winter had wanted to see his hands, either too high or too innocent to wonder.

"Tell us about Mr. Hennig," said Ryder.

"We used to play in a band together. Started in high school. After that, we drifted apart, he was getting a PhD. I haven't seen him in over a year."

"You decided to reconnect here?"

"I never really gave up on him coming back to music. I thought if he saw what it would be like if we made it big he'd want to get back together. Stupid, I know."

"Why stupid?" asked Winter.

"This," said Singleton, waving his hand generally at the house, the food. "This isn't Gerry. It would turn him off more than get him excited. He's kind of a quiet guy."

Singleton was still talking about Hennig in the present tense. Winter prodded, "You said you couldn't find him?"

"Yeah, I'd pretty much given up. I figured if he had shown, he'd be someplace quiet, maybe even in the kitchen, with the staff."

Winter didn't like parties either, and when he did go, that's exactly where he usually ended up. He felt an extra tug of sympathy for Gerry Hennig. "Sorry for your loss," said Winter.

"Thanks. I can't believe any of this."

"Anyone else here know him?" asked Ryder. "Who knew he'd be coming?"

"I asked Candy if it was okay if I invited him, she said sure, just tell Miranda. Both of them knew."

"Why were you hiding up in a closet?" asked Ryder.

"I told you, I was looking for Gerry. I was in the hallway by the kitchen and heard people talking about someone being killed. I guess I panicked, I ran upstairs and hid. A couple of women came into the bedroom talking about a dead man, but they were talking about another guy, Outta Here Dwayne. I got really confused and freaked out. I know that sounds lame, but it's the truth."

"Did you know Dwayne Coleman?" asked Ryder.

"Not before tonight."

"You talked to him? About what?"

"Music, what else? That's what the whole party was about."

Winter wasn't sure many music parties ended up with two dead men, but it did make him think. Maybe there was a music connection. "Did Gerry know Dwayne?"

"I doubt it. Like I said, we hadn't been in touch."

"Gerry into hip hop?" asked Winter.

"Music was like math to Gerry, the beats, the construction. He'd listen to taiko drumming, Baroque, you name it." Singleton's eyes glistened. "I can't believe he's gone."

RICK WAS FIGHTING to hold it together, all the questions were getting to him. Thinking he was doing okay, walking the thin line between being open but not admitting he'd been alone with Dwayne. His story about his reason for inviting Gerry sounded weak, but the cops apparently had bought it. The truth would have involved Dwayne and maybe even Doc. He'd have a hard time explaining about Doc. Doc would kill him if Rick dragged him into this. Or worse, Kevin would hurt his mother because Rick screwed up and ratted Doc out.

The cop in the suit was telling him to hang around, they'd have more questions, Rick nodding mechanically, he didn't want to appear suspicious. Behind the cops, in the main room, Candy and Miranda were looking right at him.

Shit, Miranda. *She'd* seen him with Dwayne. What had she told the cops? What was she telling Candy? As it was, Candy might not use his song once she learned the co-writer had been killed in her own house.

Rick felt like shit, worrying about his music when Gerry was lying dead upstairs. That's how fucked up his life had become, one thing after another. A little drug delivery for a customer of Doc's had led him here, one small step at a time, impossible to predict, yet looking back, so obvious his path would lead him to a heap of shit. The one guy he'd really thought of as his best friend dead, and Rick so backed into a corner all he had left was a song, a lifeline from Gerry.

The cop in the suit walked away, Rick refocusing on the other guy, who didn't look like a cop at all. Rick not quite cheering up but feeling like he'd dodged one bullet. "What's your name again?" asked Rick, more to get his head screwed on right.

"Winter. Robert Winter."

"Sorry. I'm a little out of it."

"Understandable," said Winter. "You lost your friend." The cop touched Rick on the chest. "Plus this."

Rick looked down, a telltale spattering of white powder. He didn't bother to deny it.

"That yours? Or did you get it here?"

Rick glanced over at Miranda and Candy, the two women still in view but no longer looking his way. He could tell the truth, that he'd been at the pool, that he got the drugs from Dwayne, Miranda could back up his story. That would clear him, sort of, on the drugs, pin it on Dwayne, it wasn't like he was going to get arrested for doing a few snorts. But it would put him with Dwayne, and would also burn Miranda, in case she hadn't fessed up to being with Dwayne either, which he doubted. And Candy would be pissed at Miranda, getting high at her party.

If he got Miranda in trouble, she'd turn on him for sure.

It must have been the remnants of the coke in Rick's system, giving him such heightened brainpower, all these thoughts flashing through his mind.

Couldn't burn Miranda, couldn't admit being with Dwayne, not until he found out what Miranda had told the cops. "Just a few snorts I brought," he said. "Not a big deal, I mean, it's a party, right?"

The cop said, "I've got bigger things to worry about. Not like you are the only one here getting high."

Rick wasn't sure what he meant about that, so he kept his mouth shut.

"Got to ask you though, are you carrying any on you?"

Rick said, "No, I swear." He held out his arms. "Search me if you want."

The cop gave him a pat down, asking, "How about Gerry? Would he have brought drugs?"

Rick translated the cops question as: Was Gerry dealing? Is that why he got killed? It would have been easy to throw Gerry under the bus, make him sound like a dealer, get the cops thinking it was about drugs. If they did, they might not figure out the connection between Gerry and Dwayne, which was Doc.

Doc had to be mixed up in this. Had to.

The words formed in his brain, but Rick couldn't get them out of his mouth. He'd invited Gerry here, he'd probably got him killed. He was responsible. There was no way he could drag Gerry through the mud. "I never saw Gerry touch so much as weed when I knew him," he said, truthfully.

"Okay," said Winter. "But you won't mind, will you, if I take your jacket? Just in case."

Rick filled in the rest: In case we find your drugs on Gerry. Or Dwayne.

Shit.

Yet another step he'd taken, another swipe of the brush, painting him tighter into the corner. He took off his jacket and handed it to the cop.

CHAPTER 25

WINTER PARKED in front of the old, neatly kept bungalow. Quarter to six in the morning, the grass in the yard frozen brown, reflecting off his low beams. Brooker's house. The living room light was on.

They could have used Brooker tonight. It had taken almost all night to do just the initial interrogations. Brooker was good at interviews, even better than Winter. It was surprising, since Brooker looked and talked like a cop, although not like Ryder. An old style cop. Where Winter talked *with* suspects and witnesses, often learning from what they didn't say, Brooker was the authority figure; he rarely spoke, and people just opened up, like they'd been dragged to the principal's office in elementary school.

But Brooker was out, at least for a while. Winter could still talk to him, get his thoughts. Right now would be a good time; Winter was tired, not thinking straight, and the whole mess at the Carter's house needed a clear set of eyes.

Brooker was probably up, not able to sleep, restless. That's why the light was on.

Or maybe he was in pain, and would be embarrassed for Winter to see. Not because he wouldn't let Winter see him in pain, they'd been through plenty of pain before, but rather it would confirm that Brooker wouldn't be coming back.

Winter couldn't face either one of them having to deal with that.

He pulled away from the curb and headed home.

LESS THAN THREE hours later Winter was at the station. He'd managed a few hours of sleep. In ones and twos the detectives arrived, bleary eyed, most carrying travel mugs, beelining into the break room for refills.

The detective squad conference room was too small, so they assembled in the bullpen, the long, narrow room where the uniforms did the shift change. Along with the detectives were Dickie Evans, the squad commander, a few senior uniforms, the criminologist Cindy Prague, and the data guy, Dan Cole.

Captain Logan, looking crisper and more awake than he probably was, brought them all up to speed on the deaths at the Carter house. Nothing new had been uncovered since Winter had left.

Logan pointed to the squad commander. "Rotate your best through the Carter house. I don't want to release the scene until we are sure no one is hiding out on the property or we didn't miss evidence in the dark."

Evans said, "We'll have to go open beat." A couple of the uniforms groaned, it meant the regular beats would be short patrolmen.

Logan said, "Full boat on this one, all leave and days off cancelled. Detective teams the same as I set up last night. Owens and O'Dowd on Coleman, Ryder and Crosse on Hennig, Winter in the middle. First job is to get a timeline, what the deceased were doing before the party, phone calls, texts, you know the drill. Track down anyone on the guest list who skipped out. Cindy will cross reference everything from your notes. I want one set of assignments for the interviews, on the whiteboard at all times. Let's not have two different teams running around doing the same interview."

"Priority is Jacque LaChance," said Ryder. "He popped up in the system, an arrest for assault."

"Already on that," said Evans. "He wasn't at his apartment, got a squad car sitting there, BOLO out on him and his car."

"Working on getting his cell," said Cindy.

"Miranda Dell—she was in charge of the guest list—might have it," said Winter.

"What do we know about next of kin?" asked Logan.

Winter said, "Singleton—the guy who invited Hennig, told me his parents moved to New Hampshire. We'll track them down."

"Nothing on Coleman's family yet," said Owens.

"Find out," said Logan. "Any other questions? Okay, get to it."

*   *   *

JUDY CROSSE DREW two horizontal lines on the whiteboard. "The green line is for Gerry Hennig, the red line for Dwayne Coleman. I'm labeling both lines starting at 8 p.m. for now."

"I saw a photo of Coleman at the party, with a timestamp of 8:38," said Winter. "Taken by a publicity photographer."

"Anything earlier?" asked Crosse. "No?" She drew a tick mark on the red line, marking it with the time. "What else do we have on Coleman?"

One of the uniforms said, "Talked to three young women, they had photos taken with Coleman, all right around that same time."

"Any of them know him?" asked Owens.

"Not Biblically. That's a quote," said the uniform, his face flat.

"That's all you got?" asked Ryder.

"That was the gist of it. One of them added *Yet.*"

"Gonna have a long wait," someone muttered.

"I talked to a woman with the catering group," said Winter. "She says she brought Coleman a drink but doesn't know what time. But he'd just had his photo taken."

Crosse said, "Cindy, we're going to have a million photos. Can you and Dan print them out and stick them on the board?"

"Sure. Dan's already running the guest list against social media accounts, in case any photos were posted."

"Already found a few," said Cole. "Including one showing Candy Carter with Coleman inside the house."

"Anyone have a witness putting Coleman out by the pool?"

"I do," said O'Dowd. "Five, as a matter of fact. Three women, together, were on the patio, they saw him come out with," O'Dowd looked down at his notes, "a young white male in a dark jacket or suit coat. The unidentified male and Coleman were in conversation walking toward the far end of the pool. No idea of the exact time."

"Anyone else able to lock that down?" asked Crosse.

No one could. O'Dowd continued, "A couple walking through the garden heard a man yelling on the other side of the hedge. Something about *People reading about him*. They were curious, they looked—there's this gap in the hedge from the garden to the pool area—and saw a black male with long hair near the cabana. Just standing there. They are pretty sure it was right around 9:30 because they were leaving the party early to get home, they had a sitter until ten."

"Probably Coleman," said Owens. "But put a question mark on the timeline, just in case."

"No 911 call on Coleman?" someone asked.

"No," said Owens. "Randy Kleeve found Coleman in the pool. He told me he was checking the property after the Hennig thing when he walked by the pool and saw Coleman's body. He almost missed it, it's pretty dark on that end. Pulled Coleman out, did chest compressions, otherwise he didn't think he messed things up much."

"Randy's careful," said Evans.

"His call to dispatch for another ambulance was logged at 10:40," said Owens. "So we need to fill in a little under two hours, plus the time before. Let's assume for now that Coleman was alive at 9:30, and went into the water sometime between then and 10:40. Probably earlier, unless he just happened to fall in or been pushed just as Randy was walking up. Narrows it down. Now we need to figure out who was where. That we know of, anyway."

"How about the gate?" Winter asked.

"Useless rent a cop," said Ryder. "For the first half hour or so they took names of guests who weren't on the list, but after that they just waved anyone in who was in a nice car."

"Coleman's name actually is on the list," said O'Dowd, "although we couldn't find it at first. He's listed in a notation under another man, one Terrence Jackson, who is himself listed not as a guest but in a note on Kendall DeVaughn, Candy Carter's producer. DeVaughn said he put a lot of possible attendees on the list. He confirmed that Coleman's name came from Jackson."

"We have anything on the Jackson guy?"

"Not yet," said O'Dowd. "I put him on the list for Cindy."

"You're going to need help on this," said Winter. "You'll be tracking down names and pictures for a year."

"You volunteering?" asked Cindy.

That brought widespread snickers, everyone aware of Winter's lack of skill with anything remotely computerized.

"Let's do Hennig," said Crosse. "The 911 call for Hennig was logged at 9:58. The caller is a woman, she just said a man was hurt bad. Didn't identify herself, but we're tracking the number. Another call came in three minutes later. This one from a Polly Cooke, she identified herself as the house manager and said a man was dead."

"Timing is really close," someone said.

"Got to be connected," said O'Dowd. "I mean, what are the chances? Guy gets beaten down at the same time another guy dies in a pool?"

"We don't know exactly what time Hennig got killed," said Logan. "Only the time of the call. Anyone have a witness locking down Hennig before ten?"

"Man was a ghost," said Ryder. "No one admitted seeing Hennig. Not even the guy who invited him, Rick Singleton."

O'Dowd said, "The kitchen staff saw two males, one black and one white, heading up the back stairway. They didn't pay much attention, people always wandered around the house, checking the place out."

"Coleman?" asked Crosse.

"I don't think so," said O'Dowd. "I showed them his photo, they said the guy was much thinner, no braids. No idea who the white male was. They didn't know the time, although they did say it wasn't the very beginning of the party or the very end."

"We're going to have to go back to everyone once we get a little more meat on the timeline," said Winter. "Can we get the photos organized in order, so we can flip through them with the witnesses?"

"Easy," said Cindy.

"For you, maybe," said Winter.

"Got to get the video feeds too," said Owens. "I saw a few security cameras."

"I'll talk to Candy Carter again," offered Ryder.

Owens caught Winter's eye, grinned, and mouthed, "Of course."

THE MEETING WENT ON for a few more minutes, breaking up as they got fidgety, wanting to get on with the few leads they had. Ryder and Crosse, on the Hennig's death—everyone treating it as a homicide—made a list of interviews. Jacque LaChance, the man who had an assault prior and who had discovered Hennig's body, was top of the list. Owens and O'Dowd did the same for the Coleman death. They'd focus on who had been seen with Coleman at the party.

"I'll take the staff," said Winter. "Try to catch them at home, they might be willing to say more than they did in front of their bosses."

"Works for me," said Owens. "I'm going to see if they started the autopsies."

"Might tag along on that," said Winter.

"Me too," said Crosse.

"See you there," said Owens. "On my way as soon as I grab a smoke."

On the way out Winter stopped at his desk, retrieved his tablet from the bottom drawer, and met up with Cindy in her cubicle. "For when you get the photos," he said.

Today Cindy's hair sported pink streaks. "I suppose I'll have to remind you how to use it."

"At the least," said Winter. "In the meantime, the head of the staff at the Carter house, Polly Cooke, said she'd email us a list of the workers. I gave her your email address."

"You have one, you know," said Cindy. "You can get the messages on here." She waved the tablet.

"Yeah, yeah, my VCR can be programmed too, but who remembers how?"

"Who has a VCR anymore?"

"Huh? How do people record *Barney Miller*?"

"Sometimes I don't know when you are just bullshitting me," said Cindy.

"Never," said Winter. "When you get the list, check the staff for priors. And I was serious about you getting help. There are going to be a million names to run."

"The Captain has already been calling in favors. The Sheriff's office criminologist is going to be giving us a few hours a day. Maybe help from Hampshire county. We're going to bring in Dan's uncle, he's done IT work for us before, he's been cleared."

"Call me when you get those photos," said Winter, as he headed out the door.

"You remember how to answer your phone?"

THE DRIVE TO THE medical examiner's office could either be ten minutes or twenty five, depending on the time of day and traffic. The highway was faster, but more prone to the traffic, which Winter hated more than just about anything, so he took the route through the city.

It wasn't a long enough drive to really think about the two cases. Winter avoided jumping to conclusions early on, or even forming quick hypotheses. Too easy to start fitting the facts to the idea, instead of generating ideas from the facts.

He pulled into the parking garage of the U Mass Medical Center, where the state Medical Examiner was located.

Owens and Crosse were already in the autopsy room, talking to a pasty faced, heavy set man named John Reposte, the assistant medical examiner. There were two bodies on examining tables, neither one of them Coleman or Hennig.

"What do you mean you haven't started yet?" said Crosse.

"Do you have the required forms filled out for the next of kin notification?"

"For a homicide?"

Reposte, sounding like a cross between a first grade teacher and a lecturing professor, said, "You've determined cause of death, detective? I guess you don't need the office of the medical examiner, then, do you?"

"Ours have priority," said Owens.

"These two are on my schedule," said Reposte, indicating the tables. "And there are three others—all with the proper paperwork—behind those. I'll also remind you that it is Sunday."

"Maybe we should call Kristol," said Owens. Kristol was the Medical Examiner assigned to the Marburg area.

"Your threats are not going to work on me," said Reposte.

Winter, having dealt with Reposte before, said, "Doctor, if we could just get your expert opinion with a visual, it would point us in the right direction. Right now we just need a starting place." Winter knew he had laid it on thick, but Reposte was susceptible to even the most obvious flattery.

Reposte sighed. "I suppose I could look."

IN THE MORGUE Reposte took one look at the body of Gerry Hennig and shook his head.

"Besides the fact that he was cut and likely beaten, which I assume you already know, I am not going to even attempt to deduce more than that. There is too much damage. We'll need a neuropathologist for the autopsy as well."

"We'll want a tox screen too," said Winter, thinking about the coke he'd seen on Rick Singleton's jacket.

They crowded around the stainless steel pull out drawer holding the body of Dwayne Coleman. Reposte made a harrumph sound, and the cops backed up to give him room.

Winter had seen his share of examinations and autopsies, but it was still a black box to him. Even when a pathologist pointed out findings, Winter had a hard time seeing exactly what they meant, especially with contusions, they all looked the same.

Dwayne Coleman just looked dead.

"I want to remind you this is unofficial," said Reposte. "With that in mind, I see no obvious signs of anterior external injury or penetration. There is a lateral scar in the lower abdomen, suggesting an appendectomy years ago, not by laparoscopy."

"Could he have drowned?" asked Owens.

"We'll have to check the lungs. The skin is normal, no sign of wrinkling on the soles or nails. If he did drown, he wasn't in the water long. Did someone do CPR? Did they report foaming?"

"A uniform did compressions," said Owens. "I'll check with him."

"Probably didn't notice," said Reposte. "Your training procedures are atrocious." Reposte motioned for the mortuary assistant. "Flip him."

"We should get a tox on him as well," said Owens.

"Of course. I see a small occipital contusion here," said Reposte, pointing to a spot on the back of Coleman's head.

"Could he have been struck there?"

"Perhaps. Or he may have hit his head when falling."

"It was a pool," said Owens.

"Could be the edge," said Reposte. "But don't quote me."

"Any way to tell if he was dead before he went in the water?" asked Winter.

"Not until the autopsy. And even then, I can't promise we'll know for sure unless there is no significant water in the lungs. We can probably identify other possible causes, a heart attack, a seizure, but whether they occurred before or after he went in could remain an open question."

"I doubt he was going for a swim," said Crosse.

Winter wasn't even sure of that.

CHAPTER 26

Doc REACHED OUT to the nightstand, feeling for his morning cappuccino. Nothing. He opened one eye, the blue digits of the clock confirming his coffee should have already arrived. Where the fuck was Tricia?

He didn't shout, shouting was for weak men. You only had to shout if no one was listening to you in the first place. Ask Dwayne.

Pissed, Doc dragged himself out of the bed, trying to pull his thick robe on fast enough to not get chilled. He wasn't happy, which meant Tricia wasn't going to be happy.

He plodded down the hall, knowing he looked foolish, a sagging, untanned, overweight guy in a bathrobe and slippers. Not caring. That was the benefit of age. That and a shitload of money. A dwindling shitload.

Still expecting Tricia to come running down the hall with his coffee, getting angrier with each step. If she appeared now he'd have a decision to make: immediately throw the entire cup in her face to teach her a lesson or take a few sips first.

He found her in the kitchen, bent over the two thousand dollar coffee machine, her tongue stuck out in intense concentration, cooing to the machine. She was naked except for a thin gold chain around her neck and tiny white panties with little red hearts, either oblivious to the morning chill of the floor tile, or getting ready for Doc, always serving him his coffee in a similar stage of undress.

The chain wasn't expensive or anything special, yet she hadn't taken it off since Doc had given it to her.

"Where's my coffee," he grunted, but the anger had seeped away.

Tricia twisted her head, her mouth a mixture of a smile and an apology. "I'm so sorry, Doc, it just keeps beeping."

"Use the other machine."

"I know you like the coffee from this one better."

Doc moved her out of the way, turned the unit off, then back on again. No more beeping.

"How did you do that? You're so smart." Tricia went to work on the coffee.

Those words from any other woman would have set Doc off, a gold digger buttering him up. From Tricia, it was the truth, at least as she understood things. Doc normally hated bimbos, but he had a weak spot for Tricia.

"I'll get it," said Tricia. She deftly stirred in two heaping scoops of sugar, handed Doc the cup, and slipped out of the room.

Doc hadn't even heard the phone ring. Getting old.

THE COFFEE DIDN'T help with the phone call. The kid, Rick, was blabbering about needing more time to get his money, giving Doc a headache even the caffeine couldn't overcome.

"I was expecting to hear from you last night," said Doc. "I even called you. You know how much I hate calling to ask for what I expect to get? Did Gerry sign the papers?"

"I had to turn my phone off. Wait, didn't you hear?"

"It's nine in the fucking morning, what would I have heard?"

"Gerry—Gerry's dead."

Doc had assumed as much, hearing it didn't help. "What the hell happened?"

"I went to meet him at the party to talk to him about signing over the rights to me."

"What, he said no and you roughed him up?"

"*Me?* I didn't touch him, I never even saw him."

"So how did he end up dead?"

"Somebody beat him up. Maybe a robbery, I don't know. It wasn't like I could go ask the cops questions."

"Did you talk to them?"

"I had to. They talked to everyone. I was there half the night. That's why I had my phone turned off, I didn't even have the burner with me."

"My name better not have come up," warned Doc.

"Not from me it didn't. I just said I was going to see if Gerry was interested in getting back into music."

"Did they buy it?"

"I think so. Who's to know otherwise, other than you?"

Dwayne might have, for one, thought Doc. "You sure you didn't talk to anyone else about our deal?"

"No one, I swear."

"Better not be lying to me, kid. If you got something to say, now's the time."

"Doc, I'm telling you, no one alive knows about our arrangement."

No thanks to Rick. Doc had been forced to take care of that himself. But it didn't mean Rick hadn't given up the details to Dwayne. Doc waited to see if Rick would mention he'd talked to Dwayne at the party. The kid, maybe too smart for his own good, kept his mouth shut. "This was all supposed to be low profile."

"I was just doing what you told me to do."

"You were the one who invited Gerry, right? The cops will come back to you."

"Plenty of people know I was in a band with Gerry. It's not like I picked his name out of a phone book."

Doc pressed. "What if Gerry told his friends?"

"I doubt it. But even if he did, then so what? He was meeting me to talk about music. It will all sound the same."

"You said you signed some papers with Gerry. What happens to the rights if one of you died?"

"Nothing," said Rick. "I mean, we didn't write that in there. We were nineteen, who thought about dying?"

"Never too young to think about dying," said Doc. "Remember that."

CHAPTER 27

R<small>YDER STRAIGHTENED</small> his tie as he listened to the faintly echoing chimes beyond the massive double door entry of the Carter home. The place was even more impressive during the day, the grounds immaculate, impossibly clear of leaves, the peaceful stillness of an empty park, giving little hint of the disturbances from the preceding evening.

A petite Asian woman answered the door, sharp cheekbones, dressed in a loose-fitting smock.

"Yes?"

"I'm Detective Ryder with the Marburg Police Department. I'm—"

"Mr. Carter is not home," she cut in, a hint of an accent.

"Actually, I need to speak with Candy."

"She's not home either. You'll have to come back when Mr. Carter is here."

Ryder peered behind her into the house. The foyer had been cleaned up, with no sign there had been a party. "Where's Candy?"

"I don't know. If you will excuse me, I have a lot of work to do."

"It's very important I speak with her."

"I cannot tell you anything. You have to talk to Mr. Carter. I suggest you call for an appointment." The woman started to close the door.

Ryder wondered if she'd been told not to speak to the police or if she was always so protective. "Wait. Where you here last night?"

"Yes. I live in one of the tenant houses."

"I don't remember seeing you at the party."

"I was not there. I helped with the setup and then went to bed, I had to be back very early to clean up."

"Did you hear or see anything out of the ordinary?"

"No. My house is on the other side of the property."

"How long have you worked for the Carter family?"

"Eighteen years. They are very good to me."

Ryder translated that as: No matter what I know, I'm not going to tell you if it will make the family look bad. Ryder made a show of taking out his notebook. "Please tell me your name."

The woman hesitated, then said, "Yao Lee Chen."

Ryder asked her to spell it. As he wrote it down he tried to think of how he could get her to open up.

Before he got the chance she had closed the door.

JUDY CROSSE, three desks over in the detective pen, hung up on her call and said to Winter, "I'm on my way over to see Rick Singleton for the follow up. Want to tag along?"

"If you can get me there via a Dunkin Donuts drive thru."

"Sure. You're buying, though."

"Only if you don't get one of those expensive foofy drinks."

"Foofy?"

"You know, a drink that isn't black coffee."

Owens caught them in the hall. "Winter, got time to help do a follow up on Coleman?"

"We were just off to see Singleton, on the Hennig case."

"Later, can you talk to these women?" Owens turned his cell phone for Winter to see. "They took a bunch of selfies at the party, posted them online."

"Don't they all," said Crosse.

"With Dwayne Coleman," said Owens. "I'd do it, but I'm due in court, and Jimmy is working on next of kin, otherwise we'll get held up on the autopsy."

"They the only ones who posted pictures?" asked Winter.

"The only ones who weren't on the guest list."

"That's interesting. You got an address?"

"Students at Marburg State. Same address listed for both of them. I'll text you the details."

Winter groaned. He'd have to turn his cell phone on.

*   *   *

BECAUSE HE HAD already talked to Singleton, Winter decided to do the selfie women interview first. He'd catch up with Crosse later. It did remind him of the coke on Singleton's jacket. Since he had the phone on, he called Andie, the crime scene tech, as he drove one handed cross town. He was expecting her voice mail, but she picked up, sounding tired.

"You get any sleep?" asked Winter.

"We didn't release the scene until a few hours ago. We could have been there a month, but Logan wanted us out. I caught an hour on the rack in the basement."

"Pressure from the Carter family?"

"Who knows."

"Think we missed anything?"

"Who knows?" Andie repeated. "I feel good about the bedroom where Hennig was found, and pretty good about the pool area. It wasn't like we were expecting to find a break-in point of entry. All the doors were wide open."

"I dropped off a jacket with a note."

"I saw it. It'll be a while, unless you think I should put it top of the list?"

"Not yet. But if you find any other coke trace, especially near the deceased, try for a match."

"Coke trace? At a big party?"

"Get some sleep, Andie," said Winter.

"Stop calling then."

Winter clicked off, hoping she would take his advice, knowing she wouldn't. Marburg didn't have a large crime scene staff; Andie was the full time tech, and a handful of the uniforms were trained in basic collection. They'd be getting help on this one from the sheriff's office and the state police.

Marburg State was founded just after the turn of the last century, which would have qualified it as a really old school in just about any state except Massachusetts. Over the years the city had grown around it, campus buildings interspersed with businesses and even homes. Many of those were rented to students, and that's where Winter ended up, at a three story colonial badly in need of paint.

A girl who looked far too young to be a college student answered the door, wearing a long gray tee shirt with the logo of the university. Her red hair reached almost to her waist, and she held a bunch of loose bills in her hand.

"You're not the pizza guy," she said.

"I'm with the Marburg Police," said Winter. "I'd like to talk to Ginny Matthews about the party last night. And Cecily Rogers."

"Party?"

"You know, the one you posted pictures of?"

"Oh, *that* party."

"Is that the pizza?" called a voice.

"It's a policeman."

Another woman appeared at the door, wearing a loose fringed white blouse and denim shorts. "I'm Cecily," she said. "Let him in Ginny, it's cold." She had a tattoo on the back of her neck which caught Winter's eye but he couldn't make out, making him wonder if that was the point.

In the living room, Cecily plopped on the couch. "Is this about Outta Here?"

"You know him personally?" Winter asked.

"We wish," Ginny said. "We just like his music."

"Did you see what happened?"

"Not a thing," said Cecily, sounding disappointed. "We just heard the screaming. We didn't realize until later there were *two* dead guys. I would have taken more pictures. We talked to some officer, big, uh, heavy set guy."

"You show him the pictures you had taken?"

Cecily shrugged. "He didn't ask."

Winter showed a little smile, but said, "I'm asking."

"I thought you saw them online?" said Ginny.

"I want to see any you didn't post."

"Nothing good," said Cecily, but she made room on the couch for Winter.

She spun through the pictures. They all looked similar, the two women with Coleman, lots of selfies, odd angles, Cecily's oversized face with guests in the background.

"Go back," said Winter. "To the shots of you with Outta Here."

In the selfie, Coleman had an arm around Cecily and Ginny, the three of them looking very friendly and happy. Behind them, a darker haired woman, looking decidedly not. Miranda Dell.

"You know her?" asked Winter.

"That's Candy's ass—sistant," Ginny said and laughed. "She's a fucking bitch. Excuse my French."

"She must be okay, seeing she put the guest list together."

Cecily fessed up before Winter had a chance to call her on it. "We weren't on the list. I know Candy's cousin, Maggie. She told us we could come. You can ask her."

"Anything you can tell me about the other people in your photos?"

"I assume you know about Candy," said Cecily. "I don't know her very well, just a little through Maggie." Cecily waved at the room. "We're not exactly in the same circle. Maggie is okay, though. I recognized Kendall DeVaughn. I've seen him on television."

"Anyone else with Coleman?"

"There was *always* someone with him," said Ginny. "Took us *forever* to get him for a picture."

Cecily said, "He was talking to a lot of people, including Candy. And Miranda was all over him."

"What do you mean?"

"Exactly what I said." Cecily pointed to Miranda on the phone. "She wasn't too happy about us having our picture taken with Outta Here. Probably jealous."

"She have any reason to be?" asked Winter.

Cecily made a face. "Jeez, we just met him."

Miranda Dell had been very vague on her relationship with Coleman. Winter would have to follow up with that. "Notice anyone who didn't seem like they should be there? Coleman have words with any of the guests?"

"We were just having fun," said Ginny. "The party was fine until the screaming started."

"Do you know Gerry Hennig?"

"I don't recognize the name," said Cecily.

Ginny shook her head. "Is he the other guy who died?"

Winter wasn't sure if the next of kin had been notified, so he said, "I'm going to give you my number. If you can think of anything that might help us, give me a call, or ask for one of the other detectives."

As he was leaving Cecily called out, "You're not going to make us take down our photos, are you?"

*   *   *

RICK SINGLETON LIVED in an old brick industrial building that had been converted to apartments. Crosse was already with Singleton when Winter arrived, both of them sitting on mismatched chairs at a metal topped table. A red guitar was propped on a stand next to two small amplifiers. The walls were filled with posters of rock bands and cheaply framed album covers.

"Rick, you remember Detective Winter?" asked Crosse. To Winter, she said, "Rick just gave me the contact info for Gerry Hennig's parents."

"I should call them," said Rick.

"I'll do that," said Crosse gently. "You can talk to them after, I'm sure it will help hearing a familiar voice."

Winter, like all cops, dreaded having to do a next of kin notification. If he had to choose between that and getting shot he'd have to weigh it for a while.

"They are great people," said Singleton. "They let us practice at their house when we had the band." Singleton ran his finger along the edge of the table. "They'll probably blame me for what happened to Gerry. Since I invited him to the party, I mean."

Crosse said, "If you can help us with more information on Gerry, we won't have to bother them with as many questions."

"Sure. But like I told you, Gerry and I had kind of drifted apart."

"You have a falling out with Gerry?" asked Crosse.

"Nothing like that. I just wanted to stay with the music, it's all I ever wanted to do. Gerry got the math bug, got a scholarship to MIT. It wasn't like we were making a mint doing music, even though we were getting steady gigs."

"You know who he had kept in touch with? Your band mates, maybe?" asked Crosse.

"I think he talked to Doyle—the drummer—now and then."

"Do you know any of his friends at MIT?" asked Winter.

"Not a one. I haven't seen Gerry in the flesh since he's been there. On campus, I mean. After Gerry left the band we did a gig just outside the city, and he came to listen. I tried to get him up on stage to do a song or two, but he said he had to split to study." Rick got a faraway look in his eye. "The band wasn't the same without him. We broke up after that night. We didn't even talk about it, we all knew."

"Did he carry a lot of money? Anyone he had problems with?"

"Gerry was always on the quiet side, I don't remember him ever having a fight. His family did okay, but I wouldn't say they were rolling in it. Nicer house than I grew up in, but not a mansion, you know? They bought him a car for high school graduation, a Honda. He wasn't flashy, he wasn't into clothes or anything. He did have a nice watch, a Rolex, which his father gave him. I think he got it when he retired from the bank, and he couldn't wear it, some kind of allergy. Gerry liked the retro analog look and wore it all the time."

Winter didn't remember seeing a watch on Hennig's wrist. "You said you invited Gerry to the party because you wanted to get a band back together?"

"Not specifically. I didn't think I could talk him into leaving math. Although he seemed so crushed with the studying I would have been really happy if he wanted to do a little music."

"So it was mostly to reconnect?"

"He was just finishing his big tests, I thought it would help him blow off some steam. And yeah, we could finally catch up."

"Who might have wanted to hurt him?" asked Winter.

"I can't even imagine how anyone at the party would even *know* him," said Rick. "I guess anything is possible, though. Gerry did grow up in Marburg, there might have been some guest who knew him."

"You were pretty close?" asked Winter.

"Back in high school, and then a little after."

Winter was wondering how Hennig might know someone from Marburg that Singleton didn't, if they had been so close. Why had Singleton brought that up? "You see anyone at the party you recognized other than Candy and Miranda?"

"I've seen Kendall DeVaughn a few times at the studio. A few guests I recognized from pictures on the internet. No one I had met before that I can think of."

"Was Dwayne Coleman one of the people you recognized?" asked Winter.

"I didn't, actually. But I overheard his name mentioned—he was drawing a little crowd—and I've heard his music."

After another half hour it was clear that Singleton was running out of steam. Crosse told him she'd let him know as soon as she contacted Hennig's parents.

"I still can't believe it," said Singleton. "Gerry grows up here, moves to Boston where there's so much more crime, comes back and gets beaten and killed at a party at the Carter house, of all places. Who could have imagined that would ever happen?"

CHAPTER 28

In HIS TRUCK, Winter pulled out the station directory and used his cell to call Owens.

"I talked to those women at the U," said Winter. "They have a pretty good story for being there without an invite. Might want to check it, but it sounds okay."

"Anything else?"

"They suggested Miranda Dell was closer to Dwayne Coleman than she let on."

"Closer as in how?"

"*All over him* was the term they used."

Owens said, "Some people we've been talking to in the follow-ups showed us their photos from the party. Got pics of Miranda Dell close to Coleman."

"How close?"

"All over him pretty much covers it."

"Huh," said Winter.

"Let's go talk to her."

OWENS WAS OUTSIDE Miranda Dell's apartment building when Winter arrived, having run through the Dunkin drive-thru, which he'd not done earlier, because his route from the station to the U to Singleton's had not taken him past one. It was about a million to one shot that you could drive that many miles in New England without hitting a Dunkin Donuts.

Owens ground out his cigarette as Winter drove up. "Her car is in the lot," he said. "The tags come back pretty clean, a few missed inspections."

"How do you want to handle this?" asked Winter.

"You talked to her last, be my guest."

Miranda Dell came to the door wearing a tight black sweatshirt and matching sweatpants. She looked decidedly hung over.

She rolled her eyes. "I'm sick, come back tomorrow."

"Only take a few minutes," said Winter. "This is Detective Owens. I don't think you met."

"I wouldn't know," she said. "I've never talked to so many cops in my life."

"There's a lot more of them at the station," said Owens. "In case you'd rather do this there."

Dell made a show of sighing and walked back into the apartment.

With any other interview, Winter would have started with a little small talk. Today he was a little pissed about her not being truthful with him about Dwayne Coleman. "You told me you didn't know Outta Here."

"That's right."

"We've heard you seemed pretty friendly with him."

Miranda huffed. "Were you talking to that bitch Cecily? That woman would hook up with a homeless person if she thought it would get her pictures more likes."

"I didn't talk to any Cecily," said Owens. "But I've seen a whole bunch of photos with you and Mr. Coleman."

"So what? I'm probably in photos with lots of guests."

Owens held up his phone. "You get this close to the other guests? Maybe the music was loud, you had to put your talk in his ear?"

"I told you the truth, I just met him that night."

"You get that friendly with all the guys you—"

"I'm Candy's assistant. Part of my job is making her guests feel welcome."

Winter shifted gears. "Do you know when Mr. Coleman arrived at the party?"

"I didn't see him walk in, if that's what you are asking. I was pretty busy."

"Was he with anyone? Spend more time with any particular guests?"

"He was making the rounds, just like everyone else. Getting his picture taken. Which is why you got shots with me in them. Bet you will find photos of him with a whole bunch of people. Candy. That bitch Cecily."

"He friends with Candy?"

"I don't think they've ever met. Just making a point. You going to accuse her of being too friendly too? Or just us poor folk?"

"We're going to talk to everyone," said Winter. He looked around the apartment. "You look like you're doing okay."

"I'm worth what I get paid."

"Candy treats you pretty good?"

"I guess."

"Then help us out. The sooner we get this cleared up, the better it will be for her."

"For the family, you mean."

"Everybody."

"I told you, I don't know anything."

"Let's just take it from the beginning," said Owens. "When did you get to the party?"

"I was there most of the day organizing. Making calls, see who was coming, last minute changes."

"What was Mr. Coleman doing when you first noticed him?" asked Winter.

"He was next to this black guy, I don't know if they were together or not. I lost track of him, and when I turned around Outta Here was right near me. He asked me about the house—everyone does—so I pointed out a few things. I teased him a little, saying I hadn't seen his name on the guest list—"

"I thought you said you didn't know him?" said Winter.

"Jeez, he's pretty recognizable. People recognize Candy all the time, and she's never been on the cover of a music magazine."

"Anything else you talk about?" asked Owens. "Or maybe whisper in his ear?"

Miranda smirked, then said, "As a matter of fact, he asked me about Rick Singleton. So instead of hassling me, why don't you go see if you can find any photos of Rick with Outta Here? Or better yet, go bother him and leave me alone?"

*   *   *

ON THE WAY OUT, Winter turned and said, "The black man you saw with Mr. Coleman. You didn't recognize him as a guest?"

"No. Could have been another rapper DeVaughn invited."

"See him with any other guests?" asked Owens.

"Not really. I didn't see him around for long. He might have been just leaving for all I know."

"What did he look like?"

"Kind of skinny. He was wearing a baseball cap on backwards. I didn't get a good look, but he might have had a tat on his forehead, right in that space above the strap? Dark red leather jacket. That's all I remember, I was focused more on Outta Here."

From what he had heard, Winter believed her about that.

OUTSIDE, Owens asked, "What do you think?"

"She definitely knew Coleman more than she let on to me. Could be nothing, just in shock, or not wanting to sound like she was all over a guy who winds up dead. Plus I'm pretty sure she was pretty high that night."

"Could be nothing," agreed Owens.

"I'll ask Cindy to dig deeper into Rick Singleton and also see if she can find photos of the guy with the backward baseball cap." Winter caught Owens up on the interview he and Crosse had done with Singleton. "Coleman asking about Singleton—if we can believe Miranda—would mean Singleton wasn't being very truthful about knowing Coleman either."

"Seems everyone knew this rapper except me," said Owens.

"I never heard of him. I don't listen to rap."

"Neither do I," said Owens. "I just don't get it."

"You're too old."

"Speak for yourself," said Owens.

WINTER GOT CINDY on the phone after Owens headed off for more guest interviews. "I need you to bump Rick Singleton and Miranda Dell up on the background checks. We're getting some inconsistencies in the stories. I want to know more before I talk to either one of them again."

"Anything in particular?"

"Links to Dwayne Coleman, to start. Maybe through Singleton's days in his band. See if you can find any photos of Coleman with Singleton at the party. And Coleman with another guy." Winter gave Cindy the description of the skinny black male.

"I've already started attaching names to every guest in a photo we have with Coleman. Still can't find a single photo of Hennig. Also, we've run checks for priors on all the guests who were on the list, as well as the others we've identified who showed up. It was a clean group. I mean, really clean. I bet you'd find more priors on the kids at a birthday party moon bounce. A few DUI's, a few pot possessions. The only one who sticks out is Jacque LaChance."

"Singleton?"

"The only time his name shows up at all is in a dispute with a bar owner over payment to his band. This was seven years ago. Just a big argument, no arrests."

"How about Coleman or Gerry Hennig?"

"Hennig doesn't even have a speeding ticket. Coleman has tickets, but they're five years old. Maybe he rides around in limos."

"We should check that," said Winter. "See how he got to the party."

"O'Dowd already did. Coleman used a limo service out of Boston—he's used them before. The driver picked him up at Logan, dropped him off. Went to get a bite to eat, hanging around Marburg to pick up Coleman. Never got a call, figured Coleman got a ride or was staying over. Said it wasn't the first time Coleman had done that."

Maybe planning on hooking up, thought Winter, glancing back at Miranda Dell's apartment.

"Any other record on Coleman?"

"Two domestic incidents, both old. The first, a woman—this was in Boston—said he punched her. He said, she said, and then she changed her story. Charges dismissed. The second, down in Miami, a guest in a hotel who recognized Coleman called in a report he saw Coleman hitting a woman in a restaurant. He—and the woman—denied everything."

"Coleman likes to slap the ladies around," said Winter.

"This will all be in the briefing tomorrow morning," said Cindy. "You *are* coming to the briefing, aren't you?"

"Yeah, yeah. But since I have you on the phone—are you running priors on the staff?"

"Yes, and you can hear about them at the briefing tomorrow. Which I'll never get ready for, if you keep making me give you the briefing now."

WINTER WORKED THROUGH his list of guest interviews. One couple was convinced the murders were committed by a bartender who disappeared for nearly an hour early on. Winter made a note but suspected the couple were pissed because they didn't like the way he made their drinks, which they mentioned not once but twice.

Another stop brought him to a woman who was clearly drunk in the middle of the afternoon. Her apartment smelled of cigarettes and she smelled of alcohol. She kept insisting that Winter stay for dinner.

Two hours and six interviews later Winter began to wonder if these people had been at the same party, their recollections ranging wildly. Not a single guest knew Coleman or Hennig. So far no one stood out; they all had good reasons for being at the party or for why they had left early. Only one guest had actually heard screaming just as he was leaving. He assumed it might have been the music, which all sounded like a bunch of screaming to him anyway.

Half the people on Winter's list were not home. This was going to take forever.

CHAPTER 29

RICK HELD HIS MOTHER upright with one hand, bending awkwardly to flush the toilet with the other. He tried not to think about the unnaturally green bile she had just vomited up.

"I'm sorry, Ricky," she said, the flush of embarrassment the only color in her cheeks.

"Don't worry about it, Ma. Just hold on to the sink." Rick did his best to get her cleaned up, cringing as she grimaced when he gently swiped her mouth. Her skin had become paper thin and sensitive. "There. You need to use the bathroom?"

"Not now. I'll just lie down."

Rick helped her back to the living room. This was their third trip during the night; it was after three in the morning. Each time his mother felt lighter as he half carried her and lifted her legs into the rented hospital bed.

"Anything I can get you, Ma?"

"Just leave that little tray close by, you should get some sleep."

Rick could barely stand he was so tired, but the thought of his mother puking into a metal tray on her lap was not an image he could live with. "I'll stay here. Just let me know if you have to get up."

Rick waited until he was sure she wasn't going to lose it again before plopping into the lounge chair.

He was holding things together, just barely. The cops sounded a little suspicious, but that was likely their way. He thought he had done okay with his story about why he had invited Gerry to the party. Doc's name hadn't come up. If the cops knew about Doc, they would have asked about him. At least he thought so.

Now he just needed to figure out how to get some cash to afford a night nurse. He couldn't keep showing up for work late because he was up half the night taking care of his mom.

An excited announcer with an Australian accent was going on about non-stick frying pans, jolting Rick upright. Groggily he followed the sound of the voice to the television, which was on, although his mother still looked asleep. Light streamed in through the window.

Sherry, the nurse, was puttering around the room. Rick's mouth tasted like crap. "You come in early?"

"I come in on time, just like every morning. Been here an hour."

"An hour? Shit, what time is it?"

"It's an hour after I get here," said Sherry. "And don't be using foul language around your ma."

Rick bit off another curse and ran for the bathroom. He was late for work again.

RICK WAS IN such a hurry he forgot about the pothole in the studio parking lot, his car jolting so hard he hit his head on the roof. Worse, Larry's car was already in the lot. A very full lot. Rick had totally forgot about the commercial voiceover session he was supposed to handle.

Inside, he didn't even get a chance to see what was what when Liz, in her prissy voice, said, "Larry wants to see you. *Right away.*"

Larry, on the phone, pointed to the chair in front of his desk. Into the phone Larry said, "I don't see how any of my equipment could end up in a pawnshop in Boston. Maybe it's just a mix-up." Larry listened, his eyes narrowing, settling on Rick.

Rick's formulations of an excuse for being late took a wide detour at the word *pawnshop*. He shifted to praying Larry hadn't noticed his panic.

"I'll look into it and get back to you." Larry hung up.

Rick, fearing being late was the least of his problems, tried anyway. "My ma . . ."

Larry ignored him. "That was a very interesting call. Seems the Boston police arrested some guy who had been robbing pawnshops. Care to guess what they found in his garage? No? How about a bunch of amps? *My* amps."

"I'm not sure I'm following, Larry."

"Seems pretty straightforward to me. Some of my equipment ended up in a pawnshop in Boston, and then got stolen."

"I heard you say it might be a mix-up?"

"Could be. Maybe you can help me straighten this up. Let's me and you go downstairs and see if anything is missing."

"Man, I wouldn't be able to tell."

"I'm sitting here thinking, who would pawn my equipment? I didn't do it. I know it isn't Gus, if he needs a few bucks he can just ask me. Liz wouldn't know what was worth pawning."

Rick said, "Maybe one of the musicians in here recording? The Crash Heave's were a little—"

"Save it," said Larry. "It had to be you."

"Larry, I swear—"

Larry jabbed a finger at Rick across the desk. "Don't. Just don't."

Rick didn't have the energy. "My ma is really sick. I had to hire a nurse."

"I know that. It's the only reason I didn't tell the cops about you. I feel bad for you, son, I really do. But you've been late every day, you've been hitting the white powder, and don't think I don't know you've been screwing up on the board. I got to cut you loose."

"What? You can't—" Rick couldn't think fast enough.

"Sorry kid. I always liked you, gave you all the breaks I could. But we got nothing on the schedule after Candy, and it's not like we're ever going to get back to the old days. I wouldn't be able to afford you anyway, so it was bound to happen sooner or later."

Rick wasn't too proud to beg. "Larry, please, I need this job, I *got* to work. I'll make it up to you, I'll do anything."

Larry pointed to the phone. "It looks like you already did. Now beat it before I change my mind and call the cops back."

CHAPTER 30

W INTER LEANED ON the fender of his truck in the studio parking lot as Ryder rolled in, driving one of the plain white detective cars any crook would recognize as a cop car from a mile away. Ryder came over but didn't lean, maybe thinking it would dirty his suit. The sky was as gray as the wall of the building.

"You weren't at the morning briefing," said Ryder.

"I meant to be. I forgot I had to do my weekly run to work the street. Nothing on what happened at the Carter house, although I picked up a little gossip on those car hijacks." Winter had a wide net of informants, street people, minor league criminals, prostitutes, regular citizens with good eyes in bad neighborhoods. Twice a week, Monday on the south side, Friday on the north, Winter would cruise through.

"Could have sent a uniform," said Ryder.

"They won't talk to anyone but me. Catch me up, will you?"

"Waste of time," said Ryder. "We got nothing from the witnesses. Probably a hundred interviews done, no one saw a thing. The usual. Or they saw a lot, just nothing useful. Crime scene couldn't find Gerry Hennig's cell phone. They found Coleman's in the pool. Waiting on cell phone records. The call list could tie some of these people together."

"Something's not right. We're getting mixed messages from Miranda Dell and Singleton. Cindy say anything about photos of Coleman with Singleton?"

"She found one, but they aren't really close together. Coleman is in a little group, Singleton is on the other side, you can't tell whether he can even hear Coleman."

"I heard Coleman had a little history?"

"Not much, the two semi domestics. However Hennig ties to Coleman, we haven't found it yet."

"Assuming there *is* a tie."

"Got to be a tie either between Hennig and Coleman, or between whoever did the killings and them. There was a lot of talk this morning about drugs. One of them selling, or the dealer was there."

"No drugs on Hennig, though."

"No, and if there were any on Coleman, they were lost in the pool. No paraphernalia in his pockets. Me and Crosse are going to drive to Boston this afternoon, do a search on Gerry Hennig's apartment with the Cambridge PD, then look at Gerry's office on campus with the MIT police. Paperwork is taking a little time."

"Coleman's cell phone?"

"The salt water trashed it. You really should come to the briefings. Be a lot faster."

ON THE WAY into the studio, Winter remembered what he needed from the briefing. "Did O'Dowd say anything about the limo driver?"

"What limo driver?"

"Hold on." Winter took out his phone, then realized he didn't have O'Dowd's number programmed in. In fact, other than the dispatcher, Cindy, Brooker, and his daughter, he didn't have any numbers programmed in. "You got O'Dowd's number?"

Ryder scrolled through his phone and held it up. Winter figured he might as well store O'Dowd's number, but couldn't remember how. Ryder said, "Here, I'll have my twenty before you figure out how to use your phone." He hit call and handed his phone to Winter.

O'Dowd said, "Ryder?"

"No, it's Winter. Listen, you talked to that limo driver who picked up Dwayne Coleman at the airport, right? Did you ask him if he had another passenger?"

"He didn't mention another passenger."

"Miranda Dell said she saw Coleman at the party with a black male. I don't think he's been identified as a guest yet?" Winter raised an eyebrow at Ryder, who shook his head. "Red leather jacket, backwards baseball cap, maybe ink on his forehead. Could be he got picked up by the limo driver with Coleman."

"You want the limo driver's number, or you want me to call?"

Winter now had two phones in his hands and if he tried to punch in a new number he'd screw it up. "You do it."

Winter handed Ryder back his phone. "I hate these things."

THE STUDIO door opened. Rick Singleton, carrying an overfilled brown box, slowly backed out.

"We need to talk," said Winter.

Singleton put the box in the trunk of a Kia, leaving it open. "I got one more load, but it can wait."

Winter said, "Looks like you knew Dwayne Coleman better than you let on. We got some photos . . ." Winter let it hang, and sure enough, a quick flash of worry ran across Singleton's features.

"I don't know what you saw, but I swear I just met him that night."

"You did talk to him, right?" asked Ryder.

"I told you, about music."

"What specifically?"

"The usual. What he was working on, what I was doing. Music contracts."

"Music contracts?"

"You know, how the artists and songwriters get paid, or usually get screwed, by the labels. You go to any party where there are music people, you hear the same stuff."

"Dwayne getting screwed by his label?" asked Winter.

"He didn't say, we weren't talking details."

"How about you? You having a contract problem?"

"I don't even *have* a contract with a label," said Rick.

Winter had long ago learned that when he got a very specific answer to a general question, someone was being extra careful. "You have a contract with anyone else?"

Singleton said, "Candy is thinking of using some of my songs—one of them, at least—on her album. Nothing is definite, we don't have paperwork. So, yeah, there will be a contract at some point, if she goes ahead. I don't see it as being a problem, I'm not going to ask for anything other than the standard royalty."

"We'll ask her," said Ryder.

"Go easy. Please. This could be my big break. She's got enough to deal with as it is, and with me being the one who invited Gerry . . ."

"She upset with you?" asked Ryder.

"If she is, I don't know about it. I'm going to lie low for a while. I got my own problems to deal with. I'm trying to help Gerry's parents with the funeral arrangements."

Winter felt a little sorry for the kid, but still had a sense he wasn't getting the whole story. Winter didn't know anything about music, contracts, royalties. He did know about drugs. "You see a lot of drugs at the party that night?"

Singleton looked away. "I don't want to get anyone in trouble. Especially Candy."

"Candy involved with drugs?" asked Winter.

Singleton laughed. "I doubt it. She doesn't even allow cigarette smoking in the studio."

"Besides Candy?" pressed Winter.

"Might have been a few people doing some lines," Singleton admitted. "Discreetly."

"Miranda Dell one of them?"

Singleton said, "Please don't make me go there. I can't get between Miranda and Candy."

"So, yes is what you are saying."

"I'm not saying anything."

"We're testing that powder you had on your jacket," Winter reminded him.

"I told you, that was from before. In the field, after I parked my car. I didn't think I spilled any, it's not like I'm rolling in money to waste the little blow I use now and then. It might not even have been mine, for all I know I rubbed up against someone at the party."

"Like Miranda," said Ryder. "Maybe she gave you the coke?"

"No, no, no," said Singleton. "What, you think I'm going to screw up my one big chance with Candy by doing drugs with Miranda at the Carter house?"

"Miranda seemed pretty close to Dwayne Coleman at the party," said Winter.

"I saw them together. But like I said, I didn't know Dwayne. What Miranda did with him is her business."

Another answer to an unasked question. Winter said, "Miranda and Dwayne have a thing going on?"

"I only meant that if Miranda was hanging out with Dwayne it had nothing to do with me."

As Winter was trying to figure out another way of angling in on Singleton, his eyes dropped to the box in the trunk of the Kia. On top was a photo of Singleton with Gerry Hennig and three other guys. "This your band?"

"A long time ago."

The only time Winter had ever seen anyone with a box of photos walking out of their place of employment was when they got fired. "You packing up your stuff?"

"Yeah. I need time to take care of my mother. She has cancer."

"Your boss fired you for that?"

"Let's just say we're both in a tough situation. I need to take care of my mother and can't always be here, so Larry had to let me go." Rick looked up from the photo. "Now can I finish getting my stuff?"

WINTER AND RYDER let Singleton go back for his other boxes and watched him ride off.

"You believe that story?" asked Ryder. "I bet he got fired over drugs. Candy is a client here. She doesn't like drugs, and we know Rick was snorting at the party. Kid probably has a drug problem, the boss doesn't want to lose Candy over it."

"Let's go find out," said Winter.

Inside, they found Larry in his office, staring at a poster of Led Zeppelin on the wall. Both the poster and Larry were showing their age.

Winter and Ryder introduced themselves, and Larry said, "This about my equipment?"

"What equipment?"

"Had some missing stuff turn up in Boston."

"No," said Winter. "We want to talk to you about Rick Singleton."

Larry looked momentarily confused, then said, "Yeah?"

"We're investigating the deaths at Candy Carter's house. You hear about those?"

"Who hasn't?"

"Did you know that Rick was there?"

Larry leaned back in his chair. "None of my business. Candy records here, that's all I know of her."

Ryder said, "Any problems between Candy and Rick at the studio?"

"She never said a word to me about a problem." Larry's eyes narrowed. "She tell you there's a problem with the studio?"

Ryder said, "That's between you and her. We're interested in Rick."

"Rick have something to do with what happened out there?"

"Just following up on all the guests," said Winter. "Rick knew one of the deceased. Gerry Hennig. You know him?"

"I heard Rick mention a guy named Gerry a few times, said I would have enjoyed hearing him play."

"How about Dwayne Coleman?"

"Nope."

"He's a rap musician," said Ryder. "Goes by the name Outta Here."

"Rap and musician is a contradiction in terms." Larry pointed to the Zeppelin poster. "*Those* are musicians."

Winter said, "We ran into Rick in the parking lot. Says you fired him."

Larry shrugged. "Had to. Business is slow."

"You know his mother is sick."

"Yeah, life sucks for us all. I can't do anything about his situation."

"No one saying you should," said Winter. "So no problems with Rick otherwise?"

Larry's fingers tapped out a thoughtful beat on his blotter. "He's late a lot. No such thing as a perfect employee. Feel sorry about his mother, but not much more I can do besides what I already have."

BACK IN THE PARKING LOT, Winter asked Ryder, "What do you think?"

"I'd hate to be working for him."

"Could just be he doesn't want Singleton to be badmouthing the studio and screw up his business with Candy."

Ryder said, "Or it could be he fired Singleton because he was pushing drugs around, and Candy didn't like it. Larry just didn't want to admit to us there were drugs at the studio."

"Then why'd she let Singleton come to the party?"

Ryder said, "Good question."

"Let's go ask her."

"Good luck with that, her father has her bottled up." Ryder got in his car. "You'd have known that if you came to the briefing."

CHAPTER 31

W INTER EXPECTED to get the runaround at the Carter house, but an older rather spry woman ushered him in. Wearing a light blue suit and low heels, she looked like she was on the way to a meeting of the local chamber of commerce.

In a formal British accent she introduced herself as Polly Cooke, the estate manager, and offered Winter coffee or tea.

Winter was tempted, wondering what kind of coffee they had. "Perhaps later. I'm here to see Candy, but I want to talk to you too."

"Miss Candy is with Mr. DeVaughn in the studio," she said. "I normally would not interrupt her, but for the police I'm sure it will not be a problem. You can wait in the sitting room."

Winter didn't want to give Candy a chance to brush him off, so he said, "I've never seen a home recording studio. Maybe I could just follow you?"

Cooke hesitated slightly, but as Winter hoped, bowed to both his official status and his politeness. He didn't think Ryder had taken the same approach.

"Of course."

She led Winter into a wing of the house, stopping in front of a closed door. "The light isn't on, so Miss Candy isn't recording." Cooke knocked before opening the door. Music was playing, even though Winter hadn't heard a thing in the hall.

"Miss Candy, I have a Detective Winter from the Marburg Police to see you?" Cooke held the door open for Winter.

The room was larger than Winter expected, even given the size of the house. Candy sat on the edge of a stool, a set of headphones around her neck. She was wearing bright pink sweatpants that looked more fashion-able than athletic, an oversized plain white tee shirt, and sneakers. Kendall DeVaughn was in a utilitarian chair in front of a mixing board, wearing jeans and pointy toed boots. The rest of the room was filled with neatly arrayed musical equipment.

"I wanted to fill you in on where we are," said Winter.

Candy said, "My father already talked to your captain this morning. From what I hear, you haven't learned much."

"It's early," said Winter. "That's not an excuse, it's just how things go. It would really help if you can fill in a few gaps."

DeVaughn, whose tan was definitely not locally produced, said, "Candy, maybe you'd better check with your father."

"Why?" asked Candy, pulling off the headphones. "Besides, we need a break, we're not getting anywhere."

Winter got the definite sense that DeVaughn wanted to argue the point, so he rushed in, starting easy. "The way we investigate crimes is to work backward from the victim. Who they knew best, who they spoke to last. Not only here at the party, but before they arrived."

"I told you I'd just met Outta Here that night."

"Who invited him?"

"I did, indirectly," said DeVaughn. "Terrence Jackson—Dwayne's producer—and I have worked together. He's got a couple of hot artists, and they get good publicity. Terrence and I have done cross promotion in the past. So I told him to invite whoever he thought would be good."

"Did either of you see Mr. Coleman talking to anyone in particular, maybe having an argument?"

"Not at all," said Candy. "But I was moving around."

"I saw him but didn't have a chance to talk to him," said DeVaughn.

"Gerry Hennig got invited through Rick Singleton. How long have you known Rick?"

"Not long, just since I started recording at the studio."

"He mentioned something about you using his music?"

Candy glanced at DeVaughn. "We haven't decided the final tracks, that's what we were just working on. Rick's got a song we think we can use."

"Is that how you came to know him? Through the song?"

"No, he was working the board at the studio. He let me hear his music."

"So that's your only connection to him?" Winter was working up to the question about drugs.

"That's it. I played Rick's song for Kendall, and he agreed it would be a good fit for the album. We will need to change it up, it wasn't written for me originally."

"Rick have a problem with that? You changing his music?"

"Not at all. In fact, he made a few suggestions for how to do it."

Candy hadn't offered up even a hint of Rick giving her more than just music, so Winter pivoted. "I heard about royalties? How does that work?"

DeVaughn said, "There's a simple explanation and a complicated explanation. The simple one is that just about everyone who works on a released song could get a cut. That includes the songwriter, the label releasing the song, the singers and musicians, the producer, the distributor, the retailer."

"You said *could* get a cut," said Winter.

"That's where it gets complicated. All those relationships are dictated by contracts. Studio musicians are usually paid a flat fee and get no royalties at all. The artist may have a tiered deal with the label where they only get royalties after expenses. Each deal is unique, not only for the album, but sometimes for the individual song. And there are separate royalty streams for radio play, streaming, mp3 sales, CD sales, international."

"How much money are we talking here?"

"The mechanical royalty—the amount paid out for CD and mp3 sales—is about nine cents per sale. That gets split between the songwriter and the publisher."

"Is that a lot? It doesn't sound like much."

"That's like asking how big is big," said DeVaughn. "Sell enough, and there's money to be made, otherwise no one would be doing it and investing in it. There's also money in using songs in commercials and movies."

"But for one song, are we talking thousands of dollars?"

DeVaughn laughed. "Many many thousands. If it's a hit, of course."

"It's not all about the money," said Candy.

"Not for you," said DeVaughn. "But if no one was in it for the money, the whole system would collapse. I'm not talking about the artists, but the producers, the labels, the streaming companies."

"You said the songwriter splits the royalties," said Winter, trying to follow. "What about the singer?"

"They get more if they write the song," explained DeVaughn. "It's a little more complicated, but that's the gist of it."

"So Rick would make some money if you use his song?"

"If it becomes a hit or the album sells really well," said DeVaughn.

"You think it has potential?"

Candy and DeVaughn exchanged looks. "This is Candy's first real major release," said DeVaughn. "New artists are not a sure thing. Candy is good, I'm good, the material is good, we've got a better than average marketing budget, but nothing is guaranteed."

Candy said, "Oh, come on, Kendall. Tell him the truth." To Winter she said, "Rick's song might be the best thing I have for the album."

"But don't tell Rick that," said DeVaughn quickly. "We haven't got a contract yet."

"You have any sense he's going to ask for a special deal?"

"Just the opposite," said Candy. "We didn't go into details, but he specifically said he only wanted standard royalties."

"He's looking for a break," said DeVaughn. "We could probably get him to do it for nothing. New songwriters will sometimes exchange the rights just to get their name listed as a songwriter on a successful album. To get exposure."

"You mentioned Rick didn't write this song just for you?"

Candy said, "He wrote it years ago. Rick didn't pretend he had written it for me, if that's what you are asking."

"No, I was thinking . . ." A line of connection began to form in Winter's head. "Did Rick mention where those songs came from?"

"A band he used to be with." Candy pointed her finger. "He did say something about a co-writer for the song."

"You didn't tell me that," said DeVaughn.

"I didn't think it was a big deal. Neither did Rick. He said the co-writer would be no problem, he's not in the music business any more. I told him to get it in writing, just in case."

"Who was the co-writer?" asked Winter.

"I don't know his name. Some guy in Rick's band."

Winter had an inkling. Rick had been in a band with Gerry Hennig, and he had invited Gerry to the party. Just to catch up, said Rick. Maybe it had been about this song Candy wanted to use. If there was big money to be made from the songwriting royalties . . . "How would it work with a co-writer?" Winter asked.

DeVaughn said, "The co-writers would both have to agree to the song being used. The co-writer could sign off or sell his rights for a flat fee instead of royalties. Happens all the time."

"So you wouldn't have used Rick's song without that agreement?"

"Not a chance," said DeVaughn, staring at Candy. "Rick would have to stipulate in his agreement that he was the sole copyright holder and held the rights. If he wasn't truthful about that, we could end up in a lawsuit."

"I don't think Rick was trying to hide the fact he had a co-writer," said Candy. "He was the one who brought it up. Why are you so interested in the song?"

Rick hadn't mentioned any of this to Winter. It might be nothing, but it was another potential piece of the puzzle, especially since money was involved. "No particular reason. Just looking for connections." He paused. "I have to say, I'm a little surprised you are back working so soon, with what happened and all."

"It's not that I don't feel badly about those two men," said Candy. "Really. But what am I going to do? Sit around and cry? I've been working on my music for *years*." She pulled at the hem of her tee shirt. "Plus, my father is really upset, and while I don't blame him, I don't want him to pull the plug on me. If he sees me moping around he certainly will. He might anyway—our name is going to get dragged through the mud. I just got to keep going."

Winter waited to see if she had more to add, but she had run out of steam. "I have to ask about something else. We've been hearing about drugs at the party."

"Candy," cautioned DeVaughn. "This is where you really should talk to your father."

Candy looked like she just might do it this time, so Winter said, "Look, I'm not trying to jam you up, you got enough bad publicity already. I'm just looking for a reason why these two men ended up dead. Unless you supplied the drugs, and that's what led to their deaths."

Candy said, "Let me make this very clear. I did *not* supply any drugs. I don't use drugs or condone their use. *Ever*." She'd come up off the stool and was half in Winter's face.

Winter didn't budge. "I sense a *but* there."

"What part of what I said suggested a *but*?"

Winter gave her his best ambiguous smile. "I've been doing this a long time."

Maybe Candy's stare worked on her staff, but Winter had seen far worse, and had heard far more adamant denials. He waited her out.

"You take drugs?" she asked.

"Not me we're talking about. But no."

"You ever thrown a party where other people might be snorting lines in a closet?"

Winter had never thrown a party in his life, even his ex-wife wasn't a party type. "No, but I take your point."

"There are drugs in the music business, just like a lot of other businesses," said Candy. "My friends know how I feel about drugs."

"But there were people at the party you didn't know," pressed Winter.

"That's right. Could someone have snuck off and popped a few pills or do some coke? Sure, we weren't policing. But I assure you, no one was doing anything out in the open. I don't even drink alcohol, but I know half the people wouldn't show up if you didn't serve it."

Winter turned to DeVaughn. "What about you?"

Very carefully, DeVaughn said, "Candy's party, Candy's rules."

Candy was still hot. "I'm telling you, what happened to those two men had nothing to do with me."

Maybe or maybe not, thought Winter. Candy might be right in the middle of it, although Winter couldn't quite see how, and she hadn't lawyered up.

Or she could be in the middle of it and not even know.

Winter said, "I'm not accusing you of anything. It's just that in a beating death, if it's not personal, it's often about drugs, or by someone drugged up. Did you see anyone acting strange? I don't mean a little tipsy, but really wired?"

"No one," said Candy.

"Me neither," agreed DeVaughn. "As these music promotion parties go this was really on the extremely low key and subdued side."

Not for Gerry Hennig and Dwayne Coleman, thought Winter.

WINTER THANKED them and said he'd let himself out. In the hall he turned away from the direction he'd come, wandering through the rooms, getting a feel for the house. It was huge, doors everywhere, leading to parlors, dens, sitting rooms, an office. Dozens of people could have split off from the party to do whatever. The walls were thick, the draperies and rugs plush, dampening Winter's footsteps. No wonder no one had heard or seen Hennig getting beaten up.

Winter passed through an old butler's pantry with a dumbwaiter and into the gleaming kitchen. Two women who looked related were chatting away in a language that reminded Winter of Spanish but might not have been.

They stopped talking but kept chopping vegetables. Winter was about to ask them about the party when Polly Cooke entered the kitchen from the other side.

"Found you," said Winter. "Mind if I ask you some questions?"

"We can go to the front sitting room."

"Here is good," said Winter. "I want to show you all a photo." He pulled out his tablet, flicking through the pictures. It was the one thing he had learned to do pretty well with it. He pulled up Coleman. "Do you recognize this man? He was a guest at the party."

"No," said Cooke. "But I wasn't out front much."

The other two women shook their heads. Winter flicked to Gerry Hennig. "Him? Maybe upstairs?"

The two cooks spoke between themselves, sounding to Winter like a bit of a disagreement, with the older woman shaking her head.

Cooke said, "Carlina, if you have something to say, please tell the detective."

The younger of the two, with light bronze skin, almond eyes, and long straight hair looked at the older woman, who nodded. Carlina said, "I was talking to a boy—," another glance at the older woman, "—one of the caterers, and he told me he saw a white man going up the back steps." She pointed behind Winter.

"He told you this that night?"

Another glance at the older woman, who now appeared very interested in Winter's question. "No, a few days later," admitted Carlina, sheepishly. "My mother doesn't approve of me talking to the boys."

To the mother Winter said, "I have a daughter too. She's older than Carlina and I still don't like her talking to boys. Carlina, it would really help if you can give me his name."

"Eduardo. I don't know his last name, I've only spoken to him a few times. Really."

"Is he on the staff here?"

"No," said Cooke. "We don't have an Eduardo. We brought in some extra help from Brookside Caterers. We use them all the time."

Winter showed them photos of Rick Singleton and the images of the party Cindy had loaded on the tablet. Cooke identified Miranda Dell and a few of the older guests, frequent visitors to the Carter house.

Winter said, "Can you tell me about the security cameras?"

"It would be easier if I showed you," said Cooke.

She led Winter to a stone walled basement. As Cooke unlocked a door she said, "There's not much to see, and we've already turned over the recordings we had to the police."

The room held a rack of recorders, a small desk, two dark monitors, and little else. No one was inside.

"I didn't want to talk about this in front of the staff," said Cooke.

"I understand," said Winter.

"It's not because of what you might think. Ada—Carlina's mother—has been with us forever, we totally trust her. Carlina too. But you know how word gets around. Everyone thinks we have a lot of security, and that's a deterrent. But in fact . . ." Cooke clicked on the monitors. "We have very little. This shows the drive you came in on, the other is the service road out back." She hit a button, bringing up two more views. "The back entrance to the main house and the garage." The images were not the highest quality. "Here are the rest." She hit a button a few times; the screens turned blank, although there was a flicker with each click.

"Nothing," said Winter.

"Yes, that's our little secret. We only have recordings on those four cameras."

"But I saw more cameras than that," said Winter.

"We don't record from those. We used to, but . . ." Cooke turned off the monitors. "I trust you won't share this with the staff or anyone who doesn't have to know?"

"I can't make open promises, but if it has nothing to do with what happened, sure."

"The other cameras were turned off years ago. Mrs. Carter, she, well, when she drinks . . ."

Winter got it. "You saw Mrs. Carter do something you didn't want recorded?"

"Not me, one of the security men who reviewed the recordings. He brought it to my attention. Mrs. Carter likes to go in the pools. Without a bathing suit."

"Ah. I see. And you decided to turn off the cameras by the pools?"

"Not on my own. I notified Mr. Carter the cameras might be a problem. He never wanted them anyway, something about insurance. He made the decision to turn all of them off except the ones showing the entrances and the garage. I'm not even sure if all the cameras are still even connected."

CHAPTER 32

Doc ROLLED A work stool over to the safe behind the garage circuit panel. He'd sent Gina and Kevin to make a delivery and Tricia out for new shoes. She didn't need new shoes, but he wanted the house to himself so he could take stock.

Not only of his supplies, but his situation.

On the supply side, he was in good shape. Doc eyed the bins, doing quick calculations in his head. It would take years for the average person to earn the equivalent of what was in front of him. Doc wasn't average, but even a 9 to 5 grunt got cash at the end of the week. All the coke in the world couldn't even pay for a cup of coffee if it couldn't be converted to cash.

Which meant his supply situation was actually in *too* good a shape, because his sales had been slow. Doc could move more product, but it would mean taking more risk, and Doc hated risk. Many times he'd passed on opportunities to do a big score or spread his sales connections. He'd kept his network and associations tight and as trustworthy as they could be in this business. Other suppliers had a houseful of guards, a street full of dealers. Who needed that shit?

Although it *was* time for a second house. In a warm location.

Doc was looking at enough drugs to be able to do that, except he'd need to get a mortgage. It wasn't like he could show up to the closing with a briefcase of coke.

The ironies of modern society. All this collateral, yet useless at a bank.

Good thing he still had a license to practice medicine. No bank would turn down a doctor.

*   *   *

IN THE KITCHEN, Doc spread the Marburg *Times* on the granite counter-top island, sipping an Irish coffee. The paper was a piece of crap, but did have a story about the deaths at the Carter house.

The Carter family, true to form of the wealthy, was being characteristically mum, releasing comment only through their attorney. There were the usual interviews with the local police chief, whose assurances that the cops were following up numerous leads told Doc they had nothing. Certainly nothing on him, or they would be at his door.

Only Rick could tie Doc directly to Dwayne and indirectly to Gerry at the same time. Sterling knew about Gerry, but he'd use the attorney client privilege thing.

Dwayne was no longer a threat.

One article profiled Candy Carter. She was on the board of two local charities, had given a speech at a rally protesting GMO's, and was the national spokesperson for a wildlife habitat. All gave the impression of a little bird trying to break free of her cage. On the other hand, she'd had her party at the family house and was an executive in her father's holding company.

Doc's translation: Candy wanted to make a name for herself, but she wasn't going to do that by joining the Peace Corps. She'd use as much family money and connections as she needed to make her music career take off.

Which was good for Doc. Doubly good, if Rick got Gerry's rights.

Unless Candy dropped Rick's song because of his connection to Gerry.

That wouldn't be good for Doc. Or for Rick.

Rick was the only one who could be a problem for Doc. That risk gnawed at Doc, forcing him to weigh the upside and the downside of the Rick connection. He liked the upside, but the downside was much worse.

It was time to make contingency plans to sever that connection.

Had to keep an eye on Rick . . .

RICK NEEDED TO get over to his mother's house to help out, figure out a way to cover the nurse's next check, and also look for a job. Yet here he sat, picking through the chorus of *Never Believe* on his Gibson. This was the song that Candy might use, although she might not recognize it the way Rick played it, meandering and desultory, matching his mood. The title was so appropriate, Rick never believing he could find himself in such a disastrous situation.

It was bad enough being in hock to Doc, even worse having the cops suspect him of being involved with Gerry's death. They hadn't come right out and said it, but it was pretty obvious. And the question about contracts, where had that come from? Shit, he'd mentioned it himself, telling the cops about his conversation with Dwayne.

If the cops ever found out about the deal with Doc . . .

That wasn't the worst of it. The worst was that he suspected Doc had something to do with what happened at Candy's party. Rick couldn't figure out why Doc would want to hurt Gerry. Doc would have wanted Gerry to sign the papers. Why kill Gerry? That would only bring attention on Doc. Rick had enough history with Doc to know Doc hated attention.

Rick listlessly replayed the song, a painful reminder of his past and current promising big breaks, big breaks that had not come to fruition. He should never have taken that equipment from Larry. He'd always meant to return it, now it was too late. The idea had seemed so good at the time, yet another small step on the path into his trap.

The wall of his apartment shook, the next door neighbor pounding on the wall. The guy worked at night; Rick had promised not to play his guitar during the day. Screw him. He cranked up the amp and finished the song.

He ran his hand over the cherry red mahogany as he put the guitar back in the case. It had taken Rick ten years to save up for the guitar, a somewhat rare 1963 Les Paul SG. Rick had fallen asleep with that guitar for months after he got it. It was by far the most valuable item he owned, worth more than his car.

He never would have imagined he'd ever part with it.

He cried as he wrote out the description for the Les Paul on the online auction site.

CHAPTER 33

WINTER WATCHED through the two-way mirror into the interrogation room, where Miranda Dell was applying lipstick not eight inches away on the other side of the wall. When she was finished she puckered her lips into an exaggerated kiss, dispelling any doubt about whether she knew she was being watched.

It had been Winter's idea to get Dell to the station. Her story about Dwayne Coleman had shifted from when he spoke to her at the party, and information from others, including Rick Singleton, suggested she still wasn't being fully forthcoming. The police station interview room might straighten out her story.

Owens and O'Dowd entered behind her. Winter hoped O'Dowd would let Owens do the talking. O'Dowd was a pretty good detective, but hadn't learned the finer points of interviews, which mostly involved getting the conversation going and then listening. O'Dowd was good at the first part but hadn't quite figured out when to keep quiet.

"Miss Dell," O'Dowd said. "Thank you for coming in."

"It didn't sound like I had much choice. Isn't this the part where I say I want to see my lawyer?"

"That is your right," O'Dowd said. "You think you need one?"

"No, I haven't done anything wrong." Dell looked back at the mirror, fluffing her hair. "This is so television."

Owens said, "We need you to clear up a few things. It appears you knew Dwayne Coleman much more than you let on—"

That spun Dell around. "Who told you that?"

"Pictures don't lie," said Owens.

Dell hadn't sat down, so Winter couldn't see her facial reaction, but her body stiffened. What was she afraid of having been recorded doing?

"Can't you guys come up with anything new? Like I told you and the other cop—I bet he's on the other side of this mirror, right? You two must be losing your memory. I only met Dwayne that night."

"Please sit down, Miss Dell," said O'Dowd, pleasant, like he was a restaurant maitre d'. "We're just having a talk here. You are one of the last people to see Dwayne Coleman alive. We need your help."

"Me and a hundred other people," said Dell, but she sat down. O'Dowd also sat, his back to Winter. Owens hovered.

O'Dowd leaned across the table, open. "Look, I know how parties get. These old guys," he jerked his head at Owens, "are too stiff to have fun. Tell her the truth Dave, when's the last time you got down at a big party?"

Winter grinned, O'Dowd doing a good job, getting a friendly poke at Owens along the way. Owens hated being called Dave.

"Been a while, I got to admit that," said Owens. "Not like you youngsters. Jimmy."

O'Dowd laughed. "See? He's probably exaggerating, he's never let loose. Nice party like at the Carter's—you were involved in the planning, right?—good booze, no surprise the guests have had a few, getting a little friendly. Nothing illegal about it, either."

"So?"

"So, we're just trying to get a handle on Dwayne Coleman. Even the least little thing you talked about might help us."

"Just the usual. Music, the house. I must have repeated the same conversation a dozen times that night. I can't remember exactly what I said to whom." Dell leaned back in the chair, smirking. "You know, since you've been to so many parties."

Winters could tell that Dell obviously wasn't buying the good cop routine, which is probably what prompted Owens to say in a flat voice, "Tell us about the drugs."

"What drugs?"

"Save it," said Owens. "We know there were drugs floating all over that party."

"Then you're getting your parties confused. Candy is totally against drugs. She doesn't even take aspirin."

"I told you, pictures don't lie," said Owens. "And neither do tests. We know there was at least coke at the party."

"It was a *party*. I can't control what people do—"

Owens rolled right over her. "Did you supply drugs to the guests?"

"Are you crazy? Candy would have my head."

"The guests brought their own drugs?"

"I'm not saying that. I can't believe anyone who knew Candy would have brought drugs into her house."

"*Somebody* brought drugs," said Owens. "If I was looking for a little white stuff, you'd be the person I'd go to, since you grease the skids for Candy."

"I'm not the one who supplies anyone drugs," insisted Dell.

Gotcha, thought Winter, hoping Owens caught the slip.

Owens had. "So you know who brought the drugs to the party?"

Dell bit her lip, her eyes darting to the mirror. "I don't know anything for sure."

"But?" prompted O'Dowd.

"Rick Singleton got me a little blow once. For another party. One of my parties, actually. The drugs weren't for me. I was trying to make a good impression on a few guests."

"Are you saying Singleton supplied coke to the party at the Carter house?"

"I'm not saying anything. But if you want to talk to someone who brought drugs to a party, talk to Rick."

Winter was wondering if they had it all wrong, it wasn't that Dell knew more about Coleman, it was that Dell and Singleton had something going, maybe with drugs. Too much he said, she said.

O'Dowd, still with the friendly voice: "Dave, I bet Miss Dell likes her job. You think Candy would be interested in finding out her assistant throws coke parties?"

Dell made a face. "No wonder everyone hates cops."

"What's the younger generation coming to," said Owens. "Maybe we should get the Carter family attorneys in here. They might be interested in this conversation."

"Look," said O'Dowd. "As long as it didn't have anything to do with what happened at the Carter's, we don't care about your party. But if you supplied drugs at Candy's place, we're going to find out about it sooner or later. You might as well tell us now."

"I swear, I didn't give drugs to anyone that night. I'm not stupid. Neither is Candy. Does she suspect I might do a line now and then when

I'm not at work? Probably. Does she care, as long as I do my job? No. She'd fire me in a heartbeat if she found out I was passing out drugs in her parents' house. She wants publicity, but not that kind."

"Which brings us back to who brought the drugs," said Owens. "You suggest it might be Rick. When he supplied your party with drugs, where'd he get them?"

"Ask him."

"We will," said O'Dowd. "Anything you can help us out with? If we get this cleared up maybe there'd be no need to mention our little talk to Candy."

Dell huffed at O'Dowd. "You're as much of an asshole as he is."

Winter wished he had one of those earpiece radios so he could send signals in from the bench. O'Dowd, to his credit, stopped talking. The two cops waited.

Miranda looked at the mirror. "I don't know where Rick got his drugs. I did see him once with this older guy at the studio—in the parking lot. Fat man, reminded me of a dough boy at first. I thought he was in the music business."

"Why did you think that?"

"He was in one of those really high end Mercedes, the SUV? With a driver. That, and he asked me a few questions about music royalties."

"Why would you think he was the guy Rick got drugs from?"

"I don't know for sure. But the driver—I've met quite a few record people. They have assistants, people like me. I don't drive Candy around much, she likes to drive herself, but when she does she gets a ride from this polite guy who works for her father. The fat man's driver was a guy you'd cross the street to avoid. He almost dragged me out of the studio to meet the fat man, and Rick was scared of him."

"The driver or the fat guy?"

"Both of them." Dell looked back at O'Dowd. "To tell you the truth, so was I."

That was the first thing she'd said in the interview that Winter totally believed.

WINTER RAN out the back door, jogged through the parking lot, and got into his car. Drove around the lot, pulling into a spot a few cars away from Miranda Dell's BMW when he saw her coming down the stairs.

Took his time getting out of the car, not looking her way. He wasn't that good of an actor to try to appear surprised, counting on her to see him first.

She did. "I thought you were watching."

"I wanted to talk to you myself, but I was out at the Carter house looking at the security cameras." Winter waited to see if that got a rise out of her. If it did, she was a pretty good actress herself. "Been talking to Rick as well."

With exaggerated indifference, Dell asked, "So?"

Which told Winter there was more to the story. The question was whether it was about drugs, or Coleman, or both. Owens had pushed on her directly, so Winter came in from another angle. "I'm trying to square the whole drug thing with Candy. She seems to be really straight. We know there was coke at the party. You are close to Candy, how does that happen?"

"Like I told those guys in there, Candy doesn't like drugs. But she knows it isn't exactly uncommon in the music business. And hell, who doesn't do some weed or a snort now and then? As long as no one is flashing it around or is high when they are working with her."

"That include you?"

"That includes everyone."

"No exceptions? I saw you drinking pretty heavily at the party."

"I didn't have a single drink until after the problems started. I was upset. Even Candy wouldn't blame me for that."

"Seems like she lets people get away with a lot."

Dell unzipped her bag for her keys, her eyes away from Winter. "Candy has a lot of ambition, but she also has a soft spot for people. She knows she's had it lucky. She'll give someone a break if they make a mistake."

"That include you?"

Dell hit her unlock button. "That includes everyone too."

BACK IN THE STATION, Winter caught up with Owens and O'Dowd. "I took another run at Miranda Dell outside. There's definitely a piece missing." He filled them in on the conversation. "Might be we need to consider a connection between Singleton, Dell, and Coleman."

"Drugs?" asked Owens.

"Maybe. Or even music. Candy and her producer told me they might be using one of Rick's songs. The royalties could be a money pot."

"What's that have to do with Coleman and Miranda?"

"Rick talked to Coleman about royalties at the party. I don't know how Miranda fits in."

"Drugs as royalties?" suggested O'Dowd, doubtfully.

"I don't know," admitted Winter.

"Don't forget the guy Miranda said might have been with Coleman, the one with the cap," said O'Dowd. "I talked to the limo driver again. You were right, was another guy in the car that brought Coleman to the party. He was wearing a backward cap. From what the driver overheard, he doesn't think the guy came off the plane with Coleman. It sounded like they were catching up after not seeing each other for a while."

"Maybe a Boston local?"

"I thought so too. I sent his description to Boston PD. Maybe that's who brought the drugs. Gerry Hennig could have been the buyer, he didn't like what he was getting, or didn't have the money . . ."

"That sounds more likely than some complicated music royalty thing," said Owens. "I mean, we got drugs, we got a beating, we got music people, we got more drugs . . ."

"Yeah, you're probably right," conceded Winter. "Forget it. Let's dig into the drug angle."

Which kind of sucked, because it meant he'd be out doing interviews of guests again.

CHAPTER 34

W INTER PULLED into a church parking lot, checked three names off his interview list and jotted down a few notes on his lack of success. There were still a lot of names.

His phone rang. The guy on the other end, Vernon Black, was a retired Marine who worked at the regional airport. "I've been watching the monitors on the parking lots like you asked. Car just drove in, matches that license plate you gave me."

Winters had to think for a second, not remembering which plate he had asked Vernon about. Funny, it was only a few days ago they had spoken. "Remind me?"

"Lexus sedan?" Black gave him the plate number, using the military alphabet.

It finally clicked for Winter. It belonged to LaChance, the guy who had found Hennig's body at the Carter house. "When did he get there?"

"Twenty minutes ago. I was out, just rolled in and was catching up on the recording. What should I do?"

Winter didn't doubt the man's intent or ability, but Black had lost both legs to an IED. "You got a security guy doing rounds?"

"He's over at the garage. Want me to get him?"

"Just alert him for now. The guy in the car has an assault on his record. Are there any flights scheduled to go out soon?"

"We only run eight public flights a day. The next one isn't for two hours."

"Private?"

"I'll check, take me a few."

"Thanks, call me back. Expect company."

*   *   *

WINTER CALLED the dispatcher on the radio. "We got a hit on a BOLO, out at Marburg Airport. I need two units. Anyone close?" Winter didn't mention LaChance's name; the Marburg police band was streamed on the internet.

"Thirty-four is on the ring road, Sixteen on the west side."

"Tell them both to meet me there."

Winter turned the radio up as he drove, listening to the call go out. It could be nothing, but when a person of interest went to an airport . . . Winter slowed at a red light, saw no traffic, pushed across the intersection. Three miles later he got a call back from Vernon.

"One private jet has filed a plan. The plane is out on the tarmac. The tower hasn't had a request for takeoff yet. It's heading for the Dominican Republic. Two pilots, two passengers, no names on the sheet, which there should be."

"Who is it registered to?" asked Winter.

"Mr. and Mrs. Conrad Dect."

"I owe you. On my way."

Winter switched to the radio mike. "Dispatch. Winter. Get hold of Detective Crosse, tell her our guy might be running."

WINTER FUMBLED FOR the magnetic light, stuck it on the roof, barely slowing at the next two intersections, cursing as he got caught behind a septic truck on the airport access road. Gunned it to pass, his phone ringing just as he came up to the perimeter parking lot.

"It's Vernon. That plane just wound up, it's taxiing. I told the tower to see if they can stall them when they ask for clearance, but the head controller is an asshole, says I don't have authorization. Want to talk to him?"

"Would it help?"

"Over the phone? Maybe not. He might want paper."

"What's the fastest way for me to get on the tarmac?"

"Pilots have a lot on the north side. You need a card to get through the access gate. It's not one of those flimsy drop downs, either."

"Can you get me in?"

"Already moving," said Vernon. "Meet you there."

Winter passed the main doors, no police car in sight. He got back on the radio to pass his whereabouts along to the units on the way. On the other side of the airport building he pulled up to the pilot's parking lot just as a John Deere Gator ran up alongside. Winter jumped the curb onto a strip of grass, left the car, and ran for the gate.

Vernon had maneuvered the Gator to the card scanner, the gates swinging open, Winter not breaking stride, jumping in with Vernon. In the distance he could hear a small plane revving up.

Thanks to Cindy he had Crosse on speed dial, and fortunately she picked up. "Get to the tower controller at Marburg Regional. LaChance might be on a private plane, get him to stop them from taking off."

"If it's the controller I'm thinking of," said Crosse. "He's an asshole."

Vernon sped across the parking lot, which smelled of grease and exhaust fumes. "That's the pilot's lounge. You can cut through there and be on the tarmac."

"We can't get the Gator there?"

"Not this way. Maintenance truck access is on the other side of the airport. How bad you need this guy?"

"Who knows?" admitted Winter. "He's either a one or a ten priority. He might not even be on the damn plane."

"It's going to the Dominican Republic," said Vernon.

"You should have been a cop," said Winter. "Okay, an eight."

"Hoped you'd say that. Boring around here." Vernon spun the Gator away from the pilot lounge, aiming it toward a low gray building. The Gator had been modified so Vernon could control the speed and braking with levers. "Maintenance used to bring in equipment through a gate. It hasn't been used in years. Just got a chain lock."

"Yeah?"

Vernon revved up the Gator. They were probably only going thirty, but it seemed much faster, like being in a go-cart. "I don't have a key," yelled Vernon. "Hold on."

They hit the fence at full speed, Winter hanging on to the seat, bouncing hard, the gate bursting open, one side cleanly, the other raking Winter's side of the open vehicle, the chain link grabbing at his arm.

Vernon righted the Gator, pushing across the concrete, bearing down on a small private jet that was taxiing into position.

Sirens drifted in from the other side of the airport building, suggesting Crosse hadn't had any luck with the air traffic controller.

Winter shouted over the sound of the plane. "You had too much fun doing that."

"Nah. But *this* will be fun." Vernon sped toward the plane, cutting across the runway. Though the plane wasn't likely to hit the Gator, the pilots, easily visible through the cockpit window, yanked the plane sideways and aborted the takeoff.

Vernon was grinning. "Up to you now."

Winter said, "I don't think Uber is in your future."

THE ENGINES WOUND down after Winter held up his badge. A short haired guy dressed in a white shirt and pressed gray slacks appeared a moment later at the gangway door. "What the hell was all that about?"

"Need to see your passengers," said Winter. He hoped LaChance, if he was on board, wouldn't try anything stupid, but Winter didn't have much choice. He unzipped his hoodie so he'd have easier access to his gun.

The pilot turned and had a conversation, then said to Winter, "Come on up."

"No, you come down," ordered Winter. "Then everyone else."

Another conversation, followed by the pilot dropping the stairs. Without turning his head Winter said, "Vernon, appreciate it if you could get the officers."

"Roger that."

Both pilots came down. Winter motioned them off to the side. "Two passengers?" he asked.

"Mrs. Dect and her guest."

A middle-aged woman appeared in the doorway, platinum blond, wearing a clingy dress, lots of jewelry, and even more makeup. "What's the meaning of this?"

"Mrs. Dect? Could you come down, please?"

"I don't see why—"

Her eyes jumped to the Gator pulling up behind Winter. A uniform named Lincoln jumped out, Vernon pulling away. "He's going back for the other unit," said Lincoln.

Winter had worked with Lincoln, he knew what he was doing. "Mrs. Dect? We can get this cleared up much faster if you come down."

"If you insist," she said, making it sound like Winter had just asked her to give up her first born.

Up closer, she was older than Winter thought, her jewelry large and gaudy. Her wedding ring was studded with diamonds.

"What do you want with me?" she asked.

"Who is your passenger?"

"Does he really have to be involved in this? Whatever this is?"

"I'm afraid so. Come on, Mrs. Dect, let's get this over with."

"Very well. It's Jacque LaChance. What do you want him for?"

"Mr. LaChance," called Winter. Winter rested his hand near his gun. The last thing he wanted was to have to go up into an open doorway with no cover.

A moment later a man appeared. Tall, only part of his face visible in the low door. "Yes?"

"Come on down. Keep your hands away from your pockets."

The man came down the steps, confident. He was, thought Winter, what many woman would consider handsome, square jawed, a fashionable beard, dark eyes and hair, thick eyebrows. A forty-year-old model. He wore designer jeans and a blue silk shirt, a leather jacket over his shoulder.

Winter said, "We have some questions for you about the party at the Carter house."

LaChance glanced over at Mrs. Dect. "Don't have much to tell you."

Winter read the tea leaves. A guy on a married woman's plane, no names on the manifest, flying off to the islands. Winter didn't think Mrs. Dect's husband knew about this particular passenger. The woman was either helping him get away or was off for some extra-marital activities. "We could have this conversation here, or at the station," said Winter. "Starting with where you have been the last few days."

Mrs. Dect seemed pretty interested in that as well, which might have been what prompted LaChance to say, "Sure. Be happy to go with you."

LACHANCE STARTED talking as soon as he got into Winter's car. "That was a close one," he said, looking over his shoulder. "Thanks for getting me out of there."

Winter, surprised, said, "I thought you'd be upset, losing your trip and all."

"Wouldn't have been much fun if Bertie grilled me all the way down about where I've been."

Winter had LaChance sitting in the passenger seat. He considered sticking him in the back of the blue and white with Lincoln, but had no real reason to treat LaChance that way just yet. Always time to toughen up later. "Bertie?" asked Winter.

"I don't name them, I just do them," said LaChance.

Winter headed toward the station. "Since Mrs. Dect isn't here right now, maybe you can fill *me* in on where you've been since the party."

"The party. Yeah, what a disaster, huh? Bet Candy wasn't looking for that kind of publicity. Anyway, I was supposed to have got out of there an hour earlier, I needed to drive to Stockbridge to see my girlfriend—"

"Mrs. Dect lives in Stockbridge?"

"What? No, not her. Jaime." LaChance swept some invisible lint off his jeans. "Jaime's ex had the daughter that weekend, so Jaime and I went to a B&B in Lenox."

Winter was having a hard time keeping up. "So Jaime is your girlfriend? What's Mrs. Dect think about that?"

LaChance grinned. "She doesn't know about Jamie, and vice versa. That's why I'm glad I'm not on the plane right now."

"Tell me about the party."

"A little more action than the usual Carter affair, probably because it was for Candy. Lots of younger women. That's why I was late leaving, I met this—"

Winter wasn't sure he wanted to know. "Tell me about the guy who got killed."

"I was on my way up the stairs, this woman I met was supposed to follow me up. I got to the landing, this guy is in the hall, lying on the floor. I figured he was drunk and passed out. Then I saw some blood." LaChance rubbed his hands on his thighs.

"No one else around?"

"Not that I could see. Anyway, I'm standing at the top of the stairs, you know where that balcony is? I see Candy coming up. I don't want her to see the guy, I go down and stop her. Got someone to call 911, then I split."

"Did you know he was dead?"

"No. I went right to Jaime's. The next morning we dropped her kid off, drove to Lenox. The B&B doesn't even have televisions in the room.

Not that we were watching any tv, if you get my drift." LaChance talked like he didn't have a care in the world. "Just heard about all of it an hour ago, actually. Bertie mentioned it. Her husband knows Carter too, everybody with money does."

"How exactly do you know the Carter family?"

"I like hanging out with people who have money, brings me in contact with bored wives who can take me to the islands on private jets. I was teaching tennis at the Marburg Country Club, gave lessons to both Carter and his wife."

Winter glanced over. "You and Mrs. Carter ever—"

"Not a chance. Carter isn't a guy you cross."

"Unlike Mrs. Dect's husband?"

"Man, those two are worlds apart. I'm telling you, no one screws with James F. Carter. Which means no one screws his wife." LaChance put his hands out like he was warding off an imaginary husband.

Revealing a well worn, but very heavy, wristwatch. "Nice watch you got there," said Winter. "A Rolex?"

"It is, actually." LaChance turned it to face Winter. "You into watches?"

"Not really. Had it a long time?"

"Six months, maybe? I never wear it unless I'm with Bertie. She gave it to me."

"Any way you can prove that?" asked Winter.

"What, you think I stole it?" LaChance pulled the watch off. "She got my name engraved on it."

Winter knew LaChance could have his name engraved on a stolen watch, but if he remembered correctly Gerry Hennig's watch had been a gift to his father from his job, so Hennig's watch was probably already engraved. He'd check, but if anyone could get a married woman to gift him a Rolex, it was probably LaChance.

"You had some problems before," said Winter. "Roughing a guy up."

"Man, that was ten years ago. A fight with a jealous husband. He actually came after *me*. Back when I was just getting started. Didn't know how to pick them. I'm much more careful now. Wait, you think I killed that guy?"

Winter was a few blocks from the station. "You got to admit, you look pretty suspicious from our end. Find the body, take off, disappear."

"I explained that."

"And you didn't answer your phone."

LaChance said, "What number did you call? The one they texted me the invite on?"

"I'm not sure, probably."

"That's my private phone. I don't carry that when I'm with a woman, or even give them the number."

"Really? How many phones you got?"

"A bunch, I get those prepaids, you know the ones with the monthly cards?"

"Seems a lot to keep track of. Remembering who goes to what phone."

"It's a whole lot easier than getting a call at the wrong time, if you catch my drift."

Winter was a one woman at a time type of guy, so he was having a hard time getting his head around LaChance's promiscuity. Hell of a way to live. "Will I hear the same story from Jaime?"

"Jaime made the arrangements and paid. She'll back me up. But leave out the plane and Bertie, will you? I like Jaime."

Winter said, "Seems you like them all."

LaChance spread his hands. "What can I say? Lots of women, only so many hours in the day."

By the time they reached the station, Winter had pretty much decided LaChance didn't have anything to do with the Hennig killing.

Winter walked him into the station anyway.

CHAPTER 35

Rick TIPTOED to the living room to check on his mother. She was finally sleeping. Rick should have felt relief, but her ragged breathing was terrifying.

He jumped as a voice behind him said, "You need to start thinking about hospice."

"Jesus, Sherry, don't sneak up on me like that. And don't let my mom hear you."

"It's you who needs to hear me. She needs more than pills now. The hospice people can give her stronger pain medication."

"But hospice, that means she's dying." Rick knew his mother's situation wasn't good, but putting her in hospice sounded like giving up. "I don't think she's ready."

Sherry said, "She won't be ready until you are."

"The doctor said she could live for a while yet. She might even go into remission, there was this case I read about on the internet—"

Three loud knocks on the door interrupted him. He answered it robotically. Two men on the steps, looking familiar, Rick's brain finally kicking in, cops he'd seen at the party.

"Need to talk to you," said the black cop. "I'm Detective Owens, this is Detective O'Dowd."

Through the screen Rick said, "I already talked to Detective Winter and some other cop." Rick looked over his shoulder, Sherry didn't need to hear this.

"Have to clear up a few things," said Owens. "Let's go down to the station."

From the hall, Sherry said, "Rick? I have to leave."

"Just—give me a minute, okay?" To the cops Rick said, "I can't leave my mom alone."

"And I need my check please," said Sherry.

"I—I left the studio before Larry wrote out my paycheck, if you can stay a little longer I can go pick it up and get you some cash."

Sherry appeared at the doorway, her eyes narrowing at the cops. "You know I can't do that, I have to get to my other patient."

"Please, Sherry, tomorrow, I got my hands full here."

"What else is new. I'm going to get my coat."

Owens said, "Hard to pick up a check when you don't have a job."

"Shh," said Rick. He pushed out the door. "Come on, give me a break, please. If Sherry finds out I can't pay her, she'll quit today, and my mom needs her."

Owens shook his head. "Gotta say, Jimmie, kind of hard to believe, a big drug dealer like this can't even come up with a few bucks to pay his mother's nurse."

"He's a cold one," said O'Dowd.

"What are you talking about?" said Rick, stepping away from the front door, praying the cops would follow. "Who's a drug dealer?"

"We hear you are."

"You think if I had money I wouldn't pay for my mom's nurse?"

"I don't know, maybe you just aren't good handling cash. Or the drugs, maybe you snort up all your inventory?"

"Where are you getting this?" Rick fought the panic, not only about having Sherry overhear, who was just coming out the door, but because he feared they knew about Doc.

"We heard you were passing around blow at the Carter party," said O'Dowd.

Rick shuffled his feet in the leaves, hoping the sound would cover the cop's voice, waiting until Sherry made it down the walk. "Whoever told you that is a liar. I didn't give out a thing at Candy's. That's bullshit."

The black cop said, "Not the way we heard it."

"Well you heard wrong. No way I'd bring coke into Candy's house."

"Now who's bullshitting," said Owens. "There was coke all over that party. You lie to me again and I'm going to go find that nurse lady and tell her you were fired."

Rick swallowed back his urge to shout *asshole*. Fighting to keep his voice level, he said, "I swear to you, I didn't bring drugs inside that house." Then, panicking now, remembering the coke on his jacket, he said, "I did a line in my car. One line. I never snort and drive. That's it, one line." Rick hadn't had a toot since the party, even if they tested his blood they'd come up with nothing.

"So you'll let us search your place?"

"What's this got to do with me?"

"Your friend, and another man, end up dead at a party where there's a lot of drugs floating around. We hear you and drugs and parties kind of go together. Gets us to thinking."

Rick did his own thinking. *Fucking Miranda.* She sicced them onto him.

What else had she told them? He could play that game, *she* had been with Dwayne, out by the pool . . .

He could tell the cops that, but he'd have to admit he was there as well. If he didn't, Miranda would throw him under the bus. He'd been protecting her, but she wouldn't give a shit about him.

He had to get the cops off of this. "Search all you want." He pulled out his keys. "Here. You can search my car too. I got nothing to hide."

O'Dowd said, "I'm going to get a search consent form from our car."

Rick wasn't especially worried about the search. There was nothing in the Kia. He'd cleaned it out after the party, even the CD where he kept his stash. Maybe they could do a test, find some residue, it wouldn't prove anything, would it? And he had nothing at the apartment.

"Where did you get the party drugs?" asked Owens.

"You talked to Miranda, right? She had a party, I shared a few lines with this woman. You already know I do a little coke now and then. Who doesn't?"

"Where'd you get it?"

"Around. It was like nothing worth." Rick waved his arm at the house. "I look like I got enough money to supply a party?"

Owens said, "I understand you talked to Dwayne Coleman at the Carter's. You see him with anyone else?"

"Bunch of people, chicks wanting their picture taken with him."

"How about another black man? Skinny, might have been wearing a dark red leather jacket, backward cap?"

"Don't remember him," said Rick. "I did see a black photographer, but I don't remember any cap."

The cop nodded, dug in his pocket and came up with a pack of cigarettes, offered one to Rick. Rick said, "I don't smoke in front of my mother. You go ahead though. She's asleep."

"You won't smoke even though she's sleeping?"

"You know, she's my mother, she doesn't know, about, well, a lot of stuff."

The cop said, "Hmm," and stuck the butt in his mouth but didn't light up. After a minute, he asked, "What's up with your mother?"

Rick said, "She's got cancer."

"Sorry to hear that," said the cop. "My father had it too."

"Is he—."

"No, years ago. Tough for him at the end."

The change of topic wasn't pleasant, but Rick relaxed slightly, they were off of the drug angle. Maybe the cop was going to let him off the hook.

Owens said, "Who's the guy in the black SUV?"

Rick hesitated, too long, his mouth opening and closing, not able to come up with a plausible denial, especially since he had no idea what the cop already knew. "What guy?"

"Heavyset man you met with at the studio. Has a driver."

"Oh, him. Some guy whose kid's a singer, wants to make a demo tape to send to one of those television competition shows. I told him we didn't do that sort of stuff."

"Yeah? What was his name?"

Rick desperately tried to remember if Doc had mentioned his name to Miranda, he didn't think so, that wasn't Doc's style. "I don't think he introduced himself." Wanting to appear open, he added, "Miranda talked to him, you might want to ask her." Rick doubted Miranda knew Doc's name.

The other cop came back, Rick signing the form, his hand shaking, realizing the cops finding a little blow was the least of his problems right now.

CHAPTER 36

WINTER AND THE rest of the detectives assembled in the bullpen for the morning briefing. Captain Logan, the squad commander Evans, Cindy Prague, the criminologist, Andie Pearle, the crime scene tech, the data guy Dan Cole, and a handful of senior uniforms crowded in as well. The room smelled of coffee, donuts, and cologne.

Logan gave Crosse a *let's get on with it* gesture. One of the reasons Winter liked Logan was that he didn't feel the need to stand up and give them a Gipper speech, or even worse, tell them to *do better*.

Which would have been appropriate, since it had been five days since the deaths at the Carter house, and they had basically nothing.

Crosse said, "I've read all your notes. Let's keep this short, just fill in the gaps on what might be useful across the Coleman and Hennig situations. Also, the Medical Examiner has agreed to come in."

"That's a first," someone muttered.

"She figured it would keep you all from tramping over there for preliminary findings." Crosse had a tablet in front of her on the table, along with a pile of reports and folders. "First, the drugs. Andie?"

"We did field tests in the bedroom where Hennig was beaten and around the pool area. We also found," Andie glanced at her notes, "sixteen baggies of powder in nine locations, twelve loose pills, and about a dozen rolled marijuana cigarettes either in bags or loose, none smoked."

"People dumping their stuff when we showed up," said O'Dowd.

"Looks like it. Oddly, no sign at all of drug paraphernalia beyond a few glass straws. No bowls, pipes, not even roach clips."

"Might not be that odd," said Winter. "Most of the guests probably knew Candy Carter wasn't a fan of drugs. What you found might have been what the guests just had on them. It also explains the un-smoked dope. One thing to sneak a line, another thing to light up."

"Everything is out at the lab," said Andie. "But from the field tests, we do know a few things. First, there is quite a bit of coke around the pool, specifically in and around the cabana area. Second, we found a pen of crack in the bedroom. It's the only coke we found in crack form anywhere on the property."

"Maybe Hennig had the crack," said Ryder. "Or whoever beat him up."

"Hennig's clothes are at the state lab," said Andie. "Other unknown powders were mixed with dirt and other contaminants. All that is getting tested." She looked up. "I have to tell you, there's a million samples we collected, that place is huge. It'll take weeks to even get preliminary reports. Other than on Hennig's body and in that bedroom, we didn't even bother with hair samples. Blood we got, only in the house. We already have type matched it to Hennig, and it appears it's all his, but we'll confirm. On Coleman, there's nothing from the scene to be even remotely definitive of whether it is a homicide or an accident."

They all mulled over that for a while, then Owens said, "Got to be connected somehow. Drugs at the pool, drugs in the bedroom."

"And in the garden, the walkway, near the cars," said Andie.

"What about Rick Singleton's jacket?" asked Winter.

"At the lab. I didn't want to swipe it, and there wasn't enough to scrape off."

"He admitted he'd taken a hit," said Winter. "But it sounds like he might not have been the only one. Even Candy's assistant Miranda Dell looked high to me, although she was drinking too."

"Pretty wild party," said one of the uniforms.

"Or maybe not," said Owens. "You get that many people together, there's bound to be drugs. If it weren't for the drugs near the bodies, we might not think twice about the drugs."

"The crack is what's odd," said Winter. "Fancy party, the type of guests there, I'd expect a little weed, some coke. But crack?"

"Maybe Ryder is onto something," said Logan. "Whoever beat up Hennig dropped the crack."

"Party crashers? Hard to imagine," said Evans.

"It's possible," said Ryder. "There was almost no security. Big place, lots of ways to enter, dark. There's a fence around the property, but a kid could climb over it."

"Still, a crackhead would stick out," argued Owens.

"Unless they knew the place, or came in the back way," said Evans.

"And snuck upstairs?" Owens didn't sound convinced.

"Maybe an inside job," suggested Crosse. "One of the staff tips off a friend about the party. Guests coats get put in a closet, guy comes in and works the pockets."

"The house manager, Polly Cooke, seems to be on the ball," said Winter. "She trusts her inside staff. Although there is this guy I need to track down, one of the outside caterers, who might have seen something."

There was a knock on the door, and a woman stuck her head in. "Now okay?"

"Sure," said Crosse. "You all know Dr. Kristol?"

Clarice Kristol was the state Medical Examiner whose jurisdiction included Marburg. Winter had worked with her before and thought she was very good. Methodical, a little unwilling to go out on a limb. The former was good, the latter common to most M.E.'s. She was a short black woman with smooth skin and close-cropped hair, dressed in a dark blue pants suit.

Kristol remained standing. "The usual caveats, this is all preliminary, based on physical observations and presumptive tests. First, Gerry Hennig. Mr. Hennig sustained considerable bruising and blunt force trauma. There were eight separate knife wounds. Six were superficial slashes, and one full penetration, approximately three inches deep, just below the ribcage. None of the knife wounds, including the slash to the face at the left eye, were fatal. In three places he was hit with an object, rather narrow."

"Like he was being beaten with the back of the handle?" asked Crosse.

"Yes. Or a similar object. There were bruises on the top of the scull, and considerable trauma around the neck. It's possible he was held in a headlock and repeatedly struck on the top of the head."

"Any signs indicating how many assailants?" asked Ryder.

"Inconclusive. There were defensive wounds on his hands. Other than the one deep penetration, the primary area of trauma was the neck. His carotid artery was not only compressed, but severed, and there were fractures of the cornu and the tracheal cartilage, indicating a very strong twisting. The neck did not have finger bruising, suggesting he wasn't strangled as you might normally think of it, but rather his neck was held tightly and then violently twisted sideways."

"Like a carotid hold?"

"It might have started that way, but the assailant either didn't apply the pressure appropriately or wasn't in the right position."

Ryder said, "So he might have been in a headlock, like this," Ryder curled his arm, "with one hand, and a guy beats his head with the knife, and then twists his neck?"

"That's a possibility," said Kristol. "It takes a lot of force to sever the artery. Most likely the twisting of the neck would require the entire body to be adding to the momentum, in a fall perhaps, or being thrown to the ground."

"Hennig managed to get out of the room," said Crosse.

"He would not have died instantly, even with a severed artery. And it isn't definitive exactly where that trauma took place. It could have been in the room, and he stumbled out, or the attack may have started in the bedroom, and continued on into the hall. The blood splatter supports that view."

Kristol waited for questions, then continued, "Fluids were taken for toxicology, and the liver has been sent out as well. I can tell you that nothing in the organs suggested long term drug use, and there were no indications of needle marks on the body. The blood test was completely negative for common drugs. We'll know more from the liver in a few weeks."

"You'd pick up cocaine from the blood, right?" asked O'Dowd.

"If he used in the last few days, yes. Before that, no. "

"So," said Logan, "and not to put words in your mouth, he was beaten up, cut and stabbed, and then his neck was broken?"

"That would be putting words in my mouth, Captain," cautioned Kristol, although her tone was friendly. "His neck wasn't broken in an anatomical way, there were no cervical bones severed. But the likely cause of death, pending toxicology, was the trauma to the neck area causing asphyxiation."

"And it could have been done by one person," added Ryder.

"Yes. It's possible."

"Anything else on Hennig we should know?" asked Crosse.

"Not at this point. Shall I turn to Mr. Coleman? Okay. There are no indications of extensive bruising on Mr. Coleman, with the one significant exception of a deep trauma to the left side of the head, just above the ear. This would be consistent with being hit by a hard, blunt object, but would also be consistent with hitting his head on the coping stone of the pool. The pool area showed no indication of that, although with the water being splashed around, there might be no evidence of a glancing blow."

"So he could have hit his head while falling in?" asked O'Dowd.

"Yes. Or he could have hit his head elsewhere, or been hit on the head, and fell in. Or was pushed in. Mr. Coleman had water in his lungs, which suggests he was alive when he went into the water, although that is not conclusive, since some water typically collects even in a person who is already dead. But his heart stopped as well. So he could have had a coronary attack, fell into the pool, or fell into the pool, panicked, and had a heart stoppage. However, the heart showed no sign of major anomalies. Again, the tissue tests will show more. Of greater interest to you, perhaps, was that Mr. Coleman had recently ingested a significant amount of cocaine. This was evident in his blood and in his stomach as well."

"His stomach?"

"Yes. He likely ingested cocaine not long prior to death."

"Who eats coke?" asked one of the uniforms.

"Bombing," someone said. Another voice, "Dabbing."

"I've seen cocaine in stomachs before," said Kristol. "It could also be accidental, pills mixed with coke by mistake. The most important finding is Mr. Coleman's heart stoppage. This could—and I emphasize *could*—be the result of an overdose. He had been drinking. In significant quantities, cocaine and alcohol can lead to a heart attack. Thus a possible cause of death would be a secondary drowning to an overdose. While I do not believe the head trauma killed Mr. Coleman, I have requested the assistance of a forensic neurologist. Until that and the toxicology tests are done, I cannot begin to conclude this was a homicide, or even that there was any evidence of an assault."

"You're saying he might have just overdosed, fell in the pool, and drowned?"

"It wouldn't be the first time," said Kristol. "In fact, it wouldn't even be the first time this year in Massachusetts."

"But," said Ryder, "he could just as likely been pushed in the pool after starting to OD."

"It's possible, but of course there would have to be at least one other person there. Do you have evidence of that?"

"That's your cue, Dan," said Crosse. "Thanks, Dr. Kristol. We'll try not to pester you."

"I'll believe it when I see it," said Kristol as she left.

"LET'S MOVE ON to the house security video," said Crosse. "Dan?"

Dan Cole was the youngest person in the room, sporting a failing soul patch. "The short answer is we don't have much. The video system is old, and though it works, there are two problems. The first is that while there are about a dozen cameras, only four of them are recording. The second is that the resolution is pretty bad. We spent a lot of time trying to catch license plates from the front entrance camera. Many of them are hard to read, although we've been able to use the guest list and the style of the car to identify about half the guests so far."

"How about the other cameras?" asked Winter.

"The driveway camera is partially blocked, but from what we can tell, no one walked up the drive. Out back, there's one on the garage, and no one appears in the feed at all except for one woman who walks away from the main house very early on. We've identified her as one of the staff who lives on the property who went home before the party started. The back entrance of the house—there are two, and only one has a camera, but supposedly the other door is rarely used—showed a lot of coming and going. We went through it with Cooke, and she identified most of them as staff. The rest were likely from the caterer."

"The catering company is Brookside," said Crosse. "They are cooperating and have sent us a list of who was working the party. Dan, take us through the phones."

"Hennig's phone hasn't turned up. We don't know his carrier and are working through all the cell phone companies. Coleman's phone was in his pocket, and though it probably wasn't in the water long, the salt did a job on it. We managed to pull up a few pages of his contact list. I cross referenced those contacts to the guest list, and there's not a single match except for Terrence Jackson, who Kendal DeVaughn said might be inviting guests."

"As far as we can tell, Jackson wasn't at the party," said O'Dowd.

Crosse said, "Coleman's cell records have been subpoenaed. When we went to Hennig's apartment and office, we couldn't find anything connecting him with Coleman. Hennig's parents didn't know about Gerry going to the party. They gave me a list of a few friends, his PhD advisor. He didn't have a girlfriend. They were adamant Gerry never touched so much as weed."

"They wouldn't be the first parents to not know their kids got high," said Ryder. "No paraphernalia at the apartment or office though. Or in his car."

"One thing we got from the parents," said Crosse. "They confirmed their son had a Rolex watch and wore it all the time. There was no watch on Hennig. But his wallet was still in his pocket, with two credit cards and almost a hundred in cash. No ATM card, so we are working to see if he had one and if there were any withdrawals." Crosse looked up from her notes. "That's about it on Hennig so far. We have the description of the watch out to pawn shops. We still need to talk to more of his friends. As of now, though, there's nothing to indicate he had any connection to Coleman or any other guest except Rick Singleton, and there's no evidence he was involved in drugs."

"Wrong time, wrong place?" said Logan.

"Could be," said Crosse. "Someone at the party—guest, staff person, caterer, crasher—sees Hennig, gets him alone, robs him. Hennig fights back. Whoever did it panics and grabs the watch but not the wallet."

"I'd buy that, maybe, if it weren't for Coleman," said Logan. "Any evidence *he* was robbed?"

"If he was, whoever robbed him was blind," said Owens. "Coleman was wearing three gold chains, they were still around his neck. He had a money clip with a wad of hundreds—sequential, like they came from an ATM machine. A black Amex and three other cards in his wallet. Plus the time line is tough—not impossible, but tough. If one guy did all this, he would have had to kill Hennig and make it out to the pool without being noticed, and he probably would have blood on him. Or the other way around, first the pool and then Hennig."

"Might not be one guy," said O'Dowd. "We're working on id'ing a black male who came to the party with Coleman. He could be involved. Even if he wasn't, still could be more than one person."

"We're working through Coleman's background," said Owens.

"Seems he spent most of his time in Miami, but did have an apartment in New York and another one in Belize. Coleman was born in Providence. Mother is deceased, no father is listed on his birth certificate. We found one sister, who lives in Charlotte, she says she hasn't seen Coleman for a year but he sends her money every month. From what we can tell he's pretty well off from his music. He got a lot of publicity a few years ago, he was shot at in a drive by."

"Gang?" someone asked.

"Looking into that. Nothing obvious, but it wouldn't be out of the ordinary to have a gang connected with a hip hop guy. Coleman has some ink, but nothing gang related. The mystery man who came with him may or may not have a tat on his forehead."

"The driveby—where did that happen?" asked Winter.

"I don't know," said Owens.

"Let's find out if we can. Might help us identify the gang if there is one."

"If there was a gang beef, the Carter house seems like a strange place for it to go down," said Logan.

"Someone followed Coleman from the airport?" suggested one of the uniforms.

"And, what, pushed Coleman in a pool at a fancy party?" said O'Dowd.

"If it *is* gang related," said Owens, "it's hard to see how Hennig fits into that. I haven't run into too many PhD gangbangers."

"That's assuming they are connected," said Logan.

About six voices at the same time said, "Got to be."

Winter wasn't one of them, and the voices sounded much less convinced than they had a few days earlier.

CHAPTER 37

T HIRD EYE MALCOLM huddled on the back porch of a three decker off Morton Street that had been under renovation, on and off, for two years. Half the windows were broken, the door hung ajar, but it least it cut the wind. Though it would be warmer inside, the place smelled of piss and vomit, so he stayed on the porch.

Malcolm hit redial on his phone. The result was the same as it had been over the last few days, the call jumping right to Dwayne's voicemail. Not like he and Dwayne were tight, not since Dwayne became Outta Here and moved to Miami. But Dwayne usually got back to him.

Dwayne owed him. Malcolm had done what Dwayne had asked, put the fear into that skinny boy Gerry, more than fear, gave him a good beat down, cut him too. That's what Dwayne had wanted, and now it was time to collect.

Malcolm hadn't had a hit since that morning, the last of his stash. Would have been good if he'd got the white guy's wallet. Never got the chance, the guy had slipped out of his bloody fingers, Malcolm's hand sliding down his arm, catching on Gerry's watch. Malcolm followed him into the hall, where Gerry had stumbled toward the balcony, not where Malcolm wanted to be. He yanked off the watch and went the other way.

Now nothing to show for all his work except for the watch, which Malcolm wore, wondering if the band could really be gold. Felt heavy enough. Dwayne would have known, except Dwayne was nowhere. Malcolm also had the white boy's cell, a nice iPhone he'd scooped off the floor. He'd get a few bucks for that.

The watch looked good on him, but not good enough to keep, he needed a score.

Hit redial again, nothing happened. Battery was dead.

Back into the cold.

ON BLUE HILL AVENUE, after turning away from the red brick police station, Malcolm picked out the pawnshop with the thickest security gate. Two steps inside, another glass door, locked. An older guy with a black beard wearing a smock peered at him from behind a counter. Malcolm saw his lips move, and a speaker on the wall said, "Buying, selling, or leaving?"

Malcolm held up the watch.

The old man buzzed him in. Malcolm, cool, checking the place out, maybe he'd have a fourth option, taking.

Another dude appeared from the back room, a younger guy in a leather jacket, darker skinned, maybe an Arab, Malcolm didn't know much from black, white, brown. This guy leaned against the doorway, moving his jacket aside, making it clear to Malcolm he had a gun. Or at least pretending to.

Malcolm stared him down. The guy didn't turn away, which told Malcolm today he'd be selling and not taking.

He held the watch out to the old man. "What can I get for this?"

The old man said, "Nothing."

"What, you saying it's fake?"

"If it's fake, it isn't worth anything. If it's real, it's worth something, but not to me."

Malcolm saw plenty of watches in the case. "Looks to me you like watches."

"That your watch?"

"Sure, I got it, right?"

The old man didn't answer. Malcolm didn't even bother trying to push the iPhone. He finger gun pointed at the guy in the doorway and walked out.

AT MALCOLM'S next stop, still on Blue Hill Avenue, he didn't even get buzzed in, the guy behind the counter, another old white dude, just shaking his head. Malcolm gave him the finger and walked the long blocks past Woolson. Not far from his corner now, they'd know him here.

The store he entered was a mishmash of appliances, clothing, electronics, and cheap jewelry. Three women were arguing over a blouse. On the near wall two brothers sat behind a counter, flicking over their phones, shoot up video games. A large mirror behind them reflected the entire store, Malcolm appearing out of proportion as he walked up.

"Yo, Third Eye, what you got?"

Malcolm dangled the watch. "Tick tock."

The brother, who Malcolm knew as Cadillac, took the watch, handed it to the other dude, who everyone called Flash. Flash peered at the face with one eye closed, put it up to his ear, turned it over, and pulled the band down away from the face. He dropped it on the counter. "Two hundred."

"Shit, man, worth ten times that."

"More," agreed Flash. "Except all those watches got serial numbers, and stolen ones get on a list. Not like I can eBay it."

"Who says it was stolen?"

Cadillac turned the watch over, said, "Your real name Rudy Hennig?"

Malcolm hadn't noticed the name, who looked at the back of a watch?

"Worth more if you can get one without a name," said Flash. "This one, I can move the band. Best I can do."

"Gimme a minute," said Malcolm. He pulled out his phone, hit Dwayne's contact, the screen going black. Remembered the iPhone he'd picked up. Turned it on, pressed in Dwayne's number, which he knew by heart after all the failed calls. Right to voice mail. No help or money from Dwayne.

"Two hundred," he said to Flash. "If you throw in a charger for my phone."

THEY GAVE MALCOLM a charger and let him keep his phone there to charge up. He walked out of the store, turned left, and within three blocks had a baggie of rocks. In a back alley he loaded the pipe, but the wind kept blowing out his lighter. Shaking now, really needing a hit.

Half ran back up the street, looking for the dude he'd scored from, who had moved on. Found three brothers he recognized on a stoop. They didn't have any rocks, but sold him a teener. Malcolm didn't want to wait for the buzz but turned his back from the street and did the snort from the baggie right there through his straw. While waiting for the blow to hit he asked about the pawnshop with the old man. They all knew the place, one of them saying it wasn't candy, Malcolm taking that to mean they had tried to take the place and had failed.

Malcolm getting an idea though, watches. Never even thought about them. Find some restaurant where rich types went slumming for ethnic dinners, wouldn't take nothing to yank a few in a dark parking lot. Malcolm had boosted a few cars, just too hard to move, and even harder to hide. Watches, easy on both.

The teener wasn't doing it for him, too slow, Malcolm asking if there was a spot out of the wind. Meaning not too close to their crib, giving their area respect, just like he'd expect in his own. They directed him to a closed restaurant a few blocks away. In back a set of concrete stairs led to a lower landing overflowing with wet plastic bags, garbage, lots of cigarette butts, broken pipes, a rainbow of empty plastic lighters. Malcolm finally managed to get the pipe lit, did a hit, but couldn't finish the rock, it was that windy. Finally gave up when his lighter ran out.

He laid back against the cold concrete, the high pushing away his hunger pains. Better.

A WHILE LATER, getting dark, Malcolm back at the store. No customers, Flash and Cadillac still playing their phones. Malcolm's phone, on the counter, showed enough charge, so he unplugged it and tried Dwayne again. Still no answer. With his newly sharpened brain he remembered he once got a call from one of Dwayne's posse, Polo. Malcolm had never met him, but still had the number.

Finally, a live person.

"Been trying to reach Outta Here," said Malcolm. "Did some work for him, you know what I'm saying? He owes me."

"You and me both, man. You know Dwayne won't be paying off on his debts."

"Say what?"

"Doubt he left a will."

Malcolm's high wasn't enough to help with the translation. "Something go down with Dwayne?"

"You're really in the dark, Third Eye. Dwayne is outta here for real. He's dead. He drowned at some party, or that's what the papers say." A long pause. "Hey, he was up near Boston, that's your crib, right? You see him before?"

Malcolm didn't need a translation for that, Polo asking him if he was with Dwayne, maybe had a hand in what went down. Malcolm said, "Me and Dwayne ain't that tight, since he went to Miami. Ain't seen him in forever."

He hung up. Shit. No Dwayne, no money.

He pulled the iPhone out, waving it at Cadillac. "Trade this for one of those windproof lighters?"

CHAPTER 38

FRIDAY MORNING, Winter did his informant run, hoping someone on the street might have heard who did the Carter assault. He and the other detectives had spent all of yesterday tracking down guests, looking at photos from the party, and coming up with nothing.

Winter came up blank on the informant run as well, either nothing going down or it was just too cold, the last three days unending wind and overcast. Winter had never minded the cold, but the falls and winters seemed to be getting worse, or he was feeling it more.

He figured he'd have plenty of time to catch the end of the morning briefing on the Carter house deaths. Inside the station, though, the bullpen was dark.

Winter stuck his head in Logan's office. Logan, on the phone, waved him in as he hung up. "Anything on the street?" Logan knew Winter's schedule.

"Like Siberia," said Winter. "No briefing?"

"Short one. We got—and this is not for external communication— jack shit. Phone records still aren't here on either Hennig or Coleman. Still about ten more guests to track down. Trying to put a rush on the tox tests. The Carter lawyers are pushing me to make a statement that they didn't directly invite either deceased, and after that if it were up to them we'd not have another press conference, which would be just fine by me. The Marburg *Times*, though, wants to know what color underwear the Carter family wears, and whether they have categorically denied they have drug parties?"

"And your problem is?"

Logan said, "Funny. Actually, it's *your* problem now. Last night we had a hit and run, a woman changing her tire, she died on the scene. Right after that, those assholes who've been doing the gas station convenience store hits were back at it. The store manager put up a fight that didn't end well. He didn't make it through the night."

"Should have called me," said Winter.

"O'Dowd has been running the robberies, with Hendricks, they were both on last night. Crosse is taking the hit and run. If anything gets cleared, I'll switch them back, but for now, Owens is lead on the Coleman death, and Ryder is on Hennig."

"You want me to keep on both?"

"Yeah. Focus on Hennig, we know for sure that one is a homicide."

"If Coleman comes back accidental, that means there's no connection between the deaths."

"Unless you turn up something," said Logan. "In the meantime, let's figure out what happened to Hennig. No reason why the poor guy should have got a beating over a watch. There's something going on we don't know. Find it."

WINTER FOUND Ryder hunched over his computer, music playing from the tinny speakers.

"Must be nice to have time for that," said Winter.

"Research," said Ryder. He turned up the sound. "This is Gerry Hennig's band, back when he was with Rick Singleton. I found it on a cache of their old band website."

"What's a cache?"

"It's—never mind. I can understand why Singleton wanted to get him back into music."

Winter didn't know much about music, but he had to admit it sounded pretty good. "What's next on Hennig?"

"I got interviews lined up with Hennig's roommates, Bernstein and Cheng. They weren't there when we searched Gerry's apartment. And Hennig's faculty advisor, Dr. Milov. I got the addresses of two of the other guys in the band. One of them, name of Doyle Madison, is in Boston."

"You find out anything else about Hennig?"

"Can't find the drug angle, if that's what you mean."

"If there is one."

"Got to be. Or something else we don't know. Who gets killed over a watch?"

"You and Logan are on the same page."

"We all are. We got three choices: drugs, personal, or crazy."

"Maybe we can rule one of them out in Boston."

WINTER CALLED his daughter Audrey before leaving. Audrey was with one of those grind around the clock investment advisors in Boston. He usually got her voicemail so he tuned out after dialing. His conversation with Ryder had spurred a thought, but he'd lost it.

"Dad?"

"Sorry, didn't expect you to pick up. I'm heading in to Boston. Just wondering if you might be available for dinner tonight? Save you a trip out tomorrow." He and Audrey had a weekly Saturday lunch in Marburg, and he knew she often had to go back into the office when she returned to the city.

"Tonight's not really good for me."

Winter translated that as she had a date, and while Audrey was well past the age when he should be screening her boyfriends, he still got that twist in his gut. "Okay, no problem."

"I could do a coffee though, if you are going to be near the office."

Winter flicked his notebook to Gerry's apartment address. He knew Boston pretty well, he'd gone there enough on cases. "Cambridge, just across the river, right?"

"As the crow flies. Friday traffic . . ."

"I won't keep you waiting. If I get held up, I'll call."

IN CAMBRIDGE, Winter and Ryder walked south on Third Street for two blocks. Gerry Hennig's apartment was one in a long line of similar buildings, six or so stories, retail shops on the first floor, apartments above. The street, semi busy, college aged kids in college type clothing, texting while walking. A chalkboard sign advertised a stomach roiling combination of pulled pork and oysters.

"I've been wondering how Hennig could afford this neighborhood," said Ryder, as he rang the buzzer. The door clicked, both cops frowning. They bypassed the tiny elevator and took the stairs to the fourth floor.

A dark haired, too skinny guy in black wire glasses answered the door, wearing a blue fleece zip up and chinos. "Come on in."

Ryder introduced them, then said, "Mr. Bernstein, you really shouldn't just buzz people up."

"Saw you from the window," said Bernstein. "I was expecting you, and you look like a cop." He squinted at Winter. "Although you don't."

"It's a disguise," said Ryder. "He goes undercover a lot."

Winter checked out the apartment. Small living room, kitchen along one wall, four doors, two of them open, a bath and a bedroom. A sofa bed, opened. Windows only on the street side. Not much paper, unmatched prints on the white walls. "Did you know Gerry for a long time?" he asked Bernstein.

"A year. I met him on campus, we're both math grad students."

"Nice place," said Ryder. "Pretty expensive I bet."

"Tell me about it. Almost four thousand a month."

"Kind of tight," said Winter.

"Lots of students do it, split the rent three ways in a two bedroom. Nothing illegal about it."

"What did Gerry do when he wasn't at school?"

"Not much. Study. He teaches an undergrad class, like we all do. He wasn't into video games. Did a hackathon now and then."

"You know his close friends?" asked Winter.

"Gerry's on his own most of the time."

"He must have hung out with somebody," said Ryder.

"You know what it's like to be a PhD student here?"

"Must be long hours," said Winter. "I wouldn't be able to stay awake." His way of edging into the drug question they'd have to ask.

"Tell me about it," said Bernstein. "I never knew what naps were until I became a grad student. Sometimes I fall asleep eating."

"No one using pick me ups? A little coke?" asked Ryder.

Bernstein pointed to a coffee machine on the counter. "There's my pick me up. I won't say nobody uses drugs, but I'd never take the chance. What if you had a bad reaction? Or got hooked? I've been working at this for years, no way I'm going to risk losing it all."

"How about Gerry?" asked Ryder.

"Gerry doesn't even drink coffee. Never saw him do any drugs."

Winter stepped inside Hennig's room. The bed was made, the desk empty except for a charging cord, three math textbooks, a holder of mechanical pencils, and a stack of graph paper. One wall held a white-board, with one equation at the top. He saw no indications it was any-thing but a student's bedroom. Crosse and Ryder had already been through it all, he was just getting a feel.

From the doorway, Winter asked, "Any of Gerry's music friends come around?"

"No. I haven't really seen him with anyone other than students. He did tell me and Cheng about the party he was going to, the one he—died at. Said it was about music. He didn't sound too excited, more like something he had to do."

The door opened, and a heavyset guy walked in, eating a slice of pizza. "Hey," he mumbled around the food. "I'm Cheng."

They did the introductions, asked Cheng more or less the same ques-tions, but learned nothing new.

Ryder said, "So you guys live together, what, two, three years, but don't really know much about Gerry?"

Cheng said, "We don't even overlap much at the apartment. I see Gerry more on campus than I do here, and that's just because my office is near his."

"No girlfriend?" asked Winter.

"Got less time for girlfriends than we do for drugs," said Bernstein.

Cheng said, "I did see Gerry talking to this girl now and then, she does check-in at the math building."

Winter said, "Can you think of who might have had a problem with Gerry?"

Bernstein shook his head, but Cheng said, "How about that guy on the street?"

"He was stoned."

"What guy?" asked Winter.

"The three of us were heading out, this guy came up to us, I thought he was looking for a handout. But he didn't say anything, just pushed Gerry against the wall. Aggressive like."

"Gerry specifically?"

"Seemed that way," said Cheng.

"Did it look like Gerry knew him? Did Gerry say anything after?"

"No to both. We get panhandlers all the time, people on the street just bumming money. I didn't think much of it, and I don't think Gerry did either."

"I wouldn't have remembered if you hadn't brought it up," said Bernstein. "The guy was scary, though, but it only lasted a minute, not even."

"What did he look like?" asked Ryder.

"African American man," said Cheng. "Our age. Some pockmarks on one side of his face."

"He had a baseball cap," said Bernstein. "Turned around, backward."

"He have a tattoo on his face?"

"I was trying hard not to make eye contact."

"When was this?" asked Winter.

"Few weeks ago, maybe? I lose track of time. Like I said, it barely registered. Go down on the street and hang for a while, someone will come up and ask you for some change. Well, not you in particular, but you know what I mean."

OUTSIDE, Ryder said, "You think the mystery black man was the same guy at the party?"

"And rode in the limo with Dwayne Coleman. Could be. Lots of guys wear their caps that way though."

"Might be Gerry's drug connection. Gerry might have pretended to not know the guy in front of his roommates. Maybe Gerry owed him money, or was going to do a deal with him at the party."

Winter said, "Didn't look like the den of a drug lord to me. What did the MIT police say?"

"They hardly ever get a complaint about the grad students. Claim there are not many drugs on campus. That's their story and they are sticking to it." Ryder looked back at the apartment. "Those guys said they barely saw Gerry. Maybe he had another place, moved drugs from there. Or maybe he was just a go-between, put deals together."

"Sounds like a stretch," said Winter.

"Got to be something."

Winter wasn't convinced it was drugs, but Ryder was right. Had to be something. Of all the people who could have gotten robbed at that party, why'd they pick Gerry Hennig?

*   *   *

WINTER AND RYDER grabbed an early lunch at a cafe on Binney recommended by Cheng, Winter getting the pizza. As they ate Ryder phoned the guy from Rick's band again, Doyle Madison. Madison lived and worked in Dorchester and agreed to see them after work.

"Gonna catch the traffic," said Ryder. "Let's go talk to Hennig's advisor and the girlfriend."

They decided to leave the car where it was and make the walk to Hennig's office on Memorial Drive. In the Simons Building, a girl wearing earbuds who looked too young to be in college, let alone grad school, sat at a reception table, reading a book.

Ryder tapped on the table to get her attention. When she looked up they couldn't see her eyes, her haircut one massive set of overgrown bangs.

"Can I help you?" said a voice from behind the hair.

"We're looking for Dr. Milov," said Ryder.

"Second floor."

"And maybe you too," said Ryder. "We're with the Marburg Police. You knew Gerry Hennig?"

"Oh my god yes. Poor Gerry." She pulled her hair away from her face, which was as blanched as her hair.

"You know him well?" asked Ryder.

"Not very. We'd talk when he came in and out."

She sounded disappointed, suggesting to Winter she and Hennig weren't that close. "You liked Gerry?"

Her face turned crimson. "Sure. I mean, everybody did, I guess." She bit her lip. "What happened to him? I heard he got mugged."

"We're still trying to figure it out," said Winter. "You ever see Gerry have a problem with anyone? Or people come asking for him?"

"I think you are the only people who have ever asked about him. I mean, except for a few undergrads in his math class, they come by now and then during his office hours." Her voice cracked. "I mean, used to come by."

"Is one of the students a black man, skinny, usually wears a backwards baseball cap?" asked Winter.

"I don't remember anyone with a backward cap in here, like ever."

"Maybe he took it off. Might have a tattoo on his forehead?" said Winter.

"I'd remember that. No."

Winter wondered if she paid much attention, between her book and her earbuds and her hair. "What did you and Gerry talk about?"

"The usual. School. He asked what kind of music I listened to. He actually told me about that party he was going to, at the Carter house? I never knew he had that much money."

"What makes you think he had money?" asked Winter.

"Who else would go to a party at the Carter's? They gave a bunch of money to the school."

"But you didn't think Gerry had money before that?"

"I never thought he did. I mean, if he was rich, what was he doing getting a math PhD?"

THEY ASKED HER a few more questions, got her contact information, and walked up the stairs to the second floor.

Dr. Anatoly Milov looked Russian, but had less of an accent than Winter. Late forties. He had short black hair with a hint of early gray at the temples. Behind his desk was a large cork board, filled with perfectly arranged letter sized pieces of paper with tightly packed equations. In the center, one page, blank.

"Terrible, terrible," said Milov. "Gerry had amazing potential."

"Smart?" asked Winter.

"Everyone here is smart. I bet you're smart. Math at this level is beyond smart. You have to have a grasp of—the underlying nature of what makes math work. It's not about numbers. It's about seeing the world in ways that can be described with symbols and then using techniques to see how those symbols interconnect."

"And Gerry could do that?"

"At more than the basic level. He was capable of insights. He was beyond most of his peers."

"You ever notice any problems? Late to meetings, health problems, money problems?"

"No, why? I understand he was mugged? What does that have to do with his studies?"

"Probably nothing," said Winter. "You talk to him much about his personal life?"

"He mostly talked about math. I met his parents once, they were very proud of him. Nice people."

"He mention any other interests?"

"He liked music, mostly the theory. I don't believe he played any more."

They went around it for a while, getting nothing new. Finally Ryder asked, "Did you ever get the sense Gerry had any interest in or contact with drugs?"

"Gerry? I don't see how. I had a student, three, four years ago, got hooked on pain pills after an operation. It was pretty obvious. He had to leave the school." Milov made a grand gesture with his arm. "All of this, you can't do it high. You just can't."

"Did Gerry get paid?" asked Winter.

"All grad students get at least partial tuition, and if they are teaching, a stipend. The stipend is about three thousand a month. It sounds like a lot, but it's expensive to live here. Most of the students still need outside money."

"Ever see Gerry get in a fight?" asked Ryder.

"No. It would be out of character for him."

As they got ready to leave, Winter pointed to the blank piece of paper on the board behind Milov. "What's that for?"

"Often the best way to see relationships is to work from emptiness, instead of forcing together complexity. I use that as a reminder."

"I do the same thing," said Winter. "Only I stare at my ceiling."

Milov raised an eyebrow. "Maybe you should consider math."

"I don't think so," said Winter. "Unless balancing my checkbook counts."

THE WIND BLEW across the river, most of the leaves already off the trees along the math building. "If Hennig was dealing, it doesn't sound like he was doing it around here," said Winter.

"Unless he was careful."

"Never heard of a drug dealer with a PhD," said Winter. "Although I don't know many PhD's. He wasn't hurting for money, but it didn't seem like he was rolling in it either."

"I had a case, back before I came to Marburg. Coach at a small college was supplying pills. Started out with just steroids, but he expanded. Hennig could be selling to the undergrads. Worth checking."

"Guess so," agreed Winter. "Just doesn't feel right, though. You heard the professor, Hennig was gifted, he was into the math. Why ruin all that?"

"How much can math PhD's possibly make?"

Winter was thinking about his conversation with Candy Carter. She had a lot of money, and was still pursuing her own passion. "Might not be about the money."

Ryder said, "It's always about money, for someone. We just need to figure out who."

It was too early to see Doyle Madison, so Winter said, "I'm going to grab a coffee with my daughter. Meet up later?"

Ryder said, "I'll try to find a few of Hennig's undergrad students."

"Thanks. Call you as soon as I'm done."

RYDER CALLED an Uber, and Winter called Audrey. "Forty-five minutes a good time?"

"Okay, text me when you are downstairs. You do remember how to text?"

"Hey, a professor at MIT just told me I had a future in advanced math."

Winter headed off along the drive toward Longfellow Bridge, remembered it was under construction, and wondered if he could walk across. Turned around, took the slightly longer way, across the Mass Ave bridge. He liked to walk, he didn't do it enough.

It was cold along the river, but he preferred Storrow Drive to the congestion of Beacon. Along the way he tried to get a handle on Gerry Hennig.

From what they'd learned so far, Hennig appeared to be just who everyone described him as, a hard working PhD student. Winter had dealt with plenty of drug dealers, and with few exceptions, all the people around them knew them as what they were, drug dealers. It was hard to deal drugs unless you were *known* as a drug dealer, otherwise you'd have no customers.

Of course, Gerry Hennig was likely smarter than all of them put together. But a guy that smart would probably figure out an easier cover than grinding to a math degree. It didn't fit.

On the other hand, Ryder was right: if you ruled out crazy, assaults—especially viscous ones—were usually about drugs, or were personal conflicts. Drugs and money were often tied together, although there could be another money play they hadn't figured out. As for personal, Hennig didn't appear to know anyone at the party except Singleton. Singleton hadn't beaten Hennig; he would have had blood all over him. Maybe someone Singleton had hired? But why? And why do it at a party where Singleton was?

If they didn't find a drug angle, either there was a personal connection they were missing, or it was money. Money could mean a simple mugging, Hennig in the wrong place at the wrong time. Hennig might have looked like easy prey. Winter had read about a study of violent convicts who had looked at pictures of strangers and were in almost total agreement on who they'd pick to rob. It wasn't an age or a sex or a race, but rather a look of weakness. Hennig and his Rolex get spotted by a thief at the party, it gets out of hand. Maybe the thief is coked up. It fit the facts as well as anything.

Winter was making good time, so he cut across to the public alley on the other side of Beacon and took it to the Boston Common. A half dozen kids were dribbling a soccer ball just outside the fence. A man selling lemonade from a cart looked at Winter hopefully, so Winter bought a water from him and sat for a few minutes on the bleachers at the softball field, hoping for insights into Gerry Hennig.

None came.

CHAPTER 39

WINTER MET Audrey in a small coffee shop around the corner from her State Street office. She looked harried, as she usually did, even on weekends.

"I'm afraid I don't have much time," she said as she hugged him.

"No problem. You good?"

"The usual. Not enough sleep, shit flows downhill. Probably the same as you."

"They treating you okay?"

"Treating us to a lot of work. Sound familiar?"

"I don't have to dress up, though."

"I'm sure you've been talked to about that."

"Less and less. Logan leaves me alone, for the most part."

Audrey stirred her coffee distractedly. Winter thought she wanted to tell him something. After a bit, he prompted, "You happy?"

"I like it, mostly. I know there are a ton of investment advisors, but the stuff I do is complex, and not for the sake of complexity. When I get my head around a big problem, and figure out a solution, it's like I solved a mystery."

"I get that. I just—ah, hell, you can take care of yourself."

She gave Winter a fleeting smile. "I had a good teacher."

"Speaking of which, how is your mother?" Winter was one of many divorced cops, but unlike most of the others, he actually had an okay relationship with his ex wife, who lived in Virginia.

"She's good, talked to her a few days ago. You haven't?"

"A few weeks maybe? No reason, just, you know, busy. She has her own life. So do you."

Audrey touched his hand. "I'll always have time for you."

But Winter saw that her mind was elsewhere, and felt her slipping away.

WINTER CALLED Ryder from the lobby of Audrey's office after walking her back. "Any luck?"

"I found three of Hennig's undergrad students. They didn't look like dopers. One of them admitted he smoked weed but he claimed he wasn't getting it from Hennig."

"If Hennig was dealing, someone would know."

"Yeah. I'll get the paperwork going to get the whole class list. Can you cover the Madison interview? You can take the car back to Marburg."

"How are you going to get home?"

"Since I'm here I was thinking of doing a little bar crawl. Nice rooftop place at the Colonnade to start. I'll head back in the morning."

"Pretty sure of yourself," said Winter.

"These city women go hot for cops. You should try it."

Winter hadn't picked up a woman in a bar since—he couldn't remember. Not a stranger, that's for sure. "I'm a little underdressed," he said.

WINTER MET Doyle Madison on the loading dock of an old mill in Dorchester, now a welding business. Madison wore a denim work shirt with burn marks on the sleeves.

"Seems like another life," said Madison. "The band. Out late at night, sleep in. My ears rang for years after I hung it up."

"You didn't keep in touch with Rick and Gerry?"

"For a bit. Rick tried to keep it together after Gerry left, but it wasn't the same. Gigs slowed down, the van was out of commission, little shit went bad. I had to take a day job, hurt my shoulder, couldn't play drums for a while. Never went back. I was just an okay drummer anyway, Gerry was the musical genius." Madison lit a cigarette, leaning over the railing. "Can't believe he's dead."

"He have problems in the clubs?" asked Winter.

"Gerry? If you didn't look closely, you wouldn't even know he was on stage. Half the time he stood behind the stacks. He just wasn't into the limelight. At breaks he'd be practicing licks while the rest of us were grabbing a beer or chatting up the chicks."

"No women for Gerry?"

"Not sure how it was when you were that age, but it wasn't cool for women to be with the nerdy guy."

"Drugs?"

Madison laughed. "We tried to get Gerry high for his birthday. We lit up some weed, we couldn't even convince him to take a hit. So we locked the door and all toked up, seeing if we could get him with second hand smoke. Man, that was funny." Madison voice was nostalgically sad.

Winter leaned over the railing next to Madison. "Anything else?"

Madison tossed his butt in a oily puddle. "With all the time I spent with the guy I didn't really know him that well. We'd all talk, but he was mostly a listener, and when he did talk, it wasn't about himself."

"Like he didn't want you to know?"

"No. He just didn't like to be the center of attention. It wasn't like he was antisocial, he was in a band. You should ask Rick, he knew Gerry the best."

"They were close?"

"Like glue. They thought they were going to be the next Lennon and McCartney. Even though one or the other had written a song, it had to have both their names on it."

"Whose idea was that?"

"It was Rick's idea but Gerry went along. They even signed a contract—this was before the band started. Rick always said their songwriting was fifty-fifty."

"Even Lennon and McCartney had a falling out," Winter said.

"Not these guys. They were a great team. Rick was more the organizer. Gerry did most of the arrangements, and he had a sweet voice. I can't sing a damn, so I was happy. I just wanted to pound the skins."

"What about the rest of the band?"

"Same for them. Rick would tell us where to be, the rest of us just showed up and played."

"So Rick ran the show?"

"Somebody had to. A band can't run with five guys making decisions."

What Winter was hearing wasn't too far off of what Rick Singleton had told him. Gerry was a straight, quiet guy who played music, moved on. "Did Rick and Gerry ever sell any songs?"

"Not that I know of."

Winter was thinking about royalties. "You write any of the songs?"

"I never even *tried* to write a song. Rick, though, he was into all that. I think he realized he was no different from a million other musicians, maybe good enough to make a few bucks on the local circuit, but he wasn't going be playing the Boston Garden. If he made it, he'd do it writing songs, with Gerry." Madison lit another cigarette. "Actually, we came pretty close to getting signed one time. Not locally, but with a real big label. It fell through."

"How did you all take that?"

"We were caught up in the excitement, going to New York. We just thought it was a glitch, it would work out. It didn't. Rick was devastated. Even Gerry was disappointed. We all could have been millionaires."

"You don't really mean a million bucks, right?"

"Who knows? Wouldn't be the first time someone got rich from music. Besides," Madison jerked his hand at the building, "compared to this, running a cutting torch eight hours a day? Even a slice of the pie would have seemed like a million."

WINTER GOT THE phone numbers for the other two members of the band from Madison. Winter would check them out, but he wasn't expecting much.

He stayed on the dock as Madison drove off in an old pickup. Nothing he'd learned so far about Hennig pointed to a problem in his past. There was more they could track down, Hennig's high school teachers, more of his college friends. In Winter's experience, people just didn't jump into drugs; they were in it or on the periphery for years. If Hennig hustled drugs, people would know. There were infrequent cases where, out of desperation, someone tried to make a big score. Hennig didn't seem like the desperate type, but it would have to be checked, like everything else.

If Hennig hadn't been killed over drugs, and with no one else turning up who knew him at the party other than Singleton, it was hard to imagine a personal motive either. That left money.

The only money that kept popping up had to do with music royalties.

Rick Singleton and Gerry Hennig had a deal about royalties. It sounded like a long shot, but right now it was just as likely as drugs.

The overhead door opened. Two men wrestled a forty-gallon drum out onto the dock. They nodded at Winter and went back in, speaking rapid Spanish.

The singsong cadence reminded Winter of the caterer he'd been told about who had seen a man going up the back stairs at the Carter House the night of the party. Eduardo.

Winter checked his watch. Right in the middle of rush hour. He'd never get back in time to catch Eduardo tonight.

Maybe Ryder was right, might be better to stay in the city, drink some beers, go home in the morning. Find some woman to curl up with.

Who was he kidding. He'd rather waste time sitting in traffic than sit in a bar hoping for a miracle.

CHAPTER 40

WINTER DIDN'T get back to Marburg until after eight, stuck in two separate accidents before he even got out of Boston, and then a third on the Mass Pike. He'd stopped to get bite at the Framingham rest stop, hoping the traffic would clear. It hadn't.

He swung by Brookside Caterers but the place was dark. Too late to catch Eduardo, too early to go to bed.

Winter cut across town toward Brooker's house, whom he hadn't spoken to since the Carter investigation had started. Winter wasn't quite certain whether he should keep Brooker up to date. He could use Brooker's help, but he was worried it would make Brooker feel worse for being on medical leave. Maybe worse for Winter too, making it harder for him to accept Brooker might not come back.

Brooker answered the door with a, "Wondering when the hell you'd get by," which answered one of Winter's questions.

Brooker got beers from the kitchen. "You okay on the porch? Going nuts in the living room."

"Been in the car for hours, porch sounds good." Winter nodded toward Brooker's beer. "You okay to drink?"

"I can have one a day."

"That might be worse than none."

"Tell me about it. I never watched much tv except for games, but when it was on I always would have a few. Now I watch ten times as much tv and get no beer."

"Maybe you should stop watching tv."

"You got an alternative?"

"Exercise? Stamp collecting? Crochet?"

Brooker slid open the door to the porch, dropping into one of the creaky mesh lawn chairs. "I'm walking a few miles a day, believe it or not. Which, come to think of it, is probably less than I walked on the job. My eyes aren't good enough for stamp collecting or crochet. Otherwise I might consider both."

Winter thought Brooker looked the same as always. Buzz cut, too big all over, his ears, his nose, his gut. "Any news from the docs?"

"The same. Doing more tests to see if I should get surgery, reduce stress, blah blah blah."

Winter took a hit of his beer. "Good thing you have a low stress job." Winter wanted to ask if Brooker thought he'd be coming back or not. Figured Brooker would tell him when it was time. "This Carter thing I'm working on, it's a bitch."

"Been reading the papers, which doesn't tell me much."

Winter filled Brooker in on where they were. Their beers were long gone when he finished. "More than I thought," he said.

"That's because we're not talking every day."

"About that—"

"Not a criticism." Brooker shifted in the chair. "If I lose weight, I'll need to get new furniture, I won't have all this built-in padding."

Winter said, "You lose enough weight to have a bony ass, and I'll *buy* you new furniture."

"So you figure that it's the million to one chance the two deaths aren't linked?"

"Time to buy a lottery ticket, right?"

"Remember that one we caught, maybe ten years ago? Fight breaks out at a party, that guy gets shot?"

"And when we show up his next door neighbor is dead on the side of his house. I remember. The guy was working on his air conditioner, got electrocuted. We kept looking for gunshot holes in the poor bastard until the M.E. got there."

"Point is, just because two guys show up dead right next to one another . . ."

"Yeah, yeah. I'm not trying to force it. Just don't want to miss the obvious."

Brooker said, "You never miss the obvious."

"That's the problem. There is no obvious. If there's a connection, it's not the usual. The two men didn't know one another as far as we can tell. One might have been a coke user. The other guy, Hennig, was a boy scout."

"No such thing as boy scouts," said Brooker. "Without secrets, anyway."

Brooker hadn't turned on the porch light, the only illumination from the kitchen overhead, throwing harsh shadows outside. Beyond the railing, the yard was in complete darkness, which was about how Winter felt. "Most likely answer is that it's just a coincidence. Coleman is an accidental, Hennig got robbed. Like most of what we see, it's usually just the obvious."

"Until it isn't," said Brooker.

They thought about that for a while. "Maybe I need to think about it the other way around," said Winter. "Assume it's *not* drugs, or a robbery, or personal."

"Follow the money," said Brooker.

WINTER SAT IN his truck in the parking lot of Brookside Caterers. Saturday morning, two hours after the sun had risen yet the early chill still not overcome. Winter was coming.

The window cracked, the radio off, Winter stared at the blank wall of the low whitewashed building, using it as his canvas to try to connect any dots between Dwayne Coleman and Gerry Hennig.

The party was one connection, but the line he could draw was not solid, since neither man appeared to have a direct relationship via another guest. Candy Carter said she'd only met Coleman that night, and she didn't even know Hennig. Why would she lie? If she had any inkling the two men would be a problem she wouldn't have let them be invited. The same went for Miranda Dell.

So, no direct connection, not yet anyway. How about an indirect one? Coleman knowing someone who knew Hennig? Needed to check that out.

Drugs *could* be a connection, but neither man had priors for drug offenses. Even if one or both of them turned out to be users, so what? It wasn't like all the other guests were totally clean on that score.

The only other connection Winter was sure of was music. Yet he couldn't really draw a line between Coleman and Hennig, because if he did, he'd have to include lines to Candy, to Singleton, to DeVaughn, to half the guests at the party. It was like saying all the guests at a college reunion were connected because they went to the same college. It didn't mean much.

Hennig wasn't even into music any longer, and he was the one beaten. Coleman *was* doing music, but he wasn't roughed up.

Music, though, could lead to money. And the money was doled out through royalties.

He'd heard from multiple people there could be big money in music. It depended on the royalty deal. Singleton and Hennig had some kind of royalty contract. Who was Coleman's contract with? Was there a linkage between their royalty deals?

In his mind, Winter penciled in a dark line between Hennig and Singleton, and lighter lines with a question mark between Coleman and Hennig and, then, after thinking about it some more, between Singleton and Coleman. The possible indirect connection.

Follow the money.

WINTER WAS just about to give up on the caterer when a white van pulled up. A woman wearing oversized sunglasses got out and approached the front door.

Winter caught up to her. "I'm looking for Eduardo—"

Too fast, the woman said, "We don't have an Eduardo."

Winter couldn't see her eyes through the dark lenses, but her head shifted slightly to the side of the building.

Winter thought about the number of vans and parking spaces out back, and the few in front. "You sure?"

The woman said, "I have to get ready for a lunch," and pushed quickly inside.

Which tipped off Winter something wasn't right. He ignored her, running around to the back of the building. Four cars were there that hadn't been an hour earlier. Two men wearing black pants and white shirts were on the landing, peering into the back door window.

Winter, half asking, half guessing, said, "Eduardo?"

One of the men took one look at Winter, jumped off the landing, and ran toward the cars.

Winter sprinted across the lot, another car moving now, cutting him off, Winter dodging out of the way, slamming his hand on the hood, yelling "Police!" He pointed his finger at the driver, warned, "Don't," only caring about Eduardo.

Who had managed to get in his car and get it started, Winter grabbing at the door handle just as the lock clicked, not fast enough. Winter yanked open the door and jerked Eduardo out of the car, the car still rolling, Eduardo falling out, Winter screaming at him to not move. The car plowed into one of the vans, pushing it sideways, finally stopping as the first van hit another, the car stalling.

Winter held Eduardo down with one hand, taking a fast glance to see if there was going to be a problem with his friends. "Turn off the engines," he yelled, fishing a zip tie from his cargo pants, twisting Eduardo's wrists behind his back.

"Leave me alone, I didn't do nothing."

"You run every time someone calls your name?" Winter yanked him up. "Against the trunk." Winter frisked him, nothing.

"Man, you ruined my ride."

A maroon sedan pulled into the lot, a guy wearing a blue shirt with the name of the caterer stitched over the pocket jumping out. "What's going on here?"

Winter said, "Police. Came to talk to Eduardo here and he ran."

The guy glanced toward the building. "Okay if these other people get to work? We got a lunch to handle."

Winter pointed to the driver in the car that had almost run him down. "You, stay here. The rest can go."

"Come on," said the guy in the blue shirt. "You heard him, get inside." As he came by Winter he said, "I told Linda not to hire this one, and them in the car. They probably thought you were immigration."

Winter got the message, they were working off the books. He ordered the two from the other car, who didn't look much older than sixteen, to toss out their keys and sit on the hood.

"I didn't do nothing," repeated Eduardo.

"Never said you did." Winter turned him around. Eduardo was giving him the didn't give a shit glare, either for the benefit of the two younger kids, or because he'd dealt with the police before.

Winter could play that game. "Too bad for you I wasn't immigration. Immigration gives you a court day, tells you to show up. Me, I can throw all of you in jail right now. Failure to stop for a police officer, assault with a dangerous weapon."

"I got no weapon," said Eduardo.

"A car tried to run me over. That's a weapon."

"We were just leaving," said one of the kids, but Winter could hear the fear in his voice. "I stopped, didn't I?"

"Maybe I'll believe that if Eduardo here helps me out."

Eduardo stuck with the glare. Winter said, "Maybe I search your car while you're thinking it over in this nice brisk fall air?"

"Can't just look in my car."

"Really? I see what looks to be a roach on the floor, and hey, is that a baggie of weed on the armrest? That's plenty of probable cause." Winter leaned into the car. "I'm sure I can find—"

"Okay, okay, what do you want?"

"I want to know about the party you worked at the Carter house."

"I didn't kill nobody," said Eduardo.

Winter realized the caterer had probably not included Eduardo on the list of employees they'd provided to the police. To the other two he said, "You work the party too? Don't lie to me."

One of the kids said, "We were there, just setting up."

Winter leaned into Eduardo. "Heard you were around the back stairway near the kitchen."

"Who told you that?"

Winter didn't want to finger the girl Carlina. "Lots of people. We have video."

"So we were in the kitchen. That's what we do."

"Tell me about the guy going up the stairs."

Eduardo said, "I tell you, you let me go?"

"If you don't, I won't even consider letting you go. That's the only thing you can be sure of."

"Maybe I saw a guy."

"What did he look like?"

"White guy, dark hair. Had a suit jacket on. That's all I remember."

Winter was thinking Eduardo might have been talking about Rick Singleton. "He look okay to you?" Winter wanting to see if Eduardo mentioned anything about blood on the guy's clothes. "You see him close?"

"I was in a hurry—"

One of the kids said, "He just ran up the stairs past us."

Eduardo said, "Shut up, Ray."

"Wait," said Winter. "You were *upstairs*, coming down? What were you doing upstairs?"

"We weren't upstairs," said Eduardo.

Winter didn't believe him. He backed up a half step, maybe he had stumbled upon Hennig's killers after all. "Maybe you were looking around for some easy stuff to pick up?"

"No way," said one of the kids.

Eduardo hadn't said anything. Winter prodded, "So that's it? You check the bedrooms, shove jewelry in your pocket? Didn't expect to see anyone up there?"

"Didn't see nobody."

Winter figured he'd guessed close enough, Eduardo had made a run through the house hoping for easy pickings. Maybe he'd stumbled upon Gerry Hennig wearing his Rolex and took it from him. "Let's take a ride, Eduardo."

"You said you'd let me go if I told you!"

"You're lying to me."

"Wait, okay, I was upstairs! We heard yelling, we ran for it . . ."

"*We* didn't take nothing," said one of the kids. "He just makes us keep watch."

"Shut *up*, Ray."

Winter pushed on, no idea if Eduardo might clam up later. "A guy gets killed, you are *right there*, you don't see a thing?"

"We weren't there, not on that floor. We were on the third floor, just looking around, nice house. Wanted to see it, that's all. We ran down the back stairs, didn't even look the other way. You should ask that guy I saw going up the stairs."

Winter wasn't sure he believed much of anything they'd said, the usual mix of truth and untruth common to those who had something to hide. He pulled Eduardo around. "Come on." He needed backup but he'd left his phone in the truck, still not used to carrying it around. "You too," he said to the kids.

"Where're we going?" whined Eduardo. "I told you what you wanted."

Which is what Winter was afraid of, someone else telling him what he wanted, rather than the truth.

CHAPTER 41

Rɪᴄᴋ ʜᴀᴅ ʟᴇꜰᴛ his mother's house Saturday morning the minute the new nurse had shown up. He'd found her at an agency, the last one near Marburg where he hadn't bounced a check.

His check to the regular nurse Sherry *had* already bounced, and Sherry told him she wouldn't be back on Monday unless he covered that and paid her in advance from now on.

He'd made a three-hour drive to a little town north of Albany, his guitar in the backseat. He'd got better offers for it, but all of them required shipping and then waiting for the payment escrow to clear. He needed money, like yesterday. The Albany buyer was the only one he could reach fast.

Rick followed the buyer, a pimply kid who at least looked like he'd appreciate the guitar, to his bank, where they did the bill of sale, Rick walking out with almost three thousand dollars.

His tears over the guitar were long since gone, pushed aside by the fear of losing his mom, being harassed by the cops, and Doc.

His dreams of making it big in music seemed so insignificant now. Yet he needed it more than ever, for the money to take care of his mother and get Doc off his back. Even though he'd heard plenty of stories of cops finding a scapegoat to pin a killing on, that was a big *if*. There was no *ifs* about his mom and about Doc.

As he drove, Rick kept worrying that the cops knew *something* about Doc. Why else had they asked about the fat guy with the driver? The only other person who was there had been Miranda. She might have told the cops enough to undermine Rick's lame story about not knowing Doc.

What would Doc do when he learned he'd been identified?

Rick didn't want to find out.

Which left him just two choices. Tell Doc the cops might be on to him, or tell the cops about Doc, all of it. Both choices sucked. If he confessed to the cops, what could they do, anyway? All Rick had on Doc was that Doc was blackmailing him to give up the royalties. Because Rick owed him money from a coke buy.

Right.

The cops would be far more interested in Rick's drug transactions than in protecting him from Doc.

If he told Doc, maybe Doc would agree to lie low, take off the pressure. A big maybe. It just didn't seem Doc's style.

The drive back to Marburg went too quickly, each mile a reminder of the dwindling time he had to make a decision.

RICK SAT at the same table in the park where it had all started, the fall into his hellhole. Rick's debt, getting fired, Gerry's death, all began at this very table. He wanted to tear it up, rip off the legs.

But it was just a stupid table. The table didn't start all this, he had. All he could hope for now was that his own legs wouldn't get torn off.

Rick gripped the black portfolio tightly in his lap, still second guessing his decision. If he ran off now fat Doc would never be able to catch him.

He'd actually half risen when the sun was blocked out by a looming shadow. Too late.

Doc perched on the metal chair. "I hope that's your friend's will, telling me you own his half of the rights."

Rick had rehearsed his spiel, but Doc's presence and the question had thrown him off. "What? No, I don't know if Gerry even had a will. What do you want me to do, call his parents up and ask?"

"Sounds good to me. You should get what belongs to you."

"Doc, Gerry was my *friend*. I—I can't do that."

"So you don't think your *friend* had a will?"

"I have no idea. Shit, *I* don't even have a will." Rick was thinking a will might be a good idea right about now. "And if Gerry did, he might have forgot all about the royalties."

"You better pray he didn't leave all his unidentified assets to some stupid charity."

Rick slid the portfolio across the table. "There's fifteen hundred bucks in there. Toward my debt." Rick had kept only enough to cover what he needed for Sherry's bounced check and for another week of nursing help.

Doc didn't make a move toward the cash. "Your debt is the royalty deal. *And* the cash. I'm not seeing any action on the first, and this doesn't come close to covering the cash."

The money hadn't done as much to soothe Doc as Rick had hoped. "I'm doing everything I can. But the royalty won't be worth a damn if Candy doesn't use the song, and after what happened at the party . . ." Rick froze, that hadn't come out right.

"Candy's not going to use your music?"

"No, no, she hasn't said a word about that." Rick hadn't even talked to Candy, he had no idea what she was thinking. He'd left her a text about not being at the studio, needing to take care of his mom, and all he got back was an *okay, hope she feels better*. Which told him nothing. For all he knew, Candy had found another song. "There may be another problem, though."

"You've been one big problem. If it wasn't for this Candy and the royalty, I would have solved it, you hear me?"

"I do, really I do." Shit, how to say it? Rick hadn't run off, but his re-hearsed speech had. "The cops—the cops might know about you."

Doc just sat there, not saying a word. He didn't glare, he didn't move, he didn't threaten. And yet Rick had never been more afraid of Doc than at that very moment.

Rick jumped in front of the silent train. "It wasn't me, I swear. I never said a word to the cops about you, about our—deal, anything. Not a word. They were asking me about Gerry. They seemed to be buying my story about why I had invited him, which was mostly true anyway, then out of the blue, bang, they ask about, about . . ." Rick ran down.

"They asked about me by name?"

"No. They asked about . . ." Rick couldn't say the words *fat man*, not in the big presence of Doc.

Again, Doc's silence.

Rick said, "They asked about the man in the black SUV at the stu-dio." Praying Doc wouldn't demand to know if that was the word for word question.

When Doc spoke his voice was so low Rick could barely hear it, as if even Doc had to avoid speaking in a way that would set off his barely contained rage. "What did you tell them?"

"*Nothing*. I made up a story about you—not you by name, I just said a guy had stopped by the studio to ask if we could do a demo tape for his kid. It's happened before. I think they—I'm sure they bought it, why wouldn't they?"

"They wouldn't if they know more than they were telling, trying to catch you lying. And the cops always know more than they're telling."

"Whatever they know, it didn't come from me," insisted Rick. Rick's leather jacket held off the fall chill, but not the cold Doc was throwing at him.

"You must have said something," said Doc, his voice still frighteningly quiet. "It's not like I'm advertising."

There was only one other possibility. Rick knew he'd be getting a visit from Kevin unless Doc got it out of his head that Rick had fingered him. "It had to be Miranda."

"The broad who works for Candy."

"That's right. The cops talked to her too. She must have brought it up."

"Why would she do that?"

"I have no idea." Actually, Rick had a good idea, Miranda covering her own ass, pointing her finger at everyone and anyone so she wouldn't look bad in front of Candy. Or maybe the cops knew about Miranda being with Dwayne, and this was her way of pushing their attention onto Rick. Either way, if he told Doc *that*, then the conversation would shift back to drugs, which was a detour Rick had to avoid at all costs.

"If I send Kevin to talk to this Miranda, her story is going to agree with yours? That she doesn't know anything about what you owe me and why, and how you are paying your debt?"

Rick didn't want to think about how Kevin would get that out of Miranda. Not that he was caring much for Miranda right now, but it made him think of what Kevin would do to *him* if Doc even suspected his story didn't agree with Miranda's.

"Doc, I'm in no position to be telling you what to do, but if you put any pressure on Miranda, it might—draw attention, and then who knows what might happen? Candy could postpone the album. She might not want to use my song if my name comes up. It won't be good for any of us."

"I don't like loose ends," said Doc.

"You want me to talk to Miranda? Figure out what she might have said?" Rick was digging himself a bigger hole with every breath.

"She ever mention me to you any other time? About our chat in the studio parking lot?"

"Never."

"Then don't talk to her. If you do, she'll wonder why." Doc waited until two joggers had gone past. "This woman, is she smart?"

"She looks for angles, out for herself," said Rick. "Smart enough though."

"Let it alone. I'll handle her if I have to. Which means you'll owe me more." Doc wheezed out a breath through his nose, Rick feeling it across the table. "What's her last name, and where does she live?"

Rick couldn't very well claim he didn't know the answer to the first question. "Dell." If Doc somehow was aware that Rick knew of Miranda's apartment, and he didn't tell the truth . . . "She's over at the Chatwick Apartments." It was the tightest line he could walk. The apartment complex was big, maybe Miranda didn't have her name on a mailbox . . . he was rationalizing, but what choice did he have?

Now he'd have another no-win decision to make, whether to warn Miranda about Doc . . . "The cops—if they ask again, what do you want me to say?"

"Do people know Candy records at that studio?"

"It's no secret. Larry might even have spread the word around."

"If the cops say they heard about us talking about Candy, stick to your story about the demo tape. Candy's name came up, I recognized the name, wanted to feel out her assistant about whether to make an investment."

"But you didn't talk to Miranda about that."

"Don't be an idiot. I was just feeling her out about Candy's chances, who she had behind her. Stick to the truth as much as you can."

It sounded like good advice, but Rick couldn't afford the cops, or Doc, knowing all the truth. And the *as much as you can* part was becoming harder and harder to keep track of.

Doc got up. "Don't fuck this up, kid."

KEVIN HAD THE HEATER running full blast, and it still took Doc ten minutes to warm up. The car idled, Kevin smart enough to not disturb Doc's thoughts.

The cops might have nothing, they always threw crap against the wall to see what stuck. Rick, problematic as he was, was right about one thing: calling attention on himself now was not a good idea.

He didn't think Rick had any inkling he had been at the party, Doc would have smelled that right away. Miranda, he wasn't so sure about. He'd seen her with Dwayne near the pool. If the cops suspected her, she might just be smart enough to make a trade with the cops for any tidbit of information she had.

She'd left Dwayne by the pool, gone back to the house . . .

Could she have come back? Seen him with Dwayne?

Doc said, "Kevin, does your cousin know where the Chatwick Apartments are? Not your musician cousin. The other one."

"Everyone knows them."

"Might need him to do a job."

"With me?"

"Keep you out of this one." Miranda had seen Kevin's face.

"Whatever you need, boss."

Doc couldn't make a move until he found out what the cops had been told. He clicked on the rear seat heater. He hated being in the dark as much as he hated the cold.

CHAPTER 42

W INTER, OWENS, Ryder, and Cindy Prague were the only ones in the bullpen for the morning briefing. Winter, arriving last, having spent an hour running down a useless tip from an informant regarding Dwayne Coleman, said, "Where is everyone?"

"We're it," said Owens.

"Tell me you've got something," said Winter. The projector screen was lit, showing a mug shot of a droopy eyed thin faced black man with a vague mark on his forehead.

"Actually, I do. Boston PD came through on our mystery male with the cap. His name is Malcolm Washington. On the street he is Third Eye. The ink on his forehead is supposed to be an eye."

"We sure it's him?"

"Talked to a uniform in Mattapan who has dealt with Washington plenty of times, says he always wears the cap. Has a sheet going back quite a few years, mostly possession. Weed, crack, drug paraphernalia. He's pleaded out on everything so far to time served."

"Gang?"

"The sheet doesn't show any, and the uniform said he didn't think so either, he's just a punk."

Winter said, "We need to show this around. Start with Candy Carter and Miranda Dell. Gerry's roommates. And the limo driver."

"What's a punk from Boston doing at the Carter party?" asked Ryder.

They talked about that for a while, couldn't come up with a good reason. Owens said, "It's not likely he'd be wandering around Marburg, looking for a house to rob."

"He did hitch a ride with Coleman," said Winter.

"Coleman's drug source?" suggested Ryder. "Coleman might have wanted a little coke for the Carter party and didn't want to chance carrying it on the plane. He lands, calls Malcolm Washington, does a buy."

"And takes him to the party?" asked Owens, skeptical.

"Bodyguard? Posse?" said Winter.

Owens snorted. "Small posse."

Winter said, "Cindy, we'll need to go back through the guest photos, see if we can spot this guy."

"I'll ask Dan for help, but Logan has him on the hit and run, looking at traffic cam video."

"We need more people," said Winter. "I'll ask—"

Cindy said, "Hey, you'll want to hear this. I just got an email. Gerry Hennig's phone records are in. Guess whose number came up on Hennig's phone history? Dwayne Coleman."

"Finally," said Owens, pointing a finger at Winter. "Knew they were connected."

"One problem," said Cindy. "The call was made on Wednesday. As in four days after Gerry Hennig was killed."

THEY ALL SQUINTED at the phone records on the screen. The resolution was lousy. "I'll print out copies from my desk," said Cindy.

"If Hennig called Coleman," said Ryder, "or the other way around, they are linked. Got to be."

"Or whoever took Hennig's phone called Coleman," said Winter. "Could be Malcolm Washington."

"Doesn't make sense," argued Ryder. "If Washington is the guy who was in the limo with Coleman, that means he was at the party. So he'd know Coleman was dead. Why would he call him on Hennig's phone days later?"

"Unless Coleman dropped Washington off on the way," said Owens. "The limo driver didn't mention that. I'll go back at him in case he thought it wasn't important."

"We need to get on those party photos to see if Washington shows up," said Winter. "Weren't we putting together a board of what we have so far?"

"I started to, but," Cindy looked at each of the detectives, "I keep getting called to jump on other high priority items."

"Sorry," said Winter. "Too many cooks. I think we can agree this is top of the list?"

"Fine by me," said Cindy. "But the captain wants me on the convenience store robberies."

"Damn it," said Winter. He knew that case was important too, but they finally had a good path to run down. "How can I help?"

Cindy said, "If someone gets me a good coffee, I'll give you all the work you can handle."

WINTER STOOD IN LINE at the Starbucks closest to the station. For once he didn't mind a line, it gave him time to think.

They needed to confirm that Malcolm Washington was the mystery man who had ridden in the limo with Coleman, and if he had been at the party. If he had, *and* he was the same guy who had pushed Hennig around near his apartment, then there would be an undeniable connection between Coleman and Hennig.

It wouldn't explain the connection, just that it existed, in the person of Malcolm Washington. Coleman and Washington obviously knew each other well enough to share a ride. How might *Hennig* know Washington? Maybe Hennig's friends were all wrong, and Hennig bought drugs from Washington. Washington hung around Mattapan, not far from Cambridge.

Though Winter didn't want to get too far ahead of himself, the Washington-Coleman-Hennig link opened up an whole new canvas of possibilities.

Winter reached the front of the line, where a spiky haired clerk with a pierced eyebrow waited impatiently. Winter was still thinking about the case, the possible connection washing away Cindy's complicated drink order. He looked up at the coffee menu, the array of choices as mind numbing as the possible reasons for how the rapper Dwayne Coleman could be linked to PhD student Gerry Hennig.

WINTER PLOPPED THE tray of four drinks on Cindy's desk.

"Is this an indication of how late you're going to keep me tonight?"

"I forgot your order. Hopefully one of these is close."

Cindy opened one of the lids. "These are huge, what size did you order?"

"I asked for medium."

"They don't have mediums."

"I know, dumb right?"

"Next time, I'll go get the coffee, you pull the photos together."

Winter said, "We'd get the coffee right and the photos wrong."

Cindy handed him a thumb drive. "All the photos with Dwayne Coleman are in one folder, and the general guest shots are in another. You can put them up on the bullpen screen." At Winter's dazed look, she added, "Detective Ryder knows how."

"Figures," said Winter.

"And take some of this coffee, I'll never drink it all."

"They all got milk."

"Give it to Detective Ryder, he likes cappuccino."

"Figures," said Winter.

BACK IN THE BULLPEN, Ryder pulled the photos up on the screen. "Might be faster if we each work separately."

"I like the big images," said Winter. He clicked through the Coleman photos first. There were quite a few pictures of black males, but none with Malcolm Washington.

"That's the last one in the Coleman folder," said Ryder. "Over five hundred images in the other." He took over the remote, working fast through any images that didn't show black males.

Forty minutes later, Winter said, "I should have brought more coffees."

"You didn't bring me one," said Owens.

"I didn't even get myself one. Wait, there."

The screen showed three white men toasting Candy Carter. Behind them and off to the side, two black men, one with a backwards cap, were talking to a tall dark haired woman.

Winter walked up to the screen to get a better look. "I don't remember them from the party."

Ryder and Owens didn't either. Ryder blew up the image, centering it on the screen. "Could be Washington," he said. "The note on the image identifies Candy Carter and the three men with her, not the ones in the background."

The next photo showed a totally different set of guests. It wasn't until they were half way through the folder did they find another shot of the two black men. This photo was better, the two men talking to another black man with a camera.

"I remember him," said Winter. "Works for a magazine or blog or whatever, he let me look at his photos."

Again Ryder zoomed in. The photographer was partially in the way, but they could see the face of the man in the cap.

"I can't see a tat," said Owens.

"Might be how he has the cap on," said Ryder. "How tall is Washington?"

"Five eight," said Owens. "One hundred and forty-five pounds."

"This guy looks heavier," said Winter. "And that jacket doesn't look red." He pulled his notebook from his cargo pants. "I got that photographer's name and number . . ." He found it and dialed from the bullpen phone.

"I'm Winter, from the Marburg Police, remember me? Quick question for you. We found a photo of you taking pictures at the party, two black men. One is wearing a backwards cap, clean shaven, not too tall, he's got on a dark leather jacket. The guy he is with has some chin hair, tight afro, wearing a gray sweatshirt, I can't read what it says on the front."

"That sounds like Loot," said the photographer.

"That a name?"

"They're actually brothers, go by Loot. Hip hop, out of Boston. Gerome and Hancock Ives. Don't blame them for going by Loot."

"Did you take any pictures of them?"

"Did you get me that subpoena?"

"That's a yes?"

"Get me the paper, I'll send them over."

Winter thanked him and hung up. "We might have a problem. The guy with the cap is either Gerome or Hancock Ives."

"Might not be the only dude with a cap," said Owens.

But they couldn't find another black male with a cap even after looking through the rest of the images twice.

"We'll know more when we get the photographer's shots," said Winter.

"Even if it's not Washington, still doesn't mean he wasn't there, just that there is no photo of him. Might not have photos of everyone."

"Be good to know that," said Winter. "I'll ask Cindy to get us a list of any guests we know were there but we don't have photos of."

"I thought you were going to give her less work, not more," said Owens.

Winter got up. "Better go for another coffee run."

CHAPTER 43

B<small>Y MID AFTERNOON</small> the bullpen looked like the after party at a frat house for old men, littered with half empty pizza boxes, stacks of files, and too many empty soda cans and coffee cups to count.

While Owens and Ryder kept at the photos, Winter worked through all of Gerry Hennig's phone records, cross referencing them to every number they had belonging to the guests. He'd made it through six months of records and had yet to find a single call or text from Gerry Hennig to anyone who had been at the party, except for one call from Rick Singleton and the mysterious call to Coleman. The Singleton call jibed with what Singleton had said, that he'd called his friend to invite him to the party. There were no other calls to Coleman except the one that took place after the killing.

There were three texts from Singleton to Hennig the night of the party, asking where he was. Hennig had not responded to the texts.

Winter had taken a break at that point, walking around the block a few times to clear his head from the numbers and his nose from the stale pizza. The sky, a rare bright blue, was clearer than his head. The discovery of Malcolm Washington had reopened the idea of a connection between Hennig and Coleman, but now even that was questionable.

Back inside, Winter called the Sheriff's office to follow up on the subpoena to get the photos from the photographer. They had mailed the subpoena, as was customary in cases where the paperwork was deemed a formality. Winter spent twenty minutes on the phone back and forth with the photographer and the Sheriff's secretary, finally getting it worked out. The photographer said he'd email the photos later that day.

The bullpen was neater than Winter had left it, but still smelled of cheese. "Solve it?" he asked.

Ryder said, "Did find this." He spun his tablet around. "It's from a hip hop blog covering new artists. Loot is one they mention. There's a photo of the brothers. Low resolution, but one of them has the cap."

Winter and Owens peered at the image. "Could be," said Winter. "I don't think so," said Owens.

"We'll have better pics later today," said Winter. "If it turns out to be one of the Loot brothers in the photo, it doesn't mean Washington wasn't there. If he was there, and he's the same guy who got in Hennig's face in Boston . . ."

"Could still be a beef with Coleman," said Owens.

"But if Washington drove in with Coleman, why wait until he got to the party? And what did he do, beat up on Hennig, and then drown Coleman?" Winter walked to the whiteboard, which still showed the timeline. "Hennig's 911 call came in at 9:58. Coleman went into the water about thirty minutes either side of that. So if Washington killed Hennig, he'd have to go downstairs, covered in blood, through a roomful of guests, and go out to the pool. Even if he went out the back someone on the staff would have seen him."

"Could have been the other way," said Ryder. "Washington kills Coleman first, then kills Hennig."

"But if Washington was there to rob the guests, why didn't he take Coleman's gold chains?" asked Winter. "He must have seen them in the limo."

"Unless Washington was high," said Owens. "Remember the crack in the bedroom. Washington was picked up for crack."

"What are we saying?" asked Ryder. "Washington is flying high, he decides he's going to rob guests? He just happens to pick Coleman and Hennig?"

Owens said, "Or he picks Hennig, tells his friend Coleman, who gets pissed at him for going nuts at the party, which for Coleman is work related. The two of them fight, Washington hits him on the head, pushes him in the pool."

"Works for me," said Winter. "But it's making a story to fit the scene, rather than the other way around. We could probably make up ten other stories. We need to talk to Washington."

"I asked Boston PD to put a BOLO out on him," said Owens.

Cindy stuck her head in the door. "I have good news and bad news."

"Starbucks is out of coffee," said Owens.

"I said bad news, not catastrophic news," said Cindy. "I did some more digging on Malcolm Washington. Guess where he was first arrested? Providence. Which is where Dwayne Coleman was born. Even better, I found a newspaper article about Coleman that says he was in Providence until he was seventeen."

"So they might have known each other," said Winter. "But we sort of knew that."

"Well, if you know everything, I guess I won't tell you the rest."

Owens said, "Don't tell him, just tell me."

"Well, since you asked nicely. The pics just came in from the photographer. The guy in the guest picture with the backwards cap? It's one of the Ives brothers. Definitely not Malcolm Washington."

WINTER DIDN'T DO his best thinking in the station, so after he looked at the photos the photographer had sent over—the photographer was right, the guy in the cap at the party was not Malcolm Washington—he got in his car and drove out of town to the reservoir.

He parked in a little turnoff just past the causeway. He would come here as a kid to fish, skip rocks, just fool around. He'd got his first kiss not a hundred yards from here.

He dropped the windows, the breeze off the water drowning out the sound of his engine cooling down. Time to think.

They'd have to check on the Ives brothers slash Loot, just to see if they were involved. Possible, but Winter didn't think so. He'd been wrong enough times before to know they'd still have to run it down.

More phone record checks . . .

The sun slipped down through the trees, casting the water to a dull gray shadow. The days were getting shorter, the year running out of time. Investigations didn't have a schedule, yet the more time that went by, the harder it became to figure out what really happened.

They hadn't ruled anyone out. Washington, Singleton, Eduardo, and who knows who else could have killed Hennig. They'd been assuming that whoever assaulted Hennig would be covered with blood, but it wouldn't have been the first time a killer had got away bloody. Winter once had a case where a guy had worn a thin nylon windbreaker and latex gloves, killed two people, rolled the jacket up under his sweatshirt, and walked out through a crowd of people *and* cops, no one the wiser.

He sat there until it was dark, the slapping against the causeway the only evidence he was near water. Too early to go home, too filled up on junk food and coffee to eat.

Winter started the car and drove back to the station.

CHAPTER 44

WINTER SPENT MOST of the next day looking for—and not finding—any hint that one of the Ives brothers knew either Dwayne Coleman or Gerry Hennig. It got worse as the day went on. Malcolm Washington was nowhere to be found. Crosse was still tied up on the hit and run. O'Dowd was working the convenience store homicide. Winter knew that the next major crime that came in the door would pull him from the Carter investigation.

He'd been working in the bullpen, not because the chairs were any more comfortable than his desk, but because it had a blank wall he could stare at.

Winter hadn't drawn in any new mental lines between the players; the result would have been a spaghetti lump of question marks. Spending half the day looking for connections with the Ives brothers meant they were grasping at straws.

Winter got lunch at the deli across from the station, the pony-tailed girl there giving him the extra pickle like she always did. He sat at one of the flimsy metal tables on the sidewalk, the only customer eating outside in the cold, but he needed the fresh air.

Back in the station, he couldn't deal with the bullpen again, so he went downstairs to the crime tech office. Andie was signing an evidence bag.

"You get a chance to process Eduardo Alvarez's puke green car?" he asked.

"According to the manufacturer, that would be a misty emerald. I didn't do it, my trainee did."

"You have a trainee?"

"I wouldn't need one, if you stopped the crime. Report isn't online yet, what do you want to know?"

"Drugs?"

"Bits of weed here and there, mostly droppings, probably from rolling joints in the car. A few empty cigar casings for blunts. Three pipes, only one used."

"Crack?"

"Not in the car." Andie said, "Wait here." She left the office, returned a few minutes later with an evidence box, pulling out a plastic bag with the pipes.

Winter didn't break the seal. "A little yellow. Could be. Any steel wool in the car?"

Andie checked the list in the box. "Doesn't say so."

"Could your new trainee have missed it?"

"I wouldn't be a very good instructor if he had," said Andie. When Winter didn't reply, she said, "Okay, I'll check myself."

UPSTAIRS, Winter caught Captain Logan in the hall. "We're going to need some overtime for the tech people."

"Are we now?" Logan said. "And here I thought your job was to catch criminals and my job was to decide on overtime."

"I think the tech people do more of the crime solving than I do these days. Phone records, videos. Whatever happened to finding the husband with the gun in his hand standing over the body?"

"Feeling a little old, are we?"

"I'm *feeling* just fine. I'm detecting old." Winter burped up a pickle. "Maybe digesting old, too. How do you do it? Keep up with all this tech shit?"

Logan said, "I approve overtime for the youngsters."

WINTER WANTED TO make another run at Eduardo Alvarez. If Andie found any evidence of crack in the car, it might tie Alvarez to the crack in the bedroom at the Carter house. But the drugs in the car were not enough to keep him and he'd already made bail.

Winter spent two hours making calls to pawn shops about Gerry Hennig's Rolex. At four-thirty he drifted down to Dan Cole's office.

Cole was with another guy who Winter didn't recognize. Cole introduced him as Eddie McCoy, his uncle, who was helping with the image and video reviews. McCoy looked like Santa after a successful diet, thick white beard and hair, a gaunt face over a medium frame.

"Thought you'd be younger," said Winter.

"Because he knows about tech or because he's my uncle?" asked Dan.

"Both." Winter eyed McCoy. "You really know about tech?" McCoy looked as old as Winter. Older.

"He does, so there's hope for you yet," said Cole. "He's going to pick up when I go off shift. After we finish with the traffic cams on the hit and run we can spend some time on the Carter house license plates."

Winter listened as Cole explained to his uncle how to access the files, the conversation quickly getting too technical for Winter. Winter said, "If you explain it in English, I can start on the license plates."

Cole got up. "You can use my computer. I've been in this chair for nine hours." He showed Winter how to access the security videos from the Carter driveway, and where he had started writing down the plate numbers. "Note the time, a description of the car, and any portion of the plate you can see."

"The time stamp doesn't look right."

"It's not. They either didn't set it correctly on the recorder, or the power went off and it reset at some point. But the relative time is accurate. Enter your notes in this database."

Winter had experience with videos. The database was another matter. "How about pencil and paper?"

McCoy, clattering away at a laptop keyboard, said, "You sound like *my* uncle. He's ninety-two."

TWO HOURS LATER, Winter had finished scrolling through the license plates, a much slower process than he had expected because the video quality was so poor. He had full plates for maybe a quarter of the cars, nothing at all on another quarter, and partials on the rest, but half of those he couldn't clearly identify the make or model of the car. They'd have to run the partials and get a list of the associated cars, then try to match them together.

He got up and stretched, needing a break. He said to McCoy,

"Where'd you learn all this tech stuff?"

"I was a high school history teacher, retired a few years ago. We had to do all the student grading on the computer. Just got comfortable with it, I guess. I did some free lance work for a military consulting firm and had to get a security clearance. Last year Dan told me they could use some help. I was able to get cleared, although I'm limited right now in what I can access and look at. I'm thinking of going through the auxiliary officer training."

"You want to become a cop?"

"Nah, leave that to you youngsters."

Winter said, "You think you can show me how to pull up some more videos?"

McCoy FOUND THE security footage of the other cameras at the Carter house easily enough. Like the recordings from the drive, the time stamps were all wrong, showing a date in 2002 and time in the early morning. Yet unless the staff hadn't aged in fifteen years, Winter was looking at the right video. The older woman, Ada, and her daughter, Carlina, entering the house together. Two other house staff he recognized.

It took Winter over an hour to find Eduardo Alvarez. Dressed in a white top and black pants, he was running out the back door with two others. The angle was all wrong, and the resolution poor, so Winter could not be certain there wasn't blood on Alvarez's clothes. Ten minutes after the three men left, others did as well, in ones and twos, staff and guests. It was impossible to tell if any of them had been in the kitchen when Alvarez had passed through. More likely they were simply guests who just didn't want to be there when the cops showed up.

Assuming Alvarez had run out shortly after Hennig's death, Winter was able to get a rough sense of how the timestamp correlated to the actual time. It wasn't perfect, because he didn't know the exact time of the homicide, but every little bit helped.

He went back five hours and ran through the video on fast forward, looking for any sign of Malcolm Washington, but found none.

His fingers numb and his neck stiff, he leaned back in the chair.

McCoy, who worked quieter than a monk, said, "Found what you were looking for?"

Winter said, "I wish I knew."

*   *   *

WINTER HADN'T EATEN, so he stopped at a drive-through chicken place on the way home. Suddenly starved, he worked through a drumstick and a wing on the way, trying, but failing, to keep the grease off the steering wheel.

At the house he washed down more chicken with a beer at the kitchen counter. Normally he'd be wired and wide awake in the midst of an investigation, often going out again at night. Tonight he was dead tired. It might have been the hours staring at the computer, it might have been because he felt like they weren't getting anywhere.

Usually at this point there would be a person or persons who would be the focus of the investigation. In most crimes, once the basic facts were known, the list of possibilities narrowed down very quickly.

Yet every time they had chased down a possibility it had only served to open up more. Plenty of people had opportunity on both Hennig and Coleman, yet except for a robbery, no other motive was apparent, and there was no clear physical evidence to point to an obvious suspect.

If Coleman had died accidentally, and Hennig had been robbed by a guest, the two deaths could be totally coincidental and about as close to random as you could get.

Winter didn't like random, and no cop liked coincidental.

But that didn't mean both didn't happen.

TOO TIRED TO take a shower, Winter pulled off his clothes and dropped on the bed. A complex set of noises awoke him before he even realized he was asleep. Groggily he picked up the phone, confused, because another phone was still ringing.

From his cell phone in the pocket of his pants on the chair.

Into the house phone he said, "Winter."

"O'Dowd. I'm at the Ready Mart on Sullivan and Sixth. Another robbery and shooting, three dead. I could really use your help."

Winter leaned out of bed, balancing on the floor with one hand, fumbling for the cell phone. "Yeah, okay, be right there. Getting another call."

"Probably dispatch," said O'Dowd. "You were awake, right?"

"I am now," said Winter. "Sort of."

The other line stopped ringing before he managed to get it out of the pocket. The late night call wasn't the worse of it. Now dispatch would be calling him on his damn cell phone.

CHAPTER 45

For THE NEXT two days Winter worked the Ready Mart homicides. It was almost certainly the same crew as the prior robberies. Three males, hitting convenience stores, after or around closing, forcing the clerk to empty the register and the safe.

They wore hoodies and baseball caps, keeping their heads down, so even with security video they were hard to identify. Likely white, perhaps Latino, not overweight, moving smoothly enough to suggest youth.

The only difference at the Ready Mart was that there were only two, one keeping watch, the other with the clerk. A car full of teens pulled up, unaware of the robbery. Panic all around, then shooting.

When it was over the clerk and two teens were dead. The shooters were gone, their car parked, as always, out of sight of the camera.

Unlike the Carter killings, these didn't make the national news, yet the Marburg Business Association demanded to know why the police couldn't keep them safe. Logan put Winter and Owens on it, along with O'Dowd.

Winter tried to keep a few irons in the fire on the Carter investigations, and Ryder was still on Hennig. Not that much was happening. Owens had spoken to the limo driver who had driven Coleman to the party, and no, he couldn't positively identify the man with Coleman, other than to reaffirm he had a cap and he was not dropped off along the way.

The Ives brothers, traced to a California recording studio, could not be reached, calls going back and forth to their manager. The message had been relayed, they just hadn't called back, and there was little Owens could do about it.

Friday morning Winter did his usual pass by for his informants, in the truck this time, the bed full of leaves from the oaks in his yard. Charles, the gray haired black man, was at the bus stop, but not wearing blue, so Winter passed him by. On Barton, Millie was walking her two Pomeranians across a dried out community garden. The dogs wore matching green ribbons.

Winter slowed down just a bit to make sure Millie saw him, then pulled around the corner and parked behind a row of empty delivery vans.

Millie strolled along ten minutes later, Winter pretending he was on the phone, the dogs not pretending they were pissing on his tires.

Millie had been married for forty years to a truck driver named Joey who had a fondness for backing his cab up to trailers full of merchandise waiting for transit, unloading them at his storage facility, and selling the lots in bulk. The husband was doing five to ten, and Millie was suspected of helping Joey move the merchandise. It was Joey who suggested to Winter that Millie had a sharp eye for detail and an ear for news; could he keep her out of jail if she helped Winter out?

Winter didn't think they had much on Millie, so it was like getting a freebie, and Millie had been his best eyes on the street. Who noticed a bundled up old woman walking her little dogs?

"Doing okay, Millie?" asked Winter.

"Except for the arthritis." Millie wore a white puffy parka and ear muffs even though it was in the fifties with no wind.

"You taking your pills?"

"The brandy works better. Listen, I heard these kids talking on a stoop, arguing about who was going to get to ride some car while their friend was inside."

"Yeah?" Watching a ride for a someone in prison was pretty common.

"Got the true sense the ride wasn't their friend's to begin with," said Millie.

Winter's first reaction was, *That's it?* A stolen car wasn't high on his list of priorities right now. But one thing with informers, you didn't want them to stop helping. "Okay, Millie, I'll check it out."

The two Pomeranians sat down and panted at Winter. Millie said, "I didn't tell you the best part. Seems the friend hustled drugs, and they were wondering if the car held inventory."

Getting interesting, thought Winter, but still not a big deal. "Any idea of the name of the guy who owned the car?"

Millie fished out treats for the dogs, maybe taking time to consider if she could divulge that bit of news. "Scout," she said. "I done heard that name before, used to be on the corner of Broad Street, good eyes."

Good eyes on the street meant he could spot undercover cops. "Thanks Millie. He leaned into the backseat, pulled out his thank you pack, and handed Millie a twenty dollar Petco gift card. "What color ribbons next week?"

Millie shoved the card deep in her parka. "How about pink?"

"Pink it is," said Winter. He waited until she wandered off, then made a note in his book about the conversation and Millie's next signal color. He used to be able to remember stuff like that.

WINTER SLIPPED INTO the bullpen, the morning briefing on the convenience store homicides still underway. Within a minute it was clear to him they were treading water. Winter said, "I might have something."

O'Dowd said, "Please. We're dying here."

"I heard that a kid—which might mean barely adult up to thirty, given my source—just went inside. His street name is Scout, probably over by Broad Street."

"I arrested him last year," said one of the uniforms. "Caught him with a gym bag of oxy. He must have run out of court delays."

"So I was thinking," said Winter. "A lookout goes to prison, and at the Ready Mart there were only two men instead of three? A missing Scout, maybe? Or a guy like him, who just got sent up?"

There was a long silence, and then O'Dowd said, "I would have thought of that."

"Me too," said Owens. "Next month. Maybe."

WINTER LISTENED for a while, talk about using the third robber as a way to identify the crew, tuning out. The convenience story homicides were obviously a priority, but he didn't want the Carter investigation to go cold. After a bit he got up and went back to his desk, where he called the medical examiner.

When she answered the phone, Kristol said, "I can't believe it."

"That I'm calling?"

"No, that it took you so long. I'm going to give you those preliminary briefings more often."

"If you have new news, I can save you a trip."

"I am now comfortable saying that the assault on Mr. Hennig took place only in the bedroom, and he likely then tried to leave via the hallway."

"Which means if someone else was in the hall, they might have seen him come out, but not the actual assault."

"Yes. The door was probably closed. Hennig's blood was on the inside door handle and the door."

Winter pictured it. Hennig's killer could have gone after Hennig as he tried to escape, saw someone in the hall, and ran off in the other direction, away from the balcony.

Kristol said, "We are still waiting on Mr. Coleman's tissue toxicology. At this point I have no additional information that clearly points one way or another to his death being accidental or a homicide. I found no abnormalities suggesting he had a heart condition. So it is possible he died of accidental toxicity from an overdose."

"And just fell in the pool," said Winter.

"That part you have to decide," said Kristol. "There is the bruise on the side of Mr. Coleman's head. If you find a blunt object with Mr. Coleman's DNA, that would certainly narrow down the possibilities."

"Are you saying that without a weapon, you might not be able to determine the cause of death?"

"The *cause* won't be a problem. I'm—and don't quote me yet— almost positive even now it was a drug overdose which lead to a heart stoppage. In other words, the blow to the head didn't kill him directly. But there is a possibility he was very high, was hit on the head, and panicked in the water, raising his heart rate and pressure even more, leading to death. Beyond that, it's up to you."

Winter thanked her and hung up, something she said nibbling at his brain, but he lost it.

CHAPTER 46

MARTIN RYDER didn't find the crime tech in her office, nor was she in the high ceiling room where vehicles were searched and tested. Marburg called it a crime lab, but it was nothing more than a garage bay. A guy he didn't recognize, wearing a shower cap, was collecting hair samples from a silver Toyota. Two other cars were in the bay, including the green Ford Fiesta he was interested in.

The sample collector didn't even question Ryder as he crossed the room. It never ceased to amaze him how lackadaisical the attitude was in Marburg. He couldn't wait until he moved on to a force where they knew what they were doing, with modern procedures and better technology.

Halfway to the Fiesta Ryder turned around. He'd never get out until he got credit for doing what he was brought in to do, which was to get Marburg out of the dark ages of policing. It all started with attitude and respect for policies and procedures.

Like keeping evidence protected.

The crime tech was lying on his stomach on a plastic mat on the backseat, his head along the floor, using tweezers. Ryder kicked him in the foot to get his attention. "I want to know what you aren't doing?" said Ryder.

The guy, young and pallid enough to suggest he spent all his life inside, said, "I'm collecting hair samples."

"I didn't ask what you *were* doing, I asked what you *weren't* doing."

The guy looked befuddled. "Collecting prints?"

Ryder said, "One. I walk in, you don't ask me who I am or why I'm here. Two, you aren't wearing a suit, you'll contaminate the car. And three, you're supposed to keep the extra evidence bags out of the vehicle." Ryder was sure about the first two, he just made the third one up to make it clear there should be a policy about the location of evidence bags.

"I'm sorry, no one told me . . ."

"Of course not," said Ryder.

Andie came through the door, looking from Ryder to the tech. "Can I help you, Detective?"

"Have you finished processing the Fiesta?"

"Almost. Detective Winter was right, we found some steel wool."

Ryder had no idea what she was talking about, Winter hadn't mentioned steel wool. It wasn't the first time Winter had left him in the dark, the guy was a lone ranger. "Show me."

"It's in a bag in the locker, but I can show you where I found it." She opened the door of the Fiesta. "Here," she said, pointing to the area between the center console and the seats. "Could be they got pulled over, stashed it out of sight."

"You just find the evidence, Ms. Pearle, I'll draw the conclusions." Ryder didn't know what Winter might be holding back from him, so he said, "What else?"

"The pipe was positive for crack, although we didn't find any in the car."

"Did you find any empty containers, baggies, a ballpoint pen?" They'd found a broken piece of a plastic pen with crack in the Carter house bedroom.

"Some weed in baggies, not much. No pen. A few other empty bags with no visible residue. If you want those tested I'll have to send them out, we don't have the equipment."

"Of course not," said Ryder.

WINTER STOPPED in Dan Cole's office, expecting it to be empty, since he'd just seen Cole in the bullpen. The light was on, Cole's uncle McCoy at the desk. "Must be nice, being retired," said Winter. "Now you have enough time to work whenever you want."

"Dan's mother says it's your fault he missed the weekly family dinner the last two weeks. Believe me, you don't want to be on the wrong side of that woman. I'm here to solve your case and keep family peace."

"I was going to leave a note for Dan asking when he's going to get back to the Carter videos."

McCoy gestured at the computer. "I just got a text from Dan, he's up in some meeting, he said we need to go back and start over, try to match up descriptions on the man who appears to be the look out at the convenience store robberies."

"Wonder where they got that idea," said Winter, innocently.

"You could help free up Dan by looking at some of these tapes."

Winter could think of a hundred things he'd rather do. "Maybe later."

RYDER HAD TWO lists in front of him. One, on his computer, was the spreadsheet of Gerry Hennig's classmates and professors. He'd annotated each with information on whether they had been contacted, interviewed, and what they'd said. As far as he knew, he was the only detective in the department who used a database.

The second list was on his phone, numbers of women he'd met in Boston, all with their own annotations.

From the first list it was clear they had barely scratched the surface of Hennig's contacts. Any one of them could know what was going on in Hennig's life, why he had been targeted. Hennig's acquaintances said he was clean, but what if they had lied? Or if the few people they'd spoken to were a bad sample?

The presence of the crack paraphernalia in Eduardo Alvarez's car meant Alvarez might have killed Hennig, or was there when it happened. Alvarez was gone, probably because the crime techs hadn't moved fast enough to process the car, or just as likely, were too dumb to recognize the steel wool as evidence of crack pipe use. Winter must have belatedly realized he'd screwed up, which is why he hadn't mentioned it.

Crackheads were often violent. Alvarez had been upstairs in the Carter house. They'd found crack near Hennig, but nowhere else in the house. Not a smoking gun, but worth following up on, even if Winter couldn't see it.

He'd go back to Boston, press Hennig's friends, find out if there was a drug angle. Solve it on his own, he didn't need Winter's help. Get a few more cases closed, make his mark cleaning up the department, and he'd be free of Marburg in no time.

Ryder scrolled through his list of women. He'd come up dry on his last trip to Boston, and he wasn't going to repeat that mistake.

WINTER WAS PULLING a take-out menu from his center drawer when his phone rang. Owens.

"Finally got hold of those Ives brothers. It's Hancock who wears the cap, not that it matters. They know of Coleman, and saw him at the party, but never got a chance to meet him. And Hancock didn't ride in with Coleman from the airport. He and his brother both came with their manager. I'll get a better photo of Hancock and show it to the limo driver, and get it to Ryder to show it to Hennig's roommates, but I think there's nothing there."

"Makes it more likely it was Malcolm Washington in the limo," said Winter. "Hey, it's like nine o'clock. You just assumed I'd be in the station?"

"Tried your cell first. Left a voicemail."

"Thank God," said Winter.

"That I left a voicemail?"

"That I remembered to turn the phone off."

BACK IN COLE'S OFFICE, Winter called in delivery orders for sandwiches as he looked over McCoy's shoulder. Cole had left hours ago. McCoy was watching a sped up video taken a few hours before a prior convenience store robbery.

Winter, still on the phone, pointed to the screen. "What's going on there?"

The woman taking his order said, "Nothing, why?"

"Hold on please," said Winter.

"That's what I'm supposed to say," she said, but Winter tuned her out.

Winter said, "This guy is getting into a car, then over here, another guy is getting into a car, and, go back, go back, this woman is getting into a car. But none in the front seat." The time stamp on the video was twenty-five after nine at night. Winter knew the neighborhood. "Not like they are getting picked up after work."

"Probably Ubers," said McCoy. "This first guy, see, he comes out of that apartment building, the woman from the one across the street. You think they were scoping out the store?"

Winter recalled Ryder arranging for an Uber in Boston after leaving Winter with the car. Out loud, Winter wondered, "How did Malcolm Washington leave the party?"

The woman on the phone said, "Is this a riddle?"

CHAPTER 47

W INTER WAS EATING an Italian grinder, dripping oil and vinegar as he read the arrest record of Malcolm Washington. Winter was looking for a local connection Washington might have in Marburg, someone who could have picked him up at the party. Three known associates were listed. Winter ran their names; two were currently in state prison, and the other one was deceased, a victim of a robbery in Boston.

Winter made a list on a lined pad of Washington's other arrests and who he had been arrested with, which wasn't always noted as a known associate.

Winter found six names. He pulled up the Marburg arrest files, which went back twelve years.

One of the names matched.

WIDE AWAKE NOW, Winter jolted over the railroad tracks. The streets grew darker as he made his way across town, fewer retail businesses in this area, mostly industrial, then residential.

He parked in front of what was the last known address of Anthony Davis, who had been arrested in Boston with Malcolm Washington two years ago for possession.

It wasn't that the house was empty, it was that there was no house. What might have been a house had been bulldozed into a pile of rubble, two overflowing dumpsters waiting to be emptied.

"Shit," said Winter.

The street was deserted, no one to ask about Anthony Davis. Winter tried an all-night deli and got only a broken English denial from the clerk. He drove around for an hour, a photo of Anthony Davis on the seat, then finally gave up and went home.

LIKE MOST Saturday mornings, Winter had grandiose plans. Get a project done around the house, meet Audrey for lunch, put in a few hours on an investigation, stay away from the station. He wasn't assigned this weekend but wouldn't mind working as long as he didn't have to watch any more videos.

He scrambled up a few eggs, thinking he still would have time to check out a few places near where Anthony Davis had lived, or claimed he had lived. No hurry, it wasn't like he was going to find a punk up and about at eight in the morning.

He had recognized Davis's parole officer's name, Julie Merring, and called her at home as soon as it was civil. She answered the phone with "This better be good," which suggested he had miscalculated.

"Very quick question. Anthony Davis. Three arrests for possession."

"Which Anthony Davis?" she asked, sounding sleepy.

"First arrest was in Boston?" Winter had the photo on the counter next to his wallet. "Black male, one eye bigger than the other, really wide nose, big hair, file said he was five eight, one seventy."

"I remember him," said Merring. "He's no longer on parole."

"His last known address was listed as being on May Street. There's no house there now. Was that a good address, do you know?" Winter was hoping she was too tired to notice he was basically asking if she had checked it out like she was supposed to.

"Last I heard they were tearing up that whole block. He's lived in that neighborhood all his life. Look around there."

RYDER OPENED his eyes and saw nothing but hair. Dark roots, to be exact. The woman's shoulders moved up and down in rhythm, she was still sleeping.

He pulled away quietly, deciding whether to wake her for another go around. He hadn't needed his list; he'd met her in the bar of the Four Seasons. She had the looks he went for, but missed a little on the demeanor, a bit flighty, not all there. She'd been okay in bed though.

He was putting on his pants when she said, "Leaving so soon?"

"Criminals work weekends." It was his cop talk that had reeled her in. She said she'd never been with a cop, just a fireman.

"This early?" she said, an invitation.

Ryder thought, What the hell, I'm still mostly undressed.

AT TEN, Winter was cruising the neighborhood where Anthony Davis had lived. His parole officer had been correct in that they were tearing up the block, except the work appeared to have stalled long ago. Boarded up buildings still stood on half the lots, the rest bulldozed, much of the debris still in piles.

The next block was night and day, new duplexes, many of the yards well maintained, interspersed with neglected houses, ugly pimples. Four teenage boys gave him the long stare as he drove by, Winter not bothering to stop, no way they'd tell him anything.

On the corner, two old black men in button up wool jackets sat at a metal table on the sidewalk outside a homestyle restaurant, sipping from Styrofoam coffee cups. Winter got out, said, "Coffee any good?"

"Best coffee in five blocks."

Winter played along. "Only coffee in five blocks."

The old man gave Winter a flash of teeth. "Don't make you pay the monopoly though."

"Good enough for me," said Winter. He went inside, immediately inundated with the aroma of frying onions. Another elderly black man, with gray military cropped hair and wearing an apron, was chopping onions. Winter filled a cup from the self serve pot and waited at the register.

"One dollar."

Winter put a bill on the counter, said, "You happen to know Anthony Davis?"

The man gathered the onions with his knife and put them in a large stewpot, added garlic, and began the sauté. After a minute he added in meat and the black beans. "You the man?"

"I am. Just looking to ask questions. No warrant on Anthony." Winter sipped his coffee. "Ham hock or bacon?"

The old man snorted. "Bacon be cheating." He wiped his hands on a towel stuffed in his apron. "You know cooking?"

"Just eating."

"Come around for lunch, and not just when you are looking for punks."

Winter accepted the rebuke; like many cops, he was guilty of that. "I will."

The old man gave him a long look. "You just might." He pushed Winter's dollar back across the counter. "Coffee's on the house. You'll have to pay for lunch though."

"Thanks," said Winter.

"Haven't seen Anthony Davis for a while. He must be around though. He don't go far, he doesn't have a car. Still rides around on one of those kid's bikes, the high bars."

RYDER TOOK an Uber to the MIT campus. He had already made an efficient list of his stops organized by location. No one answered at the first two, but on the third apartment he caught one of Hennig's classmates, a woman named Lyn Hsu.

She wore stylishly small glasses that barely covered her eyes. "Sure, I knew Gerry."

She didn't recognize any of the names Ryder threw at her. He gave her his card anyway.

Hsu offered, "Did you talk to Nadya Boyko?"

"No." The name wasn't on Ryder's list.

"She's an undergrad Gerry helped tutor. I think Gerry had a thing for her."

"They were dating?"

"I'm not sure. He did invite her to the after-orals party, which kind of surprised me, since Gerry wasn't the party type. I think he was surprised when Nadya showed up. They left early, together. She said she had a gift for him but it was a surprise and they had to go somewhere to get it. We were happy for him."

Ryder said, "You don't sound too happy."

"Just sad, because of what happened."

Ryder prided himself on his ability to read women. "And?"

"I thought she was too wild for Gerry."

Ryder took that to mean two things. First, that Nadya Boyko was too wild compared to Lyn Hsu, who had her own interest in Gerry. And second, that Nadya liked to party.

*   *   *

IT TOOK RYDER less than thirty minutes to find where Nadya Boyko lived. She had posted hundreds of photos on Facebook, all public, many taken in and around her dorm. The first student he spoke to identified the building.

At the dorm, three women with various shades of blond hair were just coming out. Ryder identified himself and said he was looking for Nadya. One of them, the strawberry blonde, said, "Isn't everyone."

"She missing?" asked Ryder.

The silvery blonde said, "She's popular."

The one with the dark eyebrows said, "And not just because she's pretty."

Ryder didn't need any special ability to read women to sense the hostility. He did know well enough to keep his mouth shut and wait.

"You here to arrest her?" asked Strawberry.

"She need arresting?"

"You're the police. You tell us."

"You can probably catch her at Java Jinx on Berkeley," said Silvery.

The women laughed. "Catch her," said Strawberry. "Get it?"

RYDER WASN'T SURE he had, but Nadya Boyko sounded like a better option than any of the other names on his list, so he walked over to Java Jinx.

He spotted Nadya immediately, sitting at a table by the window. She was even prettier than her online photos, long dark hair, high cheekbones, skinny jean legs crossed under the table. Two young men sat with her, one talking, the other staring.

Ryder pretended to look at the bagged coffee. Nadya's table was empty except for a coffee mug and a thin leather portfolio. Nadya glanced in the portfolio, set it in her lap as she zipped it backup, and set it on the table.

The two men got up and left. Another man, older, with very dark hair and a pea coat, got up from the table next to Nadya and also left.

Ryder stood in the line for coffee. The drinks were handwritten on an old fashioned mirror behind the bar, giving Ryder a fuzzy view of

Nadya's table. When she was joined by a student aged woman, Ryder risked a glance.

The leather portfolio had moved to the other side of the table. Nadya zipped it up and the woman left.

Ryder ordered a large cappuccino, grabbing a hightop table on the other side of the serving bar. Before his drink had cooled enough for him to drink, another woman had sat with Nadya Boyko, the subtle exchange underway.

Nadya had balls, Ryder gave her that. She had to be, because he was certain she was selling, and her product was not answers to math tests.

WINTER ASKED four more people about Anthony Davis, to no avail, and had zigzagged every street three times, now getting enough hard looks to make it obvious the entire neighborhood, or at least the criminal elements, knew he was there. It was time to go meet Audrey anyway.

The stop sign at the corner was twisted and bent. A narrow three decker with boarded up windows and missing siding cast his truck in shadow. A wire led from the second story across the street to another house. Winter rolled down the window for a better look. The wire was an extension cord.

That by itself was nothing; squatters often tapped electricity from another house. What *was* interesting was a high bar bike leaning against the side of the three decker.

Winter parked and walked along the rusted metal fence to the gate. At his first touch it hinted of a squeal to come, better than an alarm. Winter let the gate alone and walked past. A narrow driveway separated the three decker from the next house, the alley blocked by a four by eight plywood panel covered in graffiti.

Winter walked up the drive, conscious of the open porches above him on either side. As he suspected, the upright panel wasn't permanently attached, just leaning, leaving a narrow space to the alley.

He eased into the gap, sidestepping trash and litter. The back door was intact, the lock shiny and new. A brick wall of a tall garage formed the rear side of the property.

Winter retreated to the truck. Even with the bike, he couldn't be sure Davis was inside. What he *was* sure of was that no one would be coming out the boarded up front door. He drove off down the street, turned left twice. When he got to the cross street he could see the metal fence, but not the house. He figured he had a seventy five percent chance that if someone in the house had seen him and decided to leave, they would do so via the street; there was no way to get out the back way with the bike.

He'd been there barely three minutes when the bike zoomed past. Winter had the truck there in ten seconds, just in time to see a flash of white sweatshirt make the next turn.

Winter was on top of the rider, looking ridiculous on the small bike, before he could make the next block. Winter had trailed bikes in a vehicle, and it was harder than one would think. The rider dodged into a drive between two houses.

Winter pulled into the drive, yelling as he jumped out. "Police! Just want to talk, Anthony!"

The rider didn't hesitate, pushing on through a shaggy row of bushes at the end of the drive, making for a gap in the back yard fence.

"Don't make me chase you!" Winter yelled, even though he was already running.

The rider threw Winter the finger over his shoulder and shot through the opening. Beyond the fence, another three decker, narrow space on both sides, the rider making for the next street.

Winter sprinted for the gap, his hoodie catching on the fence, pushing through. The rider was maneuvering around a big pickup in the driveway, the handlebars screeching along the passenger door.

Winter caught him just beyond the truck, kicking the rear tire sideways. The bike spun out, the rider's leg catching in the pedal, going down hard. He looked up at Winter, one eye bigger than the other. "What the fuck you do that for?"

"Told you not to make me chase you," said Winter.

WINTER SAT HIM on the stoop, tuning out his whining, Davis denying everything but the Kennedy assassination. After he ran down, Winter said, "You ready to talk now?"

"I been talking, you ain't been listening."

"I got some simple questions, if you had answered them civil like a man I'd be gone by now."

"I *am* a man."

"Then ride a man's bike. Who'd you steal this from, some ten year old?"

"I didn't steal shit."

Winter patted him down, found a small baggie of weed, a well used crack pipe, four dirty dollar bills, a cheap month by month phone, and a switchblade so worn it no longer sprung open. "I normally wouldn't run you in, even with the running and the blade, but you made me rip a new sweatshirt. This is one of those nice thermal lined ones. Just for that, we're going to take a ride."

"Be out in a few hours," said Davis.

"It's Saturday. You won't be out until Monday afternoon, earliest. If you got bail money. Four bucks won't do it." Winter hovered.

Davis said, "What you want, anyway?"

"You see Malcolm Washington around?"

"Third Eye? He's in Boston."

"I was thinking more about out this way."

"I ain't seen him near here ever."

Winter recognized the street version of a lawyerly answer. "So you haven't seen him. Who has?"

"What's it worth to you?"

Winter flipped the knife, caught it. "Depends. Might be willing to call this a pocketknife instead of an illegal switchblade."

"Man, that's weak."

"What are you fighting me for, Anthony? Maybe you a part of what Malcolm did?"

Davis's smaller eye grew as large as the other one before darting away. "Don't know shit about what Third Eye be doing."

"So you say," said Winter. "We got people who say you were with him."

"They lying. I told you I ain't seen him here. He called me, needed a ride. I told him I only got the bike. He said he'd give me—something—if I got him picked up. My man Juke has wheels, picked him up."

"Where'd you send Juke to get him?" Winter didn't believe for a second that Davis wouldn't have gone along, especially since Washington was probably paying for his ride in crack.

"He was in front of some woods way out in the country. Took us an hour to find him."

Davis didn't catch his slip, but Winter did. "How'd he look to you?"

"It was darker out there than me, man. Barely see him. Same old Third Eye, always hopping."

"Where'd you take him?"

"To the Peter Pan."

Davis meant the bus station. "You see his hands?"

"He was in the back seat. He paid his fare, got out. That's all I know."

Winter figured by that time Davis and Juke were so interested in the fare they wouldn't have noticed if Malcolm was completely covered in blood. He pulled out his phone and called the station for a uniform.

Davis said, "You said you'd forget about the knife."

"I already have."

"What, you pissed about your hoodie?"

"That too," said Winter. "But mostly because I'm going to be late for lunch."

CHAPTER 48

O<small>N</small> S<small>UNDAY</small>, Winter watched the Patriots on television, wishing he had been able to go to the game. Twenty minutes after it ended he was on the phone to detectives he knew in the Boston PD, knowing they too would be home watching the game. One had seen the BOLO on Malcolm Washington, the other had not, but promised to spread the word.

Monday morning was cold, dim, and rainy. Not a single one of Winter's informants were out, not that he could blame them. Winter didn't bother making a second pass.

Owens was huddled under the overhang on the back steps of the station, tucking his cigarette in his palm to keep it out of the rain. "Ryder is looking for you. He's got something on Hennig."

"Yeah?"

"Found his drug connection. That's all he told me, I've been in the bullpen on the Ready Mart."

"How's that going?"

"We had this great idea, look for drug lookouts who had been sent up recently, see if one of them was with this crew. Looks promising."

"Never would have thought of that," said Winter. "They taking a break?"

Owens finished his drag. "They're talking about cross referencing databases. I figured if I was going to die, might as well do it from smoking than boredom."

"You can come with me to see Ryder."

Owens grimaced. "A third option. Death by gloating."

*   *   *

IN THE DETECTIVE ROOM, Ryder was pretending to look busy and failing, and not even bothering to hide his glee.

"You going to tell us, or you want to take a victory lap first?" asked Winter.

Ryder leaned back in his chair, crossing his hands behind his head. "Gerry Hennig partied with a woman in Boston named Nadya Boyko. She's known to the students as a drug dealer, and I personally saw her in likely transactions. Boston PD is surveilling her now."

"She sold drugs to Hennig?"

"Maybe. Or she could have just got him hooked. He might have wanted to score at the Carter party and got taken advantage of. Or he was dealing for Nadya. We'll find out once she gets arrested. In any case, we'll have a motive for Hennig's killing."

"His friends didn't think Hennig was a user," said Winter.

"I found a friend who said Hennig had the hots for Nadya, and went off to party with her after his exams. She promised him a special gift, and having seen Nadya and knowing what we know about Gerry Hennig, I don't think it was a roll in the hay."

Winter and Owens looked at each other. Owens said, "Could be. You hear about cases like this, high school basketball players get signed to an NBA contract, get high for the first time. Just because the guy was a math whiz doesn't mean he didn't want to celebrate."

"He'd have a tough time turning down this particular woman," said Ryder.

"So Hennig gets a taste, wants more?"

"Actually," said Ryder, "I'm thinking he might have been delivering Nadya's drugs to Rick Singleton to sell."

"Rick Singleton knows Nadya?" asked Winter.

"Don't know yet. But it makes sense. We know Singleton had a history of supplying coke at parties. Where was he getting it? Maybe from his friend Hennig, who got it from Nadya. Hennig is trying to impress her, tells her he knows a guy who can move weight out of town. She gives the drugs to Hennig, he brings them to the party. Something goes wrong with the exchange, or there's another player, Hennig gets the drugs taken away from him. Won't be the first time an amateur got in over his head."

Owens said, "I got a problem with Singleton as a big dealer. He wouldn't even smoke a cigarette at his mother's house. Most of the dealers I know would *sell* their mother's house. With their mother inside."

"Could have been just putting on a show for you," said Ryder.

Owens ignored the implied insult. "We didn't find a thing in Singleton's car or his apartment. No coke, not even weed."

"He's pretty broke," added Winter. "If he's a drug dealer, he's a really bad one."

"So maybe he's a sometimes drug dealer," said Ryder. "The only thing that matters is that Hennig believed Singleton could move product. We've got a woman who moves drugs and a witness that not only puts them together but says Hennig was into her. I've been hearing over and over no one can figure out why Hennig got attacked. This is a good reason."

Winter saw a lot of holes, but he had to admit it was as good a motive as any they'd come up with so far. It might explain why Hennig had gone upstairs at the party. Singleton had also been upstairs. Had they planned a meet to exchange money for the drugs? "Could be," he admitted.

Ryder pointed a finger at Winter. "Got to be. Told you it was about drugs."

"You're like a dog with a bone," said Owens.

"You got a better explanation?" challenged Ryder.

"Didn't say you were wrong," said Owens. "Singleton is down on his luck, that's for sure. He might try anything, even pushing drugs. He needs money."

Follow the money, thought Winter. "Even if drugs were involved, there's no evidence Hennig is a user or a dealer. It might not be about drugs, but the money."

"Same difference," said Ryder. "Hennig wanted money, Singleton needed money, whatever."

"Singleton had another way to get money," said Winter. "There's money in the music, the royalties. Candy Carter was going to use Singleton's music, he'd make money from that."

"So?" said Ryder.

"Singleton had this arrangement with Hennig to split the money from the songs they wrote. Candy told me that Singleton had a co-writer on the song she was going to use, it was probably Hennig. According to Candy's producer, he'd have to sign off."

Owens said, "You think Hennig didn't agree and he and Singleton got into it?"

"I don't know," admitted Winter. "But," he pointed to Ryder, "you said yourself, when there's a beating, it could be personal."

"Doesn't explain the drugs," said Ryder.

"Unless we got it backwards," said Owens. "*Singleton* might be Nadya's source. Hennig is there to do a buy. Singleton gets Hennig to agree on the song, or not. Either way, Singleton kills Hennig and takes the money from the buy."

"Where would Singleton be getting enough weight to interest this dealer Nadya?" asked Winter.

"Dwayne Coleman," said Owens and Ryder and the same time.

THEY ALL DIGESTED that for a while, the possibility of the connection they had all assumed. Winter said, "I found this punk the other day named Anthony Davis. He's got a story about getting a call from Malcolm Third Eye Washington one night needing a ride from quote way out in the country unquote. He and another guy named Juke go pick up Washington and drop him at the bus station."

"Heard the name," said Owens. "This happen the night of the party?"

"Says he doesn't know what night. It all fits though."

"Where's Davis now?"

"In the lockup, but the minute he gets in front of a judge, probably this morning, he's gone. I don't know if we have enough on him to get him to give us Juke."

"I'll work him," said Owens. "Got some ideas on how I can identify Juke too."

"I'm going back at Singleton," said Winter.

Ryder's phone rang and he answered. He listened for a while, said, "I'm on my way." He was grinning when he hung up. "Boston just picked up Nadya Boyko. I'm going to go and squeeze her." He grabbed his jacket and was gone.

Owens looked at Winter and deadpanned, "Told you it was about drugs."

CHAPTER 49

WINTER SAT IN his car outside Rick Singleton's mother's house. Singleton's Kia was parked in the driveway behind a stately Buick covered in leaves. The rain had stopped, the sky still a dirty gray.

The yard was small, edged by a traditional short picket fence. Remnants of a garden ran along the fence, the flower boxes on the windows empty. The neighborhood of tightly bunched Cape Cod houses was somewhere between the upper end of lower class and the lower end of middle class.

Winter was trying to decide how to come at Singleton. They'd gone easy on him before, partially because his friend had been killed, and partially because they had no specific reason to suspect he had anything to do with Hennig's death. They'd pushed Singleton after Miranda Dell had pointed a finger at him, but Winter wasn't exactly sure what to make of her motives; she had a lot to lose, and she might have been simply trying to deflect attention from her own rather unprofessional behavior so as not to upset her boss Candy.

On the other hand, Singleton had invited Hennig to the Carter's, by his own admission he did coke at parties, including that night, and had spent time with Coleman. Drugs were certainly a good motive for Hennig—and perhaps even Coleman—to be killed.

The only other possible motivation for Hennig's killing had to do with money, and the only money that had popped up were the royalties. *Potential money*, Winter reminded himself. Who got beat up over potential money?

Put that way, it sounded farfetched. Still, it had to be examined, if for no other reason than to cross it off the list.

There were still too many possibilities.

Singleton came out of the house, buttoning up a red check shirt jacket. He didn't appear to see Winter as he cleaned the leaves off the Buick and picked up a rake. Winter watched him work for a few minutes before getting out of the car.

Singleton, intent on his yard work, didn't notice Winter by the gate. When he did look up he startled back, saying, "Jesus, you freaked me out."

"Sorry," said Winter. "Got a few minutes?"

"Sure, I guess. My mom is watching the tv, so I came out here to clean up a little."

"Whose car?" asked Winter, indicating the Buick.

"My mom's, although she hasn't driven it in a year. I start it up so the battery don't run down, try to keep it clean."

"How's your mother doing?"

Rick looked back at the house. "She's just . . . drifting. She's in more pain than she lets on. I don't know what else to do."

"Any other family to help?"

"My dad died ten years ago, a heart attack. I have a sister, but she's pretty screwed up, she's in California. In rehab. My mom has a sister, but she lives in a nursing home in Florida. It's pretty much just me around here."

"Tough situation," said Winter.

Singleton gave him a funny look, then seemed to realize Winter was sincere. "Not as tough as my mother's situation. She's just lying there, she knows what's coming, she can't do a thing about it."

"You got a nurse helping, right?"

"I had to let her go after I lost my job. I can't blame her, she's actually a good person. She's come by a few time just to check in. She keeps telling me I need to put my mom in hospice." Singleton halfheartedly flicked at a few leaves. "I just can't. She's lived here for so long. And I went to one of those hospice places, you ever been? She'd be so depressed. At least at home she can see her stuff, her pictures, you know what I mean?"

Winter was now more convinced of his earlier conclusion about Singleton: if he was a drug dealer, he was an utter failure. If he was so cold he hoarded his drug money instead of using it to help his mother, what was he doing out in the cold raking leaves?

It wasn't even likely he was a big user. There was a perfectly good car in the driveway. If the kid needed a fix, he could sell it in a heartbeat. Yet Winter's only impression was that Singleton couldn't bear to sell the Buick for the same reason he couldn't put his mother in hospice, because he'd have to admit she was near death.

Singleton said, "You find out anything about Gerry?"

"We found a friend of Gerry's at school who says he was hanging around a woman who dealt drugs."

"That doesn't sound like Gerry at all."

"You said you weren't really in touch. People change."

"Not Gerry. He just wouldn't be interested. Wait, did he know this woman was dealing?"

"We're not sure yet."

"Gerry was really smart, book smart, but he—this sounds weird, but he just wasn't really into people. He just took them at face value, they said hi, he said hi. They talked about music, he talked about music. If he talked to a drug dealer ten times, but they only talked about music or math, he wouldn't have a clue."

"That true about you, too?" Winter left it vague.

"I didn't do much drugs when I was in the band, that was high school. I smoked a little weed. We snuck some beers, I bet you did too."

"Can't deny it," said Winter. "I talked to another guy, he said you were upstairs at the party before Gerry got killed."

"That's not what happened. Who said that?"

"What were you doing up there, anyway? You go up to meet Gerry?"

Rick dropped the rake. "I told you, I heard about somebody being dead, I kind of panicked, I wasn't the only one. There were people running all over the place. I didn't know what was going on. I just ran and hid."

Which was pretty much what Singleton had told Winter at the party. Winter had long learned that liars couldn't keep their stories straight more than two or three times. He went at Singleton again. "Why were you in the kitchen?"

"I couldn't find Gerry, and he wasn't returning my texts. I just looked everywhere. He didn't like parties, I figured he might be somewhere more quiet, so I tried the back rooms."

Winter put some disbelief into his voice. "Hard to believe Gerry would just go upstairs."

"I can't figure that out either. I wasn't looking up there for Gerry. I just ran upstairs to get away after these guys almost knocked me down running out the door."

"What guys?"

"They looked like waiters, they had those bright white shirts on. They were the ones talking about someone being dead. In Spanish."

"You didn't tell me this when I spoke to you at the party."

"I didn't think it was important, it wasn't like they were the only ones freaking."

"Notice anything about them?"

"Not really. I was a little out of it, you know I'd—done a little powder. Wait, did they have something to do with Gerry?"

"Notice any blood on those white shirts?"

Singleton closed his eyes for a moment. "You mean Gerry's blood? I think I would have noticed that. Man, I need to sit down."

Singleton slumped on the damp stone steps. Winter gave him a few minutes. If Singleton was putting on an act, he was very good.

If Singleton had somehow killed Hennig, he'd just let slip a perfect opportunity to pin the blame on Eduardo Alvarez. All he had to do was say he'd seen blood on the guy coming down the stairs. Instead, Winter sensed only sadness.

Singleton said, "You ever feel that everything in the world has just gone against you?"

Winter hadn't, but he'd heard this lament enough times. He waited until Singleton had gathered himself, then said, "I talked to Candy and her producer about the royalties. Maybe that will work out for you, get you some money?"

Singleton shrugged. "The way my luck is going, who knows? Plus, it's not going to happen overnight. She still has to finish recording, then the final mixing, the release, it could be a year before I see a dime."

"That song Candy is using, did you write that with Gerry?"

"Yeah, way back. Candy will likely change it up though."

"But Gerry would have to sign off on her using it?"

"Sort of. Gerry and I signed a contract a long time ago. Everything we would ever get would be split fifty-fifty."

Winter pressed. "But would he have to agree? Could he stop it?"

"Why would he? I mentioned it to him on the phone when I invited him to the party, he wasn't going to object."

"So how would that work? Would he have to sign a contract with Candy too?"

Singleton got up, wiping off his pants. "I guess. Listen, I need to make my mom some lunch, can we talk about this another time?"

"The sooner we finish up the faster I can get to what happened with Gerry," said Winter. "That's what you want, right?"

"Sure. But what's the music got to do with it?" Singleton opened the storm door. "Listen, just don't talk about this in front of my mom, okay?"

Winter, taking that as an invitation, followed him in. The house was stuffy, both in atmosphere and knickknacks, too much furniture. Singleton turned into the living room and said, "Ma, you hungry?"

Winter checked out the kitchen. Brown wood cabinets, a well worn formica countertop. A case of meal replacement shakes next to a blender. Wheat bread and peanut butter on a tray. A laptop, closed.

On an open shelf next to the sink, a dozen prescription pill bottles, all made out to Judith Singleton. Winter recognized at least three potent pain medications including fentanyl, all of which were common street drugs.

Behind him, Singleton said, "You can't believe how many meds she's on."

"What are these for?" asked Winter.

Singleton started shaking pills out into a small cup. "One for appetite, one for nausea, one to offset the chemo drugs, a few for pain. Drugs to counteract what the other drugs do, I don't understand all of it." He held up a bottle. "I had to get these anti-anxiety pills for her after she found out I lost my job."

Singleton finished with the pills and made a watery shake in the blender. As he was spooning peanut butter onto the bread, Winter said, "About those royalties."

"I told you, Gerry wasn't going to have a problem."

Singleton's voice was shaking as much as his hands. Winter, knowing he had to do it, bore down. "Maybe he needed convincing?"

"For the millionth time, he wouldn't care!" Singleton pushed past Winter, not meeting his eyes. "I got to go feed my mom."

Winter said, "Tell me about Nadya Boyko."

"Who?"

Winter waited to see if Singleton filled in unnecessary details, but all he got was a look of bewilderment. "She's a friend of Gerry's," he prompted.

"Not when I knew him. I'd remember a name like Nadya."

Winter let him go, the kid obviously concerned about his mother. Winter felt sorry for him, and though it didn't seem at all likely that Singleton had killed his friend, he could be wrong. It wouldn't be the first time he'd seen a murderer who also loved his mother.

And Winter sensed Singleton was clearly worried about more than his mother, and it had to do with Gerry and the royalties.

RICK MANAGED TO get his mother to take a few sips of the shake and one bite of the peanut butter sandwich, his latest desperate idea to get calories in her. He waited with her until he was sure the cop had left.

"Was someone here?" his mother asked.

"Just a guy I know, stopped by to talk," said Rick. He still hadn't told her about Gerry, thankful she didn't like watching the local news.

"You don't need to be here all the time. Go out, see your friends."

Rick wasn't so sure exactly who his friends were any more. He'd probably spent more time talking to the cops than anyone else in the last few weeks. His life suddenly seemed small and confining. "I'm good, Ma."

She grabbed at his hand, her fingers cool even in the warm room. "I know what you are doing, Ricky. And I love you for it, but you have to get on with your life."

Rick tried to smile, to reassure her. "I'm not always sure what I'm doing," he admitted. His life sucked so much right now that getting on with it meant going to Gerry's funeral the next day.

She tightened her grip, surprising him with its intensity. "Sure you do. You are doing what you think is right."

Rick wasn't so sure about that, either.

LATER, after she fell asleep, Rick cleaned up the uneaten food and quietly did the dishes. The cop's questions worried him. They obviously suspected he knew more than he was telling.

Winter didn't seem like the type to give up. Rick didn't think the cops knew about Doc yet, but they were sniffing around about the royalties, and that wasn't good. Rick hadn't ever been in real trouble before, but he knew the cops wouldn't miss the fact that he had probably been the only person at the party who knew Gerry and who had also talked to Dwayne. Rick couldn't figure out how Dwayne was involved, but he obviously knew Doc, and Dwayne had mentioned Gerry's name specifically.

Dwayne said he knew Gerry was at the party. Gerry hadn't been near the pool; Rick figured Dwayne was just using that to lure Rick outside. Now he wasn't so sure. Why *did* Gerry go upstairs? Could *Dwayne* have killed Gerry?

He tried to remember how long it had been from the time he left Dwayne with Miranda to when pandemonium broke out. It all ran together now.

It had to be Doc who told Dwayne about Gerry and about the royalties. Yet Doc hadn't mentioned Dwayne at all, and Rick was too scared to ask. Right now, he was at worst in debt to Doc, and at best, a money ticket. The last thing he wanted was for Doc to see him as a *problem*, especially with the cops all over the place.

He was still more afraid of Doc than the cops. He couldn't help shake the feeling that Doc had something to do with Gerry's death, but he couldn't see how or why. Doc wanted Gerry to sign over the royalties, killing him wouldn't help with that.

Rick did some internet research, trying to learn how to determine if Gerry had a will. He was surprised to find out that probate records were public. If Gerry had left the royalties to him, he could maybe get Doc off his back . . .

He typed Gerry's name into the search box, but even before the results came up his hands started shaking, his gut twisting into a knot, his body recognizing a few seconds before his mind what he was doing. He ran to the sink, dry heaving.

He coughed and coughed, then cried, bent over the sink staring at the drain. His once best friend wasn't even buried and here he was, clawing over his will. And for what? To get himself out of the mess he had got himself into. A mess he couldn't blame on Gerry, or the cops, or even Doc. Only on himself.

His stomach lurched, foul bile rising in his throat. He ran the water and splashed it on his face and neck.

On the shelf, his mother's anti-nausea pills were right in front. They might help . . . His tears blurred the name on the bottle until all he could see was *Singleton*.

What was *wrong* with him?

He turned away. He'd face Doc before he stole his mother's medication.

CHAPTER 50

W INTER WAS JUST pulling into the parking lot of the station when Owens came down the steps, way too fast to be on a smoke break. Winter rolled down his window. "What's up?"

"The databases say a dude named John Lander, aka Lighthouse, got sent to MCI Concord three days before the Ready Mart for possession. He was arrested two years ago with one George Crowe for armed robbery of a gas station. Crowe got off. Evans is putting together a team to hit Crowe. You coming?"

"Hop in," said Winter.

Owens tossed his vest in the back seat. "Granville Street," said Owens. "Off of Post. Forming up at The Presidents Hotel."

"The databases say?"

"If this is good, the technology will get the credit. If it's a waste of time, it will have been your idea."

Winter cut onto a service road behind a strip mall, working his way through the neighborhoods, avoiding the lights.

"Got a line on your man Juke," said Owens. "Real name is Walter Weese. Supposedly he has a crib somewhere on Harral, over by St. Raphael's."

"Not far from Anthony Davis."

"We can pay him a visit if this don't pan out."

Winter said, "What, you don't have faith in technology?"

Owens patted his gun. "My faith is in this."

"Anthony Davis might have been lying through his teeth, but his story about Juke is too complicated to make up on the spot."

"That would put Washington at the Carter party, assuming the woods they picked him up by weren't the evergreen bushes in Marburg Park."

"Washington has a record, doesn't want to be around a couple of homicides when the cops show up, I get why he would want to run," said Winter. "Now we need to find out if Coleman mentioned anything to Washington about the party, like meeting up with Hennig."

Winter slowed at an intersection, checked the cross traffic, ran the light, his adrenaline flowing. They reached the hotel right behind the SWAT van.

Three minutes later the squad commander, Evans, unrolled a very old technology map over the hood of O'Dowd's car. The SWAT team leader, Jerry Symond, did the talking, pointing at the map. "Crowe's house is here, around the block. We got a picture?"

O'Dowd had a tablet. "Here, street view." He passed it around.

Symond said, "We'll split into two groups, one for the front door, on me, the rest around back." He held up a mug shot. "This is the guy, five ten, one eighty. House is owned by a Simon and Joanna Pierce. Crowe might be a renter."

Winter was looking at the house photo on the tablet, a neat two story shingled Victorian. "I've been in houses like this. Some of them have a walkout basement on the side."

Evans had the tablet, spun the view. "Can't see it here. If there is, someone could exit that way, jump into the next door yard, cut across and be out the next street."

"We can cover that," said Winter.

"Okay," said Symond. "You and Owens, over on Lincoln. Crowe has two priors for assault, and he used a gun on the robbery. Assume he is armed and dangerous. "

OWENS GOT A SWAT frequency portable radio and he and Winter pulled on their vests before getting back in the car, leaving off their seat belts. Through his open window, Winter said to Symond, "If you give me three minutes we can get to the side street without driving right by the house."

"We need that long to get to the corner," said Symond. "Go."

Winter turned and made a big rectangle, coming in on the side street from the opposite direction. He parked in front of a white colonial that he estimated to be about even to where the target house was one block over.

They were just getting out of the car when the radio squawked, "Two minutes."

Owens took out his gun, checked the magazine, and held the gun down by his leg. "Homeowner's going to be pissed if we bust down the wrong door."

"They'll feel better once they find out their house was identified by a database," said Winter. He held himself loose, keeping his breathing steady. They weren't in the thick of it, but the tension was still there.

TEN MINUTES LATER it was all over. Evans, on the radio, said, "Lady of the house says George Crowe rents the basement, he hasn't been around for two days."

"Shit," said Owens. He leaned against the car, fishing for his smokes.

A young teen wearing a blue sweatshirt, jeans, and pristine white sneakers appeared from a backyard two doors down. The kid was walking fast, looking back over his shoulder.

Owens ground out his cigarette. "Today's a school day, right?"

"Last I heard," said Winter, starting up the street. Behind him, he heard Owens's raspy whisper into the radio. "This George Crowe, he rent the basement by himself?"

Winter didn't wait for the reply, trotting to intercept the kid, who saw Winter, stopped.

Winter edged forward, figuring the angles, where the kid would run. Owens called out, "Thomas Crowe?"

The kid backstepped, his eyes darting from Winter to Owens. Winter said, "Lots of police with guns back that way."

"I ain't done nothing," said the kid.

"No problem, then," said Owens, nice and easy, walking toward the kid, freezing him in place like a runner caught between bases. "We can drive you to school."

Winter went left, blocking the only exit lane. The kid tensed, then deflated. "George didn't do those robberies," was the first thing he said.

Owens unbuckled his vest. "Out of the mouth of babes."

*   *   *

AT THE STATION, Owens took care of the kid. Winter hit the bathroom, and after he came out he found Dan Cole waiting at his desk.

"Might have found a connection between Malcolm Washington and Dwayne Coleman," said Cole. "Better if I show you."

Winter followed him to his office as Cole said, "I've been watching Coleman's music videos. One of them is really popular, we're talking millions of views on YouTube. The rap he does is about a drive by."

"Wait, you're going to tell me I have to listen to rap?"

Cole swung his screen around so Winter could see, then pulled up a video. "Just one." The video was jerky, interspersed with the lyrics on the screen in unmatched lettering. It was a good thing the text was there, otherwise Winter wasn't sure he would have been able to follow the words. *Down and dirty hustlin' rustlin' on the street shootin' up bang bang beat.*

Right after the words *bang bang*, a spray of gun shots, a white limo flashing by, the window down, Dwayne Coleman looking right at the camera, pointing his finger like a gun, as if he were firing back, laughing. *Took your shot punk ass fool be hittin' back ain't be missin'.*

Cole muted the sound. "That's the key part."

"I must have missed it," said Winter, perplexed.

"Watch it slowed down." Cole reran the video, clicking through frame by frame. "See where the shooting scene starts? How the image streaks from frame to frame? That means it was recorded with a lower quality camera. At first I thought it was just to make it look more realistic, like a street scene. But see all these people in the background? They look pretty shocked. They are either really good actors, or . . ."

"It was real," said Winter.

"Right. So I did some digging. Turns out Dwayne Coleman *was* shot at in a drive-by, about four years ago. Down in Miami. Not much came of it, since no one got hurt."

"Police report?"

"That's another funny thing. Yes, but the limo company reported it first. It was a rental limo. Coleman only admitted to the shooting when the Miami cops talked to him. They figured he knew who did it, warned him not to do his own retribution. Coleman never said a word, but the video went viral. The song became his first hit."

"Okay, so the guy takes advantage of some drive-by," said Winter, still not getting it.

"I didn't think much either," said Cole, "until I watched more of the videos and checked out the increasing mentions of Outta Here in the music press. I found two interesting things. First," Cole clicked through some photos. "This is Coleman's car, a 2014 Bentley Flying Spur. He probably paid over a hundred thousand dollars for it. It became his signature ride, just about every photo I could find of him near or in a car is with the Bentley. In fact, I can't find a single photo of him in a limo other than in the drive-by."

"Pretty lucky," said Winter. "Guy not in his expensive car when he gets shot at."

"That's what I thought. Like maybe he knew the shooting was coming? Which meant it might have been faked, just so they could use it in the music video later. The second thing I found is even better." Cole went back to the music video, zooming in on an old-fashioned pedestal clock in front of a bank. "That's Capital Bank of Miami. As part of the investigation, Miami PD pulled their security video which showed the street. They had installed a camera on the roof to take videos of a parade the bank sponsored. It has wonderful resolution."

Cole pulled up another video, cars flowing back and forth across the busy street. "The drive-by happens way down the block," said Cole, "so you can't see much of it. But," he froze the screen, "this is taken about five minutes before the shooting."

The image showed a large dark green SUV pulling to a curb. A black man emerged from the shadow of a doorway, looked up and down the street, and got into the SUV. Cole froze the video on the figure.

Who was wearing a backwards baseball cap and looked very much like Malcolm Washington.

"Damn," said Winter. "How'd you do that?"

"Technology," said Cole. "And four painful hours staring at videos."

CHAPTER 51

THE TASTE OF ACTION in the search for the Ready Mart robber had Winter itching to be back on the street. He forced himself to eat a quick lunch across from the station, sitting inside this time, a steady stream of cops coming in and out of the sandwich shop.

He was still bothered by the fact that Coleman's gold chains hadn't been taken. They'd probably be much easier to move than Hennig's Rolex. It was hard to believe the chains would have gone unnoticed if robbery was the motive for the two deaths.

Winter had mixed success trying to put himself in the position of criminals. Usually he at least understood the motivation. He wasn't smart enough to know what made one person without money steal and another person without money work harder.

What he *could* do was figure out what a crook might do after the crime. Steal a Rolex? Sell it for money. Where? At a fence or an ask-no-questions pawnshop. They already had the description of the missing Rolex out, but that didn't mean it would turn up or be reported if it did.

Crooks rarely changed their favored theft—guys who stole cars kept stealing cars, guys who stole jewelry stole jewelry. Maybe whoever killed Hennig and perhaps attacked Coleman had stolen jewelry before. If he had, what would he do with it?

Go to a pawnshop or jeweler.

AFTER LUNCH Winter signed out from the evidence room the chains Coleman had been wearing, transferring them to a gym bag he kept in the trunk.

He grabbed a coffee at a Brazilian deli and sipped it as he drove to a pawnshop with a history of buying stolen goods. Winter knew just about every pawnshop in Marburg, although there were an untold number of people and businesses who bought and sold used goods. These could be anywhere, private homes, discount shops, even pizza parlors. Winter was sure that for every one he was aware of, there were ten times more in the shadows.

The pawnshop was closed up tight. A builder's permit sign flapped on the door. Winter turned around and headed across the river to East Main. Jackie's Pawn was a sprawling industrial building flanked by a used car dealership and a tire repair center. Behind the metal protective window grates a wide assortment of old style televisions and stereo equipment lay under a layer of dust.

The security guard, a former Hartford cop, gave Winter a nod and jerked his head toward the back room. Winter waved a thanks and passed through the thick steel door as the guard buzzed him in.

Jackie Stein was sitting with his feet propped up on a metal desk that was older than he was, and Winter figured Jackie for his eighties. Jackie had in fact been a fence back in the day, but had gone straight after a stint in prison, turning his eye for resale into a legal skill. He was dressed in a white shirt buttoned all the way up, gray wool pants, and comfortable looking shoes that probably cost significantly more than all his office furnishings put together.

Stein raised his hands. "I didn't do it," which was the same thing he said to Winter every time he saw him.

"Well, don't look at me," said Winter. "I didn't do it either."

Stein pointed to a mini fridge. "Help yourself to some Dr. Brown's Cel-Ray."

"I swear you keep that there just to get me to gag," said Winter, sitting down in a creaky office chair.

"I guess I'll have to share then." Stein pulled out a bottle of Jack Daniels from his desk.

"I'm driving," said Winter.

"I start drinking alone, I'll think I'm old," said Stein, but he only splashed a dash into Winter's glass.

"You *are* old," said Winter.

Stein raised his glass and sipped.

Winter did the same, he wasn't much for JD but it was all part of the ritual. For all he knew, Stein really didn't drink in between visitors. "Help me with something?"

"Don't I always?"

Winter pulled the brown envelope with the chains out of the gym bag. He set them down one by one on Stein's desk. "How hard would it be to turn these into cash?"

"Chains are generally easy. They pretty much look the same, since most come off a big roll anyway, even the thick stuff. And the gold ones can always be melted down. Gold is gold."

"Would a street guy know that?"

"Sure. We get the random crackhead wandering in, usually with a lightweight chain."

"A lot of money here? Never seen chains this thick."

Stein swirled his drink. "Two of them are worth money. The really thick one is fake."

Winter frowned at the chains. "Because it's thick?"

"Because it's nickel or an alloy."

"You can tell that by looking at it?"

"By listening." Stein picked up one of the chains and dropped it on the desk, then the second. The third, the thickest, was the loudest, landing with a thud. "Hear the difference?"

"Nope." They all sounded heavy to Winter.

"Don't buy any chains from strangers," warned Stein.

"Why would a guy wear fake chains?"

"Save money. Look rich. Both. Some rapper?"

Winter, trying to keep a straight face, said, "Hip hop. It's more than just rap."

"Don't buy chains or play poker," said Stein. "These from that guy who died out at the Carter house?"

"Might be. Would some pawnshop owner not as savvy as you buy the fakes?"

"I'm a high value product reseller," said Stein. "It's more than just pawn." He splashed more JD in his glass. "I doubt it. You're talking thousands of dollars of gold, even if it's hot. No fool would lay out that much money without testing it."

Winter said, "Who sells the fakes?"

"Not me. Why don't you ask a jeweler?"

At the door Winter said, "High value added product reseller?"

"Like a recycler. Doing my thing for the environment. It's all the rage."

"Might want to redecorate your windows," said Winter.

MCKAY'S JEWELERS looked tiny tucked between a Subway and a bank. Winter had bought the engagement ring for his wife at this store, the older man McKay, now deceased, letting Winter pay off twenty dollars a week. No paperwork, just a handshake. Those days were long gone, but Winter always brought his business here on the few occasions he bought jewelry.

The business was now in the hands of McKay's daughter-in-law Charlotte, an attractive, well coiffed silvery blonde who might be in her forties or even fifties, Winter never fell into the trap of guessing. She was behind the counter with another woman, about the same age and brunette, but who looked like she got her hair done by Charlotte's stylist.

"Don't tell me," said Charlotte. "You're finally getting married again, and are here to buy a diamond to show her how big your love is."

"Is *that* what diamonds are for?" said Winter. "I was thinking of a Hallmark card."

Charlotte visibly shuddered. "You poor man."

"I'd be poorer if I bought diamonds."

Charlotte said, "Denise, this is Detective Robert Winter, an infrequent customer, as you can tell, but we love him all the same. What can we do for you, if it isn't to buy diamonds?"

"How common is fake jewelry? I don't mean costume jewelry, but fakes of the good stuff."

"More than you would think. Those million dollar necklaces you hear about? A lot of them sit in a bank vault. The owner gets really good looking fakes, and that's what you see them wear around. Partially for insurance, partially because they can look like they own more than they have." Charlotte leaned forward on the counter, her eyes and tone suggesting an impending secret. "You might be surprised to know that some wives take the expensive glitter their otherwise stingy husbands give them, get fakes made, and sell the real ones."

Nothing really surprised Winter when it came to money. "Another reason not to buy diamonds."

"Another reason to choose the right spouse," said Charlotte.

"How about chains?"

"Chains aren't really that expensive, even for a diamond necklace. Not relatively speaking. The fake diamond would cost more than a real gold or even platinum chain."

"I mean big chains," said Winter. "Like these." He pulled out the chains, setting them down on the sound absorbing velvet pads. "I've been told these get faked too, for the same reasons you mentioned. The thick one is fake."

Denise picked it up. "I can't tell."

"Do you know who might make a fake like this?"

"No. I don't imagine there's much demand in Marburg for either the fakes or the real thing."

"Any ideas on who might help me find a source?"

Charlotte picked up a silver pen from the counter, jotted on a pad, and slipped the folded sheet to Winter. "Call this man. Be as discreet as you can please. You can use my name. He might be able to point you in the right direction."

"Thanks," said Winter.

Denise was running the fake chain through her fingers, feeling along the links. "Hey, this is neat." She held up a section of the chain that had a series of decorative looped bulbs. Denise twisted one of the links and it opened, revealing a hollow shell. "Hiding place?"

Winter said, "What the hell?" He moved the pad onto the velvet, set the chain on the paper, and slowly untwisted another one of the links. A light dusting of white powder flittered out. Winter looked up at Charlotte. "Hope you are paying her good."

Denise gave Winter a big smile. Charlotte said "Don't fall for him, honey, otherwise he'll shower you with Hallmark cards."

CHAPTER 52

BACK IN HIS CAR, Winter decided to call the number Charlotte had given him from his cell phone instead of from the station. He suspected the guy wouldn't want to see Marburg PD pop up on his caller ID. Winter didn't get an answer, just a beep, no recording. Winter said, "Charlotte said I could call you with a question."

Winter decided to wait fifteen minutes, in case the guy was checking it out with Charlotte. The phone rang in ten, but it was Owens.

Owens said, "Finally got the photo of Malcolm Washington in front of the limo driver. He's pretty sure it's the same guy who rode in from Logan with Coleman. Boston PD also showed the photo to one of Hennig's roommates. No positive ID. They still haven't caught up with the other roommate."

"We—," said Winter. His call waiting beep cut in. "Got to take this." Winter, always afraid of hanging up on the wrong party, gingerly pressed a button.

"I was told who you are," said the voice, quiet and calm. "No need for names."

"Works for me," said Winter. "I came across a large gold chain, I mean, really large. I'm told it's fake." Winter stopped there to see what came to the guy's mind without more prompting.

Either nothing much, or he was extra circumspect. "And?"

Winter framed his question carefully. "Is that something that could be sourced locally?"

"How good are they?"

"I'm told good quality. Two others were real, a little less thick, but about the size of a man's thumb. Wait, let me check something." Winter looked at the evidence envelope. The description box had a notation for the weight, not always filled in, but this time it was. "Four pounds nine ounces. For all three."

"That's a lot of gold. I doubt you'd find a local source, not even Boston. You see those more on the west coast, maybe Miami or New York."

"For the real or the fakes?"

"The real ones you can buy anywhere, this is the age of the internet. I don't know about the demand around here. Big chains are flashy, big city. What I come in contact with is more refined."

"Thanks."

"Anything for Charlotte," said the man, and hung up.

WINTER DROVE BACK to the station. In the crime tech's office he asked Andie to take photographs of the chains separately, and for the fake chain, close ups of the hollow links—there were six—opened and closed. Winter wasn't surprised the links hadn't been discovered; the chains hadn't been used to strangle Coleman, so they were just being held for next of kin to claim after the investigation was complete. He asked Andie to run a test on the powder residue.

Winter returned the real chains to the evidence envelope, added a notation about one of the chains being fake and the number of the bag it had been transferred to, signed the bag and returned it to the evidence locker.

Upstairs, Cindy was on the phone, so Winter hovered. Into the phone, Cindy said, "Got to go, one of my many nasty bosses is here to give me even more work."

"Technically, I'm not your boss," said Winter, when she hung up.

Cindy smacked her gum. "Does that mean I can decide not to do the work?"

"You'll like this, it's jewelry. Andie just took some photos of the chains Dwayne Coleman was wearing. Turns out one was a fake. Can you send the photos around to New York, LA, Hollywood Division, Miami, and, well, anywhere you think guys would wear big chains."

"And I'd know that how?"

"Damned if I know. Certainly I don't. Try those cities. Send it to robbery, not homicide. And fraud, maybe people claimed fakes as real for insurance."

*　　*　　*

WINTER WENT back out, this time to look for Walter Weese, the guy known to Malcolm Washington as Juke. Owens had given him a general location of Weese, a neighborhood on the cusp of the poorer section of Marburg called Hallows, where Anthony Davis also lived.

Walter Weese had been picked up six times, all as a juvenile, the last being four years ago. None had led to an arrest, so there was no photo. Although Anthony Davis claimed Weese had a car, there was no record of him having a license in the DMV, nor was a car registered to him.

No one Winter found on the street admitted to knowing Walter Weese or a Juke. It wasn't like the people who lived here were especially transient, someone had to know him, but no one was talking.

As Winter was leaving the neighborhood he passed by a Cuban restaurant, which made him think of Miami even though he'd never been there, which made him think about Brooker, who had.

Brooker answered before the first ring ended. "That was fast," said Winter. "Expecting a call?"

"Yeah, from the lottery. Going stir crazy. Tell me you got something for me to do."

Winter explained about the chains. "We sent photos down, but who knows if they'll get looked at and when. Maybe you could make a few calls?"

"Beats waiting for the lottery," said Brooker.

WINTER COULDN'T THINK of anything productive he could do at the station other than paperwork, so he drove around trying to spot any of his on and off informants who might lead him to Juke. He found only one, a tall skinny woman with a bright blond wig named Melody who was standing in front of a construction site near the river. She was wearing a gold tank top, a white miniskirt, and spike heels.

She got in the car gratefully, and Winter turned on the heat. "Thought you were off the street."

"My boy needs braces, you know what braces cost?"

"I can't even imagine," said Winter, cracking his window to release Melody's perfume.

She rubbed her hands in front of the heater vent. "Gonna be a tough winter."

"You need a coat? I could drop you at the donation center."

"Wear a coat, no one sees the merchandise. I'll survive. You just driving around warming up the girls, or you need something?"

"Looking for a guy goes by Juke."

"Know him for sure. Little dude, always twitching. Ain't seen him for a while though."

"Heard he had a place in the Hallows."

"Don't spend time there no more. They can't even afford me."

"What's Juke into?"

Melody flipped the visor down, checking her makeup. "Whatever. He's got wheels, or had. He might rent rides."

Not everyone could afford a car, and Marburg had no local mass transportation other than buses. Car owners could make a few bucks ferrying people around, or even rent their car out for a drug buy. "Thanks."

Melody said, "Fair trade for the warm up."

The cold air from his open window blew into Winter's ear. "When I went by the ministries, Pastor Jason's car was out back, he probably has the heat on." The New Ministries was a soup kitchen and shelter, run by a man who may or may not have been a real pastor, but did what he could and kept the place clean.

Melody stared out the side window. After a block she said, "What the hell. Construction guys won't get off work for another hour anyway."

Winter headed that way. It was the best he could do for her.

AFTER DROPPING OFF Melody, Winter stopped for another coffee, and his phone rang as he took the first sip. Brooker.

"Got lucky. Caught one of the Miami homicide detectives at his desk. He hadn't heard about the photos you sent down, but after I told him about the chain he connected me to a guy on the street in narcotics."

"Narcotics?"

"That's what I thought. Turns out they've seen jewelry like that a few times before. With compartments. Pendants, big rings that slide open, even chains. Any place you can hide powder or even a few pills. They've heard about this guy, supposedly specialized in this fake jewelry, who also moved oxy on the side. Goes by Doc. Never put a name or a face on him. Thought he might be a real doctor, but there are so many shady doctors moving pills in Miami they couldn't find him."

"So he's not a priority?" Meaning Miami wouldn't be looking for him.

"Worse, they heard he moved."

"That's not good," said Winter. "Although I guess we can try to track down other sources there for the fake jewelry."

"I'll make some calls. There is one other thing. When I asked if they knew where Doc went, they didn't have anything specific, but thought it was up north. Not like northern Florida, but out of state. New York maybe? Boston?"

"Who moves from Florida to the northeast?" asked Winter.

"Got me. I felt warmer just being on the phone with them. I hit that lottery, I'm in the sun. I'll let you tag along if you want."

"Just as long as I don't have to see you in a bathing suit," said Winter.

CHAPTER 53

W INTER FOUND the detective room full, the day shift filling out reports. Owens using paper, Crosse on her keyboard.

Winter did a search in the national database for arrests with the alias Doc or Doctor, and found four thousand and eighty. He narrowed the search down to New York, almost a thousand. For the hell of it he tried Massachusetts, and got twenty-two. Most were men in their thirties and forties, probably got their nicknames because they wore glasses or finished high school or read books. Six were real doctors, in the system for insurance fraud or moving pills on the side. None of them showed Miami priors or even addresses; the latest arrest had been in Lawrence almost two years ago.

That didn't help much.

He forced himself to write up his notes, then clicked through his emails. One was from Cindy about the license plates he'd identified on the Carter house security camera. She'd taken his notes, entered them into a spreadsheet, and added notations for the car owner or, for a few of the partials, possible owners.

Halfway down the list was a Doctor Eric Poole. Since he'd just been looking up doctors, that stopped him. Winter pulled up the guest list from the party and there it was. He spun in his chair. "Hey Judy, you remember a guy from the party named Poole, a doctor?"

"Think so. Bow tie. Not a doctor doctor, but a professor. Teaches at the U."

"He clean?"

"From what I could tell. Older guy, been there forever."

Winter was already looking back at the list. No more doctors. He did see three cars registered to companies, maybe leases. Two of them he recognized, a local accounting firm and the *Marburg Times*, which he ignored.

The third company, Stannis Hill LLC, was listed alongside a partial plate, and also had three names of individuals associated with it. None of the individuals were on the guest list. Winter ran them quickly through the system, none had priors.

Winter had a note in his desk from a prior case where Cindy had shown him how to look up corporate information. He found the note and was feeling proud of himself for successfully accessing the online record. The address of Stannis Hill LLC was on a stretch of Warren Street that definitely had no residences. Probably an office. Winter went out to the hall, found Cindy packing up.

"Thanks for the licenses. One led to an LLC. I know they don't have to list the owner, but can you remind me how to find out who set it up?"

"Not necessarily who set it up, but what is called a resident agent, where they can get their mail." She scribbled on a pad. "I showed you this once before."

"I already did that," said Winter, trying to sound modest.

"Ooh, look at you," said Cindy. "A computer geek. Did you go through all the filings?"

Winter said, "Uh . . ."

"I'd look them up for you, but I have an appointment for my hair."

"Don't tell me, you are going to get it dyed," said Winter. Today Cindy's hair was sky blue.

"Thinking of going natural," she said.

"Really?" Winter was surprised. "What color is that?"

"I don't remember." She took back the pad from Winter, wrote more. "Scroll down on the corporate page. Sometimes there's a filing for a name change or other paperwork that the resident agent asks a paralegal to submit, and they screw up and enter the real name of the owner."

WINTER USED Cindy's computer after she left, it had a bigger monitor. The registered agent for Stannis LLC was an address on Main Street. Winter googled it and found it belonged to a law firm he'd never heard of. He wrote the name down but doubted they'd tell him anything.

Back on the state corporate website, he found a filing for an amendment to the business entity, recording a member's change of address. The member's name was Doctor Rudolph Miles.

Winter went back to his desk. This doctor *wasn't* on the guest list. "Anybody talk to a Doctor Miles?" he called out.

"He's not on the interview list," said Crosse. "Was he there?"

"He or his car. Maybe." The license spreadsheet indicated it was a dark colored SUV. Winter switched databases, looked up Miles in the DMV. He didn't have a Massachusetts license. But the car was registered to the same LLC with the Warren Street address, Stannis Hill.

He'd run around in one big circle.

Winter had reached the limit of what he could get out of technology. At least he had a name and an address.

WARREN STREET was at the edge of an industrial area, low, wide brick buildings with smokestacks that hadn't been used in decades. A few of the old factories had been converted to other uses. There were a lot of *For Lease* signs.

A block-long, two-story building with a new façade had been split into multiple rentals. Behind glass doors, a stairway led to an open walkway on the second floor. The lot had spaces for maybe a hundred cars, but only six vehicles were there.

Winter cruised through the lot. Four of the cars, all sedans, were clustered in front of a tax preparation center. At the other end of the building sat two SUVs, both silver.

Winter parked and found the Stannis Hill office, on the corner of the second floor. The windows were tinted, and slatted wood shades blocked his view. He was about to go in when a black SUV entered the lot and pulled up to the glass doors.

Winter couldn't see the entire license plate from where he stood, but the first letter matched the Carter house security footage. No one got out of the SUV.

Winter headed off away from the office. It was times like these he wished he smoked, so he could pretend to be on a cigarette break. He found another set of stairs, open to the air. He went halfway down, his head at eye level with the second story landing.

A very heavy set guy in a charcoal sweater came out of the Stannis Hill office. He locked the door, turned away from Winter, and went through the glass door leading to the opposite stairs. Winter continued down the stairway at his end, and was in time to see the driver holding the back door open for the big man to get in the black SUV. The driver, tall, with a buzz cut and a leather jacket, closed the door and got in the car.

Winter waited just long enough for the SUV to get out of the lot and then ran for his car, watching which way they turned.

He caught up to the SUV at the light on Park, scribbling the license plate on his hand with a ballpoint. The plate looked like the right one, but he didn't want to chance looking it up in his notebook. The SUV was a Mercedes.

The SUV stayed on Park, heading north. Two miles later, Park became residential. Cars began peeling off into the neighborhoods. The blocks became longer, the houses larger. Just past a private golf course the SUV turned onto Old Town Road.

There were far fewer cars, the houses set back and stately, some behind stone walls. Winter slowed, his lights still off even though it was getting close to dusk.

The SUV pulled into a two story white stone house behind a gated entry. Winter drove on past as the solid gates closed.

Winter parked a block down the street. He wrote down a description of the house along with its address.

A half hour later, it was too dark to see. No one had come out of the house. Winter drove home, his mind on a conversation he'd had with Miranda Dell, about a fat man in a Mercedes SUV who had met with Rick Singleton at the studio.

CHAPTER 54

Rıck awoke at the gonging sound, a crick in his neck. The tv was on, the only light in the room. His mother was in the bed, her eyes closed. He'd fallen asleep in the lounge chair. An old black and white movie was on, but that wasn't the source of the bell.

Someone at the door, at . . . eight p.m. The cops again?

Or Doc?

Rick tiptoed across the room and peered out through the window. The yard was dark, and he didn't have a good angle on the front door. Shit.

Pretend no one was home?

The cop Winter wouldn't be fooled, Rick's car was parked outside. Doc could have Kevin with him, who might bust down the door. He couldn't risk that, not with his mom there.

The doorbell rang again. His mother stirred, and that got Rick moving, it was hard enough for her to fall asleep. He ran out into the foyer to head off another ring.

He steeled himself and opened the door.

It wasn't the cops or Doc or Kevin but a short woman in a brown heavy duck jacket with a no nonsense haircut and an even more no nonsense look.

"You Rick? I'm Patricia. Detective Winter told me about your mom."

"What about her?"

"That she could use some help."

"You a nurse?"

"You want to talk about it through the door or let me in? It's freezing."

Rick opened the door and she brushed by, giving off an aura of authority and competence. By the time he closed the door and returned to the kitchen she was already peeking in on his mom.

"Got the tv on, that's good, if she likes those old shows," said Patricia. "Cancer, right? How far?"

No one had ever been so direct with Rick with the 'c' word, yet he found himself answering, "Metastasized, into the bones too."

"Are you able to get her to eat?" Patricia had unzipped her jacket and was looking at his mother's medications.

"A little," he said. "Say . . ."

Patricia waved a prescription bottle. "Did you notice a change in her eating when she started these appetite pills? Throwing up a lot?"

"Quite a bit."

"Try stopping these for a few days. They often cause nausea."

"The doctor gave her those . . ."

"The doctor isn't here. If she stops eating, it's all over. You won't even be able to get the pain meds in her, because she'll throw them up."

Rick, reeling from her straightforward manner, said, "Who did you say you are again?"

"I'm a hospice volunteer."

"I don't want hospice."

"It's not about what you want, it's about what your mom needs. You want help for her or not?"

Rick was so tired he couldn't stand up, but that didn't stop him from being wary. "What would you do exactly?"

"Do what you've probably been doing, but much better than you can. Give you a chance to get some sleep. Give you about ten years of experience on helping people like your mom."

"And Detective Winter sent you?"

"Nobody sends me. He told me about your mother, and I'm here." Patricia started going through the cabinets. "You giving her this shake?"

"She doesn't do well with solid food."

"This shake—it's got dairy. Might be okay, might not. We'll need to experiment."

Rick looked back and forth from Patricia to the food to the medications and back to Patricia. Something about her directness allowed him to say, "If we do the hospice, she's going to die."

Not unkindly, but in her straightforward manner, Patricia said,

"She's going to die at some point. The question is, do you want her to be in pain or as comfortable as we can make her?"

Rick wasn't sure what Winter would be expecting for sending Patricia his way, he'd deal with that later. He watched her as she separated out the food, bustling around the kitchen like she owned the place. She certainly sounded like she knew what she was doing.

God he could use some sleep . . .

DOC'S DAY IN the office hadn't been productive. He'd made a dozen calls, going deep into his client list, trying to drum up business. It was like the whole world had decided to take a break from drugs.

Kevin sensed his mood and kept his mouth shut, just driving, no music. Doc worked through his options. It had taken him longer than he expected to set up shop outside of Florida. Maybe he needed to get back down there, not to resettle—still too risky—but put in an appearance, get face to face with his customers, the phone calls weren't working.

He still had unfinished business here. To Kevin, he said, "What's up with the Rick kid?"

"He's always at his mother's house. I don't think he's working no more."

Doc immediately jumped to the implications of what that would mean for him. If Rick wasn't working, he wasn't with Candy, which meant he might be on the outs with the song deal.

"Another thing," said Kevin. "He got a visit from a guy. They talked in the yard, then the guy went into the house with Rick, came out about a half hour later."

"What did he look like?"

"Older than Rick. They talked like they knew each other but weren't buddy buddy. He gave off a vibe like he was in charge. Guy used to getting his way."

"A cop?"

"Wasn't dressed like no cop. He was wearing a hoodie, and I didn't see no cop car."

"Undercover?"

"Never heard of no undercover cop that old, but what do I know?"

Doc figured Kevin knew plenty. Worst case it *was* a cop Rick had been talking to, and Doc always prepared for the worst.

"What happened after he left?"

"Nothing. I hung around for a bit, but Rick never came out again. Thought about following the other guy, but didn't want to miss Rick in case he went off somewhere because of whatever happened with the guy. Got his plate though."

"Anybody see you?"

"Doubt it. I was in my brother's pickup."

Doc grunted. If he'd been in Florida, he could make a call, he had more than one customer in the DMV, they'd track the plate in a second. Not here, though. Another hole in his organization he had to fill.

"Want you to bring me Rick," said Doc. "Time for a heart to heart."

"Tonight?"

They'd just pulled through the gate at the house. The lights were on, Tricia would have the hot tub turned up, a scotch waiting. Doc wanted to salvage the day. "Tomorrow."

RICK WAS AMAZED at how quickly Patricia got his mother to perk up. Patricia had repositioned his mother on the bed, worked a heating pad under her hips, and even got her to eat, all while carrying on a conversation.

Patricia had gently guided him out of the room into the kitchen, where he listened in on their talk. Patricia wasn't dealing with his mother any differently than she had dealt with Rick, talking directly about her condition, her pain, asking questions, interspersed with a discussion about books and movies. His mother seemed to be taking it all in stride. Maybe she wasn't just tired physically but also tired from the pointed avoidance of the elephant in the room. Not only from her few friends who visited, but from Rick.

He was as guilty as all of them.

He made himself a few eggs, but when they were done he was too drained to eat. He was scraping them into the trash when Patricia poked her head in the kitchen. "I think I can get her to eat a little more, you got eggs?"

"I just used the last one." Patricia just stared at him, and Rick said, "I'll go get some more."

"I'll give you a list of other things to pick up."

Rick wasn't sure he should leave his mother with a stranger. From the living room his mother called, "Patricia! Come see this part!" And then his mother laughed.

It was the first time Rick had heard her laugh in—he couldn't remember. Strangely, it made him start to cry. He turned away from Patricia.

He splashed water on his face, just as he had before, yet for a very different reason.

When Patricia came back into the kitchen with the list, Rick said, "I know I haven't been that thankful, I'm sorry. Now that you're here—is there any way you can sit with my mom tomorrow during the day? It's important."

"For your mom?"

Rick thought about lying, he could make up a story. Getting some money to help his mom, something. He knew immediately Patricia would see right through him. And he was so tired of lying.

"No. For me. It's just something I got to do, a one-time thing. After I do it, I'll be much better helping out around here."

Patricia gave him a long look. "Do what you got to do," she said. "As long as you go get those eggs."

CHAPTER 55

W INTER STARED into his refrigerator. There was food enough, and he was certainly hungry enough, but nothing except the beer called out to him, and he wanted to keep his head clear. He'd picked up a lot in his long day that he needed to let wash over him. He settled on simple crackers and peanut butter.

In the living room he sat in the lounger, working through the crackers. He had turned on all the lights, not that he was worried about falling asleep, his mind was buzzing. He wanted the big white ceiling, his blank canvas, to work on.

The big breaks in cases came from being on the street, but when you were on the street, you didn't always recognized them as breaks. A piece of information here, leading to a tidbit, another piece of information, doors opening and closing, both literally and figuratively. Usually you were stuck between too much useless data and not enough relevant facts.

Cops looked for suspects who had motive and opportunity. It was a good approach because it worked. Yet it was often hard to identify the motive if you didn't know how all the players were connected—or even if you had all the players identified. A lot of police ran down fruitless paths because they thought they had all the players and chose the most logical suspect out of them. The problem was that there might be a much *more* logical suspect who wasn't on their radar. Winter had made this mistake enough times that he risked keeping too many options open.

The prime suspects in most homicides were pretty obvious: the jealous husband, the gang turf fights, the trigger happy robber. When it went beyond that, it took far longer to find all the possible connections to the victim—connections you needed before you could figure out who might have reason to do a killing.

Which led to the ceiling.

When he was young, Winter and his father would listen to baseball games on the radio in this very room. Even after he had learned the names of all the players he found it difficult to follow the plays. So his father had taught him how to use the ceiling as a way to picture the field, the players. Tie game, bottom of the eighth, two out, a man on second, the announcer excitedly calls out a line drive to left, and Winter, even at eight, able to picture the ball on the ceiling, but it's not a ceiling now, it's green grass, the shortstop leaping in vain, the runner on second already on the move, the ball bouncing twice, the left fielder getting in position, Winter *seeing* him release the ball toward the plate even before the announcer yells *Here's the throw!* and it's obvious there's going to be a play, because a runner wouldn't try to score from second on a hard hit ball to left unless there were two outs . . .

He missed those days, those games, his father.

Winter couldn't get them back, but he still used the ceiling visualization trick. This was how he figured out the hidden connections between the players in his most difficult cases, this is where he connected the dots he often could not see in the mass of words and interviews and witnesses and suspects and victims.

All the technology in the world couldn't compete with what he could often do right here, staring at his blank ceiling.

The initial assumption was that the deaths of Coleman and Hennig were connected. But with no apparent ties between the two men, no obvious suspects, and the Coleman death possibly accidental, it seemed more likely they weren't connected at all, that it was just one of those weird, random coincidences. Cops hated coincidences, but that didn't mean they weren't real.

All the digging hadn't turned up anything to tie the two cases together. Until today.

Now he just had to make sense of it all.

Winter arranged the players on his ceiling canvas. On the left, Dwayne Coleman, on the right, Gerry Hennig. Next to Coleman he placed Malcolm Third Eye Washington. Winter connected the two men with a solid line in his head; that connection was firmly established because they'd arrived at the party in the limo and from Coleman's music video. In a large box next to Coleman were the guests he had definitely spoken to at the party: Miranda Dell, Rick Singleton, Candy Carter. A final box, this one for Doctor Miles, who might have been supplying Coleman with fake chains.

They still had very little information on other people in Coleman's life. Some had been identified: his manager, other guests in photos with Coleman, the limo driver. Yet those people either hadn't been at the party or appeared to have just a passing contact.

Winter shifted his attention to the Hennig side of the canvas. Closest to Hennig was Rick Singleton. Though Singleton claimed he hadn't been in touch with Hennig for a while, a firm line connected them. Winter had no reason to put Candy Carter and Miranda Dell with Hennig; there were no photos of them together at the party or any evidence they had known each other.

Ryder had found the possible drug dealer connection, Nadya Boyko. She got her own box and a light dotted line to Hennig. So did Malcolm Washington, who might have pushed Hennig around outside his apartment. There were others who could be worked into Hennig's circle, fellow students, roommates, the young woman who had eyes for him. Yet none appeared to have either reason or opportunity to kill Hennig.

The only names appearing in both sides of the canvas were Rick Singleton and Malcolm Washington.

Winter rearranged his picture. He moved the boxes for Singleton and Washington to the middle, in between the two dead men. Singleton had a tight connection to Hennig, but only a weak one to Coleman. Washington was the opposite, a hard connection to Coleman, but only a weak one to Hennig, and that assumed the man who had accosted Hennig at his apartment had actually been Washington.

Winter noodled over that, tried moving the boxes around, ended up back where he started. That was all the *who*. How about the *what*?

First, drugs.

Drugs were all over the place. Coleman had been doing drugs at the party, probably his own, hidden in his chain. Singleton admitted he done coke at the party. Perhaps Miranda Dell as well, although she might have just been drinking. Hennig's possible connection to drugs was through Nadya Boyko. Singleton was a user, and according to Dell, had brought drugs to her party.

So a box in the middle of the map, labeled *drugs*, with a thick line to Coleman and lighter lines to Singleton, Dell, and Hennig. Hennig's line had a question mark.

The other possible tie was the music.

No, not the music, the *royalties*. People didn't get killed over music, they got killed over money. *Follow the money.*

On the Hennig side, a connection to Singleton from their royalty deal. A line to Candy Carter, since if there was money to be made from the Singleton/Hennig song it would come from her.

Winter couldn't see how any of the royalties connected to Coleman at all.

He got up, stretching, taking a break. Went into the kitchen, took a drink of water, didn't even think about the beer. Back to the lounger, getting into it now.

He started over, this time not with Coleman and Hennig as the centerpieces, but with the other players. He did the easy ones first, Candy Carter, Miranda Dell, even Nadya Boyko. All their links appeared to be limited to one side of the map, or where they connected to the other side, the connections were fleeting.

Malcolm Washington again.

Washington was with Coleman at the party, and he was a crackhead. He could have robbed Hennig of his watch and then got in a fight with Coleman. The timeline was tough, but it was at least possible. Motive and opportunity.

Rick Singleton.

Singleton had motive and likely opportunity for Hennig, but why would he kill Coleman? And could Singleton cold bloodedly kill his friend, clean himself up, and deal with the police, all over a possible share of royalties he might not see for a year?

Winter went back through the players and their connections to either Washington or Singleton. He got a little stuck on Doctor Miles. Miles possibly connected to Coleman through the fake jewelry, perhaps even the drugs, if the suspicions about him in Miami were true, although that was about oxy, not coke. Miles might be the mystery man who Miranda Dell had seen talking to Singleton.

If so, then Miles created another connection between Coleman and Hennig. Miles knew Singleton from their meeting in the studio parking lot, and, according to Dell, Miles might have supplied Singleton with drugs. Singleton was closest to Hennig. So Miles to Coleman directly, and to Hennig via Singleton.

And it was possible that a car registered to a company Miles had an interest in had been at the Carter party.

Winter went at it again and again, mixing and matching. He finally quit when two things were crystal clear.

First, there *were* possible links between the two cases, through Malcolm Washington or Rick Singleton. Washington he couldn't do a thing about yet, other than to keep trying to find him. Singleton was another matter. Winter hadn't pressed him enough on the big man in the SUV. That could lead to drugs, it could lead to Coleman. Winter would go back at Singleton, push him really hard. Get him out of his mother's house to put the pressure on.

The other thing crystal clear was that Winter had sat too long in the chair. He had no idea what time it was, but he had to take a wicked leak.

CHAPTER 56

MALCOLM WASHINGTON LEANED up against the brick wall of an old factory building on Tremont Street. In other neighborhoods he might have looked out of place. Here he was just a part of the landscape the slummers came to see.

He was facing the parking lot of a dance club. Malcolm wasn't into this kind of club, all flash, and it was out of his neighborhood. But rich types meant expensive watches.

The watch thing had worked out okay. Sure easier to trade for cash or rock than phones or computers. Problem was, he could never tell which watches were worth anything. Some he couldn't give away.

He'd been hanging with Chilli, freebasing while Chilli smoked a joint. Malcolm tried to trade Chilli a watch for a dime bag, Chilli rolling up his jacket, showing Malcolm three watches on his arm. Malcolm said, "What you need three watches for?"

"I got so much going on, I need them to keep track."

Malcolm didn't get it but it was funny, the two of them laughing, Chilli telling him he was already onto the watch thing and how he got them. "Be on the street, good street, dig? Ask the person, 'Hey, what kind of watch is that?' When they show the watch, squeeze it into their wrist, then just pull it off, say nice and friendly 'Thank You' and keep walking. They'll think the watch is still on their wrist because it *feels* like it's still there."

So Malcolm had tried it. Nobody was sporting good watches on his streets, so he went up past South End. Except no one would show him a watch, just walking on past. Malcolm did score twice in a shopping mall and was able to trade the watches for a few rocks.

All too slow for Malcolm.

He stuck out too much in shopping malls, but here, outside a mostly black club, he looked right at home even at one in the morning.

Four chicks came out of the club, but before Malcolm could make a move a car pulled up and they jumped in. A couple more people got in their cars, none looked good.

Finally two very white women popped out of the club, weaving across the street toward the lot, tight dresses and high heels.

Malcolm waited until they were unlocking their car. "Hey," he said.

They turned, too drunk to be alarmed. Malcolm could see a fine metal watch and sparkly earrings.

"Gimme your fuckin' watch," he said.

The woman closest to him handed it over without a word. The other one backed up against the car. Malcolm gave her the hard look, and she stuttered, "I don't have a watch."

"Whatever you got," said Malcolm.

Two blocks away, Malcolm checked out his haul. A watch, two diamond earrings, a necklace, a hundred and twenty dollars.

Moving fast now, time to score. Go find Chilli, he wouldn't turn down cash.

MALCOLM COULDN'T FIND Chilli, but he scored anyway, using the cash, did a nice pipe, and then went into Drifter's. Nice long haired sisters at the bar, not giving him much attention until he flashed a baggie of the white stuff. Blow was too slow for Malcolm, but it impressed the ladies. It was all the same, but they looked down on the rock.

Malcolm and the two ladies partied all night, sucking up Malcolm's score like vacuum cleaners, but he didn't mind, he got as much as he gave. He woke up in their bed, one of the women gone, the other draped across his chest.

He found his pipe and was done with the rock before she woke up. She still looked fine in the morning, and when he told her he didn't have any powder left she didn't turn down the pipe.

By the time he left he was cleaned out. He looked for Chilli, the man not in his usual spot, so Malcolm made it back up to Blue Hill Avenue, where Cadillac and Flash were in the store, happy to take the watch and earrings, giving him a cool two hundred.

Malcolm had to walk five blocks before he scored again, too early in the day. He did a quick snort through his pen to keep him up, made it back to his current crib and settled in.

Feeling good, the crystal not as shiny as the earrings he'd taken but far more useful. He stayed there all day, not even turning on a light, just hitting the pipe.

His phone went off, maybe, he was flying. The second time, just as he was coming down, he fumbled in his coat for it. Missed the call, nobody important called him anyway, now that Outta Here got himself dead.

Many pipes later, the phone rang again, this time Malcolm got the swipe in on time. "Yeah."

"Third Eye, been calling you all the time."

"Who this?"

"Anthony. Listen, you in trouble man, the cops looking for you."

Malcolm, out if it, looked around the room. "No cops here."

"They coming. I just got out of jail, the cops know about how you got picked up by Juke."

"Ain't seen Juke," said Malcolm.

"When he took you to the Peter Pan, you were out with Outta Here."

"Ain't seen Outta Here either. He got drowned."

"Shit, you listening? The cops found me, they're going to come for you."

"What you talking 'bout, fool?" Malcolm had done nothing lately to get the cops on him, no way those two white chicks went to the police. He couldn't think past last night.

"I'm helping you out, Third Eye. You owe me."

"Don't owe you shit," said Malcolm, dropping the phone and reaching for the pipe.

NIGHT, the room dark. Malcolm rolled over on the floor. His phone lit up.

In the back of his head he vaguely remembered a phone call, not who it was with or what they had talked about.

Found his pipe, but he was out of rock. Fell asleep, woke up, looked again for his stash, it finally registering he was out. Back on the street, time to score another watch, maybe more shiny earrings.

CHAPTER 57

WINTER HUDDLED with Ryder, Crosse and Owens in the detective room. Except for the occasional cough from Owens, he and Crosse sat quietly as Winter took them through it. Ryder interrupted constantly until Owens said, "Let him tell it his way," which didn't quite get Ryder to shut up, but knocked the questions down by half.

Winter finished by saying, "So the two dead men *are* connected, either through Rick Singleton or Malcolm Washington, or both. Singleton claims he just knew Coleman from the party. But if Singleton knew Miles, and Miles is connected to Coleman, we've got a possible link between Singleton and Coleman. Washington could be another link between Hennig and Coleman."

"We got to nail down Washington," said Owens. "I'll follow up again with Boston PD."

"I've got Cindy digging deeper on Doctor Miles," said Winter.

"Still sounds weak," said Ryder. "Even if Washington or Singleton knew both the dead men, what's that prove?"

"Nothing yet," Winter admitted. "But it gives us a new way to go. We get a picture of Miles, show it to Miranda Dell. If she puts Miles with Singleton, then we have something to go after Singleton with. Either way, I'm going to press him, make him think we already got them together."

"Be easier to just go at Miles," said Ryder.

"With what? We heard a rumor a guy nicknamed Doc in Florida moved drugs and fake chains?"

"We could go back to all the party guests, see if they saw Miles at the party," said Crosse.

"We going to do that with the owners of every partial plate on the security cameras?" said Ryder. "I got a much faster way. Hennig was celebrating with Nadya Boyko. She's a pretty woman, he wants to fit in. She gets him hooked. Or he's just trying to impress her. He tries to score drugs at the Carter party, hell, he could even be moving product for her, who would suspect him? Washington sees what a newbie he is and rips him off. Hennig tries to act tough, holding out, Washington gives him a beating."

"Doesn't explain Coleman," said Owens.

"Washington goes nuts—maybe he taps Hennig's stash. He gets really high with Coleman. They get in a fight over the drugs, Coleman ends up in the pool."

"I'm open to both," said Owens. "What I can't figure is how Washington even knows about Hennig? If it's drugs, who tips him off that Hennig is carrying weight?"

"Nobody," said Ryder. "Hennig tries to sell to Washington, who sees how over his head Hennig is, and just takes what he has."

Crosse said, "Works for me. Anything new on Boyko?"

Ryder got up. "Her lawyer wants to talk. That means she has something to give up. I'm going back to Boston this morning to find out what."

Cindy popped into the detective room. "The house you followed that doctor to is owned by Stannis Hill, LLC."

"That's his company," said Winter.

"Right. The house was purchased last year for eight hundred thousand dollars. I can't find a lien on the property, which usually means it was bought for cash."

That's a lot of cash, even for a doctor," said Owens.

"See?" said Ryder. "Drug money. Miles either buying or selling, using Hennig as the mule to Boyko via Singleton or Coleman."

Winter looked at Owens, who shrugged. "Not sure about what moved where when, but he's got a point, the drugs keep popping up."

"Just because he buys a house with cash doesn't mean it's drug money," said Winter. "But I hear you. Cindy, can you see if there were any sales in Florida by that LLC or by Miles himself? He could have sold a house down there, used that money."

"I can do that," she said. "Anything else?"

"Find a photo of Miles?"

"Been looking. Nothing yet. He doesn't have a website."

Ryder said, "Another reason to talk to Miles."

"Not yet," said Winter. "Let's find out about the house first."

Ryder muttered something Winter didn't catch and walked out.

Owens said, "Never going to hear the end of it if he's right."

OWENS WAS DUE in court. As he was packing up, he asked Winter, "What now?"

"Go at Singleton again."

Winter was picking up the phone when Cindy reappeared. "Those tox reports you've been waiting for on Dwayne Coleman are in."

"You got it?"

"It's in your email. They copied me on the notification, not the report. I figured you might not have checked."

Winter pulled it up, Owens looking over his shoulder. Winter said, "Cocaine hydrochloride, point zero one grams net weight, 81 percent purity . . . high quality. It's cut with a little mannitol and lidocaine."

"Zero point one grams? We found way more than that by the pool."

Winter scrolled up the screen. He was on the tox report, but not for Dwayne Coleman. "Wrong report, this is the trace on Rick Singleton's jacket." He clicked open the second report.

They both stared at it, then Winter said, "Son of a bitch."

The composition of the coke from around the pool was exactly the same as that from Rick Singleton's jacket.

"The man is lying to you," said Owens.

"No shit," said Winter. He scanned a third report. "Look at this, there was fentenyl mixed with some of the coke around the pool, and also in Coleman's system."

"Guy mixed fentenyl and high purity cocaine? No wonder he went into the pool," said Owens.

Winter jumped back to the Singleton report. There was no mention of fentenyl. He picked up the phone, punched up Andie on the speed dial. "I'm looking at Rick Singleton's trace. Would fentenyl show up on a standard substance test?"

"I don't know," said Andie. "I'll find out for you."

"If not, have them rerun the Singleton trace for fentenyl."

Winter clicked off, pulled out his small notebook where he kept phone numbers, and dialed. "Patricia? I got a really big favor. I need to get Rick Singleton into the station. Is there any way you can get out to his mother's to watch her while he's here?"

"I'm there now."

"What?"

"Rick left early this morning. Said he had to go deal with something, he asked me to stay."

"Did he say where he went?"

"No, said he'd be gone for a while."

"When he comes back, don't mention I called."

When Winter hung up, Owens said, "You think he's running?"

"I don't know. Can't see him leaving his mother. But he lied to my face about the coke. He had to get it from Coleman, or give it to Coleman, or get it from the same source, maybe even at the party."

"Or bumped into Coleman, got it on his jacket."

"You believe that?" asked Winter.

"Not for a second," said Owens.

CHAPTER 58

R YDER SUSPICIOUSLY EYED the available vehicles in the unmarked car pool lot. Four of the ancient Crown Vics and one newer Taurus Interceptor. Ryder hated the boat like ride of the Crown Vics. The Interceptor was underpowered but marginally better. In Derry the detectives got the newer cars. Here, they were stuck with hand-me-downs, which is why many of the detectives drove their own cars. No way Ryder was going to take his own car to Boston.

Ryder got the keys for the Interceptor, transferred his overnight bag from his own vehicle—in case he got held over in Boston, or even better, hooked up—and headed for the nearest Starbucks.

Winter pissed him off. Just when they finally had a break in the case, Winter was getting in the way, taking over, controlling the tempo. This Miles had to be the drug Doc from Miami, who else bought a house for eight hundred thousand cash? Miles was likely the source of Nadya's drugs, his deals arranged through Singleton's Boston friend Gerry Hennig or Dwayne Coleman. Hennig representing Miles, Coleman moving the product to Boyko for distribution. Or any one of other possible combinations. Even without the details pinned down, any idiot could see the connections, it didn't take any special skills.

Putting a little pressure on Miles was the right move, tell him his circle was collapsing on him, that Boyko was in custody, whoever talked first got a deal.

He'd clear this himself. Get Boyko to give up Miles, have it all wrapped up by the time he got back from Boston, Winter still waiting to move. No way Ryder should take a back seat to a guy who couldn't see the writing on the wall that it was time for him to retire.

*　　*　　*

RYDER WAITED UNTIL he got on the highway to drink his cappuccino, not wanting to take the chance of spilling it on his shirt. He'd gone only a few miles when his phone rang.

He deftly answered the call and put it on speaker. "Detective Martin Ryder."

"This is ADA Henderson. Nadya Boyko's attorney is in court and will not be available until the late afternoon, so we won't be able to interrogate Boyko."

"I'm already on my way," said Ryder.

"That's why I'm calling, save you a trip."

Ryder hung up, noticed he was doing eighty, dropped it down. He took the next exit, pulled into a small gas station, frustrated. Maybe he should just go on to Boston, be in position for when Boyko's attorney showed up.

He was too wired for that, things were finally coming to a head. He just needed to push it along before all the other players lawyered up. Miles was the obvious one to see, catch him off guard, just ask him about whether he'd been at the party, if he knew Coleman and Hennig. Winter should have done it when he had spotted Miles.

Ryder punched the street where Miles lived into his GPS. Winter had mentioned the street, although not the exact number. Cindy would have it, but she was close to Winter, she'd tip off Winter for sure. No matter, Winter had described the house and the gated entry.

DOC MILES HAD HIS second cup of coffee in the bedroom. Usually he was an early riser, but Tricia had been especially attentive and frisky this morning, and he'd let her do her thing.

He took a long shower, planning his day. He had a good lead on a few Boston contacts, which meant he could finally move more product. If he could replicate even half of what he had in Miami, he'd be fine here for a few years. Try a new approach, leave someone in charge while he set up shop again in a warmer location.

Gina could handle it, she had the brains and she worked good with Kevin. Too bad Dwayne had been such a problem. He had access to the

Miami music industry; if things had worked out differently he could have moved product down there. But Dwayne, though smart enough, had been both a heavy user and a egotist, neither one boding well for the long term.

In a perfect world Doc would supplement his drug business with a few new legitimate enterprises, like the bling rentals. Who knows, maybe he'd even see a few real patients, as long as they invested in his other businesses.

Like music. If this deal with the royalties worked out he could probably find some musicians who would trade good quality blow for royalties. Dwayne had tried to hone in on Doc's deal. It would be sweet poetic justice if Doc ended up making money on an idea Dwayne confirmed was worthwhile.

First he had to get a handle on Rick Singleton. Maybe Rick had been talking to a cop, maybe not. Rick talking to the cops probably had nothing to do with him, but this was no time to take chances.

Doc had no direct ties to Rick's dead co-writer Gerry. Dwayne had enough knowledge to make the connection, but Doc had taken care of Dwayne. Now only Rick could tie Doc to Dwayne and to Gerry.

Doc pulled on his cashmere sweater and headed back to the kitchen. He'd have another coffee while he waited for Kevin to get to Rick. With a little luck Rick would spill his guts to Kevin, and Doc wouldn't even have to deal with the kid face to face.

Not that he wouldn't if it came to that.

RYDER DRIFTED along Old Town Road, a nice neighborhood. Not Carter estate nice, but nice enough. Wide yards, the second and often third stories of well kept homes peaking up from behind tall fences or stone walls.

The road was over a mile long and, unfortunately for Ryder, half the houses had gated entrances. He spotted two dark SUV's, one black and one forest green. Winter might not even have got the color right.

The road ended in a cul de sac. Ryder parked in the circle. Using his phone he easily found a real estate website listing recent local sales. He searched on Old Town Road. There it was, number 47, eight hundred thousand dollars.

Ryder entered the address into a map program and realized he was sitting almost right across from the house, the first one on the cul de sac. A stucco stone wall, too high to see over, ran along the side and around toward the front. Ryder couldn't see much, just the top story.

He walked around front. The wall rose up in an arch over the drive, the entrance blocked by solid gates that looked like wood but were actually metal. There was a small gap between the gates and Ryder peered in. A light green Audi was parked in front of a three car garage, the doors closed.

Built into the curved wall was a small box with a keypad and an intercom. A circular glass pattern suggested a camera. Ryder was debating whether to flash his badge, which could go either way, getting buzzed in or totally ignored, there being no law saying you had to answer your door.

Maybe they'd seen Winter when he had followed the SUV here, scared them off. Doc Miles could be running even now.

A quiet thud from behind the fence pulled his eye back to the slit in the gate. A young woman, wearing tights and a pink tee shirt, stepped out onto the porch. She held her hand out like she was checking to see if it was raining. He yelled through the gate, "Hello!" but she must not have heard him and went back inside.

Ryder hovered his finger over the call button. Maybe the girl was the daughter, home alone, and she wouldn't want to answer.

He turned at the sound of an approaching vehicle. It rolled on past, a dark haired young woman at the wheel, staring straight ahead. It was a black Mercedes SUV.

DOC HAD FINISHED his coffee when Tricia came into the kitchen. "I think it's going to rain," she said. "I'll get you a raincoat."

Doc hated cold rain, but he was having a good morning, he wasn't going to let it get him down. "The black Burberry," he said.

One of his two personal phones bleeped as Tricia brought him the coat. It was the phone he always had on him and used for legitimate business. The text was from Gina and said, *Number two.* He said to Tricia, "Grab number two."

Tricia ran to get the burner, and it was ringing when she handed it to him.

Gina, on the burner, said, "I was just about to drive in. There's a guy outside the gate, peeking in. No car, but there is one parked in the circle, I think it's a cop."

"What kind of car?"

"Ford Taurus, has a small whip antenna."

"He see you?"

"He might have. I didn't slow down to look at him, but he could have seen me drive past. I think he's alone."

"Hold on." To Tricia, Doc said, "Anyone ring the gate buzzer when I was in the shower?"

"No, I would have said something." Tricia worked the tablet built into the kitchen wall, pulling up an image of the front gate. A man in a suit coat and tie was reaching toward the camera, his face distorted by the wide angle lens.

The bell chimed in the house. Doc ignored it, studying the man's face. Gina was right, he was probably a cop, she had good instincts.

He mentally inventoried what he had in the house, too much, but he couldn't see how the cops would have probable cause for a search. And cops on a search didn't show up alone, doing a Peeping Tom through the gate.

The bell chimed again. Into the phone, Doc said, "Swing around the block, see if you see any more cars."

"Want me to cruise by the house again?"

"No. Park at the end of Old Town, the opposite end. If you see other cars roll up, let me know right away."

RYDER RAN for his car, just in time to see the SUV turn the corner near where he had parked. Maybe Miles wasn't the only one with a Mercedes SUV in this neighborhood. But he had a feeling it was the right one.

He sped up the quiet street, the SUV gone. At the next intersection he spotted it down the cross street. He made the turn, deciding whether to call for backup. For what? To pull over a woman in an SUV? If she had nothing to do with Miles he'd be the laughingstock of the station, using uniforms to help him catch some rich soccer mom's kid driving the family car.

He'd follow it for a bit, just to be certain. If the car circled back to the Miles house he'd ask the woman why she had driven by him. If she lived in another house, no one needed know he was even here.

The car took another left, Ryder idling at the curb, not wanting to pull too close behind. There were so few cars on the quiet streets she'd notice him.

The SUV turned into a driveway. Ryder half spun making the turn, pulling up in time to see the woman get out of the car, a phone to her ear. She was wearing tight jeans and a form fitting soft shell jacket. She disappeared onto the side porch.

TRICIA HANDED Doc the phone. "Trouble," Gina said. "The guy must have seen me drive past, he followed me. I pulled into a house over on Rutland. The family is away. He might think I live here."

"How do you know the family is away?" asked Doc.

"I don't just sit around doing my nails when you're out," said Gina. "Never know when you might need a place to bail. They leave the driveway gate and side porch unlocked for deliveries."

"Can he see you?"

"No, but he can see the car. I parked it so the plate isn't visible, and I locked the gate, I'm okay for now."

"After he leaves, come on back. If you get stopped . . ."

"No problem. I'll make a food run, tell him I forgot to pick up milk before coming to the house. If he says he saw me turn into another driveway I'll tell him he must have mixed me up with another car. Play dumb."

Doc hung up. Gina was just smart enough to be able to pull that off.

RYDER WAITED twenty minutes, but the woman didn't come back out. It started to rain. He had on one of his better suits, a nice wool from Barneys, so he stayed in the car.

There was no particular reason to suspect this was anything other than what it appeared to be, a woman driving to her house. He hadn't been able to catch her plate. That would be good to know.

He called the station, got Cindy. "My appointment in Boston got held up," he said. "Anything new on that Miles property in Florida?"

"I'm still working on it."

"Okay, thanks. I have a little time, thinking I'll go swing by that Miles house, just see what I can see. Maybe find out if that black SUV is there. Can you give me the address and the plate?" Ryder had the address, but didn't want to admit that.

"Sure, hold on."

Ryder wrote it down in his notebook and hung up. Now he wished he had his own car, because he'd have a nylon windbreaker to keep the rain off his suit. If he could find a way to see the plate on the SUV he would know for sure whose car it was.

He was just slipping out of his suit jacket when his phone rang.

"This is ADA Henderson. Nadya Boyko's attorney is on the way over. He's got a few hours recess before he has to go back to court. If you want to be here for the interrogation, you'll have to hurry."

Ryder gritted out a thank you, hung up, cursed, and tore out of the neighborhood.

CHAPTER 59

WINTER AND CROSSE took the steps two at a time. Winter was on his phone, calling Singleton, it went right to voicemail. In the station parking lot he hit redial. This time he left a message. "Meet me at your mother's house. Right *now*. I'm on my way." Winter didn't need to try to sound angry, it was right there.

To Crosse he said, "Can you get over to Singleton's apartment, in case that's where he went?"

"Bring him in?"

"Yeah." Winter ran for his car.

WINTER RARELY USED the siren unless it was an emergency, but he did now, the magnetic light on the roof, pushing through traffic across the city. He was as mad at himself as he was at Singleton, letting himself get snowed, feeling sorry for Singleton because of his mother and because he'd lost his friend.

The coke match between Singleton's jacket and Dwayne Coleman meant Singleton had been lying to him all along. Even if Singleton had done the blow in his car, he probably gave coke to Coleman at some point at the party.

Ryder could be right. It was about drugs. Singleton the supplier, bringing drugs to the party, drugs Coleman might have OD'd on. Or Hennig told Singleton he could get drugs, that's why they met at the party, Singleton making a buy, perhaps bankrolled by Coleman. That would explain why Hennig was upstairs; he trusted Singleton to follow him to a private spot. Singleton tries to get Hennig to give up his source,

Hennig refuses. They fight. Maybe Singleton even pushed Coleman into the pool. Doc Miles in the mix as a buyer or seller via Singleton.

It made just as much sense as his idea about the music royalties.

Winter had seen Singleton's desperation. Just because he needed money to help his ailing mother didn't give him a pass.

Winter tried Singleton again, the cell jumping to voicemail. He gave up. No need to panic Singleton into running if he wasn't already. When Winter pulled up in front of the house the Buick was in the drive, Singleton's Kia nowhere to be seen.

Patricia was at the door, letting Winter in. "He's not here."

"I need you to get in touch with him, he might be dodging my calls."

Patricia gave him a long look, nodded. "Judith is sleeping. Let's keep it that way."

They stepped outside, Patricia holding the phone up so Winter could hear. Voicemail again.

"Damn it," muttered Winter. "He give you any indication what he had to do?"

"None, although he told me it wasn't for his mother. Needed to get something done, was all he said. He left right after I got here. He was in a hurry."

"He have a bag?"

"Not that I could see. It might have been in the car."

What could Singleton have to do that would make him leave his mother? "You okay to stay?" Winter asked.

"I'm good for today. What's going on?"

"Damned if I know," said Winter. "If he calls, tell him . . . tell him I need to talk to him. Try not to scare him off from coming back."

"You better not talk to him then," said Patricia. "You're scaring me. What did this boy do?"

Winter couldn't take the chance Singleton had brutally murdered his own friend. "I'm going to have a patrol car sit out front," he said. "Lock the doors and don't let him in if he shows up." Winter checked the deadbolts on both doors. "Look, I shouldn't be asking you do to this. If you want out . . ."

"I'll be fine. Listen, Rick . . . he seems okay. I've seen the ones who go through the motions, or don't help at all. He's doing everything he can for his mother."

"That's what I'm afraid of," said Winter.

*   *   *

WINTER COULDN'T THINK of any other place Singleton might go except the studio, so after arranging for a uniform to sit in front of the house, he drove there. As he pulled into the lot his phone rang. Dan Cole.

Winter answered while checking the lot for Singleton's car, which wasn't there. Cole said, "I finally got a chance to look through the rest of the Carter house security videos. Remember some of the date stamps were wrong? The power had probably gone off. I found a bunch of videos all with a date of January 1, 2000, which is what the recorder had reset to. We'd assumed they were old footage, but I found a video of the party."

"From the back door?"

"A little. But also from a pool camera."

Winter said, "I thought there were no pool cameras. Or they'd been shut down."

"Not all the feeds are marked by source. Two other cameras had been running all the time. They either didn't get shut down, or whoever was taking care of the system didn't notice these files because they assumed the cameras were off."

"And?"

"One camera is from the back patio area, looking out toward the pool. The image isn't stellar, but it's pretty easy to spot Dwayne Coleman coming out."

"He with anyone?" asked Winter.

"That's the thing. I can't be one hundred percent, because their backs are to the camera, but it sure looks like Coleman is with Rick Singleton. Heading for the back end of the pool where the cabana is."

THE RECEPTIONIST at the studio said she hadn't seen Singleton since he'd been fired. Winter checked with the owner Larry anyway, and he told Winter the same thing.

Back in the car, Winter steamed. He'd go look at the security video himself, but he was now certain Singleton had been with Coleman by the pool. He called Andie. "Did you get a chance to find out about those tox reports?"

"The fentanyl wouldn't have shown up in a regular trace test. I'm trying to get a rush on a new test for the Singleton jacket."

Winter thanked her and hung up. He called Crosse. "Anything?"

"No. I asked around, no one has seen him, but that might not mean much. His car is not here. I can stay."

"Good." Winter told her about the security video.

"Why run now?" asked Crosse. "Singleton couldn't have known about the tox report and the video."

"I might have scared him off when I saw him the other day. Patricia shows up to watch his mother, he takes advantage of the opportunity to run."

"Cold," said Crosse.

Winter was having a hard time reconciling the Singleton who had seemed so concerned about his mother with the one who had lied to him repeatedly and who might have skipped town. "Listen, instead of staying there, I'll swing by." He explained to her where Doc Miles had his office and the layout. "Cindy is having a problem finding a photo of him. You think you can hang around his office, maybe catch him on the way in or out, get a picture?"

"I can try."

"If the black Mercedes SUV isn't there, that doesn't mean Miles isn't, he got picked up by a driver. He might not leave until after five, but maybe he goes out for lunch and you can spot him then."

Winter hung up and pulled out of the lot, trying to piece it together. Something was missing, he just couldn't figure out what.

CHAPTER 60

Kevin Leary sat in the passenger seat of a white panel van. His cousin Liam, at the wheel, was one of the few people Kevin trusted to drive him. Liam had proven himself in the past, not bolting as Kevin finished up a job even though the sirens were only a block away.

Liam hadn't asked any questions when Kevin told him to get a van. Liam did part time work for a construction company and had a key to the vehicle lot, this particular van supposedly down for repair. There were so many white vans on the street no one thought twice about them.

Liam grunted around the ever present toothpick he mouthed as he guided the van through the narrow streets toward Rick's mother's house.

"Doc's still looking for help," said Kevin.

"Don't like being tied down. Be there for you when you need me, but you know I don't do good waiting around."

"Just offering. This works too." Kevin fit his earbuds in. "You finished up that other thing you were working on?"

"Got messy. I don't like messy, either."

Messy was Liam's shorthand for someone getting dead. Kevin knew his cousin could handle trouble, so it must have been pretty bad. Kevin had done his share of messy, and was sure he would again, if not for Doc, then someone else. There was always someone else.

Kevin swiped through to Bob Marley, a little cool reggae to chill.

Rick pulled into the lot of a small food mart gas station, two uncovered pumps out front. Rick used the porta potty and went into the store.

He stared at the revolving pizza and rolling hot dogs, going round and round in circles, just like his life. Getting nowhere except used up.

He turned away, not able to think about food even though he hadn't eaten all day. He bought a soda, his way of thanking the owner for at least having the porta potty. The man who took his money looked about seventy, Rick wondering how long he'd been behind that counter, whether this was his entire life, seeing customers come in an out, the same thing every day, going around in his own circle.

Maybe the old man never had any dreams, so it wasn't so bad for him. Maybe he was the lucky one.

Rick leaned on his car in the gravel lot. He pulled out his phone, still turned off because of where he'd been. There was no one he could call for help. He tossed the phone on the seat.

He watched the cars go by, not tasting the soda. Wondering what he could possibly do to fix his screwed up life.

LIAM SAID, "Drop down."

Kevin didn't hesitate, sliding down in the seat far enough so his head was below the window.

The van didn't change speed, Kevin watching his cousin, the shifting toothpick the only indication of trouble.

After a minute, Liam said, "Okay," and Kevin sat back up. "Cop car in front of the house," said Liam. "Didn't see the Kia."

"Marked?"

"Yeah. One cop at the wheel. Looked bored."

"Watching the house," said Kevin. "Not good." He pulled out a burner phone, called Doc. "Blue eyes on the mom," he said. Even with the burner he was careful.

"The guy you were there to see?"

"Don't know. No wheels. We'll check the other spot."

"Need to find out what he's been saying," said Doc.

"I hear you," said Kevin. Doc had hung up. Kevin said to Liam, "The apartment."

Liam nodded and turned the corner.

Kevin said, "Might get messy."

Liam said, "Better than waiting around."

*　　*　　*

RICK DROVE ANOTHER HOUR, his mind going around in circles. If only this, if only that. If only he hadn't got hooked up with Doc. If only he hadn't tried to make a score. If only he hadn't invited Gerry to the party.

Even the *if only* things that seemed to be great had turned out bad. If only he hadn't convinced Miranda to get his music to Candy. If only he hadn't played the other song for Candy. If only she hadn't liked it.

Would it change a thing if he'd made a single different decision along the way? Or would he have always ended up in the exact same horrible place?

Every decision seemed like the right one, and yet here he was. Gerry dead, the cops thinking he had something to do with it, his future a mess. And he was going to lose his mom.

He couldn't do anything about those other decisions, not now. But Patricia was right, he could at least help his mother.

RICK PARKED in the lot in front of his apartment and turned on his phone. The missed call icon was blinking, Rick scanning quickly through the calls. Multiple calls from Winter and Patricia.

Panicked, thinking something was wrong with his mom, he called Patricia, the call rolling over to voicemail. His fingers tight on the phone, he texted her, in case she was on another call. Another call came in and he answered without looking, thinking it was Patricia.

Winter.

"Is my mom okay?" Winter might be at the house, Patricia calling the ambulance . . .

"Last I heard. Patricia is with her. Where are you?"

Rick's hands were still shaking. "I just stopped by to pick up a few things at my apartment, then I'm heading over to my mom's."

"I've been trying to reach you."

"I just got back, I had my phone off. What's going on?"

"Are you really at your apartment?"

Rick caught an undercurrent of suspicion and anger. "Wait, you thought I'd left? That I'd leave my *mom*?" The hesitation on the line told Rick that's exactly what the cop had thought.

"Where were you?" asked Winter.

"I drove up to New Hampshire. To Gerry's funeral."

An even longer silence on the line. "Just stay there," said Winter. "I'm coming over."

"I want to see my mom," said Rick.

"Better we don't have this conversation in front of her. I'll be there in twenty minutes."

Rick sat numbly in the car after the call. They were going to arrest him.

He didn't even think about running. He'd made too many bad decisions already.

KEVIN SAID, "There's his car. Just drive past."

Liam took the van to the end of the row, turned left, slowly rolling to the far side of the lot. "Now what?"

"They might have apartment cameras showing the front door. If I ring his bell he's not going to let me in."

"I'll find out," said Liam.

Liam parked in the corner of the lot. He got out, leaving the van running. He was back in less than a minute.

"Definitely a camera," said Liam. "Even if we get in, be tough to take him in that building."

Kevin didn't bother calling Doc back for instructions, he knew what he had to do. "Let's wait a bit."

"Afraid you'd say that," said Liam, turning off the van.

WINTER WANTED Singleton at the station, there was nothing like a barren interrogation room to rattle a suspect. But it was one thing to be dragged into a police station, another thing entirely to drive there willingly. Singleton wouldn't be the first suspect who had decided to keep driving.

Winter pulled out of the studio lot, moving fast. On the way he called Crosse to update her, and also left a message for Owens.

If Singleton held out on him, Winter could always dangle the promise of a last visit to his mother to get some truth. Singleton wasn't the only one who could be cold.

*   *   *

RICK UNZIPPED HIS OVERNIGHT BAG and dropped it on the bed. The empty bag taunted him. Why bother packing if he was going to jail? For what, he wasn't sure, but with the way his luck had been going he had no doubt he was in trouble with the cops as well as with Doc.

He felt like crawling into the bag and pulling it closed over his head. Hiding from everyone, everything.

He had no idea what the cops knew. Maybe they really did think he killed Gerry. Or Dwayne.

He'd made so many bad choices he even screwed up being innocent.

No matter what happened, he needed to figure out how to take care of his mom. He got out a pad and began making a list of the few items he had left of value. His Martin guitar. His amps. His collection of Beatles ticket stubs, worth a few hundred. He found the title for his car, at least that was paid for.

He put the title and the list in an envelope. He'd get his mother to sign over her car, beg Patricia to turn it into cash, see if she'd help getting his mother into hospice.

On the way out he didn't even turn to look at his apartment. There was nothing left for him here.

"HE'S COMING OUT," said Kevin.

Liam had the van rolling before Kevin pulled out his earbuds.

"Get to him just before he reaches the car," said Kevin, pulling his ski cap down low and slipping into the back of the van. He grasped the inside handle of the sliding side door. "Ready."

Kevin watched through the front window as Singleton crossed the row to his Kia. The van moved slowly down the lot, Kevin losing sight of Singleton at the last minute.

"Now," said Liam.

The van jolted to a stop and Kevin yanked open the door.

WINTER PULLED INTO the apartment lot, still not sure if Singleton was going to actually be there, already looking for the red Kia.

There it was, in the second row. A white van was blocking it in, an odd place to park, too far from the door for a delivery. Singleton changing cars? Winter cut over into that lane.

Two men were in a violent struggle in the small space between the Kia and the side of the van. Winter leaned on his horn, the two men freezing for a second, Winter recognizing Singleton. The other man, in a dark ski cap and a leather jacket, grabbed Singleton by the hair and pulled him into the van.

Winter was out of the car, pulling at his gun, yelling "Police!" too late, the van in fast reverse, Winter racing after it, the driver ignoring him, Winter reaching for the sliding door, jamming his hand to block it just as it closed, pain shooting along his arm.

Winter yelled again, the only response an increase in speed, Winter desperately running along side, tearing at the door with his free hand.

Finally yanking free, the van past him now, Winter's eyes jumping to the plate, running back for his car.

A muffled thud, followed by a sickening scream, a door slamming. Winter spun around. Singleton lay on the pavement, the van roaring around the corner, heading for the other exit.

Winter ran to Singleton, who lay on his back, his mouth moving, no sounds coming out, his leg twisted, a gash on his neck spewing blood, gravel dug into his cheek. Winter pressed his hand to the wound, couldn't get the right angle, had to lean over Singleton, who screamed when Winter bumped his leg.

Winter's hand was on fire from being caught in the door, he couldn't get enough pressure on the wound, his mind registering the fading sound of the van, repeating the license plate number in his head, losing it, too distracted by Singleton's condition.

Winter awkwardly struggled out of his hoodie, switching hands, pressing the jacket to the wound. "Rick! Listen, I got to get you an ambulance, you have to hold this on here, can you do that?"

"My leg, my leg . . ." Singleton grabbed at Winter's hand.

"You got a cut on your neck, you need to hold this."

"Cut?" Singleton's stared at his fingers. "Blood?"

"Hold this!" said Winter, pushing Singleton's hands onto the hoodie. Only after Singleton's grip tightened did Winter let go, and even then he lingered for a few seconds.

The blood wasn't spurting, Winter didn't think it was an artery, but he couldn't be sure.

Winter ran back to the car, grabbed his phone, had 911 dialed by the time he got back to Singleton, putting pressure on the wound.

"This is Detective Winter, Marburg PD. I need an ambulance, fast, man with a neck wound, at . . ." Winter couldn't remember the exact address.

Singleton croaked out, "Four-sixteen Dupont."

"Four-sixteen Dupont," repeated Winter. "In the parking lot." He dropped the call, hit the speed dial for dispatch. "Winter. I need a BOLO on a plain white van, no side or back windows, plate Delta five nine . . ." Winter had forgot the rest. "Last seen vicinity of four hundred block, Dupont, felony suspects, two white males. Hold on. Rick, you know those guys?"

Singleton had passed out.

CHAPTER 61

"MIGHT HAVE seen the plate," said Kevin.

"Got it covered." Liam pulled the van into an alley behind a strip mall. He reached under the seat and came up with two license plates.

Kevin was dialing as Liam switched the plates. When Doc answered, Kevin said, "The meeting got complicated when another party in blue showed up. We had to leave. You might want to prepare."

"How bad?" said Doc.

"Won't be a good idea for me to be dropped off near your place. The third party may have seen me." Kevin was calm, he'd run into this situation in the past. If the cops rolled up on Doc when Kevin was there, and they identified him as the man in the van, it would tie what went down to Doc.

Kevin would protect himself and his cousin first, but if he could avoid pulling Doc down it would count for a lot later.

SINGLETON CAME TO as they were loading him onto the ambulance, Winter climbing in with him. He tossed his keys to the uniform, a guy named Booth who had just rolled up. "Move my car out of the way then follow us to the hospital," he said. Just as the ambulance door closed he yelled, "And grab a hoodie from the trunk."

The EMT's were working on Singleton's neck wound. "Bad, but could be worse," said the female EMT. "Good thing you got pressure on it right away." She kept working as she talked. "What's your name?"

Singleton was trying to raise his head. "Rick. What about my leg?"

"Can you feel it?"

"If you call excruciating pain feeling, yeah."

She said, "Believe me, much better than not feeling anything."

The other EMT, a thin guy with a hooked nose, was cutting off Singleton's jeans, revealing a bloated and purple calf. The EMT probed at the shinbone. "You're lucky. Looks like the tire caught the edge of your calf, squeezed it bad, but didn't run across the leg. It's not broken that I can see. They'll take x-rays at the hospital."

Winter said, "Who were those guys?"

Singleton dropped his head back onto the gurney. "One of them is named Kevin, I don't know his last name."

"Where can I find him?"

"I don't know, really. He works for Doc."

"Doc? As in Doc Miles?"

Singleton stared up at the roof of the ambulance. "Yeah, that's him."

Singleton seemed out of immediate danger, his eyes clearing. Winter didn't want him to get a chance to make up a story. "Things don't look good for you. Not just this, everything. We know you were with Dwayne Coleman near the pool. And the coke on your jacket matched what he probably OD'd from. Now you got guys trying to kidnap you. Better let me help you."

Singleton was shaking his head from side to side. "I don't know what happened to Dwayne, I would never hurt Gerry . . ."

"Come on, Rick. You invited him to the party. He ends up dead." Winter played the guilt card. "You got to feel responsible for that."

Singleton closed his eyes, Winter glancing over at the EMT, who was giving him one of those *Now is not the time* looks. Winter didn't think he'd have a better chance, so he gave her his *Don't fuck with me* look.

Winter won that battle, but knew it would be harder once they reached the hospital. "Doc Miles is the guy you met at the studio, isn't he? We know he's a drug dealer. If you're in the middle of that, getting drugs from him to the party, we're going to figure it out. Even if Candy isn't involved in this she's going to avoid you like the plague. You won't get a dime from her, and you'll go to jail. Who's going to take care of your mother?"

Playing *that* card was even harsher, but Winter had had enough.

Rick didn't respond for so long Winter thought he had passed out again. He shot a quizzical look at the EMT, but she just shrugged. "He's okay."

When Rick finally opened his eyes he looked even worse than when he had been thrown out of the van.

Rick said, "Patricia. You trust her?"

"She does what she says she's going to do. You must trust her too, you left your mother with her."

"You're right. She was right too." Rick lifted his arm, winced. "Envelope inside my jacket."

Winter took it out. "What's in it?"

"You can look. It's everything I have that's worth anything. I'll sign it over to Patricia or you or whoever. Sell my stuff, get my Mom in hospice. If you promise to do that for me, I'll tell you everything."

DOC MILES LOOKED around for something to hit. Tricia came into the room, took one look at him, and retreated fast.

Doc didn't have time for her. He had to prepare. Not that he wasn't always ready for this, having to bolt.

He could be in trouble if the cops tied him to Rick. Rick knew about the drugs, but he'd have to implicate himself to finger Doc. Doc couldn't figure out why Rick would do that, unless the cops had something else to hold over his head. Doc could deny any accusation from Rick, what proof did he have?

Gina was the only other person who could tie him to Rick with drugs. She had no reason to open her mouth either.

There was the royalty deal. Sterling knew about that, but he was safe, and what could he say? That he'd drawn up a contract. Even if the cops found the contract, it wouldn't mean anything. He could always claim he'd given Rick cash for his share of the royalties.

Still, Rick with the cops now, and another cop showing up at Doc's door, couldn't be coincidence.

Time to take a trip, go somewhere warm until he figured out what was going on. Let Kevin deal with Rick once and for all when the heat died down.

WINTER LEANED back against the side of the cramped ambulance, giving Rick a chance to talk.

Rick said, "You ever made a decision, it doesn't seem like a big deal at the time, but it leads to another decision, and then you're in trouble, and you don't know how it started?" His voice was weary.

Winter said, "Probably a lot of things start that way."

"I was just trying to move along, you know? Make contacts, impress the right people. Get my music noticed. Then I meet Candy in the studio, she needs a song, but I can't figure out how to get one of mine in front of her. So I try to get in good with Miranda. I didn't have her price."

"What did she want?"

"Coke for a party. Not Candy's party, her own party. I got it for her, from Doc. I'd made pickups for customers of his before. The first time, I didn't even know I was picking up drugs, I was just running a favor. That sounds like an excuse and it is, because I figured it out pretty fast and did it again. I never dealt, ever. But when I needed to get what Miranda wanted, I went to Doc."

"He gave you the drugs directly?"

"Not that time. He had this chick meet me. I don't even know her name."

Winter was thinking of ways to get to Doc. "Before that?"

"I'd meet him, put cash in a binder, he'd have one too, we'd exchange."

"You ever see drugs actually in his hand?"

"No . . . only with the chick."

"What's she look like?"

"Reddish brown hair, my age. Brightest green eyes I've ever seen. Really good looking." Rick's head dropped back on the stretcher.

Doc Miles sounded pretty slick to Winter. Miles could always claim he'd picked up the wrong binder. You couldn't arrest every person who was accused of being a dealer with no corroboration. "What about Miranda? She help you out when you gave her the coke?"

"Yes and no. Doc didn't trust me, he thought I was just an errand boy. I told him I might be able to introduce him to some customers at the studio, maybe even Candy. He fronted me some product for her. Turns out she doesn't touch the stuff. Miranda—she took the drugs Doc had given me, and I had nothing to pay him back with."

"So Candy has nothing to do with this?"

"No. Miranda doesn't either, not really. I mean, she screwed me, but she didn't even know Doc. I got my music to Candy, but Doc wanted his money. I didn't have any, so I pawned some of Larry's equipment to pay Doc back. But it wasn't enough. I thought he was going to kill me—Kevin came to the studio and banged my head against the wall. I gave Doc the only thing I had that might be worth anything, my share of the royalties for the song Candy was going to use."

"How did you do that?"

"Doc made me sign a contract. When he found out I wasn't the sole owner of my song, he tried to get Gerry to sign over his piece too."

"Doc knew about Gerry?"

"I opened my big mouth. That's what I'm really feeling responsible for, as much as inviting Gerry to the party. If I hadn't said anything about Gerry, Doc never would have known."

Singleton closed his eyes again. Winter looked out the back window of the ambulance, recognizing where they were. He leaned toward the driver. "Slow down," he said.

The driver said, "What?"

"I need a few more minutes with this guy before we get to the hospital."

The driver looked back over his shoulder, first at Winter, then at the female EMT. Winter turned to her. "Unless he's going to die, I need a little time. He's a witness in a murder investigation."

The EMT, who'd been probing Rick all during Winter's interrogation, said, "He's not going to die." Her voice was flat.

"Slow it down," repeated Winter to the driver, then turned back to Singleton. "Doc went to Gerry?"

"He told *me* to. That's the real reason I invited Gerry to the party. I was going to tell him about the song deal. Doc wasn't the only one who wanted a contract. I'd told Candy that Gerry had rights to the song, and she wanted his agreement too. I didn't think it was going to be any problem."

"What's Dwayne Coleman got to do with all this?"

"Nothing that I know of. He did seem to know about the royalty deal. I couldn't figure out his angle. I thought he was trying to hone in on Doc's arrangement with me."

"Dwayne knows Doc?" Another line connected in Winter's mental map.

"Yeah. At the party he told me he had just spoken to Doc. And that's where he got his coke."

"So you *were* out at the pool with Dwayne?"

"He dragged me out there. He told me he had Gerry waiting outside. I thought Doc had sent Dwayne, to make sure I got Gerry to sign. But Gerry wasn't at the pool. Dwayne kept talking about the royalties, then he shared some of his coke. That's where I did the blow, not by my car."

"You give Dwayne any drugs?"

"No, he was loaded. I didn't have any."

Pieces clicking into place for Winter, remembering his conversation with the M.E., about Coleman perhaps dying from a toxic overdose. Possible with just coke, but much more likely if mixed with another drug . . . "Not even fentanyl?"

"Where would I get—." Rick's head jerked up, hard eyes on Winter. "No, no, I wouldn't. Not from my mom. And even if I had some, no way I'd mix that with blow, you think I'm crazy?"

Maybe not you, thought Winter, *but someone was*. "How did you leave things with Dwayne?"

"I got out of there when Miranda showed up. They started to party. Personal like, if you catch my drift."

"Wait, you left Dwayne with Miranda?"

"And went back into the house, to look for Gerry. A little later I heard all this yelling about a dead guy, and I ran upstairs, just like I told you. I didn't even know Gerry was there until I got upstairs, he was already dead. I didn't hear about Dwayne dying until later."

"So this was all about the music? Gerry had nothing to do with the drugs?"

"I told you, no."

Winter let it sink in. It could be the truth, most of it not too far from what Singleton told him in the past, except for the parts where he'd been involved in the drugs. And, of course, Doc and his connection to Coleman.

On the other hand, Singleton had been lying a lot, or at least leaving a lot out.

Winter pictured the party with the new information, Singleton and Coleman in the house, Miranda floating around, Coleman telling Singleton that Gerry was outside . . .

"What exactly did Dwayne say to you when he took you out to the pool?"

Rick said, "Something about having a mutual friend, Doc. He said somebody was getting Gerry, that he'd meet us by the pool. Shit, I think he said the name, I forget what it was."

Winter knew. Malcolm Washington.

THE AMBULANCE made a turn. "We're here," said the driver.

The back door opened, a hospital orderly there. The EMT's began sliding Singleton out.

Winter hurried. "Where does this Doc get his product?" Singleton's story was plausible, but there was still the possible Nadya Boyko connection.

"I have no idea," said Rick. "But he could get his hands on it fast."

"What does Kevin look like?" Winter had only caught a glimpse.

"Mean looking. Marks on his face, really short hair, like a military guy."

Probably the driver Winter had seen picking up Doc Miles at his office. "Going to need you to testify," said Winter, as the EMT's released the accordion legs on the gurney.

"Only if my mom is safe. I saw Kevin near her house once, you saw what he'll do for Doc."

"I'll take care of it," said Winter.

THE UNIFORM, Booth, who had been following the ambulance, pulled into the emergency entrance. Winter said, "You know Old Town Road?"

"Up off Park, past the golf course."

"That's it. I got some calls to make, no siren." Winter crammed himself in the front seat next to all the mobile equipment, pushing a laptop out of the way.

"Sorry," said Booth. "Downside of all this technology."

"Tell me about it," said Winter. His first call was to the DA, a guy named Villeson. They did not have a good relationship.

Villeson wasn't in, so Winter explained what he needed to one of the ADA's, a woman named Quinn who he did know. She said, "So you want to try to get a search warrant based on the say so of a guy who admits he moves drugs? What did you promise him?"

"Nothing. He gave it up voluntarily. Not only is this Miles a dealer, but my witness is in fear of his life from a man who works for Miles, for reasons that have nothing to do with drugs, and aren't even criminal."

"I got to run it by Villeson," said Quinn. "He's a stickler."

"I know. Uh, what would you do if Villeson wasn't around? Could you help us out with the justification for the probable cause?"

"Sure."

"Well, he's not around, is he?"

Quinn said, "Is this going to bite me on the ass?"

Winter had three possible ways to get at Miles. As a dealer to Rick. For the attempt on Rick, through Kevin. Maybe even through the drugs themselves. But Miles might also skate unless Winter could put the drugs *with* Miles.

"You going to help me, or try to get me to say nice things about your ass?" Winter normally wouldn't have talked like this to an ADA, but he and Quinn had a little history.

"You were always such a charmer," said Quinn. "I'll see what I can do."

WINTER HUNG UP, knowing she'd come through. His next call was to Cindy.

"I left my notebook in my car, and I'm with Officer Booth. We are heading up to the Doctor Miles residence. I need the street address for a warrant."

"Forty-seven," said Cindy.

"You memorize that?"

"No, but Detective Ryder asked for it a little while ago. He's out that way now."

"Wait, what? He's at the residence?"

"His Boston thing got delayed. He was looking for something to do, said he'd cruise by, keep an eye out for the black SUV. He wanted the address and the plate number."

"Shit," said Winter.

"Excuse me?" said Cindy.

Or that's what Winter thought she probably said, he'd cut her off, spinning through his contacts for Ryder.

His phone rang, Winter flustered, thinking it had to do with his scrolling. Ryder's name came up on the screen, Winter hitting send, but when he put the phone to his ear nothing happened.

"I think you hung up on an incoming call," suggested Booth.

"I hate these things," said Winter. "How do I get it back?"

"Beats me," said Booth. "I'm an iPhone guy."

The phone rang again. Winter hit the button carefully.

"It's Martin. I need to tell you something."

"No shit," said Winter.

"You know?"

Winter didn't have time to argue. "What did you see?"

"There was a young female at the house, she came out on the porch for a few seconds. I didn't know if she saw me, but since someone was obviously at home I rang the intercom. No one answered." After a beat Ryder added, "I didn't identify myself as police. If they saw me through the camera they might have thought I was lost or selling something."

Fat chance, thought Winter. "Anything else?"

"A black Mercedes SUV drove by. There was a dark haired female driving. I followed her. She pulled into another house. By the time I got there she had locked the gate and went inside. I couldn't see the plate. She was probably just a neighbor with the same kind of car, weird coincidence. But I thought you should know. And that I'd been there."

Winter was picturing the neighborhood he'd driven through, he was good with streets. "Where was the SUV coming from?"

"Driving south, probably came in off Park."

"After the woman drove by you, which way did she turn?"

"Left. There's a cul de sac there—"

"I know. Which way after that?"

"Straight for a half mile or so, then another left. I wrote down the address, twenty-four Rutland, I'm going to check who lives there—"

"Don't bother," said Winter.

"What?"

"She doesn't live there. If she was going to get to Rutland she wouldn't have gone down Old Town at all, she would have just kept going on Park and hit Rutland. She went a mile out of her way. She must have seen you and kept going."

"And just pulled into a random driveway?"

Winter was thinking about the connections between Doc and Coleman and Hennig, about how Doc was in the middle of the drugs and the music royalties. Maybe even the killings. "Might not be random. They might have planned for this."

"I'll check the home owner anyway," insisted Ryder.

"Fine. Where are you?"

"On the Pike, heading for Boston. Nadya Boyko's attorney wants to talk."

Winter could have used Ryder back at the Miles place. But Winter was so pissed he just said, "Great," and hung up.

CHAPTER 62

"Push it," said Winter.

Booth flicked his lights, got past a few cars. "Code 3?"

"In a minute." Winter dialed Crosse. "I think the SUV is near the Miles house. They might have seen Ryder."

"What was Ryder doing there?" When Winter didn't answer, Crosse said, "Shit."

"Rick Singleton told me a story. Might not be all of it, but Miles is in the middle of Hennig and probably Coleman. He's also got muscle working for him who could show up at the house. The ADA is going to help with a search warrant. Could you work it, meet me there?"

"On my way."

Winter gave Crosse the details for the warrant, then called dispatch. "I need two cars to meet me at forty-seven Old Town Road. Tell them to bring a ram." The dispatcher confirmed his request, and Winter said, "Anything on that white van BOLO?"

"It's out, nothing yet."

"Let me know." Winter thought for a few seconds. Singleton said Miles sourced drugs. Even if Miles wasn't stupid enough to keep them in his car, he or his driver Kevin might have transported them. "Make one of the units a drug K-9."

Winter hung up and said to Booth, "Light it up."

Doc called Tyler Sterling, got his secretary, told her it was about Dr. Greenwood, the code to let Sterling know it was an emergency. Doc headed for the bedroom, yelling out, "Tricia!"

Doc pulled out his travel bag, started packing. Tricia finally appeared in the doorway, nervously hopping from foot to foot.

"Get a bag packed," he said, "We're taking that trip."

"Where are we going?"

Doc turned to her. "If you keep asking questions, I'll leave you here."

Tricia gave him a sad look. "I just want to know what to pack."

He gave her a pass, he didn't have time. "Someplace warm."

She smiled and scampered off. Doc was starting on a second bag when Sterling returned his call.

"Had a visitor," said Doc. "Formal guy at the gate, peeking in, ringing the buzzer. Looked like the police."

"He have a warrant?"

"He didn't show one or even identify himself."

"You don't need to let him in without one."

"Tell me something I don't know."

"Any reason the police might want to talk to you?"

Doc could think of a hundred reasons, but none the cops should know about. "Not particularly."

"If they show up again you can safely ignore them, even if they see you outside. That's true even if they identify themselves. Of course, it might make them more likely to be inquisitive. You could also just have a conversation through the gate, be polite."

"Yeah, yeah," said Doc.

"If they have a warrant, read it carefully, make sure they only look where they are supposed to. Understand?"

What Sterling was saying, in his client confidential but still careful way was: If you have anything in your house that could get you in trouble, get it out of there fast.

Doc said, "I hear you. I may take a trip."

Sterling said, "Sooner rather than later would be good."

Doc hung up, went out into the hall, called down to Tricia. "Put my bags in the foyer." He continued on into the garage and threw the deadbolt to the house.

He opened the hidden compartment and checked over his inventory. The compartment could easily be missed in a cursory search. Doc took care never to spill powder, everything well bagged, the compartment itself airtight. He'd been promised it could fool a drug dog, but there was no real way to test that. If it got that far he was screwed.

He could leave it all behind, ready to sell when he returned. Or he could flush it.

He had money stashed away. He'd be fine for a while, but it would be a waste to lose it all.

Doc took the most offending—which meant the most valuable—product and stuffed it in gallon baggies: the coke, the oxy. He filled a large gym bag with the rest.

The gym bag went into the trunk of Gina's white Honda parked in the garage. The baggies he took into the half bath off the garage.

One by one he emptied the product into the toilet. Doc grimaced with each push of the handle, his only consolation that it was better than flushing his life away in prison.

"JUST ROLL ON BY," said Winter. They were on Old Town Road, the siren off for the last two miles. As Booth drove past the Miles house Winter wasn't able to see much, the gates closed.

He directed Booth around the corner, the same route Ryder had described following the black SUV, onto Rutland. "Stop here," said Winter.

The Mercedes was parked in a drive, clearly visible through the wrought iron fence. Winter jumped out, pulling on his hoodie, and tried the gate. It was locked. He pushed the buzzer, got no reply. He stood there in the light rain, thinking.

"House is owned by a Josephine Andrews," said Booth through his open window.

"Can you get a phone?"

"Sure, if they have a landline."

Winter got back in the car, dialed the number, it went to an answering machine. "Drive down to the end of Rutland," said Winter. "Park on the corner of Old Town. If you see a car pull out of forty-seven, hit the horn to warn me. If I don't get there in time, pull them over."

"On what?"

"Be creative."

Winter jogged to the next house, one of the few without a gate. A middle aged woman answered the door. "Can I help you?"

Winter identified himself and said, "I'm trying to get hold of your neighbor Josephine Andrews."

"She's away on a cruise."

"She have anyone else in the house? A daughter?"

"She lives alone, her husband passed."

"You wouldn't happen to know what kind of car she drives?"

"I've seen a dark blue one there. Sorry, I don't know cars."

"But a car? Not an SUV?"

"A car."

Winter thanked her and ran back down the drive. The rain was picking up, Winter wishing he had his cap. Might be nothing, the black SUV at that house, a house sitter. Or could be that whoever was driving that Mercedes was pretty smart.

GINA'S VOICE was calm. "A cop car just drove past the house I'm at. A guy got out, not in a uniform, he's wearing a hoodie, he came up to the gate."

Doc, looking at the screen showing his front entrance and part of the street, said, "He see you?"

"I doubt it. I'm on the porch, they got those roller windows. I cracked one a little."

Doc worked it out. Rick had probably opened his mouth. He doubted they could arrest him based only on whatever Rick had blabbed, otherwise the cops would be banging at his gate. "Can you get here without the car?"

"I think so. I can go through that wooded area, get into your yard from the back. I'll have to cross the road, they might see me then."

"No problem, you're out for a walk."

"It's raining."

"For a fucking cigarette break," said Doc. "Don't go dumb on me now."

There was a silence, then Gina said, "I don't need that."

"Okay, okay. Look, if it's clear, do what you said. Call me when you are close, but don't come in the house, you understand? I'm going to get Tricia to drive out, they'll probably follow her, then you can—"

"Tricia doesn't drive."

"What?"

"She doesn't drive. She'd crash before she made it a block."

Doc wiped at his head, for once he was hot. Tricia cracking up the Audi would be a small price to pay if it created enough of a diversion for him to get away. "Just get here. I'll drive myself. I'll call you when it's clear. The cops will likely pull me over up the street. Take your Honda, drive out the other way. There's a bag in your trunk. I'll call Pedro, make a deal for the bag. Then meet us in Boston, at Logan."

Gina said, "Going to look odd, leaving your SUV in this driveway."

"Can't be helped."

"Maybe I can pull out, park it on the next street, say it just died on me, I pulled over."

"Don't risk it if the cops can see you. If they pick you up . . ."

"What? There's nothing in the Mercedes, is there?"

"No, it's clean."

"I'll figure it out," said Gina.

WINTER CALLED CROSSE. "Talk to me."

"We've got a problem," said Crosse. "Villeson came back unexpectedly, he's giving your girlfriend Quinn a hard time."

"She's not my girlfriend," said Winter.

"Well, if she was, she'd wouldn't be for long after the shitstorm she's getting laid on her."

"Damn it. You think it's worth waiting around?"

"You think Villeson is the type to change his mind?"

Winter said, "Owens is in court. Ask him to hang around in case we can get something that might fly to a judge. I could use you over here."

Winter clicked off and said to Booth, "Get dispatch to tell those other cars to come in quiet. Call me if the SUV leaves." Winter wrote his number on a pad clipped to the dash. "I'll be back in a few minutes."

Winter ran down Old Town, stopping short of the Miles house drive, looking for the intercom camera Ryder had mentioned. It wasn't on the wall facing him, so it had to be on the left side of the entrance, which meant anyone watching from the house couldn't see him yet.

Winter retraced his steps to the corner of the wall. Tall stately oaks lined the street along the sidewalk. Winter eyed the lowest branches, took three steps back and jumped up. The bark was slick, and he slipped off, skinning his hands. He tried again, this time holding on.

He pulled himself up, straining. Trees blocked most of the house, but he was able to see a late model green Audi parked in front of the garage. Winter dropped back down, skinning his palms again, and swore.

*   *   *

DOC MADE THE CALL to Pedro, who was happy to take the product off Doc's hands, but of course he needed a discount. Doc expected that, haggled for a minute just out of principle, then made the deal.

Tricia came out with a roller bag. Doc said, "Watch the monitor while I finish up." He went into his office, going through the desk quickly to make sure there was nothing incriminating.

Then the safe. Doc never kept drugs there, it was the first place the cops would search. The house deed, financial papers, a few thousand in cash. Doc took all but a few hundred.

The music royalty contract was there as well. That could tie Doc to Rick, but it was a business deal, nothing more. It would legitimately explain any contact he'd had with Rick.

The contract would actually look more suspicious in the safe. He took it out, put it in his file drawer marked *Investments*. The legitimate ones.

WINTER JOGGED BACK to the cruiser. Booth said, "The SUV is still there."

Winter filled Booth in on what he had seen. "Let's wait to see who moves."

Ten minutes later, Quinn called from the DA's office. "You heard?"

"Yeah. Sorry."

"You owe me even more for *not* getting the warrant than if I had. Villeson might bend, but he wants some kind of corroboration or a direct link to the house. Do you have information that the alleged assailant Kevin is there?"

Winter knew what he had so far was a gray area for probable cause, which is why he had called the DA in the first place instead of going directly to a judge. But he tried anyway. "I told you I saw a man matching his description drive here."

"Today?"

"No, it was yesterday."

"No good. Too long ago. You can ask the owner if Kevin is there, but it won't fly for a warrant."

Winter said, "What about for drugs?"

"Has your witness seen drugs there?"

Quinn's tone had gone professionally cold. "I don't think so," Winter admitted.

"Did you find drugs in the possession of your witness who says he got them directly from Miles?"

Winter thought about the dusting of coke on Singleton's jacket, which he said came from Coleman, which supposedly was sourced from Doc. It was weak and Winter knew it. "No."

"You need something else," said Quinn, and hung up.

DOC ANSWERED the burner. "Where are you?"

Gina said, "Still on Rutland. The cop car is parked down the block. I might be able to get out the back, but I have to cross part of the yard, they could see me."

"They're either here to just spook us or they are waiting for a warrant. I'll get that cop car to move. Be ready."

Doc hung up and said to Tricia, "Let's go."

They rolled the luggage out to the Audi and packed up. Doc said, "Why didn't you tell me you couldn't drive?"

"You have Kevin for that. You have me for other things."

Doc couldn't argue with dumb logic. He hit the button for the gate and eased out, turning right, toward where Gina said the cop car was parked.

He accelerated to the crest of a small hill, and there was the cop car, about a quarter of a mile away. Doc slammed on the brakes, backed haphazardly into a driveway, and sped back toward his house.

"What's the matter?" asked Tricia.

"You forgot something, we're going back," said Doc.

"I didn't forget anything."

"Sure you did. You forgot to bring some clothes for Gina."

Doc clicked the gate open and pulled into the drive.

"HE'S RUNNING," said Winter. "Get on them."

Booth tore down Old Town, Winter expecting to see the Audi at the other end of the street, but nothing.

They reached the house, the Audi in the driveway, the gate closing . . .

Winter yelled, "Stop!" and fortunately Booth listened, because Winter was already out the door. A hint of exhaust from the Audi told Winter it was idling, a woman in a pink top disappearing into the house.

If that gate closed, Winter might not be able to talk to Miles. Winter jumped into the gap between the two sides, praying it had a safety sensor. The gate stopped just before hitting him, Winter grinning like an idiot in the rain, thankful for once for this little bit of technology.

GINA SAW THE COP car move off fast, heading in the direction of Doc's. She didn't think she'd have much time, getting to Doc's by foot would be too slow.

She wasn't that worried, not yet. Even if they saw her in this yard the worst thing they could charge her with was pulling into the wrong driveway.

Still, much better if Doc's car wasn't here. She ran out the back, around the house, and along the fence to the gate. A quick peek, no cop car. She unlocked the gate, opened it, and ran back for the Mercedes.

In less than a minute she was around the block, on the street behind Doc's house. For a brief moment Gina considered just driving away. Hooking up with Doc had been okay, she'd had much worse. He'd never hit her, bought her what she wanted, and had great drugs. What she had to give up in return wasn't the most fun, but she had a man on the side, which Doc let slide; a lot of other men in his position wouldn't, she'd learned that the hard way.

If she left now she'd be starting over with the clothes on her back.

She'd done that before, and it sucked.

She'd let it ride a little longer. Had to be careful though, she'd be driving with a trunk load of drugs . . .

No way she was going to jail for Doc.

She parked the Mercedes at the end of the block and disappeared into the woods.

INTO THE PHONE Doc said, "Are you clear?"

"I'm in the woods, just behind your house."

"The cop car is here. I'm going to get them out of the way. Stay off the property for now, just in case. I'll leave the line open, you should be able to hear."

Doc got out of the car like he didn't have a care in the world, pulling up the collar on his Burberry. There was a guy at the end of his drive who'd stepped in the path of the gate, preventing if from closing. He didn't look like a cop, just a guy in a hoodie, although a police car was just behind him, blocking the drive. A uniformed cop was standing by the car.

Doc said, "Can I help you?"

The guy said, "My name is Winter, I'm a detective with the Marburg Police. Are you Doctor Rudolf Miles?"

"I am."

"I'd like to ask you a few questions about an investigation I'm working on."

"What investigation?"

"Do you mind if I walk on up?"

Now Doc understood why the cop had stopped the gate. Once Doc let him in, no telling where that might lead. The cops would make it impossible for Gina to get away with the drugs. Just to make sure, Doc said, "Do you have a search warrant?"

"Why would I need that?" asked the cop. "I just want to ask you a few questions."

That was all Doc needed to know. He figured an innocent man would ask, "What's this about?" so he did.

"We're looking for a guy who works for you. Kevin."

"I don't have an employee named Kevin."

"There's no Kevin here?"

"Definitely not."

"Mind if we look?"

It was easy for Doc not to sound guilty on this. "You see the wall and the gate. I like my privacy. I'd know if there was a Kevin here."

"We'd also like to talk to you about Rick Singleton. And Dwayne Coleman."

Doc kept his cool. "Singleton is a musician I'm investing in. Dwayne Coleman rings a bell, I might have met him at a party. Is that what you need to know?"

"It's a start. Be easier if we did this out of the rain."

Doc pretended to consider, then said, "It's not that I don't trust the police or have anything to hide, but I'd prefer we not do this at my home. No offense."

"You could come to the station," the cop offered.

Fat chance, thought Doc. Keep me there for hours while you figure out a way to search my house. "There's a restaurant on Park, Anthony's Grille. Should be quiet this time of day."

The cop said, "Works for me."

Doc opened the door of the Audi, but the cop said, "I'd prefer if you drive with us. No offense."

Doc didn't flinch, he was half expecting this. "Sure," he said. Polite, just like Sterling suggested.

He walked down the drive. The cop still stood in the opening of the gate. Doc stopped short. "You're not suggesting I ride in the back of a police car."

"Afraid of getting that raincoat dirty?"

Doc couldn't hide his disdainful glance at the cop's multi pocked pants and hoodie. "This might be hard for you to believe, it did cost a few thousand dollars."

The detective leaned out and looked up the street. "I'll get you a better ride."

WINTER WASN'T surprised by the doctor's hesitation to let him into the house or get in the police car. Even innocent civilians often balked at both. Yet it was pretty clear Miles's caginess had more to do with not giving Winter a chance to look around than it did with fear of an innocent man being taken advantage of.

Winter got the definite sense this guy didn't get taken advantage of very often.

Winter lingered in the drive, looking over Miles's shoulder, hoping to see some reason, even half-assed, for enough probable cause to enter the property. Miles hadn't given consent, the Audi turning around was not enough . . .

Crosse had just reached the house. Winter said, "We can take that car."

Miles was on top of him now, a big man, as tall as Winter and much heavier, yet he didn't walk like a man out of shape at all, as much muscle as fat, no loose skin on his neck. Miles didn't shy away from Winter, just stood there, waiting for Winter to move. Winter gave him a hard look, Miles didn't flinch.

Winter said, "Detective Crosse, Doctor Miles is going to ride with us in your car up the street to Anthony's, have a chat."

"You'll have to move out of the way," said Miles, his voice hard and flat.

And right then Winter knew for sure that Miles was fully aware of what Winter was trying to do, that it was all a charade, Miles knowing Winter didn't have probable cause, and Miles wasn't going to do a damn thing to give him a reason to be on the property. Which told Winter that something *was* at the house that Miles didn't want discovered.

Winter caught the slightest move on Miles's lip, not a smile, not a smirk, but there it was, Miles thinking he'd won this battle.

Winter stepped aside, letting his shoulders slump, pretending he'd been defeated. Let Miles feel good. There would be other battles.

Winter gestured for Miles to go ahead. "You want to close your gate?"

"It stays open for a few minutes, safety feature. It'll close."

Miles stepped to Crosse's car. She looked at Winter and he said, "Doctor Miles and I will sit in the back."

Crosse opened the door for Miles. As Winter went by Booth he whispered, "Park across the street from the drive. If that Audi pulls out, give me a call."

Miles hesitated getting in the car, watching Booth back up and park. Miles said, "Is that police car going to stay parked right in front of my driveway?"

Winter said, "Just until we're done."

"Is that necessary?"

"You worried about what the neighbors will think?" asked Winter.

"I don't care what anyone thinks," said Miles gruffly, and Winter fought back a grin. He'd won round two.

GINA, trying to stay dry under one of the few large evergreens, and not succeeding, heard Doc's clear warning about the cop car and said, "Shit."

She needed a Plan B. Wait for Doc to leave, get into the house from the back yard, grab the drugs, come back through the woods, take the

SUV instead of her own car. Risky, because the cops might come looking for the Mercedes.

Still better than driving her own car out of Doc's house with a load of drugs in her trunk right in front of a cop.

WINTER WAS STILL pissed about the search warrant, but wasn't letting it get to him. He sensed Miles didn't have a lot of patience. He'd keep Doc tied up for a while, wear him down. Maybe Miles would lawyer up, that would tell Winter a lot. He'd interview Miles, then call Rick Singleton and press him to get enough probable cause for a search while Crosse kept Miles company.

Crosse was guiding Miles into the back seat, telling him to watch his head, an old habit from being a beat cop, putting a criminal in the car. A pink streak flew out of the driveway, a blonde woman in tights and a vibrant shirt, her hair flashing behind her like a cape, Winter thinking it was the woman he'd seen go into the house, but before he finished the thought she flew at Crosse, her arms windmilling, Crosse's eyes wide like she'd turned to see a tornado that had mysteriously appeared out of nowhere.

"Get your hands off him bitch!" screamed the woman, leaping up, wrapping her legs around Crosse and pummeling her face from behind. "I got her Doc, run!"

Crosse spun around, trying to break free, twisting up the drive. The woman was screeching like a wild cat, tearing at Crosse's hair. Crosse slammed the woman back against the gate, the gate swinging back, dumping them both on the ground. Crosse flipped atop the woman and pinned her to the ground, Booth rushing over to handcuff her. The woman clawed at Booth, ripping at his face with her nails, Booth swearing as they worked to subdue her. They prodded her down the drive into the street.

"Run Doc!" the woman cried, her eyes wide with pleading.

Winter and Miles locked eyes over the hood of the car. It wasn't Miles who ran, it was Winter.

Back to the gate, catching it again just before it closed.

CHAPTER 63

T HE GATE BEEPED a warning. Winter ignored it, holding it open with his foot. Booth read the woman her rights before locking her in the cruiser, which barely muffled her screaming. Miles was stoic throughout the chaos, letting himself be put in the back of Crosse's car.

Winter had made a mistake not having more backup, leaving him with a difficult choice. The detective cars didn't have a screen on the back seats; if they left Miles alone he could get out of the car.

Crosse said, "I got this, go."

Winter said to Booth, "Get those other units here and see if you can find something to block this gate." His eyes went back to the house. Nothing moved.

Booth ran across the road with a small metal container from his trunk. "I emptied out the flares." He jammed the container in the gap between the two sides of the gate. "Should hold."

Winter knew even the assault was unlikely to give them probable cause for a search, but he could at least check the vicinity to see if there were other threats. "Let's take a quick look around."

"Wait for backup?"

"We should," said Winter, "but if you're good . . ."

Booth unholstered his weapon. "Better if we go the same way though."

Winter nodded, feeling better about Booth. To Crosse he said, "Watch for anybody coming from the other side." He waited until Crosse had drawn her weapon and was in position over the hood of her car.

The front yard was manicured lawn, a dozen trees too small to hide behind, although dense shrubs lined the wall and garage. Winter wasn't exactly sure how far he could legally venture onto the property. Winter's gun was in his hand, his finger alongside the trigger. The neighborhood didn't seem the type where you'd expect to be shot at, but Winter wasn't taking any chances. They checked the bushes by the wall. Nothing.

Winter flipped a mental coin. He could argue the bushes near the garage were a good hiding place and close enough. He approached cautiously.

More nothing along the garage.

Winter took a quick peek through the side window of the garage. Three bays, two empty, a white sedan in the third.

Winter eyed the front door, he *really* wanted to get inside.

CROUCHED BEHIND the evergreen, Gina wiped the rain from her eyes. From her vantage point just beyond the wrought iron gate leading into the back of Doc's property she could see past the corner of the house. A man in a hoodie with a gun was searching the bushes. He was the same guy she'd seen earlier.

Gina's uncle had been a hunter, and had once told her it was movement that exposed the prey. She fought the urge to run back through the woods to the Mercedes.

She had the phone on her knee, the volume turned down. Moving very slowly, she put the phone to her ear.

Gina heard Doc's voice. "How long are you going to keep me in here?" He was yelling, not at all like Doc.

No one answered, and Doc said, "I want to call my attorney. You just can't keep me in the back of a car on the street in front of my house."

Doc was sending her a message. He was telling her it wasn't safe to go onto the property.

Gina couldn't go forward, couldn't go back. She eased down onto the cold ground, waiting.

WINTER SUSPECTED Miles had wanted him away from the house. But the doctor's quick return was confusing, the Audi racing back, drawing attention. Odd, if Miles was trying to give someone time to get rid of evidence or get away. Like Kevin.

The two empty garage bays were completely clear, no junk, indicating they were often used. One was likely for the Audi, one for the Mercedes SUV.

Someone could be in the house, waiting to escape in the white sedan.

Or Miles wasn't trying to give an accomplice time to get away, he was giving them time to get *to* the house. That's why Miles had been so amenable to meet at the restaurant. Miles wanted the house clear.

The question was: Why?

No one was going to move with a police car parked out front. Which gave Winter an idea.

DOC KEPT UP HIS one-sided conversation with the woman cop outside the car. She hadn't given any indication she could hear him, even when he raised his voice. It didn't matter, all his chatter was to let Gina know what was going on.

Across the street, Tricia's face was pressed against the window of the cop car. Stupid Tricia had ruined his plan by jumping on the cop. If she hadn't, they'd be away by now, giving Gina time to get the drugs and get away. Now they were all screwed unless he figured something out.

He could no longer see Winter and the uniformed cop. He didn't know if they'd go into the house. Tricia should have locked it, but who knew with her. Could the cops go in without a warrant? He didn't know.

Sterling would.

Doc said, "I guess we're all just staying right here for a while, so I'm going to call my lawyer." Gina should get the message to stay put.

He'd probably run if he were in her place. That would be the smart move. And Gina was the smart one.

He hit the speed dial for Sterling. "Where are you?"

"In my car, on my way to you. Figured you might need me."

"It's complicated here. One of my woman friends thought I was being arrested and went a little nuts, scratched a cop. They've got us both in separate cars."

"Is she under arrest?"

"Probably, I couldn't hear it all. They haven't said a word to me. Two cops are on my property. Can they go in the house?"

"Unlikely. Even if they claimed it was for their safety, they can't search through your belongings though, only for people."

"No one is inside," said Doc.

"Good. I'll be there within an hour. Don't say a word."

THE BACKUP CARS ARRIVED, two additional units, one of them a K-9 officer named Jacoby who Winter had worked with. The other car had two officers, a rookie and her training officer. Winter told Booth to stay where he was and went out to fill them in.

Winter called Owens. "Any luck on the warrant?"

"No. I'm standing outside Villeson's office. You want to talk to him?"

"Yeah." When Villeson came on, Winter explained the situation. "The woman who assaulted Detective Crosse came out from the Miles house. Can we go in?"

"Do you have any reason to suspect there is imminent danger to you or the officers, or that a crime is in progress?"

"We know that a man who works for Miles tried to kidnap Rick Singleton. I've seen him here."

"Quinn told me you didn't see him there today."

"He could be here," argued Winter. "It's the best and only place we know to look for him."

"Can you get consent?"

Winter doubted Miles would let them in. "Unlikely. Come on, help me out here."

"I might have, if you hadn't pulled that stunt with Quinn. Get consent, or get out of there."

GINA CURLED HERSELF into a ball, watching the cop on his phone at the end of the drive. The gate still hadn't closed. If they walked around the house and came through the back gate they'd find her for sure. It would be hard to explain why she was sitting behind a tree in the rain.

On the other hand, she wasn't exactly doing anything illegal. Trespassing maybe. She wasn't sure who owned this wooded lot.

She muted the phone and shivered in the cold rain.

CHAPTER 64

W INTER SAT IN Booth's cruiser to talk to the blond woman. "What's your name?"

"Screw you," she said.

"That's not going to help you or Doctor Miles," said Winter.

"Why did you arrest him?"

"He's not under arrest. Should he be?"

"I don't have to talk to you without a lawyer."

"That's right. You don't have to, but you can if you want."

"I've got nothing to say."

Winter thought she looked way too young to be hanging out with Miles. "You live here?"

"None of your business."

The woman, defiant, didn't seem scared. She also didn't seem like she was going to give Winter a probable cause to search the house. He would deal with her later.

Booth transferred the woman to the other unit for transport to the station for booking. He opened the door on Crosse's car and said to Miles, "Now that we have that under control, you still up for that talk at the restaurant?"

"If it will get this over with."

The doctor hadn't asked about his blonde friend, suggesting the connection might not be that tight. Winter filed that away for future use. And the fact that Miles was still willing to leave the house confirmed Winter's suspicion that Miles wanted the cops away from the property. "Detective Crosse will drive you. I'll follow along."

Winter closed the door, pulled Crosse aside, and told her what he had in mind. Crosse whispered, "He's going to figure it out."

"It doesn't matter. Just make up an excuse for me not being there, stall him as long as you can, and take your time driving back."

Winter walked Booth and Jacoby away from Crosse's car. To Booth he said, "I want you on the corner of Rutland, where we were before." Winter pointed in the other direction. "Jacoby, if you park down there your car won't be visible from the house. That way we'll have both ends of this street covered. There's a white sedan in the garage. If it comes out, I'll call and let you know which way it's headed and who is driving. There's a white male named Kevin . . ." Winter explained the rest of it and got Jacoby's cell number. "Watch for a white van and a black Mercedes SUV too."

"You want me to take you to the restaurant first?" asked Booth.

"Just partway," said Winter.

WINTER TOOK his time removing the container which blocked the gate and getting into Booth's cruiser, wanting to be seen in case someone was watching from the house. If there were more cameras his plan was shot, but he didn't bother looking, they didn't have much time before Miles figured out what was going on.

Booth made a three-point U turn. Once clear of the Miles property, Winter said, "This is good."

Winter jumped out of the cruiser and ran back toward the corner of the Miles property, using his momentum to propel upward. He got his hands on the tree branch on his first attempt and pulled himself up. Nothing had changed, the garage door was still closed.

If the white car did leave, which way would it turn? Right would bring it to where Booth waited. If whoever had been in the Mercedes had seen either Winter or the cop car earlier on Rutland, it was unlikely they'd go that way. Which meant left.

The problem was that Winter was on the wrong side of the gate. If he walked by now, he'd be visible to the camera.

The property across from the Miles house was walled, but the houses on either side were not. Winter dropped down, ran across the street and into a backyard, rosebush thorns tearing at his arms. He cut across three properties, emerging well past the Miles front gate.

He walked across the road and slid along the wall, sinking into the soft mulch. When he reached a spot where he'd be able to hear the garage door open, he crouched down and waited.

GINA WAS CRAVING a cigarette. The phone had gone quiet since she'd heard Doc say 'If it will get this over with.' There was another voice before that, but she hadn't caught it all, something about a restaurant.

There had been no sign of the cops for ten minutes. She'd wait a little longer, then decide which way to go.

WINTER SAT WITH his back against the wall, his hood up against the rain. He'd been on stakeouts in much worse conditions. He didn't think he'd have to wait long. If he was right about Doc trying to draw the cops away from the house to give someone a chance to get in or out, they had to be close by.

Winter called Booth. "Is that Mercedes still in the driveway on Rutland?"

Booth said, "Wait, let me check." A minute later. "It's gone. It must have pulled out when we were down at the house."

Not long now.

GINA LOOKED back and forth from the house to the woods. She could get in the Mercedes and drive away. Even if they stopped her she was just running an errand. Doc said the car was clean, and she believed him. He was in it all the time and wouldn't risk being caught with drugs.

Drive out of the neighborhood, ditch the Mercedes. Get her friend to come get her. She could be out of the state in an hour.

With no clothes, no money, starting over.

The other direction meant dry clothes, a bagful of cashable drugs, her car. And the risk of the cops.

If they arrested Doc, they'd find out about her soon enough. Nothing in the house would identify her, except her car. Without that, they might never find her. Gina couldn't imagine the cops would let Doc skate free just to get to her; she was smart enough to accept the fact she was small fry. The cops would be smart enough too.

Her car was the problem.

She stood up, her legs cramped. She walked back into the woods, away from the house. No one yelled out, no cops came running.

At the edge of the woods Gina saw the Mercedes, exactly where she had left it.

She lit a cigarette, shielding it from the rain, and worked it out.

WINTER HEARD THE unmistakable sound of a garage door opening. A moment later the gate clanged and the front of a car peeked out of the drive. The driver, a female brunette, had her head turned, looking up the street the other way.

The car turned left.

Winter crouched behind a tree as she slowly drove past him, his phone already in his hand, dialing Jacoby. "Coming your way. Female driver, white Honda. Can't see if there is anyone in the back."

Winter jumped up, sprinting to follow the car, keeping behind the row of trees. She'd see Jacoby's car any second, and there would be a decision to make. Winter was hoping she'd panic and speed off, giving Jacoby a reason to pull her over.

But the Honda was driving slower than a walk, coming to a complete stop at the intersection, the smoking tailpipe a harbinger of indecision.

The car eased into the intersection and turned right.

Winter ran as fast as he could, cutting across the lawn on the corner property, jumping out in front of the Honda waving his badge.

The woman stared at him with startling green eyes, her face totally devoid of the frenzy displayed by the blonde who had run out of the house. Calculating.

"Don't," Winter warned. "It's not worth it."

The woman's eyes darted away briefly to the rear view mirror, then back to Winter, still calculating.

She turned off the car.

GINA, still figuring a way out, rolled down the window. "Can I help you?"

"Do you have some identification?"

"Why did you stop me? I wasn't speeding. And I stopped at the stop sign."

"You didn't signal a turn."

Gina couldn't hide her disbelief. "You're not serious. There's no one around!"

"There's a car right down the street. A police car, actually. You must have seen it."

"You've got to be kidding."

"Do I look like I'm kidding?"

Though the guy wasn't in uniform, he had that same hard look and tone of just about every cop she'd ever met. She pried her wallet out of her pocket, the leather damp from her being in the rain. "The registration is in the glove compartment," she said. Gina waited until the cop nodded before she reached over, moving her hands very carefully.

She got a good look at him as he glanced at the papers. He was in his fifties maybe, with a very relaxed and confident air. He reminded her of the way Kevin carried himself, a toughness that didn't have to be put on display.

"Is this your current address?" the cop asked.

"No, I haven't had a chance to update it."

"Where do you live?"

"Here and there."

The cop waved his arm back toward Doc's house. "Here as in the house you drove out of?"

"I guess." The cop didn't say anything else, giving off the vibe he was wondering what Gina and Doc did together. For some reason she felt drawn to explain. "I have my own room."

The cop smiled like the answer pleased him for some reason. "That's good. Who else lives there?"

"Doc has a friend named Tricia."

"Blonde woman, a little excitable?"

Gina wondered why the cop thought that. "Sometimes."

"On the blonde or the excitable?"

"Both." Gina had a few run-ins with cops, this conversation wasn't like any she'd ever had. He looked like an uncle. Just a guy.

She could handle guys.

"I need to get somewhere now," she said, calm as she could be. "Maybe you could take my contact information, we could talk about this later?" And then, so he wouldn't think she was flirting, she added, "When you don't have to be standing in the rain."

The cop tilted his head a little, as if he were considering, and for a moment Gina thought she had him.

"We could go inside together," he said.

He'd thrown her ploy back at her, his own improper suggestion. Her heart beat faster, her body realizing before her mind that she was in bigger trouble than she thought. "It's not my house."

"If you have a room, you can give consent."

"Why do you want to go inside?" There, let him lay it out. Gina wished she had turned on her phone recorder, she'd beat whatever rap the cops wanted to pin on her if she caught him propositioning her.

"We made an arrest there. And we're looking for a man named Kevin."

"You arrested Doctor Miles?"

"That's not your concern. Are you going to let us in the house?"

Gina wasn't sure about the law, but she *was* sure how pissed Doc would be if she let the cops in. "I don't think I can do that," she said.

The cop said, "Look, this isn't about you. Although you look very much like a woman Rick Singleton described to me. A woman who sold him some drugs."

Gina didn't think she flinched at the mention of Rick's name, but the car seat suddenly felt like quicksand, sucking her down. "I thought you said this wasn't about me."

"It doesn't have to be. Why don't you make things easy for yourself. Let me look in the trunk to make sure you aren't sneaking Kevin out."

Gina didn't like that idea at all, even though Kevin wasn't in the trunk. The drugs were.

Gina tried to buy time. "You think some guy is in my trunk?"

The cop shrugged. "I've seen it before."

Gina glanced in the rear view mirror. The cop car had eased up behind them, no one getting out. No way she could drive off.

"Please step out of the car. We're going to run your license."

Gina realized she'd been trapped. She didn't think she had a choice now. She got out of the car, working out a new plan.

"Your clothes are all wet," said the cop. "Been out in the rain long?"

"I was out for a smoke. What's your excuse?" Bitter now, she was going to be left holding the literal bag.

"I was waiting for you," he said, and now his voice had turned as cold and hard as the rain.

Not many options left. If the cops found the drugs, she was done for.

The cop had asked her about Kevin. If she could keep the attention on him . . .

"I'll let you look in my trunk, just to see that I don't have some guy in there," she said.

The cop nodded, and she popped the trunk release, holding her breath.

The cop pulled out his gun, went to the side of the car, lifted the trunk and quickly stepped back.

"Satisfied?" said Gina. "No one in the trunk. Now can I go?"

The cop put his gun away. "You know Kevin?"

"The name rings a bell, I'm not too good with names. Guys are guys."

"Will you give me consent to search the house?"

"If you had some reason to believe this Kevin was there, wouldn't you have a search warrant?"

The cop waved his hand at the trunk. "What's in the bag?"

"I didn't know there was a bag in there. I haven't driven this car in a while, and other people use it too."

"Who?"

Gina realized she needed to shut up. The fact that the cop hadn't simply opened the bag told her he wasn't allowed to for some reason. "Unless this Kevin can fit into whatever bag you found, I want to leave."

"Sure," said the cop.

She was stunned. "Okay."

"Just as soon as Jackson takes a look in your trunk."

"Jackson? Who the hell is Jackson?"

The cop jerked his hand over his shoulder. Gina was confused until she saw the other cop get out with a dog. She forced herself not to look at the bag, but didn't for a second believe the dog wouldn't find the drugs.

The cop with the dog said, "Let's go to work, Jackson."

"Jackson is a name you won't forget," said the cop in the hoodie.

Gina turned on him. "You're an asshole."

The cop held out his arms. "I've been told that by a lot of criminals."

They stood there, the rain falling heavily now, Gina's hair plastered to her head, belatedly realizing she should have gone for the Mercedes.

"Maybe we can work something out," she said.

CHAPTER 65

Booth and Jacoby went in the house first, wearing their vests. Winter followed behind with the woman Gina Harrington.

Winter said to her, "If Kevin or anyone else is inside, now would be a good time to tell us."

"I wasn't here. I don't know who is in the house."

"Where's your room?"

"Upstairs, second on the left."

"The office?"

"Back side of the house."

"You know all this because you've been in all the rooms?"

The woman had turned sullen. "Yes."

"Dr. Miles's bedroom?"

"Yes."

Winter sat her on a sofa in the living room while the two officers cleared the house. It was big and took a while, Winter expecting to get a call from Crosse at any moment.

Jacoby came back and said, "It's clear."

"Watch her," said Winter. He took Booth into the kitchen. "We don't have much time. Let's do another walk through. Look for guns, drugs, and jewelry. You do upstairs, I'll work through this level."

"Jewelry?"

"I'll explain later."

Winter started in the office. The woman had given him consent, but even after he had found the drugs in her car Winter didn't trust that the DA Villeson would back him up if the lawyers got into a pissing match about whether she had a right to let them in the house.

Still, he lingered, getting a feel for Miles. The room was what he'd call comfortable, deep leather seating, a plush oriental rug, big oak desk, walnut paneling. Upscale, but not decadent. Miles no doubt had money, but he wasn't flaunting it.

The desk was bare except for a blotter, a gold pen, and an old fashioned rolodex. A cigar humidor sat on a low wooden credenza. No computer, not even a telephone. Winter had seen six cell phones in the sunroom, likely burners.

Rick Singleton had described Miles as a drug dealer who kept product nearby. The place didn't have the feel of a drug den, where low level dealers usually left product right out in the open.

Winter found two safes, one in the floor under the desk, one on a wall, unadorned and unhidden. Both were locked.

Booth stuck his head in the office. "Something upstairs you need to see."

Booth led the way to a messy bedroom, clothes strewn on the furniture, haphazard shoes, a vanity with a drugstore full of makeup. The predominant color was pink.

The top of the dresser looked like a jewelry store, a full earring display, bracelets, pendants, and chains. Lots of chains.

Most were thin and dainty, what you'd expect a woman to wear. One stuck out like a sore thumb, a long thickly woven gold chain with bulbous links. The chain had a small tag affixed which said *Hold for Dwayne*.

Winter felt that rush when the connections in his head solidified in the real world. "Got him," said Winter.

"This stuff stolen?" asked Booth.

"Worse," said Winter.

BACK IN THE OFFICE, moving fast now, Winter eased one of the credenza drawers open, rationalizing that it was large enough for someone to hide in and could easily hold records of a drug dealer's transactions. Nothing but a row of hanging files, neatly marked. Winter flipped through the first few, which held what appeared to be paperwork for real estate deals.

The next drawer had a folder marked *Investments*. The first item was a contract between Miles and Rick Singleton, both their names in the signature space. Winter scanned it quickly, did a mental balancing act, folded the contract in half, and stuck it in his cargo pocket.

THE CALL FROM CROSSE came as Winter was working his way through the master bedroom. Crosse said, "Miles has called his lawyer. He bent my ear, threatening all sorts of stuff if we don't let Miles go. And reminded me in no uncertain terms we have no right to search. He's on his way to Marburg from Boston."

"I got consent," said Winter.

"You want me to tell Miles that?"

Winter thought about Gina. If he burned her now, Miles might turn on her, which could give Winter a wedge between them. On the other hand, if he didn't burn her, she might be smart enough to cooperate, because she'd fear Miles would let her take the fall.

"Not yet," he said. "How long can you stall?"

"Miles won't answer questions without his lawyer. I don't see how I can hold him. We've been staring at one another the whole time. I'll have to drive him back to his house. Five minutes, tops."

Winter went back out into the living room, where the woman sat on the sofa, feigning indifference. She was good, but her eyes had jumped to Winter when he walked in.

Winter said, "You've got two minutes to decide whether you're going to help me or whether you are going down with Miles."

Harrington gave him a long look. "Doc gets very upset if he gets crossed."

Winter returned her stare. "So do I."

"IT'S THIN," said Villeson.

Winter could tell by Villeson's tone that he was still upset about the end around with Quinn. "Look, if it's about that other thing . . ."

"That's not it," said Villeson. "If you rely on the label on the chain for the arrest, and they argue you didn't have enough probable cause to even be *looking* at jewelry during your search—and they will—then the arrest will fall apart."

"The woman gave consent. And the drugs in the bag—"

"She doesn't live there. I'll buy the consent to enter the house, but not to search for jewelry. If you knew the chain was stolen, okay. Do you have reason to suspect that?"

Winter didn't. He was in the entry hall of Miles's house, looking at the security screen showing the front entrance. Crosse's car pulled up. Miles got out, his image filling the screen. The gate started to open.

"Rick Singleton will testify that Miles sold him drugs. I now have another witness who will corroborate that." Winter hadn't gotten that far with Gina, but it was a possibility. "Can we at least get a search warrant for drugs?"

"This other witness, is she the one who gave consent to enter?"

"Yes, and she lives here. She has her own room, plus I saw her car leave the property just before we pulled her over."

Winter moved to the window. Miles was heading into the house.

After a pause Villeson said, "I'll have a search warrant for the drugs ready for Owens to sign and take to a judge in a half hour."

Winter, surprised, said, "Thanks." Then, "That's fast."

"Quinn said you know what you are doing. Most of the time. So we've been working on it. Don't take advantage of me."

"I won't," said Winter, meaning it. "And that thing with Quinn . . ."

"I won't say to forget it," said Villeson. "Because *I* won't. Don't do it again." Villeson hung up.

Winter opened the door just as Miles reached the steps. "Back so soon?"

Miles made to push by into the house, but Winter didn't move. Miles said, "I'm not talking to you until my lawyer is here."

"Change of plans," said Winter. "We have a search warrant on the way over. You can wait in the car or here in the entry."

Miles leaned forward, his eyes narrowing. Winter understood why Gina was afraid of this man. Winter had seen men like him before, dense pent up energy and pure meanness, more intimidating than a gangbanger with a gun.

Miles's eyes flicked past Winter, maybe weighing his options, maybe looking for Gina. Winter didn't want to play that card just yet.

Miles stared at Winter, his face a mask of rage. Winter didn't budge.

Miles turned around and went back outside.

CHAPTER 66

MALCOLM WASHINGTON shuffled along Blue Hill Avenue, hands in his sweatshirt pockets, jangling the handful of watches and necklaces. He'd scored big the night before, but it had been too late to sell the bling. He'd caught a bunch of women in the back of a club, a bachelorette party too drunk to find their limo. They hadn't moved fast enough for Malcolm, so he had to show them the gun. That got their attention.

He'd lost track of how many guns he'd had in the past, never keeping them long, always trading for cash or rock. Taking the watches and jewelry had kept him in enough money to hold on to the latest one. It could hold ten shots, which Malcolm liked, although it was only loaded with six, and it wasn't like Malcolm was going to be able to walk into some gun store and buy ammunition.

He'd fired it once, in a field behind the projects, hitting a garbage can. He'd never had to shoot anyone, but he'd be fine when the need came, just pull the trigger.

He was out of rock, the need on him, a little jittery, so he yanked at the door of the store. It took him a few seconds to realize it was locked.

Inside it was dark, Malcolm peering up at the sun, way overhead, the place should be open.

A voice behind him said, "They closed."

Malcolm didn't see where the voice came from, until a cardboard box along the wall moved. A wino stuck his head out. "Flash and Cadillac got themselves picked up by the police."

"Shit," said Malcolm. He stood there blinking, trying to remember who else he had managed to sell bling to.

Malcolm kicked the wino in the leg to get his attention, lifting his sweatshirt to show the gun tucked in his jeans. "You got any rock?"

The wino held up a dirty wine bottle. "I just do the juice."

Malcolm kicked him again and moved off down the street.

FRIDAY MORNING, Winter walked into Captain Logan's office and dropped a folder on his desk. "The report on the pills we found in the bag of drugs from the Miles house. Very interesting collection. One of them is fentanyl."

"As in the drug found in Dwayne Coleman's system?"

"One and the same." Winter plopped down in the chair in front of Logan's desk. "There's more. See the chemical makeup of the powder we found in the bedroom? It matches the coke found near the pool at the Carter house."

"You think Miles was there?"

"Either him or his man Kevin. The chain and the fentanyl and the coke all tie Miles to Coleman."

"You think Miles had Coleman killed?" asked Logan.

"Or did it himself."

"What's the motive?"

Winter shrugged. "Still working on that."

"Work fast. Miles is having a bail hearing this morning."

"We'll get him on the drugs at least." Winter had been vague on the gym bag, still thinking he could use that to hold over Gina. If he found out she wasn't involved in the homicides, he'd trade away the charges against her for the drugs in her car if she testified.

"Any tie-in to Gerry Hennig?"

"I have a few ideas about that."

Owens stuck his head in the door. "We just got a call from Boston PD. Our friend Malcolm Third Eye just showed up at a pawnshop trying to lay off a half dozen women's watches."

"They get him?"

"No. Pawnshop called it in. Said Third Eye looked strung out. By the time they got there he was long gone."

"Doubt he'll give up trying." said Winter. "Let's go for a ride."

*   *   *

THEY TOOK WINTER'S CAR, Winter pushing it on the Mass Pike. Owens worked the phone, getting updates from Boston PD on the search for Washington.

"They got word out to all the pawnshops," said Owens. "We might get lucky, they'll have him before we get there."

"Be nice," said Winter. He was doing eighty until he almost rear ended a minivan in the left lane. The minivan ignored his horn and his lights, so he blipped the siren, finally getting them to move over.

"The nerve," said Owens. "Going the speed limit."

"You got someone lined up for us to meet?"

"Detective named Ridley, at the B-3."

"I know it," said Winter. "Blue Hill Avenue."

"You think we've got enough to nail Miles for Dwayne Coleman?"

"Who knows," said Winter. "Villeson isn't convinced, but he's a pessimist. He won't go to trial without more than we've given him. Dan's been going through the security video again from the party. If Miles doesn't show up on it, we need more."

"Maybe Malcolm Washington will fill in the pieces."

MALCOLM STUMBLED out of the alley, the light overwhelming his eyes, trying to remember exactly where he was. He'd been forced to leave his own neighborhood, having run out of places to sell the bling. Finally found a buyer for the earrings, probably getting screwed, but he needed a hit.

The rock gone, he crossed the street, ignoring the blaring horns. The chill wind cut into his cracked lips. His mouth was so dry he couldn't feel his tongue. At the corner, he pushed into a deli, grabbing two orange sodas.

At the register the clerk asked, "You need anything else? Candy maybe?"

Malcolm didn't think he meant chocolate bars. "You do a trade?"

"I don't do nothing. I might know someone, is all. You got something worth trading?"

Malcolm lifted his sweatshirt to show the gun in his waistband. "Got good bling, too."

"Deli store called Quick Bite over on Humboldt. Ask for Lewis."

Malcolm said, "Where's Humboldt at?"

*   *   *

WINTER AND OWENS met up with Detective Ridley at the station on Blue Hill Avenue. Ridley had graying brown hair and was tall and wide, looking more like a retired football lineman than a cop.

"I went over to the pawnshop that called it in and looked at his security tape. It's your man Third Eye. He's long gone, but I know a couple of other places near there he might try."

"How do you want to work this?" asked Winter.

"Washington doesn't have any assault or weapons charges on his sheet, just drugs. Might be good to bring along a uniform or two though. If he sees a cop car and runs, we could lose him in that neighborhood."

"Your house, your call," said Winter.

"Okay," said Ridley, the chair creaking when he got up. "I'll drive."

MALCOLM GOT LOST on the way to Humboldt. Just a few miles from his crib, he could have been in a different city. At a bus stop he asked a woman for directions, and she pointed.

"Just came from there," said Malcolm.

"Big street. You can't miss it."

Malcolm would have hit her but the bus pulled up and she jumped on. He turned around and went back. The street was there, just like she said.

Problem now was he forgot the name of the deli. The first two he went in had no Lewis. One of them had no customers, just the cashier. Malcolm fingered the gun, figuring how much cash they might have.

"You got any candy?" he asked.

The cashier guy pointed to the rack of snacks. "It's right in front of you."

Malcolm took one of the candy bars and walked out of the store.

"PLACE IS A MAZE," said Winter, squeezed into the back of Ridley's car.

"You get used to it," said Ridley, driving with one hand through the narrow streets. "Parking is a bitch though." Ridley deftly pulled into a spot in front of a stone church, marked *No parking*.

Across from the church was a brown brick apartment building with three stores on the ground floor, a check cashing place, a laundry, and a pawnshop.

As they got out of the car Ridley said, "The last place Washington was seen was a few blocks from here. This isn't his usual neighborhood, so he might be trying places at random."

"This one have stolen stuff?" asked Owens.

"It's a pawnshop," said Ridley.

Inside, it looked like every other pawnshop Winter had ever been in, bursting with the riffraff of riffraff. A man in Rasta braids was on the phone, hanging up as soon as he saw them.

"Relax," said Ridley. "We're just looking for a guy."

Owens showed the clerk a photo of Washington. "Seen him?"

The clerk shook his head. "I don't look much at faces. What's he selling?"

"Probably watches."

The clerk pointed to a display. "We got watches from like five years ago. Who wears watches any more?"

"I do," said all three cops at the same time.

MALCOLM KEPT GOING on Humboldt. For two blocks there were no stores, only a spread out housing project behind a brown plastic fence. Three hustlers were at a gate, looking open for business.

"What you need, man?"

"The rock," said Malcolm. "You trade?"

"Cash is king," said the brother. One of his posse moved his jacket aside to show a gun, telling Malcolm they wouldn't put up with no take down.

Malcolm kept his hands away from the sweatshirt pocket with the bling, he wasn't going to be taken down either. "Only got me four dollars. You fix me up?"

"Take what you got," said the hustler.

Malcolm took out his singles, and they did the exchange. The hustler pointed down the street before Malcolm could even ask where he could go do the rock.

A few blocks down, Malcolm found a really big boarded up house behind a rusted wire fence, the yard overgrown with weeds taller than him. The house had been white but every inch had been tagged. He squeezed in between broken sections of the fence and did his pipe right on the front steps, totally screened from view by the jungle of weeds.

A while later, the edge was off but it had awakened the need, so he worked his way back to the street.

Just when it looked like he was going the wrong way again, the street widened, the houses giving way to stores. Malcolm still couldn't remember the name of the deli he was looking for. He didn't even see any delis.

He did see a pawnshop, which was even better.

RIDLEY WAS TELLING Winter and Owens a story about a guy who had stolen a television set from a house and had walked home with it. It had just snowed, and Ridley had followed nice new footprints in the snow, catching the guy hooking up the set to watch a football game.

"Thing is," said Ridley, "he already had two televisions. He was betting on football, he wanted to see three different games at the same time. He was stealing the cable, too."

"Hope he was a better gambler than a thief," said Owens.

Ridley's phone rang. He answered the call, listened, then said, "Okay. We're going over too." He turned his head over the seat. "Got a report from a pawnshop over in Roxbury that a black male with a backwards baseball cap and a forehead tat is trying to move some watches. That's B-2, they'll meet us there."

"You know the place?" asked Winter.

"Driven by. Haven't been inside. It's pretty big."

THE OLD, BALDHEADED foreign-looking guy peered at Malcolm through thick eyeglasses. "These are both nice watches."

"How much?" asked Malcolm.

"This one has a new band," said the old man. "Gold. It's worth more than the other one."

"How much?" repeated Malcolm.

"I need to go check on the gold price, and get an okay from my boss. Wait a minute."

The guy shuffled off into a back room before Malcolm could stop him. There were too many people in the store, so Malcolm let it go. He shifted over to a big display of jewelry, lots of necklaces and earrings.

The old guy finally came back. "My boss is on the phone. I think he'll be done in a minute. You have anything else you want to show me?"

Malcolm's hand was already in his pocket, but he didn't show the rest of the watches, knowing he'd get the question about where he got so many. Instead he pulled out a pair of earrings. "Bought these for my woman," he said. "She's allergic or something."

The old man nodded. "We get that a lot. These look nice, but I don't know much about diamonds."

Malcolm was about to grab the bling and the watches back and look for another store, but the man said, "These could be worth more than the watches."

"Let me guess, you got to ask your boss," said Malcolm.

"Sorry," said the man. "I just work here. I think it will only be a few more minutes."

RIDLEY SAID, "Washington might remember me, you guys should go in first. A B-2 detective named Morgan should be—wait, here he is." Ridley rolled down his window as a dark brown sedan pulled up alongside. "These are the guys from Marburg," Ridley said, jerking his head toward the backseat. "They're going to go in first."

The black detective in the other car said, "There's a back entrance. I can have a squad car here to help cover it in five minutes."

Ridley's phone rang and after he took the call he said, "The owner says he can't stall him any longer. We don't have five minutes."

Winter was already out of the car. "Ask him how many customers are inside."

"Lots," said Ridley.

Winter looked up and down the street. There weren't as many pedestrians as he expected. He was the only white guy in sight. To Morgan he said, "We'll go in the front door. Can your squad car cover the rear?"

Morgan said, "I'll take it. We'll put the uniforms on either end of the block. Ridley can stay out front. That should cover it if you don't scare him off."

Ridley, listening on his phone said, "The owner wants to know if he should offer Washington something for the watches."

"Tell him to be careful," said Winter. "Don't offer too much." Winter was trying not to look directly in the window of the pawnshop, picking up the front doors in his peripheral vision. The window display blocked a good view of inside.

Owens said, "This neighborhood, better if I go in first."

"Okay. I'll head toward the rear of the store."

"Give me a minute to get around back," said Morgan.

Morgan parked, walked halfway down the block, and disappeared into an alley. Owens nodded at Winter and stepped inside.

Winter counted in his head, pulled open the door, and walked straight ahead. In front of him, along the far wall, was row upon row of shelves filled with merchandise. Owens was moving toward Winter's right, heading for the glass counters along the side. Winter risked a quick glance. A black man was alone at the counter, his back to Winter, although the bill of his cap faced out into the store. Washington. The wall behind the counter was mirrored. Washington's entire body was fidgety, his head bouncing, the cap jerking like a bobblehead.

Winter marked an exit door in the left rear corner. He swung into an aisle of lit televisions, pretending to look at a screen. Owens was casually making his way toward Washington.

Two women entered the store, talking loudly about jewelry, Washington's head swiveling in their direction. The women headed toward the counter. Washington's body suddenly stopped, his head snapping around, maybe catching sight of Owens coming up behind him in the mirror, Owens slowing down, his hand on his gun, Winter doing the same. Owens was on Washington now, saying, "Police, take it easy Malcolm."

Washington didn't even turn to look, he ran along the counter, Owens grabbing for him, missing, Washington shoving his way between the two women, snatching one by the hair and whipping her around so fast she didn't scream until she hit the floor.

Winter pushed past a shopper into the aisle, blocking the path to the exit, but Washington ran behind the counter and through a door. Owens got tangled up with the woman as she was getting up. Winter vaulted over the counter, smashing his shin painfully against the display case. He and Owens reached the door at the same time, pushing it open then ducking through, Winter going left, Owens right, they'd done this before.

A woman and a bald man huddled behind desks in the small room, the man wordlessly pointing to an open steel door. Before Winter could take two steps there was a shout from outside, "Stop, police!" then a shot, Winter pulling his gun as he reached the door, Owens right behind him.

Another shot—a different gun—as Winter went through the door. Morgan was hobbling down a narrow service alley, his gun out, Washington halfway down the street dodging garbage cans.

"Fucker shot me," said Morgan.

Winter said, "How bad?" his eyes still on the retreating Washington.

"Through the calf I think. Shit, that hurts." Owens was there, pulling off his tie, lifting Morgan's pant leg and wrapping the tie around the wound.

"Small hole, not much blood," said Owens.

"Go!" said Morgan. "Go, go, I'll make the call."

Winter ran down the alley, not bothering to yell at Washington, the guy had just shot a cop, it would just waste breath. Owens was moving behind him, Winter hearing Morgan on his phone, getting the backup in position.

The narrow lane was walled in on both sides, the rear of stores on the left, metal security gates, air conditioning units, dumpsters. A tall brick wall on the right, forming an echo chamber, Winter hearing his own footsteps slapping on the broken concrete.

Washington was fast, Winter just able to keep up. The service road narrowed ahead, a short chain link fence, Winter thinking Washington was going to jump over it, but Washington turned left and disappeared.

"He's heading back to the street!" yelled Winter, hoping Morgan could hear him.

Winter reached the corner, stuck his head out and back quickly, just catching a glimpse of Washington at the end of a narrow alley.

Winter burst out onto Humboldt, a few doors down from the pawnshop, Washington a block away heading in the other direction. A Boston PD squad car was on the other side of the street trying to make a U turn, horns blaring.

Winter pounded down the sidewalk after Washington, people turning to look, shouts of "Hey!" Winter ignored them, kept on running, a quick glance over his shoulder, Owens about fifty feet behind, the squad car finally turned around.

The commercial section ended abruptly, a school on the left, a bright blue painted wall and a playground, empty. At the next corner Washington turned again, the squad car coming up next to Winter, Winter pointing. The squad car screeched around the corner.

When Winter turned the corner Washington was nowhere to be seen, the squad car edging down the street past a row of old single family homes, most behind short chain link fences.

Winter ran up to the squad car. Two uniforms were inside. Winter panted, "You see him?"

"No, he wasn't there when we made the turn, what happened to Morgan?"

"Caught one in the leg, didn't look too bad."

"Ambulance and backup are on the way."

Owens pounded up to the car, rasping. Winter said, "He might have slipped into one of these houses."

The uniform in the passenger seat said, "I know which one to look in first." He pointed down the block. "At the corner, house has been abandoned forever."

Winter said, "Let's try to hole him up until we get help. One on each side."

The cop said, "We'll park on the corner, cover the front and the far street side. Be careful going around back, the place is full of weeds."

Winter and Owens jogged behind the cop car, sirens in the distance. The house stood out like a sore thumb in the reasonably neat neighborhood, a three story colonial, every window boarded up, covered in graffiti. More than weeds in the yard, a jungle.

The squad car reached the corner, the cops out fast, one taking up position on the street, the other heading around the other side. Winter said to Owens, "I'll take the back," running low along the fence, his eyes toward the yard. Washington could be twenty feet away and Winter might not even see him, the brush that thick, briars and ailanthus trees, most still with leaves.

The next-door house was a tidy two decker, not pristine, but decidedly incongruous next to the mess. Only twenty feet separated the house from the fence, a row of trees in the gap. Winter ran the gauntlet, knowing he was in trouble if Washington was on that side of the yard and took a shot at him.

In the back of the other house a tool shed blocked his way. Winter stuck his toe in the flimsy chain link fence between the houses, grabbed the top, and leaped over into the brush.

MALCOLM WASHINGTON crouched down behind the short wall of the side porch. He was riding high, he'd shot that cop, hit him too, this was as good as the rock, better. He could smell the gun, warm near his face.

Heard the sirens, not caring, let them come, only wishing he had more bullets and that he was in his own neighborhood.

The cop had shot at him, missing, Malcolm running like the wind. No one could catch him, just like they hadn't caught him at that party after he'd beat down the skinny white guy, Malcolm walking down the stairs and out the back door, keeping it cool, no one with the balls to look him in the eye. Once outside, he'd walked down the back drive, putting on the Rolex, the metal nice and heavy.

Then into the woods. Made a call and was out of there.

He always knew he could do it, put a man down, shit, he just shot a cop. Could be good money in that, give up stealing watches and bling, get paid the big dollar to take care of business. Outta Here was gone, too bad, he could have sung a Third Eye rap so the street would know what he could do.

The idea gave Malcolm a new rush. He was ready to shoot it out, right here and now, but the thought of walking down his own street again, brothers pointing to him, giving him cred, that was better.

Malcolm stood up on the porch, one more run to make, get back to his crib, plan it out.

WINTER EDGED THROUGH the thicket on his hands and knees, briars tearing at his clothes. His left hand sunk into the ground, which shouldn't have been this soft in the cold, Winter picking up an odor, wet trash. He ignored it, staring at the back of the house, all boarded up on this side too. A set of stone steps led up to a covered porch. Nothing moved.

Washington might not even be here, they might be surrounding an empty house, Washington blocks away.

Nothing Winter could do about that now. He trusted the local uniform who had pointed out this house. It was a pretty good place to hide up.

Winter couldn't see Owens, but he should be on the side street, off to the left. The siren grew louder, maybe a block or two away, then Winter heard car doors opening, the siren silenced. Voices from that way, Owens talking to the backup.

Winter used the sound of their arrival to move ten feet closer to the back of the house.

MALCOLM SAW THE cop car, two cops getting out, pulling guns, another guy, black, waving toward the house Malcolm was at. No way he could get out the front or side now. Right ahead of him, past the backyard weeds, a gray house. If there was a fence it couldn't be very high.

Malcolm had five shots left, not enough to take out the cops. No matter, he wasn't going to go down here. More sirens, had to go now before they surrounded him. There was another cop around, the white guy in the hoodie who had chased him, he was probably around the front.

Malcolm rose up on his toes, ready to make his move.

A SOUND BEHIND Winter made him spin around, dropping onto his side, his gun out, shit, Washington had got behind him, but there was no one there, just the brush, scraggly trees, and a short picket fence, a gray house beyond. Winter frantically searched for the source of the sound, a metal screeching, a female voice yelling out, "What you doing sneaking around that yard?"

Winter's eyes jerked to the voice, a woman was waving a pan at him from a window on the second floor of the gray house, looking down on him over the fence. Winter tried to wave her off, making a quieting motion with his hand, but she kept yelling at him. Sound, again behind him, from the graffiti house, Winter twisting on the ground, too late, Washington had appeared of nowhere, crashing through the brush right toward him. Someone shouted from the street, now everyone yelling, Winter, the woman, Owens, the uniforms.

Washington turned his head toward the street, his gun coming up, shooting blindly. Winter fired, a fusillade from the street, Washington's body jerking, but he was still running, more shots, Winter not able to hold his aim, Washington twenty feet away, still firing as he stumbled, his body twisting, and he fell on his face, the gun flying off, his head smashing into the ground right in front of Winter, the impact a sickening thud.

Three eyes stared at Winter. Two of them were dead.

CHAPTER 67

WINTER LEANED AGAINST the counter in the kitchen as Patricia made herbal tea. The kitchen was too small for him, a cooped up sense that had nothing to do with the dimensions of the space. Winter could see into the living room, where Singleton was sitting by his mother's bed. She hadn't moved since he'd been there.

Winter turned away, less because of the dying woman, and more the helplessness of the situation.

"That stuff work?" he asked Patricia.

"Depends on what you mean by work. Is it going to cure her? No. Will it make her son feel better for getting her to drink it? Maybe. Will she feel better that he's sitting next to her, caring? Definitely. You pick."

Winter gave her a sad smile. "You don't even sugar coat . . ." he waved his arm toward the living room.

"This time of life, people don't need bullshit. The living don't deserve it, and the dying don't want it."

Winter wondered what he'd want when his time came. He thought he'd want the truth, but who could tell?

Patricia took the tea into the living room, Winter not hearing the words, just the tone, matter of fact, no sense of impending doom. She was right. If he was in that bed, the last thing he'd want is everyone sulking around like the world was going to end.

Back in the kitchen, Patricia said, "Are you here to arrest that boy?"

Winter said, "I'm here for the truth."

WINTER SAT outside on the steps, the brisk air a welcome relief from the house. The yard looked better, raked clean. Winter hadn't given much thought to what would happen to his yard when he was gone. He'd leave Audrey the house, even though she wouldn't want to live there. Her days in Marburg were over. The house would move on too, another family, more memories.

Singleton came out, zipping up a fleece. He sat down next to Winter.

"How is she?" Winter asked.

"She seems the same as yesterday, but yesterday she seemed the same as the day before. Every day seems the same, but she's way worse than she was month ago. Isn't that weird?"

"I guess," said Winter.

"Kind of like my life." After a bit Singleton said, "I expected to see you a week ago."

"I had some things to take care of," said Winter. "Figured you did too."

"Thanks for that. I really appreciate it. My mom still doesn't know anything. I've been trying to decide what to say. Doesn't feel right, her having this idea of me that isn't true. That I'm this altar boy, the perfect son."

"You sure that's what she thinks?"

"Maybe you're right. She's pretty smart." Singleton stared at his feet. "I just—wanted to have everything work out, you know? The music, my career, get help for my mom. I tried to do too much. Every thing I did seemed to be right at the time, but I just kept digging myself in deeper."

Winter said, "The man who killed Gerry is dead."

"What? Who?"

"Guy by the name of Malcolm Washington. He's from Boston, into drugs."

"How do you know he killed Gerry?"

"He got picked up by a car after the party. We tracked down the car. There was some blood in it. Gerry's blood. We also found a tooter on Washington, made from a ball point pen, same as we found in the bedroom where Gerry died. DNA tests aren't back yet, but I'm sure they'll match."

Singleton slowly shook his head. "I don't understand. I really can't believe Gerry was into drugs. What would he be doing with this Malcolm guy?"

"That's what I need you to help me figure out. Let's say it's not the drugs. Maybe not even just a robbery. Malcolm came to the party with Dwayne. It wasn't a coincidence Dwayne was at the party. We found out from his producer that Dwayne had asked for an invite. You told me Dwayne said something to you about Gerry and about your deal with Doc—"

"Ah, shit," said Singleton, staring off into space. "The contract. It's about the stupid contract."

"The contract Miles made you sign?"

"No, the other one. The one between me and Gerry. Doc was bleeding me, he didn't only want my share of the royalties from Candy's song, he wanted Gerry's too."

Winter mulled it over. "I think Malcolm was there to put a scare in Gerry, and put a scare in you too."

"I was already scared of Doc. I still am. Nobody needed to hurt Gerry . . ."

"This Malcolm guy wasn't what you'd call in control."

"Oh, man." Singleton's shoulders collapsed as he covered his face, pulling at his hair. "This is all because of me."

Winter didn't agree, it was Malcolm Washington who had killed Gerry Hennig. But he couldn't really soothe Singleton's feelings because he understood where Singleton was coming from. If Singleton hadn't gotten involved with Miles, Gerry would never have been at that party.

Yet that kind of thinking was a slippery slope. Winter had seen plenty of people pay terrible prices for even good decisions. Offering to help a stranger stuck on the road and getting beaten up. Volunteering at a drug clinic and getting robbed.

Rick wasn't to blame. He'd made his mistakes, but Gerry's blood was on Malcolm Washington.

And maybe on Dwayne Coleman and Doc Miles.

TWENTY MINUTES LATER, they were still on the stairs. Winter needed a few more answers, but Singleton had been crying, and Winter couldn't deny him his grief.

Winter was convinced Rick had nothing to do with the deaths of either Dwayne or Gerry. Not directly. Not even indirectly, not really. If you blamed every person in the world who set off a chain of events, every mother for giving birth to a rapist, every man who missed the signs of a disturbed co-worker, every patient who got hooked on pain-killers after a surgery and bought drugs from a guy who bought them from a guy who got killed in a drug buy—it never ended. If every one of those people were guilty, then no one in the world was innocent.

Winter had set enough wheels in motion to know. One in particular, one that, like Rick had said, seemed like the right decision at the time, yet had led inexorably to a deadly ending. A decision of his own he'd been second guessing for years.

Singleton blew out a long breath. "What happens now?"

"What do you think should happen?"

"You said this Malcolm guy is dead. Good. Everyone else involved needs to pay for their piece. Doc, Kevin." Singleton's voice grew more resolute. "Me."

Winter gave him a reappraising look. "Seems like you've paid a lot already."

"It's not enough. It won't bring Gerry back." Rick gazed out into the yard. "A long time ago I was sitting right here. That big tree was just as big, it's been big since I first remember it. I was watching the leaves fall off, it looked almost dead. But I knew it would come back in the spring. I wrote a song about it. About starting over. Keeping the best of what you had, all the knowledge, so you wouldn't make the same mistakes again. A clean slate."

"Sounds like a good song," said Winter.

Rick let out a dismissive laugh. "Except I got nothing, less than nothing. I don't have a dime. Even if Candy still wants to use the song, Doc owns the rights. And now I'm going to lose my mom."

WINTER STARED UP at the oak tree long after Singleton had gone back into the house. The kid was right about the tree, and yet wrong. It had lost its leaves, it was bare, dormant. Yet it still retained its majesty.

Trees didn't get a clean slate, and though everyone dreamed of them, they were just that, dreams. Singleton would have to live with his memories and his history and the realization of what he'd been part of, just like everyone else.

Still, as far as dreams went, it was a good one. Not to have all your problems magically disappear, only to make the same mistakes again, but to get back on your feet and make better decisions.

Singleton didn't have any money, he'd maybe lost his chance at making a life in music.

His mom was going to die.

Winter couldn't do anything about death. No one escaped that.

The rest of it . . . maybe. Winter couldn't have a clean slate for the things he'd done, but that didn't mean other people shouldn't get a chance. Especially people who realized their mistakes and were willing to take responsibility, to make amends.

People like Rick Singleton.

Winter took the papers from his pocket, the contract he'd found in Miles's house. Winter didn't know about contracts, what might be enforceable. The contract—this insubstantial set of papers—might just be the one impediment between Rick Singleton and his clean slate.

Winter wondered what he'd do if *his* name was on the contract. Rip it up? Or hang it on his wall as a constant reminder of how easy it was to rationalize even the worst choices?

It wasn't his name on the paper, it was Rick's. His name, his decision.

Winter folded up the contract and stuck it in the mailbox.

CHAPTER 68

"MARIA IS going to smell these onions on my clothes," said Brooker, digging into his black beans.

Maria was Brooker's nurse. "You not supposed to eat onions?" asked Winter.

"Damned if I know."

They were sitting in the small restaurant Winter had discovered while searching for leads on Malcolm Washington. Though it was way too cold to be sitting outside, the same two elderly black men he'd seen on his first visit were at a sidewalk table, like they had never left. Winter and Brooker were the only whites in the place.

In between bites, Brooker asked, "You think there will be enough of a case against Doc Miles for the Coleman killing?"

"We still don't have a witness who puts Miles at the party. It will help if the coke residue we found in his jacket matches what was out by the pool."

"That only shows Coleman got the drugs from him, not that he was there."

"You're starting to sound like Villeson," said Winter. All in all, he wasn't unhappy. Malcolm Washington was dead and Miles was in jail. Maybe they wouldn't get Miles for the killing of Coleman, and maybe he'd beat the rap on the drugs in the gym bag. But for now, things were good.

"Ballistics come back from the shooting?" asked Brooker.

"Washington was hit twice, one from Owens and one from a SWAT guy."

"You missed him from twenty feet?"

"Less," said Winter, flashing on the image of Washington's third eye tattoo.

"You need me back more than you know." Brooker wiped at his mouth. "You said the coke you found in the woman's bedroom at the Miles house was the same as the coke at the pool. Maybe *she* killed Coleman."

"She has a temper, that's for sure. You should see the scratches on Booth's face. But she's not exactly an under the radar type. She would have been noticed at the party."

"Need to find that Kevin guy and his partner," said Brooker.

"Kevin has vanished. The plates on the van were stolen. We don't even have his last name. Miles must know, but it isn't likely he's going to give Kevin up, especially if Miles told him to kidnap Singleton."

"What about the woman you caught with the bag of drugs?"

"*Near* the bag of drugs," corrected Winter. "Gina. Ryder is working on her, that might work."

Brooker looked up, disbelievingly. "Ryder?"

"He's actually pretty good at laying out a deal."

Brooker snorted. "Will she buy it from him?"

"He just needs to lay it out. Then I'll talk to her. The only question is whether she's more afraid of jail or Miles."

"What's going to happen to Singleton?"

"Nothing legally. He lied to us a few times, who hasn't? He's not really a bad guy, and he's paid a pretty big price. He lost his friend, he's got his mother to take care of. Candy might still use his song, but he'll always wonder if it had been worth it."

"He made a lot of bad decisions."

"It's easy for him to see that now. He told me how each decision he made didn't seem like a big deal at the time, but it led to another decision, and he painted himself into a corner." Winter looked up at Brooker. "Sort of like what we did."

Brooker pointed a finger at Winter. "Don't go down that path. That decision—all of them—were the right ones. I'm sleeping just fine, and you should too."

Winter and Brooker had kept that particular secret for a long time. Unlike Rick Singleton, they had yet to face any repercussions, but who knew what corner they had painted themselves into.

Brooker stared at Winter for a long time. Winter didn't want to talk about it now. He finished up his beans. "Want to hear something funny?"

"There's a funny part to this story?"

"You tell me. Dwayne Coleman had a ton of money. And a will. Guess who he left a bunch of it to?"

"You're shitting me," said Brooker.

"Nope. Malcolm Washington. He was out stealing watches for nothing. Got himself killed when he didn't need to."

"Guy like that needed killing," said Brooker. "Even if he hadn't been at the party, sooner or later he was going to kill someone else."

Winter was thinking about his conversation with Singleton. Could men like Washington ever get a clean slate?

"Yeah," said Winter. "Maybe you're right."

BROOKER LEANED back in his chair. "Damn, that was good. Any heartburn I get will be worth it."

"Going to keep this place on my lunch list," said Winter.

After a bit, Brooker said, "Want to thank you for letting me play on this one. Even just making a few calls. Maybe I can work my way back with Logan."

"What does your doctor say?"

Brooker waved his hand. "The usual, watch what I eat, limit drinking, no caffeine, no stress."

"You feeling okay?"

"Yeah. Really." Brooker hesitated, then said, "How about you?"

"Fine, why?"

"Nothing. No reason, just asking."

Winter couldn't remember if Brooker had ever asked him how he was feeling. Maybe he was just making conversation, bored with his layoff. Although Brooker had never been much of a talker.

The man who had made them lunch came around the counter to their table.

"You were right," said Winter. "Ham hocks are much better than bacon."

"Coffee?"

"Sure," said Winter. "But decaf today."

The man cleared their plates and returned with two mugs. "Cream?"

"This is good," said Winter.

After he walked away, Brooker looked at his cup morosely. "Good? It's fucking decaf."

Winter raised his mug in agreement. "Fucking decaf."

~ ~ ~